The Law of Bound Hearts

ANNE LeCLAIRE

. . . .

The Law of
Bound Hearts

A NOVEL

BALLANTINE BOOKS • NEW YORK

A Ballantine Book
Published by The Random House Publishing Group

www.ballantinebooks.com

Library of Congress Cataloging-in-Publication Data
is available from the publisher upon request.

ISBN 0-345-46045-6

Manufactured in the United States of America

2   4   6   8   9   7   5   3   1

First Edition

FOR GINGER
Sister and Friend

So much to do today:
kill memory, kill pain,
turn heart into stone,
and yet . . .

—*Anna Akhmatova*

The Law of Bound Hearts

Libby

. . . .

Autumn finally came again. The world slowed down and the prairie air grew clear. As if this year were the same as any other, Elizabeth Barnett performed her annual chores. She shopped and packed and got the twins off to their respective colleges. She sorted and washed the summer cottons and packed them away. She replaced the batteries in all the smoke detectors and emptied and stored the terracotta planters that lined the front steps and back patio (twenty in all). She arranged with the yard service to rake and bag fallen leaves, to mulch the perennial beds against the coming winter. Days, functioning at a certain level of competence, she managed for the most part to fend off panic. Nights—when even sound became a fear—nights were different.

She woke to the clutch of panic in her throat, to a racing heart and sweat-dampened gown. It was a moment before she could breathe normally again. Even before she turned and slid her palm over the linen on Richard's side of the bed, even before she touched the cool sheet, bereft of his body heat, she knew he was gone. His absence provoked in her commingled feelings of betrayal and relief, an emotional dichotomy typical of her lately. She wanted connection but pursued isolation, was obsessed with her illness but found refuge in denial, wanted the support and understanding of friends but refused to let Richard tell them she was sick.

Finally she rose and padded barefoot down the hall. His study door was ajar and she nudged it open an inch more. He had opened the drapes. Moonlight poured in, providing the room's sole illumination. His back was to her, and there was a snifter of brandy at his side. He was listening to Bach. The Mass in B Minor, she recognized, always his selection when he was distressed: all through the frightful period of the twins' pneumonia, through his denied tenure at Wesleyan, through her parents' deaths, and Matt's experiments with drugs the summer before his senior year.

These things, the crises of married life, they had handled together, had found strength in doing so. Why wouldn't she allow it now? What would it cost her, after all, to cross the room, take his hand, let him console her and find the solace that comforting another can bring? Why couldn't she permit this simple mutual comfort? Her illness, God knows, hadn't been easy for Richard. Just that morning, he'd had to turn away to steady himself before picking up the syringe. From the beginning, although near phobic about needles, he had insisted on giving her the erythropoietin injections that were supposed to stimulate red cell production, this act his mute and nervous offering of love and support.

She tried to summon gratitude, tenderness, some trace of softness toward this man—her husband—who sat in moonlight with only Bach for comfort, but all she felt was fear, as if her emotional gearbox were fixed in one position. Although he never talked about it, she assumed Richard was afraid, too. What had her doctor, Carlotta, told her? When one system is diseased, it affects all the rest. As true of a family as of a body, she thought.

The flow of light through the windows suddenly reminded her of another night. Had it been only one year ago? It might as well have been a century. In that very room, she and Richard had lain naked in a moon pool. There had been music, as well, that night. Saint-Saëns?

Or was it Schumann? She still confused one with the other. And brandy, too. And a hunger for each other they'd not experienced in a long time. It might have been farcical—their haste to strip, to bare their middle-aged flesh while their nearly adult children slept down the hall—but it had been lovely. She remembered that now. How lovely it had been, although she could not recall what precipitated their passion. They had just returned from a party; she did recall that. (Whose, she could not say for love or money. Another professor's, she supposed. The college circuit pretty much defined their social life.) In that small mirror of lunar light, they had coupled and moaned like newlyweds, momentarily innocent of the knowledge that passion, like love, is friable and transient. In the morning, she'd had rug burns on her shoulders. When she showed them to Richard, he had blushed.

That couple was far distant tonight, as removed and illusory as a scene she might have read in a novel or seen on-screen. Now she knew too well the fragility of life, knew that in the breath of a second, the future you'd planned for could be altered beyond imagination. She thought about opening the door wider then, going in, taking his hand, asking him if he remembered that night. Instead she eased the door shut and retraced her steps to their room, walking carefully, as if the floor were made not of wood but of some thin and insubstantial substance, ice that at any moment might fracture, plunging her into brumal depths.

She would have liked to watch television and let the inanity of a late-night show wash over her until she was lulled to sleep, but she knew the sound would draw Richard. So she climbed into bed and drew up the duvet. Finally, feeling foolish, she tried something she had read about in a magazine she'd picked up in Carlotta's waiting room. She pictured a white light, an amorphous glob, suspended overhead. She concentrated on it, pulled it toward her, imagined the feathery weight of it settling on her body. Was she doing it right? Were there special instructions she was forgetting? She wished she'd paid closer attention to the article. It was ridiculous anyway. If healing were accomplished as easily as that, doctors would be selling Chevys instead of driving around in Jags. Still, she continued. She visualized the light entering her body, washing through her, flooding blood and bone and tissue, then flowing to her kidneys, cleansing and healing each cell. Eventually she fell asleep.

In the morning, Richard slept at her side, his breathing heavy, just short of a snore. Today will be better, Libby promised herself as she looked over at him. She would practice patience, learn courage. She eased herself out of bed. He did not stir. On the way down to the kitchen, she paused at the door to his study. The drapes had been drawn again, the brandy glass rinsed and put away. Every trace of moonlight and music was gone from the air.

Sam

. . . .

On the day the reporter showed up at her door wanting to interview her for a feature, Sam had nearly turned him away. She was too busy and she didn't trust reporters—end of story. But before she could toss him out, her assistant pulled her aside and told her not to be a goddamn fool, this was the kind of publicity a person couldn't buy. Stacy also said she'd boil her shoe and eat it if the guy wasn't a Taurus. She could tell by his jaw. She said that Taurus was absolutely the most trustworthy sign in the entire zodiac. Honest as real vanilla.

Feeling like a fool—nothing Stacy said could ever convince her that there was any validity to all that astrology stuff—Sam gave in. And that was how the article, a full-page feature in the food section of the *Boston Globe*, had fallen into her lap, a pin of pure platinum. It was luck that had brought the reporter to Sippican in the first place. He'd been visiting his sister's summer rental cottage when his ten-year-old niece told him about "the cake lady," a cute bit he used as the lead for his article: "The neighborhood children call her the Cake Lady."

At first that line bugged Sam; it sounded as if she were some grandmotherly Mary Poppins instead of a thirty-eight-year-old pastry chef whose wedding cakes went for nearly the price of a compact car. But then the reporter also said that the sugar flowers on her cakes were so lush, so botanically correct—roses with twenty-five petals, each petal a different shape or size—that wedding guests marveled they did not wilt; that helped make up for the Cake Lady quote. He went on to say that some of her other creations were more like miniature cathedrals than cakes—brilliant, bejeweled, and dramatic, towering nearly five feet in height, fabrications so extraordinary they might have been inspired by Gothic churches or Fabergé coronets or Byzantine necklaces.

Her mother, were she still alive, would have voiced concern about how such over-the-top praise leads to a swelled head, but Sam didn't need to worry about that. Any chance of an overblown ego was forestalled by the catalog of her weaknesses and faults, a litany she knew by heart: She was too stubborn for her own good, was prone to self-sabotage and procrastination, wasn't athletic, was too self-conscious to dance well. Abilities that came easily to others—parallel parking, singing on key, balancing a checkbook—eluded her. So she would gratefully accept the reporter's praise for this one thing she excelled at. She made cakes worthy of being called art.

After the *Globe* piece ran, her phone rang steadily for a month, dozens of calls, some from caterers and brides as far away as New York and Philadelphia. And all because a reporter—a food writer—came to town to visit his sister. Pure luck. When she was younger, Sam used to think luck was something you could earn or influence, but now she knew better. Luck just happened. Both the good and the bad, and she'd had her share of each, although lately, knock wood, she'd been on a promising roll, a fact Stacy attributed to her birth planet's current position in the Second House.

Now she inserted the number 18 shell tip into the pastry bag, spooned in royal icing, and started piping, the tip at a precise forty-five-degree angle. Over the past six months she'd formed at least a zillion scallop shells and she could do this in the dark. Blindfolded. She hummed while she worked, touching the tip to the sheet of parchment paper, then lifting it slightly to create a rise. The melody helped her maintain a sense of rhythm, which was more important than people might think. That was the secret. Rhythm and momentum. She completed a dozen rows, fourteen to a row, then flexed her right hand and shook off a cramp.

A year ago, when she had relocated to Sippican and opened the shop, every bride that walked through the door wanted fresh flowers on her cake, but now that was passé. These days it was the whole seashore motif. Shells. Mermaids. Sand castles.

As if reading her mind, Stacy looked over and said, "At least no one has wanted one of those creepy little bride-and-groom things stuck on the top like midgets."

"I think we're safe on that score," Sam said.

"You hope."

"Unless some food editor decrees retro is in."

"Just shoot me with a gun," Stacy said.

Stacy. Now there was another piece of good luck. The very day Sam had propped a Part-Time Help Wanted sign in the front window, Stacy Dunn walked in to order a birthday cake for her mother. Minutes later, with only faint misgivings, Sam had hired her. Who would have thought this twenty-nine-year-old amateur astrologer who believed in past lives, this biker-chick look-alike and two-time divorcée at work on her third, would turn out to be the ideal assistant, the second-best thing to happen to Sam in years? (Although even Sam had to admit Stacy's attitude could use an occasional tweaking. For instance, she maintained that most brides' militant belief in until-death-do-us-part True Love could give a person heartburn. "Don't they know the statistics?" she'd ask. "Haven't they looked around?")

In spite of her own complicated romantic history, Sam admired the brides' courage. She respected their bravery in the face of the dreary statistics Stacy was so fond of citing. All the time she was decorating a bride's cake, she poured wishes into it, good thoughts that would protect her and shield her from disillusionment, harm, deceit. She felt tender, nearly maternal, toward these brides. All of them: the confident ones and the nervous ones and the drama queens. The brides who wanted to be her new best friend—at least until the reception was over—and the ones dressed in empire gowns that barely concealed pregnancies. Even the bride who had met her husband-to-be in Jamaica and wanted their cake made in the shape of a green-and-purple Rasta hat. (That one about sent Stacy out for a case of Sam Adams. "A Rasta hat," she pronounced after the girl left. "Why doesn't she just order a cake from Carvel?")

These women, some still girls really, came in alone, or with fiancés, or in the grip of overconfident mothers who acted as if it were their wedding, not their daughter's, women who made it clear they were footing the bill and calling the shots. Lately these mothers, almost without exception, had been whippet thin, with the well-tended look of women who spent far too much time having their nails done and their hair foiled. Women who made her conscious of her own inadequacies in the looks department. Women like Libby, she suddenly thought.

Libby. Caught totally off guard, Sam was unprepared for the pain—the actual physical pain—the name caused, even now. Her hand quavered, ruining a scallop shell. *Libby.* It had been six years. Six years. Nearly a sixth of her life. She had thought time, the reliable anesthetic, had done its work, but now a deep ache of regret and loss swept over her, scoring her raw with its familiarity. She closed her eyes, forced memories of Libby resolutely from her mind. She had done this before; it could be done. She took a sip of water, scraped the misshapen scallop shell off the parchment paper, and returned to piping shells, willing the rhythm to calm her.

Outside, moths fluttered against the window, adding a counterpoint to the Hobart that chugged away on the far side of the kitchen. Like every other piece of equipment in the place, the mammoth mixer was beyond old, ancient really, with a bowl large enough to bathe a child in. The Warrior, she called it, both because it was such a workhorse and because its original tour of duty was on a U.S. frigate in the forties. Still, you couldn't pay her to trade it for a newer model. This was a practical consideration as much as a sentimental one.

Sam did tend toward sentimental gestures—a quality of Aries, Stacy said—and knew that most people saw her as the essence of romance, probably because of her wedding-cake business, her home (a lavender-trimmed Victorian), and her appearance. According to Lee, her looks were *très, très* romantic. Botticelli-like, he said. In every other way admirably sane, he actually said things like that. As Stacy would say, totally OTT. Over the top. He was besotted with her, he said. *Besotted.*

She tried to hear this—she *did* believe in romance—but the word and its terrifying implications were enough to make her sweat. "Besotted" was best left for brides. She preferred plain, ordinary "in love." It was hard enough to accept love without inflating it like a blimp.

She checked the clock, amazed to see it was after six, then looked over at Stacy, who was stirring melted chocolate into a double batch of batter. There was a dusting of flour in her gel-spiked hair and a smudge of chocolate on her pointed chin.

"You don't have to stay," Sam told her. "Barring disaster, we're on schedule."

"I'll just finish this up," Stacy said. It was the second day this week she had stayed late, but she refused overtime.

"I can't believe I booked three weddings on the same day," Sam said by way of apology. "Of course it wouldn't be so bad if it weren't for the Van Horn order. All those mini-cakes for the individual tables. What was I thinking?" They both knew she would be glad enough for it come winter. So far there were only two weddings in the book for February, none for March, and three in April, a long stretch until the cash flow began again in the spring.

When the phone rang, the fifth time in the past half hour, she let Stacy pick up and went back to forming shells. While Sam worked she made mental notes. She needed to check her supply of pearl dust, since she would probably need more for the Sanderson order. Now *that* was a cake to get excited about. Sam looked up at the sketch tacked on the board over her workstation. Designed to incorporate details from the bride's gown and bouquet, the cake featured ivory fondant ribbons and bows that cascaded over four tiers. Each layer was trimmed with tiny seed pearls of royal icing, each gem brushed with pearl dust. A spray of white roses, their centers softened by a hint of ivory, decorated the top.

Stacy placed the receiver in the cradle. "Mrs. Gillis," she said. "From the Yacht Club."

"Let me guess," Sam said. "Sheet cake, right?" In a perfect world, sheet cakes would be outlawed.

"For Saturday. I told them you couldn't do it." Stacy was unable to hold back a sigh of disapproval. She had made it clear that she thought Sam should take every job that came along. Sheet cakes for lodge meetings, birthday cakes for one-year-olds, twenty-fifth-anniversary cakes with the couple's names spelled out in silver dragées. Well, there were a lot of things Sam *should* do, but wouldn't. Stay within budget. Cut back on coffee. Lose twelve pounds. Okay, twenty.

"Listen," Sam said. "Why don't you go on ahead? We're really fine. By the time I finish up here, the last batch of cakes should be ready to come out."

"You sure?" Stacy said.

"Positive."

"If you're sure." Stacy removed her apron.

Sam readjusted the parchment paper and began a new row—all concentration, hoping to avoid Stacy's end-of-the-day ritual—but there was to be no escape. Her assistant crossed to the extra chair by Sam's workstation and plunked down.

"I'll go first," Stacy said. "You," she said, as she always did. "I am grateful for you."

Sam scratched a suddenly itchy arm. Her face reddened at the compliment.

"Okay," Stacy said. "Your turn."

"Is this necessary?"

"Absolutely." A therapist had told Stacy, after her second divorce, to take time every day to list all the things she was grateful for. He'd told her to adopt an attitude of gratitude. Sam could just imagine the therapist's syrupy tone. *Adopt an attitude of gratitude.*

Stacy had told her that this practice had gotten her through some rough times, although there had been days when she had to scrabble to think of even one item for her list. She said she had come to believe that gratitude held a transformative power. Stacy believed in gratitude just as deeply as she did in the idea that Mercury in retrograde caused machines to malfunction and tires to go flat.

"You want abundance in your life, don't you?" she said to Sam. "Gratitude is the key to abundance."

"I'm grateful, okay?"

"Then let's hear your list."

Sam rolled her eyes.

"And be specific. It's important to be specific."

"Okay," Sam began. "I'm grateful I don't have to clean toilets for a living."

In spite of herself, Stacy laughed.

Sam began another shell. "I'm grateful I never married a man who wore a toupee. Or a ponytail." Now she was warming up. "Let's see. I'm grateful I have my own teeth, that I don't have warts, and that my kids didn't die in the Johnstown flood."

"You don't have kids," Stacy said.

"Another thing to be grateful for," Sam said. Not true. A too easy flippancy. In truth, she did want kids—someday. And there were many things for which she was thankful. But she would sooner have died than articulate them to her assistant. Okay, it was superstitious, but Sam was afraid that if she acknowledged her blessings aloud, it would attract the attention of the gods or fate or whatever/whoever was out there and, in a flash, all would be repossessed. If she had learned anything from her life's experience it was that the things you most loved could be taken away in the space of a breath and that there was nothing as fragile as happiness. Not the wings of the moths fluttering against the window. Not the thinnest, most delicate thread of spun sugar.

Here is what Sam was truly grateful for: Lee.

Last night, lying in his arms, she had looked at him and said, "You know that song from *The Sound of Music*?"

He laughed. "*The Sound of Music*? You're kidding me."

"The solo Maria sings," she persisted. "In the gazebo."

"I guess I missed out on that part of my musical education." He stroked her hips, his fingers strong, slightly calloused. Sailor's hands.

She jabbed his ribs. "You should talk. The Doobie Brothers? Foghat?"

"I have yet to sink to Broadway shows." He had no shame about his musical taste.

She straightened up and her auburn hair, unpinned, spilled over her shoulders. Too self-conscious to sing in her off-key voice, she spoke the lyrics: " 'So somewhere in my wicked, miserable past . . . I must have done something good.' "

He pulled her down onto him. " 'Your wicked, miserable past'?"

"That's how you make me feel," she said. "Like here you are in my life, in spite of everything."

"So is this when I get to hear about your illicit history?" he said. "Murder? Embezzlement? Bank robbery with an Uzi?" He truly believed there was nothing she could ever have done he couldn't forgive. If she had been Lizzie Borden incarnate, he probably would have offered to wash the blood from the axe.

The phone rang again and Stacy headed for it.

"Let it go," Sam said.

"You sure?"

"It's after five. Officially, we're closed. Let the machine pick up."

They listened to the lilting, opening notes—Debussy—and then her voice: "Golliwog's Cakewalk. We are unable to come to the phone right now. Leave your name, your number, and a message, and we will return your call." Stacy had wanted Mendelssohn in the background. Or Pachelbel's Canon. She had also tried to persuade Sam to rename the business. She said "Golliwog's" made it sound like the name of a place that sold tropical fish. When Sam explained about its being the title of the Debussy piece, Stacy said that even with the music for a hint, ninety percent of the customers wouldn't get it. She thought Sam should choose something with some pizzazz. "Flour Power" would be good.

There was a click, then the signaling tone, then nothing, as if the caller had hung up, and then, after a pause: "Sam?" The voice was hesitant, soft. "Sam, are you there?"

Sam caught her breath.

"It's Libby. I need to talk to you. It's important." There was another long, humming pause.

Sam froze.

"Will you call me?" the voice continued. Then, so soft Sam could barely hear the word: "Please."

The *coincidence* of it absolutely leveled Sam, as if by thinking of Libby minutes before she had somehow created this contact, willed it, conjured her sister up by the power of memory. She set the pastry tube aside, saw Stacy look at her hands, saw them tremble.

She is six, Libby eight. In the background, someone is playing the piano.

"Who was that?" Stacy asked.

The piano plays on, slightly out of tune. The tune is lilting, hypnotic. "Tea for Two."

"Nobody," Sam said. "Nobody at all."

Libby

. . . .

ibby had never been good at waiting. Give her an answer, don't just leave her hanging out to dry in a limbo of unknowing. She stared at the phone, as if by will alone she could compel it to ring. For two days now, she hadn't been more than five feet from it, had even carted the cordless into the bathroom while she stood at the sink and gave herself an awkward, unsatisfactory sponge bath. (Because of the sub-clavical catheter and the attendant danger of infection, showers were forbidden.) The silence of the phone mocked her and she felt, beneath her impatience, buried beneath guilt, the mounting heat of resentment. Typical of Sam not to call back. Typically selfish. Libby should have known better than even to have tried that avenue. She transferred her anger to a spot of tarnish on the lip of the silver creamer. It was the second Wednesday of the month, the day set aside for polishing the silver. Spread out on the table was an array of antique napkin rings, her mother's tea service, eight ornate candle-holders of various heights, and flatware—service for twelve.

Even now she clung to her household schedule. Over the past months, it had kept her steady, providing a compass for uncharted waters. Bed linens and laundry on Mondays. Dusting and vacuuming on Tuesdays. Wednesdays, depending on the week in the month, were for ironing, mending, cabinets to be straightened, or the silver. Grocery shopping and errands on Thursdays. Fridays were for appointments and the odd tasks that were always arising. Richard used to encourage her to hire help. With his trust fund, they could certainly afford it, but she had never liked the idea of a stranger poking through her life, nosing about in her cupboards, handling her things. The twins teased her about her cleaning routine—she once overheard them call her Anal Avis—but they were quick enough to make use of the clean clothes and meals that resulted from her organization and work.

She screwed the cap on the can of polish, snapped off the rubber gloves and replaced them on the shelf beneath the sink. It took three trips to return the silver to the dining room sideboard. Usually the gleaming surfaces brought her a measure of satisfaction, but today she was too aware of the silent phone to take pleasure in completed tasks. She knew that tonight Richard would urge her to phone Sam again, but there was little or no chance of that. It had taken every ounce of courage to call once; she hadn't the reserves to try again.

She checked the clock. Eleven forty-five. On Wednesdays, Richard's class ended at eleven thirty. It took him five minutes to gather the students' papers, another ten to drive from the campus to their door. He would be pulling into the drive any minute. A year ago, he might have stayed on campus, using the free time to grade papers or meet with one of his advisees, but not now. There is no need to come home, she'd told him. I want to, he'd said. Over the past month on these Wednesdays they had gone out to lunch or taken a walk. Once he suggested they go upstairs for a nap. She refused. She couldn't imagine he really wanted to make love to her. She could barely stand looking at herself in the mirror, seeing the disfiguring catheter that jutted from her chest. No, she certainly wasn't interested in going upstairs for a nap.

"A nap" was Richard's euphemism for sex. Just turned forty-three and he was still shy about making love. Even now, married twenty years, he would kiss her in public only under protest and would only really let loose after three or four drinks. When they were young she had found his shyness endearing. In fact, it had been one of the things that attracted her to him. That and his music.

They had met during Thanksgiving break at Oberlin. The campus was nearly empty that weekend, but Libby stayed on, since there was no sense in making the long drive back to Massachusetts for the four-day break. She passed the time sleeping and studying or in one of the practice rooms with her flute. Her playing was passable—she didn't delude herself into thinking otherwise—but it relaxed her and swept her head free of troubles and concerns. A mind vacuum, she called it. That Saturday afternoon, as she was heading for the practice room, flute case tucked under her arm, she heard music from one of the other rooms. A cello.

Her steps slowed, stopped. The cellist was good, the playing confident. There were no mistakes or hesitations, no tirelessly repeated passages. Something stirred, vibrated deep in her belly, the yearning, the ache that the bowing of strings always aroused in her. She leaned against the wall. She had no idea how long she stayed like that—long enough that at some point she slid down the wall, sat on the floor. She closed her eyes and drank it in. Chopin's Polonaise Brillante. Tears pooled behind her lids, slid down her cheeks. She remained there even after the last notes were no more than an echo. A passage of Chopin—just that—but it set in motion a meeting that changed her life.

"Are you okay?"

He was tall—over six feet, she guessed—and older, possibly a professor, with craggy good looks. He wore pleated pants, a crewneck sweater in a green that set off the flecks of green in his hazel eyes, and a sports jacket. His voice was gentle, filled with concern.

"Yes," she said, mortified to be seen like that, crumpled on the floor, weeping like a child. With guys her own age she was confident, intimidating even—there were guys she had *leveled* with one look— but not with him, not from the beginning. She scrambled to stand, swiped at her cheeks. "Really, I'm fine. It's the music."

He reached out, helped her to her feet. "Is it that bad?"

She flushed, started to protest, then saw he had been teasing.

"I'm Richard Barnett."

"Elizabeth," she said. "Libby."

"Nice to meet you, Elizabeth Libby."

"Just Libby," she said. "Libby Lewis."

"A pleasure to meet you," he said.

God help her, she nearly curtseyed.

Over coffee, she learned he was a grad student from Shaker Heights. She told him that she was from Massachusetts and that she was, or hoped to be, a poet. Later, he walked her back to her dorm, asked if he might read her poetry sometime. Another week passed before he tried to kiss her.

Back then, tired of too-persistent males who were always trying to get her into bed, she had welcomed his sexual reticence, but as the years passed she had found it less appealing. Teenagers walked around joined at the lip, practically doing it parked in the school lot, in daylight, for heaven's sake—once she saw a car actually *bouncing*—but he acted like kissing her in a restaurant was cause for arrest. PDA, he called it. Public display of affection. As if she wanted him to lay her out on the table rather than share a kiss, perform a small act of tenderness. When she allowed herself to think about it, she could almost appreciate the irony. Well, there were ways she had disappointed him, too. Twenty years built up lots of tarnish in a marriage, and it was not always possible to buff it away.

She checked the time again—eleven forty-eight—and listened for the car, but found herself hoping Richard had stayed in his office. Lately his solicitousness had been driving her mad. The way he jumped up to get her tea before the water had come to a full boil, or massaged her legs while she read in the evenings—something he hadn't done since she was pregnant with the twins. Or the tone of his voice when he asked how she was doing, the timbre hushed, like the tone you'd use at a concert or in church. Or the way he studied her when he thought she didn't notice, averting his eyes when she caught him. It made her want to scream, just hurl words across the room at him. What the hell are you staring at? You want to know how I'm doing? Well, why don't you just get up and pull a blood sample, check my urine? Sometimes the words nearly escaped, but she managed to hold them back. Richard didn't understand that caring too much could be a fault, could feel smothering.

The thought of his concern closed in and Libby wanted to bolt. She scrawled a quick note and pinned it to the message board, knowing he would be hurt when he saw it. Once that would have stopped her, but now she gathered her shoulder bag, car keys, jacket. She was nearly through the door when the phone rang. Although she had been waiting for a call, hoping for it, now she was unprepared. She let it ring again and again as she steeled herself to lift the receiver. The words she had carefully rehearsed faded. Her mouth turned dry, ashy, and she had to swallow twice before she managed a simple hello.

"Hey, Mrs. Barnett." Her heartbeat calmed, returned to its normal rhythm. It was not Sam. "It's Patrick. Patrick Cooper." Patrick the Prick, she thought. "I've been trying to reach Matt. Leaving messages at his dorm. I was wondering if he's coming home this weekend."

She made her voice careful, neutral. "I don't think so, Patrick. As far as I know he doesn't plan on flying back until Thanksgiving."

She checked the clock. Ten to. "I'll tell him you called," she said before she hung up, although she wouldn't. She didn't like Patrick. She could never see him without remembering the afternoon years before. She hadn't meant to eavesdrop, but her bedroom door had been ajar and the boys' voices reverberated, vibrant with testosterone. (Honestly, sometimes she thought a girl could get pregnant just walking by a teenage male.) "So where's your mother?" Patrick had asked. "Off with the other hockey sticks?" "What?" Matt said. "You know, the hockey sticks. My mother and the others. I mean, isn't that what they look like? Skinny as sticks and dressed all in beige." Libby waited for Matt to say something—defend her—but he laughed. "The hockey sticks," he said. "That's a hoot."

She had wanted to march down the stairs and slap Patrick, slap Matthew, too. Would they be happier if mothers all went around letting themselves go? Getting fat? They didn't have any idea how hard it was. Pilates. Yoga. Jogging. Free weights. And the *vigilance*. Training yourself to eat half what you'd ordered, watching every mouthful you swallowed, not even remembering the last time you had a piece of chocolate. Counting calories or grams of fat, or points, depending on which weight-loss system you were using at the moment. Did that little prick think it was fun to spend most of the time hungry while you lived with the tyranny of the scale and mirror? In that she had been luckier than most, a size 8 her entire adult life, just as she had been in high school. A perfect 8, according to saleswomen, as if perfection could be found in a dress size. No breast reduction for her like Suzanne Mason, or lipo'ed stomach like June Duncan, who maintained you could do sit-ups from now to the next millennium but it wouldn't repair the damage of having kids. Well, Patrick would be happy now. With her puffy face and swollen legs, she looked like anything but a hockey stick. A marshmallow was the more apt simile.

She heard Richard's car pull into the drive. Too late for an easy escape.

He came in, closed the kitchen door quietly behind him, as if the least noise might trip an alarm. He set his briefcase and the newspaper on the counter, then crossed to her and kissed her cheek. His smile was tentative, his eyes were watchful, gauging her mood. He was getting a little paunch, and the flesh beneath his eyes was puffy—his fall allergies—but he was still handsome in a Michael Caine kind of way, still good-looking enough to be the center of at least one or two coeds' fantasies. At the annual autumn mixer, Libby could pick them out by the way they fluttered around him, smooth-skinned and smiling, bodies ripe as pear flesh. Suddenly she wondered if right now on the Brown campus Mercedes was performing a similar dance around some middle-aged professor. She hoped their daughter was smarter than that, but of course lust, or whatever it was these girls were experiencing, had less to do with intelligence than with the dangerous and heady temptations of first independence and, on another level, of exploring the cruel power granted by youth alone. Richard was not totally unaware. He reassured Libby that he kept his office door open whenever one of them dropped by. Of course, if they provoked fantasies on his part, he would never confess it. She had a momentary flash, a quick and painful memory of a time and betrayal she never managed to erase from recall.

Richard noted her jacket, her pocketbook. "Going out?" he asked. His face was neutral but she knew him well enough to catch the flicker of hurt. For a moment she softened. He was only trying to negotiate the slippery terrain their life had become. She knew he wished she would handle this whole thing differently, knew that he wanted to be partners in this. She couldn't allow that, because he wasn't a partner. Not in this. He reminded her of the young men who announced "We're pregnant" when their wives were expecting. No, she always wanted to tell them. *You* are not pregnant. Your *wife* is. At least Richard hadn't tried to usurp that. In fact, when she went into heavy labor with the twins, he had fainted. Well, not exactly fainted but turned so white Dr. Glass insisted he leave the delivery room.

"Yes," she said. "Just a couple of errands."

"Want me to go with? We could do lunch at Southgate after."

Go with. Do lunch. The words sounded ridiculous coming from him, he so precise with language, and she knew it was a sign of how hard he was trying. She shook her head. "I'm not really hungry." She didn't ask him to join her. Not long ago it would have been taken for granted that he would go with her. "There's soup in the fridge."

She was at the door when he asked.

"Have you heard anything? Has she called?"

"No."

He nodded, his mouth tight. "I'm sorry," he said. "But what can we expect? Samantha's true to course."

Libby felt a stab of anger, an impulse to defend that took her completely by surprise. She let it go. Not Richard's fault. He was only parroting judgments she had voiced, opinions she herself was entertaining only moments earlier. She knew he was angry because rage was easier to feel than fear. Didn't she know the truth of that. Fear was the black beast they had been trying desperately to keep at bay for months.

In the car she had no destination in mind, but she was aware of Richard watching from the kitchen window and so backed out of the drive like a woman with a mission. Once away from the house, she drove aimlessly through town, away from the lake, up Deerpath, past the library, onto Western, up Illinois. She was so edgy that for a moment, as she drove by the Deer Path Inn, she actually considered going in and ordering a glass of wine. One wouldn't kill her, but it wasn't one glass she wanted. It was five. Ten. Oblivion. She thought next of heading north on 94 toward Wisconsin—maybe stop at Gurnee Mills, pick up a sweater for Mercedes, something for Matt. Not too long ago she would have spent an afternoon like this in a frenzy of shopping. She would have bought a pair of new leather boots for herself, high-heeled ones to show off her legs. Shopping, like slim ankles, was one more pleasure that had been taken from her.

She looped around town again and then, without conscious intent, pulled the Volvo into the parking area for the Open Lands. The lot was empty, unusual for a midday in October, and she was surprised to find herself here. This was Richard's spot, not hers. He was the one who loved the prairie, volunteered each fall for the seed collecting, knew its history like he knew his own. Imagine, he had said to her, imagine the first time white settlers laid eyes on this place, coming from the east, the land of forest and trees, and seeing this expanse, this sea of grasses. Imagine how it was back then, grassland that was unending. It would be unlike anything they had ever experienced, no matter the country from which they had immigrated. An ocean of grass. The opening edge of a new world. Imagine.

Richard saw poetry in the prairie, in its history and botany, and he was familiar with the works of the poets and writers and naturalists who had sung its song. He could recite word-perfect Sandburg's lines. All she could remember was the beginning, the part about "The prairie sings to me in the forenoon," and she's wasn't absolutely certain she had that right. Richard knew the names of the grasses: big bluestem, switchgrass, Indian grass, the prairie sedges, prairie dropseed. He knew the grasses by season and height, just as he did the scores of flowering plants—purple meadow rue, drooping coneflower, swamp milkweed, wild bergamot, prairie dock—and he had informed her that the roots on some grasses reached a depth of eighteen feet. In spite of his patient tutelage, Libby still couldn't tell them apart. In truth, the prairie made her nervous. It was too untamed. She didn't like the idea of what might be hiding in the tall grass, where there were always rustlings. Mice and voles and rabbits, and that was the least of it. There were foxes, too, she knew. And coyotes and snakes. If she had been a pioneer, on that first sight of the tall grass she would have turned right around and fled to the security of forested land, which, while wilderness, didn't threaten her in the way the prairie did. She couldn't explain what impulse had brought her here this afternoon.

She sat for a minute, gathering energy, then opened the car door. The ground gave underfoot—it had rained on and off for weeks—and she went to the trunk and retrieved her gardening boots. She had not hosed them off after her last walk with Richard and soil caked the soles. As she leaned against the fender for balance, the warmth of sun-heated metal radiated through her slacks, spreading across her thighs. Robbed of so much this past year, she was surprised at the rush of pleasure that simple sensation brought. She closed her eyes and lifted her face to the sun, then after a minute bent to replace her shoes with the boots.

She took the path leading directly through the center of the prairie, walking between the fall-dried stalks and frost-blighted seed heads, the desiccated blossoms of goldenrod and milkweed and other plants she couldn't identify. Grasshoppers flitted around her ankles. Dragonflies fed in grasses turned autumn gold, wine russet. At least today the path was deserted and she didn't have to contend with the usual horde of dog walkers. Dopey-grinned retrievers straining at their tethers, desperate to be freed and pawing at you, slobbering drool. Jittery Irish setters. Mr. Bagley and that nasty little cocker spaniel.

She had walked only a mile when she grew winded. Her stamina faded quicker these days. As recently as July she was able to make the three-mile loop without problems. Carlotta had warned her about this, but still Libby was surprised at how quickly she was losing ground. She sat on a bench beneath the gnarled limbs of a fire-stunted bur oak. A brass plaque on the wooden back proclaimed it had been given in memory of "Buddy Who Loved This Land." Man or animal? she wondered. Half the benches erected along the paths had been given in honor of dogs. Overhead, two crows dove at a red-tailed hawk. She sat for a minute, felt her chest rise and fall with the beating of her heart.

"I'm dying," she said. It was the first time she had spoken the words aloud.

Sam

. . . .

Tea for two. Two for tea.
Me for you and you for me alone.

Flap, flap, flap, ball change. *Sam relies on Libby's feet for directions and thus is a half beat behind. They are dancing too close, nearly touching, but Sam ignores Miss Nickels's instructions, hissed from the wings, telling them to* space it out. *In dress rehearsal Sam knew the steps* perfectly, *but now they have vanished from memory. She is one breath away from damp humiliation, though they were told to visit the girls' room just before they went on, because, "We don't want an accident, now, do we." Their parents promised they'd be in the front row, but Sam can't look out. Her brow is furrowed in concentration, and although their teacher has told them they must count only in their heads, she thinks it might help if she says the beats aloud.* One and two and three and four. *The joy she usually finds in the metallic clicking of her tap shoes is eclipsed by fear.*

Flap, flap, flap, ball change, ball change. *They're dressed in identical outfits, bear costumes their mother stayed up all night to finish. Brown terry-*

cloth ears perch on their heads and are anchored by elastic straps beneath their chins. Libby hates these costumes and has begged Miss Nickels to let them wear leotards like the older girls, but is told, "No, this number is always performed by dancing bears."

Adorable, a woman in the audience says. A happy voice. Not their mother's. The chinstrap cuts into Sam's flesh. Inside the costume she is sweaty. Her stomach prickles. Offstage, two older boys begin to argue. She stares desperately at Libby's feet. Finally, finally, Mrs. Bowman strikes the last notes on the piano keys—how happy we will be—hitting the "be" with a thud. Sam keeps going a few steps after the music ends. Libby stands center stage. They have practiced the bowing part at rehearsals, but now Sam is too bashful. Independent of her, Libby bends forward, her bow so deep her hand sweeps the floor. Their mother will say Libby is showing off. Above the applause, Sam hears their father calling their names and dares to look out at the upturned faces. He is standing, making a loud whistle with two fingers in his mouth. Their mother remains seated. Sam can almost hear her whisper to their father, For heaven's sake, Peter, don't encourage the child. Their mother is always scolding Libby, telling her to behave like a lady. Libby waves at the audience and then bows again, defying both their mother and Miss Nickels, who at the dress rehearsal yesterday warned everyone that they were to take just one bow each.

With an impatient swoosh, the curtain cuts off the audience. A group of toy soldiers push and stumble onstage while Mrs. Bowman makes a production of switching sheet music. Miss Nickels motions to them, urging them to hurry, to get out of the way, but Libby takes her time leaving the stage. In the wings, she pulls off Sam's bear ears, as if she knows how much the strap is hurting, the way she always knows what Sam is feeling. "You were great, Sam-I-Am," Libby says, swooping Sam up in a big hug. A bear hug. A bear hug from a bear. Sam smiles to herself at the joke. The welt beneath her chin, the hot suit, the way she couldn't remember the dance steps and didn't bow at the end, all is forgotten in the comfort of Libby's embrace. She loves Libby best in the world.

Yesterday can't be undone. And eventually all things—even things you don't want to remember—come to the surface. Sam leaned against the table, as if bracing herself against a past she could not bear and a future she could not know. Her throat closed, so tight she feared she would never be able to swallow again, and heaviness settled in her chest, as if she had swallowed stones.

Libby. The sister who had taught her how to play hopscotch and French-braid her hair, who had thought up names for her PlaySkool people and protected her. Words from a bumper sticker she had recently seen sprang to mind: *Embrace the Past.* As if that were possible. Well, screw that. The past was just that, past. Today was what mattered.

Across the room, the oven timer dinged. Resolutely, Sam tuned out memory—the *unembraceable* past—and turned on automatic pilot. She set the final batch of cakes out on the baker's rack. Steam wafted up, and she inhaled the scent of cocoa, let it bathe her, as if its sweet moisture contained power to heal. *Automatic pilot.* While the chocolate rounds were cooling, she returned to the sugar shells and finished up the last of them. *The Sanderson order,* she remembered, and got up to check the supply of pearl dust, which was low, after all. She needed glycerin and almond paste, too.

She filled the sink with soapy water and started scrubbing the beaters and mixing bowls. It took a good thirty minutes to clean up. Upstairs, her living space was totally cyclone headquarters, but here, on the first floor, she was disciplined about order and cleanliness. By the time she had finished, it was after seven, later than she expected, but Lee would still be at the boatyard. She sectioned two limes and grabbed a six-pack of Beck's from the walk-in. They could order out for pizza.

She was nearly out the door when she realized she had forgotten to leave a note for Stacy. She scrawled the list—pearl dust, glycerin, almond paste—and added a reminder to order from Beryl's, the most dependable of the suppliers, and a notation to add extra for overnight express. She'd need a double order of the dust, since she'd be using it for the Weaver cake as well. (Her favorite trick: pearl dust mixed with lemon extract painted on a cake to make it come to life.) As she finished the memo, her eyes fell on the message light, which was blinking obsessively. She reached to press ERASE, hesitated a second, then surprised herself by punching MESSAGES.

"Sam? Sam, are you there?" Six years since she'd heard her sister's voice. She swallowed, reminded herself to breathe. "It's Libby. I need to talk to you. It's important. Will you call me? Please."

She sank down onto the desk chair, stared at the phone as if there were more. *Please*, Libby had said. Her voice sounded soft, but something else, too. If it had been anyone but Libby, Sam would have called it vulnerable. She hardened herself to this thought.

She reached over and jabbed ERASE. This time she didn't hesitate.

A half block away from the boatyard, Sam saw shafts of light shining up through skylights, beckoning her. From the parking lot, she smelled wood smoke and was cheered by the idea of the stove—and Lee—waiting inside. Okay, here was one for the gratitude list. Alice Hardwin. Sam was deeply, eternally grateful for Alice Hardwin.

When she relocated from Mattapoisett to Sippican a year before, Sam had chosen Alice to help her find a place for her business. The other agents in the realty office—all women—were slender and well turned out, but Sam felt immediately comfortable with Alice, a middle-aged widow, overweight, careless with grooming, but radiating good intentions and kindness. At that moment, Sam needed kindness more than slick professionalism.

They weren't in Alice's Mazda more than a half hour—one property seen and rejected—when Alice got to the point. Are you single? she asked. Sam answered yes, not bothering to fill in the sorry details of her marital history. Alice beamed. "I have a son," she'd said. Don't they all, Sam thought, barely suppressing an eye-roll.

His name was Hurley. Hurley Hardwin. That alone told Sam all she needed to know. She pictured a sad sack of a man, stoop-shouldered and doughy, like Alice. Hurley, burley, pudding and pie, she thought. God. She might be thirty-seven and divorced, with no prospects in sight, but she had *standards*. Single but not desperate, that was her motto. She shut out the rest of the Realtor's ramblings.

On the third day, when Sam had given up all hope of finding a place, Alice said there was one more property she could show her, a Victorian located three streets west of Front Street in a block zoned for business. Although it was more than she could afford, Sam thought what the heck and agreed to drive by.

She laughed when she saw it. The house, boasting a fresh coat of lavender, *was* a cake, in the way gingerbread-trimmed Victorians were. Inside, everything was perfect. There was a spacious kitchen running the length of the back that would be large enough for commercial equipment, a paneled dining room that could be transformed into an office, and a sunlit parlor with an oversize bay window where, once she stripped the truly atrocious wallpaper, she could meet with prospective brides. On the second floor were three large bedrooms where she could live. It was too perfect, but what made Sam decide on it, despite the price, were the foundation plantings on both sides of the central entrance. According to Alice, the shrubs were a spirea called bridal wreath. Some signs were too obvious to ignore. Sam made an offer that afternoon and by five, barely time for regrets or second thoughts, it was accepted.

To celebrate, Alice insisted on having her to dinner. They settled on six thirty, and when it was too late for Sam to back out gracefully, Alice mentioned that Hurley would be joining them. Sandbagged, Sam thought.

Sam didn't dress to impress, barely bothered with makeup. The wine she picked out was a cheap Chablis. (Surely Alice stuck to the whites.) Sam would eat, claim exhaustion, make an early escape. She was late arriving and as she headed up the walk, the aroma of brewed coffee and cooked meat wafted toward her. She could picture the entire meal: pot roast, mashed potatoes, canned vegetables, homemade relish. Packaged rolls.

Alice opened the door before Sam had even raised a hand to knock. "I can't wait for you two to meet," she said.

Save me, Sam thought.

Hurley was in the kitchen. He stood when she entered, then smiled. He was just shy of six feet, his body compact, muscular. His eyes were brown and calm. She had to catch her breath.

"Samantha," Alice said, "meet Hurley."

"Lee," Hurley corrected. "Most everyone calls me Lee." He took the wine from her. She smelled the citrus scent of his aftershave. He wore a blue work shirt, freshly ironed, and Levi's, just the right side of snug. She wanted to sink through the floor. She wanted to start over, wanted to take a shower, shampoo and blow-dry her hair, put on her black jeans, the ones that made her look thinner, and her good gray cashmere turtleneck. And earrings. Jazzy dangling ones. And makeup. At the very least, lipstick and eyeliner. She wanted to have chosen a good merlot. Her stomach was heavy with that pulsing heat she hadn't felt in a long time.

He smiled again and she actually felt her knees weaken. Not a good sign. Jesus, she thought. A guy says hello and you're ready to start ordering the monogrammed towels. If she knew what was good for her, she'd get out of there so fast there would be burn marks down the center of the drive. Instead she accepted a glass of wine.

And that was the beginning.

Later, Alice said it was inevitable that Sam and Lee should fall in love. She maintained it was because of all the good karma Sam had accumulated creating wedding cakes for brides while she herself remained single. Alice believed in things like karma, or her understanding of it, which was pretty much gleaned from daytime TV. The Gospel According to Oprah governed Alice's life. Although Sam wasn't about to make light of Alice's beliefs (she had her own rites and rituals that saw her through), she was banking on there being no such thing as karma. She didn't even want to think about all she might have to answer for.

By moonlight Sam made out the hulks of two boats resting in yard cradles. They had been delivered the week before and were, she knew, rotted and worm-eaten. One had been vandalized.

It always amazed Sam that these wrecks could be salvaged. It seemed it would be easier to start from scratch with a new boat than to go to the labor and expense of attempting to restore these disasters. To the average viewer, to her, they looked beyond reclamation, but not to Lee. He saw in them the possibility of new life, or, more precisely, a return to their former glory, a careful restoration, every step undertaken with the integrity of the original vessel in mind. "Boats have feeling and personality," he had told her. "Start screwing around with that and who knows what's going to happen to you." He worked on these projects with a patience that astonished her. He talked about antiquated tools the way another man might talk about a perfectly executed double play or about Elle Macpherson. He claimed he could tell if a hull was wood or fiberglass not with his eyes but with his ears. Wooden boats were smoother under way, he said. And the sound of water hitting a wooden hull was much more real and pure than the slapping of water against plastic. He was truly sad-dened that there were entire generations who would never learn the tradition of wooden boats. He was a rescuer. A rescuer of boats and cats. And her, although, before Lee, she hadn't even known she needed rescuing.

She stood in the lot a moment inhaling the salt-heavy air that blew in off the harbor. She had grown up in the western part of the state, in the shadow of the Berkshires, but she had never felt a con-nection to the mountains like the one she felt to the sea. After a week in Sippican she'd vowed that for the rest of her life she would never live more than an hour's drive from the ocean. She took one more deep breath and then she slipped in through the office door, holding it open so the two yard cats could sweep in. A Phish CD was on. At least he wasn't playing Ricky Martin. A string hammock holding rolled cylinders of boat designs hung over the drafting table. A brack-eted shelf on one wall sagged beneath the weight of books, empty champagne bottles. Stacks of *WoodenBoat* magazines were piled on the floor beneath.

In the workshop, Lee was fairing the mahogany planking of his current project, a twenty-foot ketch, which was nestled in cradles. He was building it from scratch. It was commissions like this that en-abled him to take on the restoration jobs.

"Relief arrives." She held the six-pack aloft.

He put aside his sandpaper and embraced her, leaving sawdust on her shoulders. He kissed her neck, inhaling her scent. "Ummmm. Sugar and chocolate. My weaknesses."

She kissed him back, hungrily. He smelt of raw wood, epoxy, sea air. "Does that mean you want to eat me?"

His smile could have sent her straight to a cardiologist. "Count on it."

"I am," she said. Her belly was heavy with longing. She pressed against him, felt his breath on her cheek, turned her face up for his kiss.

He kissed her softly, then pulled back and studied her. "Is every-thing all right?"

"It's been a long day," she said, avoiding his question. One of the cats brushed against her leg, then settled down beside the woodstove. "Want a beer?" She uncapped a Beck's, pushed a wedge of lime through the opening, handed him the bottle, opened one for herself. "Shall I order pizza now or wait?"

"I've got about fifteen more minutes here. If you can wait, I'll take you to Vic's."

"An offer I can't refuse." She moved a wooden mallet out of the way and sat on a sawhorse, happy to watch him. The thing was, he made her feel good inside.

She finished the Beck's, opened another. Lee was still working on his first. She felt the beginning of a buzz coming on. The sound of sandpaper rubbing wood lulled her. It was quieter than usual, even with the CD going. She reached over and stroked the cat. "A funny thing happened today," she heard herself say. She had not planned this, had not considered or prepared for the complications, the explaining it would give rise to.

"Yeah?" Lee concentrated on the fairing.

"My sister called."

He looked up. "Your sister?"

"Uh-huh." She continued to caress the cat. It stretched beneath her hand. She had always wanted a kitten. A white Angora would have been her choice, but their mother had been allergic.

Lee swiped wood dust from the mahogany. "I didn't know you had a sister."

She took another swallow of Beck's, attempted a laugh. "Yes, you did."

"Sam," he said, looking straight at her. "This is the first time I've ever heard you mention any sister."

"I told you," she said, forcing herself to meet his eyes. Shit. Why had she started this?

"Not to put too fine a point on this," he said, "but you've never told me you had a sister."

"Of course I did." Too late to recant now. She took a deep swallow, unable to maintain eye contact.

He returned to the sanding. "I know you have a brother," he said after a minute. His tone was reasonable; they could have been talking about anything. Plans for the weekend. Weather forecast for tomorrow. Anything. "His name is Josh, he's forty-eight, married to his second wife, Cynthia, a woman you're not particularly fond of. He's the father of two sons and coaches high school hockey." He stopped and took a swallow of his beer, set it by his feet. "They live in Colorado."

"Up yours," she said.

He stared at her and, under his steady gaze, she flushed.

He lifted an eyebrow, waited a beat, and when she remained silent, returned to the work. With any other man, she would have been out of there. *Don't screw this up*, a wise voice counseled. She forced herself to remain. An awkward silence stretched between them.

An ache began somewhere in her insides. She wanted to explain, to apologize, but the words wouldn't come. (Sam's stubborn as a mule in mud, her father used to say.) Lee sanded the final coat of epoxy, put his tools away, shut down the damper on the stove, fed the cats. When he had finished up, they drove to Vic's.

In the restaurant, Sam headed for their favorite booth. Instead of sliding in next to her, Lee sat on the opposite bench. She wasn't the only mulish one. She hated the tension but was too proud to apologize first, although she knew she must eventually.

Andrea, Vic's youngest daughter, came over and handed them menus. "Whaddaya want to drink?" she asked Lee. Usually the girl's obvious crush on him amused Sam, but tonight she found it irritating.

They decided to stick with beer.

"What's tonight's special?" Lee asked.

"The mushroom, onion, and sausage."

Lee didn't eat red meat. "Can Vic make mine without the sausage?"

"No problem. You?" she asked Sam.

"I'll have the same," she said. "*With* the sausage," she emphasized. She was being childish. Lee didn't have a problem with her choice of food or the politics of her choice.

"How about splitting a Caesar?" he asked her. "That okay with you?"

"Fine." Her voice was careful. She missed the easy way they usually had with each other, realized suddenly that they had never fought, not in all the months since that first dinner at Alice's. Someone had carved a diamond into the maple tabletop and she traced the design with her forefinger, wondering not for the first time what urge led people to mar a perfectly fine surface, what desire to deface.

Andrea brought their beers and the salad.

"You still going up to Scituate tomorrow?" Sam asked. There was a customer there who wanted to talk to Lee about constructing a yacht, a thirty-six-foot ketch based on a Herreshoff design. A dream commission.

"We had to reschedule. For next week."

"Disappointed?" She nudged a crouton to the side of the salad dish. He reached over and speared it.

He shook his head. "If it's meant to happen, it will happen without me pushing the river." He said things like that, *pushing the river*, old hippie sayings that would have driven her mad if anyone else said them.

Andrea brought their pizza. Sam ordered another beer. She was already over her limit, heading from lightly buzzed to the next stage, not exactly drunk but warming up. She would probably have a headache in the morning. She couldn't drink as much as she used to. God, in her twenties she could polish off an entire six-pack and walk, draw, or sing a straight line, no problem.

"Hey," he said. He reached over and entwined his fingers with hers.

"Hey, yourself," she said, and suddenly things were all right again.

She told him about the coming weekend, the three weddings, just the thought of which was now making her slightly panicked. He offered his help—purely moral support, she knew, for the delivery and last-minute on-site assembling and decorating weren't something that could be delegated. Still, she was warmed by his offer. For the first time since they left the boatyard, Sam felt as if she could fully breathe.

"So what did she want?" he said after a while.

"Who?"

"Your sister."

She disentangled her fingers, withdrew her hand. "I don't know." He waited.

"She left a message. She asked me to call her."

"And you haven't."

"No."

"Are you going to?"

"I don't know."

He reached across again, reclaimed her hand. "Sam," he said. "Are you going to tell me what this is about?"

Her throat ached. "I don't think so." She wished he were sitting next to her instead of opposite her, but she couldn't bring herself to get up and move to his side.

He shrugged, withdrew his hand, picked up another slice of pizza, ate it.

Finally she said, "Her name is Libby."

He nodded, waiting.

"It's been a while since we talked. We had a falling-out."

He waited a moment and when she didn't go on, he said, "A falling-out?"

"Yes." The words sounded so simple—a minor tiff, a quarrel over a borrowed sweater.

"That's it?"

She nodded.

"Do you want to talk about it?"

"Not really."

He studied her for a moment. "Okay," he said. "Whenever you're ready."

"Are you ready?" Libby's arm is around Sam's waist, holding her close. They perch on the edge of the webbed lawn chaise. Thigh to thigh, skin to skin, their legs are bound together by three of their mother's silk scarves.

Libby

. . . .

I'm dying.

Such an overdramatic statement was utterly unlike her. She abhorred histrionics. She looked around to see if anyone had heard, but no one was in sight, thank God. The prairie was vacant, except for the hawk overhead, and whatever rodents lurked hidden in the grass. And, she now noted, a spider—black with yellow stripes. Richard had told her the name but she'd forgotten. It sat in the center of a large web latticed on stalks of grass, a huge web really, nearly two feet across. She was grateful that only the spider and the other prairie creatures had been witness to her ridiculously maudlin and melodramatic statement, one verging on martyrdom, something to which she had sworn she would not succumb.

She was *not* dying. She was ill. Although the disease was not curable, there was treatment, she would live. So why was she sitting here on a bench in the prairie acting like a soap opera heroine? It was the isolation. Illness set her apart from others. Everything had changed. She could no longer take the ordinary workings of her body for granted.

In truth, she had to admit, she was responsible for a large part of the isolation. She had shut herself off from Richard, shut out their friends, most of whom didn't even know that she was sick although Richard urged her to tell them. He believed that if people knew, a network of support and sympathy would rise up, along with casseroles and offers for drives to appointments. She had refused, unwilling to be the recipient not only of their chicken pies and cookies but of the satisfying pity of which even she herself had been guilty in the past: the head tilted slightly to one side to indicate sincere concern, the voice pitched softer and higher than normal. *How are you doing, dear? I'm fine. No, how are you really?* All the time grateful it was someone else's turn at bat for cancer or betrayal.

She thought of Joyce Latch and her breast cancer, the lymph node involvement. Or that pathetic Mary Hudson whose husband ran off with a counter girl from Starbucks—really, a counter girl. *How are you doing, dear? I'm fine. Fine.* But clearly Mary was not fine. She was eating herself into oblivion; at the rate she was going she would have to be buried in a piano case.

Libby was *not* dying. Carlotta—Dr. Carlotta Hayes—had emphasized that. Just as Carlotta had reassured her that it would have made no difference if Libby had gone for a checkup when she first noticed symptoms, symptoms she hadn't even recognized as significant. If there had been pain, she might have been troubled, but there had been only the swelling, a slight puffiness in her face and hands and ankles, similar to what she'd experienced when she was pregnant with the twins. Salt retention, she'd thought, or maybe an odd and early sign of menopause. Pain—backache or headache or even the slightest tenderness—would have been a definite sign of something amiss, but not a little edema. Even the first time she saw foam in the toilet bowl after peeing, she wasn't particularly alarmed. Startled, certainly, but not panicked. She explained that away too, telling herself some food had caused it, the same way beets turned your pee red, or asparagus made it smell. Still, it *was* odd. And it persisted, even after she increased her fluid intake. When she finally mentioned it to

Richard, she was resolutely casual, saying it was probably something she'd eaten. What, he said, you've been eating soap? He insisted she set up an appointment with Jack Dixon, their family physician. She postponed making the call. (Once, at a cocktail party, she overheard Jack complaining about the women needing nothing more than attention who filled his waiting room. He said more than sixty percent of the patients who came to see him didn't really need to be there.) *There wasn't any pain.*

When she finally phoned Jack's office, she emphasized that it wasn't an emergency. The day of the appointment, she went shopping first and even made a date with Sally Cummings for lunch. That was how certain she was that there was nothing seriously wrong.

Jack listened to her symptoms and took her blood pressure, which was unusually high, 170 over 115. He frowned at the reading. (One year earlier, according to his records, it had been 115 over 70.) He checked her lungs and heart and palpated her abdomen and then sent her off with one of those little waxy cups to get a urine sample, that humiliating part of the routine exam: squatting splayed-legged over the toilet, haunches trembling from the effort of keeping her flesh from touching the toilet seat, the too-small cup clutched between thumb and forefinger, so nervous she couldn't relax her sphincter muscles, whistling to release the flow—her mother's trick—hoping the patients in the waiting room couldn't hear. After she finally managed to pee, she checked the sample, half expecting to see it perfectly natural and foam-free. Didn't that always happen? You made an appointment at the dentist's, but when you got there the toothache was gone. Or you frantically carted a toddler to the pediatrician but no sooner walked through the door than the temperature that had been spiking all night dropped to normal.

After she dressed, Jack came back into the examining room, avoiding her eyes for a moment. In that second, the first tendril of fear curled in her belly. There is elevated protein in your urine, he told her, which—with the high blood-pressure reading and the edema—was cause for concern. On the plus side, there was no blood or sugar and this was certainly a good sign. She grasped at these words. *No blood or sugar. A good sign.* He wanted more tests. Full chemical and renal panels. He made out a prescription for the lab and told her to cut back on salt, to eliminate it as much as possible, see if they could get a start on bringing her hypertension under control.

At home, while she waited for the results of the blood work, Richard researched kidney diseases on the Web. He reported that since Jack had detected no sugar in the dipstick test they could pretty much eliminate diabetes. He also thought they could reject polycystic kidney disease, which, more than ninety percent of the time, was inherited. They could rule out congenital abnormalities and trauma, as well. Finally she had to tell him to stop, he was driving her crazy.

When Jack called, he suggested Libby and Richard come in together. That was *not* a good sign, but Libby clung to her hope line. *There was no pain.* Surely nothing could be seriously wrong if there wasn't pain. On the drive, Richard put a Fauré composition for cello, a deliberately lighthearted selection, on the Volvo's CD player. Whatever it is, he said, we can handle it. We'll get through this together. He drove with his left hand, his right holding hers. She knew he was thinking *cancer.*

Jack wasted no time. "Your BUN and creatinine levels are abnormal," he said, reading from a lab report.

"What's BUN?" Richard asked, but before Jack could answer Libby said, "What does that mean?"

"You're experiencing kidney failure," he said.

She stared at him, uncomprehending. Impossible. A mistake in the blood tests. She barely listened as he listed the diseases that could directly or indirectly cause renal failure. Lupus, diabetes, hepatitis B and C, HIV. He talked about the need for additional tests. An MRI, more blood and urine work. A kidney sonogram. Tests to obtain a more accurate picture of what was going on. He was referring her to a nephrologist—a kidney specialist, he explained—and had his secretary set up an appointment. The best in the Midwest, he said.

Richard wanted to tell the twins right away, but Libby persuaded him to wait until they had more information. Why worry them needlessly? She was still hoping there had been a mistake. Lab results mixed up. It happened.

She watched the spider weaving its web, the zigzag pattern in the center. Its name came to her now: garden spider. Innocuous name for such a large insect. Part of the macrocosm of the prairie. Which was one of the things Richard appreciated about this place. The order of it. Everything playing a part. Even things like fire, he'd told her, things that seemed like devastation, were a necessary part of the overarching plan, which was why each year, in early spring, a part of the prairie was set aflame, whole swatches of grass and plants reduced to nothing more than charred stubble. The fire prevented trees from encroaching on the grassland, he had told her. It returned nutrients to the soil.

What was the role that made sense of this devastation in her body? What if one's physical order went awry?

Dr. Carlotta Hayes was a surprise. Libby had not expected the "best nephrologist in the Midwest" to be a short, dark-haired woman with the fingers of a pianist, a woman who urged them to call her by her first name and held both of Libby's hands in hers the first time they met. Libby, not charmed, had withdrawn her hands. She wanted a male doctor, someone tall and strong and with a trace of arrogance, someone to whom foreign potentates would send their ill sons, not this woman who acted like someone's grandmother.

Richard *was* charmed, especially when Carlotta mentioned that she had heard him play two years before. A violin and cello concerto with the Chicago Symphony. She was on the CSO board of directors, she told him. Then she looked at Libby.

"There's no easy way to say this," she said. "Your kidneys are failing."

"Okay. That's what we *do* know." Libby tried to soften her rudeness, only an attempt to gain control, with a vestigial smile. But she *hadn't* known that. Not really. She had been hoping that the new test results would prove otherwise. She had hoped that the changes she'd made recently were all that was needed. (She'd eliminated salt, every speck; she'd *meditated*, for God's sake.)

"We'll need more tests," Carlotta said. "And a biopsy. We'll talk about treatment when we get the results." She left the room and was gone for several minutes.

"What a coincidence," Richard said as soon as she disappeared.

"What?"

"Her being on the CSO board, hearing me play."

"Yes," Libby said, her jaw so tight it ached. "How lovely for you."

"I'm only saying she seems nice."

Libby didn't want nice. She wanted professional. She wanted someone to cure her.

Carlotta returned with a folder, which she handed to Libby. "I've put everything in here," she said. "You've got an appointment tomorrow for the biopsy and I've set up a time to see you next week. By then we'll have a clearer idea of our protocol."

The days passed slowly. Libby slept late, moved cautiously, stopped having wine with dinner. When she returned for the next appointment, she had lost three pounds.

It wasn't lupus or HIV or hepatitis.

"You have a disease called focal sclerosing glomerulonephritis," Carlotta told her. "FSGS for short."

Richard asked her to repeat it, to spell it for him. He wrote it down carefully, parroted back the spelling to ensure he had it right.

"We usually find it in African American patients," Carlotta continued, "but certainly not limited to them. Caucasians can contract it, as well."

"How long have I had it?"

"That's impossible to say. People can have the symptoms for years and years and not know. The first symptoms you would notice were exactly what you experienced: swelling in the legs, puffiness in the face and hands, foamy urine."

"How did I get it?" Libby thought of the traveling she and Richard had done. The trip to Guatemala to see the ruins at Tikal. Snorkeling in Belize. The Yucatán. She was meticulous about what they ate and drank on these trips, even insisting they brush their teeth with bottled water, no matter what reassurances the hotel gave. She had always been so careful of everything. She had tried to do everything right.

"There are three ways we get diseases," Carlotta said. "Bad habits, bad genes, and bad luck. With FSGS it's purely a case of bad luck."

All that care and it came down to luck.

"What's the long-term prognosis?" Richard asked.

"FSGS is chronic, not acute."

Hope warmed Libby's chest. "Acute" sounded serious, the word itself sharp as a knife. "Chronic" sounded like something she could deal with. Something pesky like a sinus infection or strep throat, something cured with a double course of antibiotics, but certainly not anything life-threatening. Not cancer.

"Which means?" Richard said.

Carlotta was straightforward. "Which means we can't reverse it. There are treatments, but there is no cure."

Hope cooled and fell away. She had it wrong. "Acute," the sharp-edged word, was the more benign. "Chronic" was the one she had to fear. Later, she realized that was the moment everything changed. The Before-and-After moment. The plane-crash moment. The dividing line between the ordinary—the blessedly ordinary life in which all the minute and unconscious workings of the body flexed and pulsed and flowed on—and the perilous extraordinary, when nothing could be taken for granted ever again.

Richard reached for her hand, squeezed it, but she was unable to respond. She felt brittle, betrayed.

"What do we do?" he asked.

"We start with medications—drugs to get your numbers lowered." Carlotta spoke at length about chemistry levels and numbers—creatinine, BUN, blood pressure, protein—and what they signified. Libby's hand lay lifeless in Richard's.

"Long-term?" he said.

"Long-term we are looking at more dramatic treatments. Once we reach end-stage renal disease, which is without doubt where we are heading, we'll be looking at treatments to replace lost kidney function. Almost certainly hemodialysis."

"Dialysis?" Libby said. Just the thought made her nauseous. Hooked up to machines for hours. She couldn't do it.

"How soon?" Richard asked.

"Hard to say. Anywhere from a year to five." She turned to Libby. "A lot depends on how you respond to medication. But let's not get ahead of ourselves. That's a way off."

She went over the treatment plan. Control the swelling and high blood pressure with prednisone, minimal dosage. Control the edema with diuretics. Careful diet. No salt. Less protein. Erythropoietin injections to stimulate red blood cell production.

We'll beat this, Richard said to her as they drove home. He went back to the computer, checked Web sites, printed out pages of information. He located numbers for support groups and brought home books that she couldn't bring herself to read. She still wouldn't allow him to tell the twins. "Why worry them needlessly," she said.

The year passed in a seesaw of hope and discouragement, all predicated on test results, the creatinine numbers and protein levels that rose and fell. Finally, over spring break, she'd told the twins. A pesky health problem, she said, making it sound like a minor imbalance, something easily cured with drugs. She didn't want them worried.

At her last appointment—she'd assumed it would be a routine checking of her numbers—she was stupefied when Carlotta told her she would have to begin dialysis.

"Let me think about it," Libby said. She was not ready for this.

"It's not an option," Carlotta said. "You're in end-stage."

"You said five years." Rage overtook her.

"One to five. No promises." Carlotta reached for Libby's hands. "I know it sounds scary. It's the unknown. The thing to keep in mind is that most people on dialysis start to feel better almost immediately."

Is *that* a promise? she wanted to ask.

"I'll make the arrangements," Carlotta continued. "We'll set you up at the clinic for three times a week, either Monday, Wednesday, and Friday or Tuesday, Thursday, and Saturday, depending on what works best for you. You'll need to plan on four hours each day."

"Four hours?"

"Books or knitting help pass the time. Some patients have found it helpful to talk to someone who is actually undergoing treatment before they begin," she said. "Would you like me to get you a few names?" Libby did not.

Carlotta explained that Libby would need to see a vascular surgeon for the creation of an arteriovenous fistula in her left arm. She gave her a leaflet that detailed this procedure, how it would establish a connection between an artery and a vein in her wrist through which blood would leave and return to her body during dialysis. And she also would need to have a temporary catheter implanted in the sub-clavian vein, below her collarbone.

"Why?"

"For access until the shunt is properly healed and ready for use."

Shunt. Catheter. Fistula. Just the words made her feel queasy.

"Kidney patients live long, full lives on dialysis," Carlotta went on, "but I want you to be considering other treatment options, too."

"Like what?"

"Transplantation. The ideal situation is a living donor. There is less chance of rejection than with a cadaver donor."

Cadaver donor. For a moment she feared she would faint.

"Think about family and friends who might consider it. Your husband might want to be tested to see if he's a match. Do you have siblings?"

Libby paused. *Sam,* she thought. "One," she said, glad Richard wasn't there to contradict her. "A brother."

"You'll want to contact him. Let him start thinking about it. Getting things in place. Pretests for compatibility. How old is he?"

"Forty-eight."

"Not a twin, huh?" Carlotta had said. "A twin would have been perfect."

A breeze had come up. It rippled over the grasses, caused the spider-web to sway, chilled Libby. She rose from the bench and headed back toward the car. Her legs ached and she was out of breath by the time she reached the parking lot. She hated this, the betrayal of her body. She ran a finger over her breast, felt the hump of the catheter. She tried to imagine what it might feel like to have part of another person's body—another's organ—inside her. The thought made her slightly ill.

A twin would have been perfect. A memory splintered in. Her mother used to call her and Sam the Siamese twins. They were inseparable. Once.

Sam, she thought.

She felt numb with regret and sorrow and loss.

Sam

. . . .

Are you ready?

They sit on the chaise, legs trussed at thigh, knee, and calf by three of their mother's square floral scarves. Are you ready? *At this signal, they stand in unison, wobbling for a moment until Libby curls her arm around Sam and steadies them both. They are playing Siamese twins, a game they made up after they had seen a picture of conjoined brothers. They discovered the photo one day when they were playing in the basement, leafing through the pages of a musty* Life *magazine and clipping pictures to furnish homes for their paper dolls. Refrigerators and stoves, couches and tables. Plates of food. Boxes of Band-Aids. The photograph of the twins, fused at the chest, stopped them short. Sam ran her fingers over the picture, stared at the brothers, while Libby read the text aloud: Their names were Chang and Eng; they were from Siam; such twins occurred only once in fifty thousand to eighty thousand births. The brothers stared straight out at the viewer, their expressions as happy as those of Sam and Libby in the picture right upstairs on the mantel in the living room, the one taken last Easter at their grandparents'.*

They have picked names for themselves: Missy (Libby) and Sissy (Sam). When they are playing this game, they refuse to answer their mother if she doesn't use these names. They love imagining themselves connected, actually yoked by a band of flesh. In the game, they picture a future with them bound together in this way. Sometimes they decide they will be famous—singers or actors or scientists—and other times they determine they will marry. To twin brothers, they decide. They will have a double wedding. (Missy read in the article that Chang and Eng had both been married.) Naturally they will live in the same house. They will take turns choosing their clothes each day. They will never allow anyone to separate them even though Missy has informed Sissy that sometimes an operation can be performed to sever Siamese twins.

All afternoon they walk as if actually connected at the leg. They like the idea of being connected forever. Even at ten, Sam cannot picture a future without Libby at her side. She is pleased when strangers comment on how alike they look, say how if it weren't for their heights it would be nearly impossible to tell them apart. Sam likes seeing them as mirror images and sees any difference— even of height—as a betrayal. They insist on eating dinner tied together, although this annoys their mother, who thinks they take the game too far. At bedtime she puts her foot down, and in the sharp-edged voice they know better than to defy, she demands that they remove the scarves.

Later, as Sam brushes her teeth, she feels off balance, as if a part of her is lost. They were together and then they weren't. When she puts on her pajamas, Sam sees that the skin on her calf is still crimson and sweaty from where it had been pressed against Libby's. In bed, without Libby next to her, Sam has trouble falling asleep; after a while she rises and crosses to her sister. Although Libby's bed is narrow—a twin—she does not complain when Sam climbs in with her. They nestle, spoon fashion, and, with the touch of Libby's breath wisping against her neck, Sam feels complete again.

Many years later Sam would read a phrase in a novel that encapsulated how she had felt when she and Libby were playing their game of Siamese twins. The Law of Bound Hearts: Separate them and only one—at most—would survive.

Sam woke in the dark and reached out for the figure beside her. Caught in that groggy moment of half sleep when a dream can still seem real, she believed for a moment that it was Libby she was reaching toward, that they were again in their childhood home, sleeping in Libby's bed. She knew, in those brief seconds, a thrill of joy, of all being right; then her hand registered the contour of Lee's shoulder, the bulk of his muscles, and the spasm of joy evaporated. Tears suddenly rose and caught in her throat and she swallowed against the burn of them. She *would not* cry. She was done with crying. She'd done her share of that; what was past was past.

Except, the past wasn't something you could simply close your eyes and wish away. It refused to stay buried. It was always, inescapably, irrevocably a part of the present, an accumulation of decisions and actions and choices, each bearing its own consequences. She knew this, Lord knows, she knew this, had known it even when she moved to Mattapoisett and then to Sippican and began with fierce determination to build anew. Yet all the days she had spent working toward a future, some part of her had been waiting for the past to come knocking at her door; all that time, she had been waiting for word from Libby, knowing that sooner or later it would come. She had *known* this but still she had been caught unprepared.

She had to pee—all that beer—and her mouth was parched, the first sign of the hangover she would have in the morning. The bedside clock said it was eleven. They'd been in bed barely an hour. Lee slept soundly. In the darkened room, she made out the length of him beneath the covers. Oblongs of fractured moonlight fell through the window blinds, striping his body.

Eventually she would have to tell him about Libby. She wondered if he would understand. How vulnerable love was, she thought, how little it took to damage it. She knew that now. Once, she believed that the love she had for Libby would withstand anything. She could never have imagined it would turn into this loop of love and hatred.

When she was in grade school she would listen to her classmates talk of how their older sisters were mean to them, and she would hold proudly and possessively to the preciousness of Libby's love for her. How was it possible that out of such love could come rivalry and hate? Or had she been mistaken? All those years, had she just been a tedious responsibility for Libby? While Sam had believed her fierce love returned in equal measure, had Libby been resentful, annoyed at always having a younger sister tagging along, complaining to *her* classmates about her sister, the pest? Had what Sam seen as joyful been a burden to Libby? Had Sam been blind to it, seeing only what she wanted to see? Was that the explanation, then? All those years, Libby had been harboring a resentment that festered and rankled until it mushroomed into betrayal. All those years Libby had resented the closeness. Fearing what? That she would be consumed? Well, in the end it was Libby who had devoured Sam.

She slipped out of bed and went downstairs. In the kitchen, air still sweet with the scent of chocolate, she negotiated her way to the sink using only the glow from a small night-light plugged in over the desk. She ran the tap until the water was cold, then drank, assuaging thirst. She swallowed two aspirins—an attempt to derail the morning's hangover—and drank again.

Please, Libby had said. Her independent and stubborn sister, who seldom asked anyone for anything, must need her. In spite of herself, Sam couldn't hold back the glow this knowledge brought. What could have led Libby to break six years of silence? Sam tried to recall the exact tone of Libby's voice, the exact words. There hadn't been panic or shock, no urgency, unlike the call informing her of the plane crash that had killed their parents. If it was something about one of the twins, Libby would have mentioned it. Sam was certain of that. Why had she been so cryptic? Why hadn't she said more? Now Sam regretted erasing the message. She wanted to hear Libby's voice again. A wave of longing, kept at bay for years, washed over her.

She checked the clock again. A little after eleven. Ten in the Central Time zone. Not too late. She crossed to the phone, picked up the receiver. Even after all this time, she knew the number by heart. She stood, receiver in hand, for several long minutes before replacing it. In the end, pride—or stubbornness—was stronger than desire.

All possibility of sleep gone, she flicked on the overhead light and started a pot of coffee. At the desk, she took up her sketchbook. She flipped to her preliminary drawing for the Chaney wedding. Both bride and groom were architects and Sam had chosen vertical stripes for the cake. In hyacinth and apple green, edged with silver. The stripes would be sharp and stylish, confident—architectural— but softened by an overlay of curlicues and sugar-paste tassels. Yesterday she had been pleased with the design, but now, as she considered it, she frowned, dissatisfied. Perhaps something more baroque, each layer a different design. She stared up at the bulletin board over her workstation; on it were dozens of photographs showing couples posed by cakes four and five tiers tall, preparing for the ritual of the cutting.

There were so many traditions surrounding the wedding cake. According to her research, the bride and groom fed each other cake as a symbol of how they would care for and nurture each other through-out their new life together. Originally, she'd learned, small cakes were piled, one on top of the other, as high as possible, and then the newlywed couple kissed over the tower of cakes, trying not to knock them down. If they succeeded, it meant a lifetime of prosperity. So many traditions designed to ward off the perils of life.

Sam should have done that. Was that her mistake? Not to have stood by a cake and joined hands, held with her beloved a broad ster-ling knife, kissed over a tall cake. Would that have been enough?

She'd been wrong earlier. She wasn't done with crying. She bent her head to her hands and wept.

This was how Lee found her.

He came up behind her, wrapped her in his arms.

She let him hold her, felt the comfort of his embrace, felt his thighs against hers, his muscles as strong as pilings beneath a dock.

His touched his lips to her head. "I think it's time you told me," he said into her hair.

"Told you?"

He rocked her. "About your sister. About your 'falling-out.' "

She closed her eyes, leaned back against him. "I don't know where to start."

"At the beginning." He lifted her hair back from her face, kissed her temple. "Just take your time. Start at the beginning."

What was the beginning? This was the problem. Sam wasn't even sure exactly when or how it began. She was only sure of the betrayal of the end.

Libby

. . . .

It was such a betrayal, this failing of her body. No one could understand how such treason felt.

Across from her, Richard was engrossed in his menu. Libby's lay unopened. She looked around the dining room. At linen-covered tables, people were sipping drinks, talking, partaking of their meals. One laughing quartet was drinking champagne. Overhead, chandeliers sparkled, their light reflecting off the crystal glassware that graced each table. Richard had insisted they come here, not as a celebration, certainly not that, but as a way in which to pass the evening, to take their minds off what waited in the morning, as if that were in any way possible, as if she could forget for an instant. *Dialysis.* The word haunted her constantly. At the next table, a man dug into a chocolate concoction heaped with a soft mound of whipped cream. Real, not from some aerosol can. Even from a distance she could tell that. His wife, clad in a cream-colored dress, one Libby had seen the week before in the window of Talbots, picked at a slice of lemon pie. Watching the woman—the *hockey stick*—nibble at the yellow filling, she was reminded of a story from the Talmud, something about an old Jew being called before the Almighty and held to account for all the pleasures he hadn't enjoyed. (Where had she heard this tale? She and Richard had no Jewish friends.) She thought of all the sweets she had denied herself. Pastries and all manner of confections. Custards and crullers and cakes. Chocolate bars with almonds. For God's sake, she wanted to scream at the woman, just eat the fucking dessert. Eat it all. Lick the plate. Order another.

She picked up her menu and scanned the offerings. French Onion Soup with Gruyère. Pan-Seared Foie Gras with Fall Garnish. Gemelli Pasta with Roast Duck and a Port Wine Sauce. Grilled Filet of Beef with a Cognac Veal Sauce. Black-Sesame-Seed-Encrusted Tuna with Balsamic Reduction and Chive Oil. The things we take for granted, she thought. The things we accept as our just due, until they are taken from us. Simple things like a night out, a meal. Complex things like the miracle of a functioning body. Except for her. She no longer took things for granted. She had been stripped of that right. Now she had to watch everything. Food was no longer about pleasure or nourishment, celebration or diversion, or even denial. Now it was about chemistry. A precise monitoring of sodium and potassium, of phosphorus and protein.

She set the menu down. It had been a mistake to come.

As if reading her mind, Richard looked up. "Is there anything you can have?"

Mentally, Libby ran through the booklet the nutritionist had given her, "The Healthy Food Guide: A National Renal Diet," pages that had become her new bible. "I'm sure there's something," she said, forcing a smile. Potatoes were out, of course. Too much potassium, as was anything with tomatoes. The roast chicken would be all right, but not the cherry veal sauce. She would have to ask that they skip that. And there was always a tossed salad, undressed. The kitchen here was accommodating. They would provide something, but for what it was going to cost she and Richard might as well have stayed home.

"You sure?" he asked.

"Absolutely."

"We could leave."

"For God's sake," she said, her voice sharp. "I said it's all right."

He looked down, chastened.

"I'm sorry."

"No. My fault. I'm sorry."

"The chicken looks good." It was not his fault. Not his fault. She kept reminding herself of this.

"Yes," he said, openly relieved she had found something.

"How was your day?" She'd pretend everything was normal. Really it was the best way.

"Busy. We had the department meeting."

"And your lesson with the James girl? That was today?"

"Yes," he said, his face lighting up. Usually the truly talented musicians went east. Juilliard. Curtis in Philly. Berklee or the Conservatory in Boston. When someone like Sarah James landed in his care, he behaved as though he had been awarded a Nobel.

She was relieved and sensed he was, too, when the waiter came for their order. The chicken and salad for her. The veal chop with mushroom-and-white-vermouth sauce for Richard. And a glass of cabernet. "Do you mind?" he asked, his face all apologies about the wine.

"Of course not," she lied. She minded that everyone in the place was eating and drinking whatever they desired. She railed against the unfairness of it. For days she'd had this craving for hot dogs. The worst possible thing. She didn't even like them and hadn't eaten one in years. God knows what they put in those things. Everyone had heard the horror stories. Pig intestines. Rats. Still, the craving persisted.

The food restrictions were bad enough, but limiting fluids was really a bitch. Four cups a day, no more; everything counted. Gravy, ice cream, ice cubes. Even the liquid in string beans. She had learned to suck on ice chips and chew gum to moisten a dry mouth, to take her pills with applesauce, saving water for the times when she was desperately thirsty.

Richard's wine came and he raised his glass. For a moment she thought he was going to offer a toast—to what, she could only imagine, certainly not to what lay ahead. She escaped before he could speak. "I'll be right back," she said, rising.

The restrooms were on the basement level, along with a martini-

and-cigar bar, and as she made her way down the steps, the aroma of tobacco enveloped her. Unlike most people, she liked the smell of cigars. It triggered memories of her father. His favorite chair, a brown leather wingback, was currently at home in her den and occasionally, even now, she would bury her face in the crease where one of the sides met the back, and inhale. The aroma was still there, deep in the pores of the leather, the cells of the stuffing. The faint, very faint, scent of him. Of cigars.

There were four men sitting in the lounge, smoking and drinking amber liquid from short glasses. They looked up when she entered, then returned to their whiskeys and conversation, dismissing her. There had been a time when she was not invisible to men, when they would have smiled, nodded, their eyes lingering, acknowledging her looks. Well, *men*. She had read recently about a survey where ballplayers were asked at what age women were at their absolute peak. Thirty-five, she had thought they'd say. Or maybe twenty-eight. The majority of men had said seventeen. *Seventeen*. She was a long way from that. Now she might as well be a clothes hanger, a construct of sexual insignificance.

She skirted their table and wandered over to the glass cases that lined the walls, shelves filled with space memorabilia. The owner of the restaurant had once been an astronaut, a part of the Apollo 13 mission. Or *was* an astronaut, she corrected herself. Once you did something like that, she supposed, it was part of you forever. Wherever you went, it was a component of your identity. You were a Man Who Had Been in Space. She scanned the exhibit. There were letters from presidents (Harry Truman, Lyndon Johnson) and celebrities (Princess Grace, Tom Hanks). She looked at the exhibits and read the bold banner headlines of newspapers, each trumpeting words of man's conquest of space. A cover photo from *Time* showed the astronauts after splashdown. Praying. So they had been religious. Was that important? Could you do something like that and remain an atheist? How did it feel to them to orbit the moon, to look down on their planet? These men—this fraternity of the moon-bound brothers (of course, it had been all men back then)—had they caught a glimpse of some great organizing principle, had they seen a part of some divine harmony? Or had it been only ideals and science and a sense of adventure that had lured them and given them the courage to be locked in a capsule and hurled from the earth. She looked again at the photo of the praying astronauts. Whatever it had been, she could use some. All she felt was fear.

Feeling sorry for yourself, are you? Her father's voice stopped her. It had been months and months since he had come to her, but now she heard him clearly; he'd been summoned perhaps by the aura of cigar smoke that had kindled her memory of him. She swallowed against the sweetness of it. Behind her, one of the men laughed. The others joined in. She shut her ears to them, focused on hearing her father. She longed for him, his strength, his advice, his comfort. What could he tell her now? How could he console her?

He wouldn't condone self-pity, she knew. You deal with the cards that were handed you, he would say. Play the hand and hope for better next time.

Hope. The word tasted ashy in her mouth. Maybe that was what people lived on, what led them forward. Hope. Not faith.

"Libby?"

Richard's brow was creased with concern. He took her hand. "I was worried. Are you all right?"

She was conscious of the men, of their curious stares. They had stopped talking.

"I'm fine."

"They've brought our dinner."

"I was just coming."

He moved his hand to her elbow. She allowed him to guide her from the room as if she were a child, permitted him to lead her up the stairs, to their table. She sat, allowed the waiter to grind pepper over her chicken, pretended everything was perfectly all right, pretended tomorrow would be like any other day. Pretended there would be no dialysis.

Then she heard her father again, telling her what she had known all along she must do. Call Sam.

She wanted to. She looked around at the other diners, at her husband, busy carving a bite-size piece of meat, and what she wanted above all was Sam, wanted this with a hunger that shocked her. She wanted everything to be the way it once had been between them, before she destroyed everything.

Call Sam, her father whispered.

I can't, she said to his ghost. No one understood. It had taken all her nerve to phone once. She couldn't try again. Long ago, she had lost the right to ask anything of Sam.

Sam

. . . .

They had returned to Sam's bed. Sam was wrapped in Lee's arms. His hand stroked the length of her back. His fingers and palms were just rough enough to feel good against her skin. Her head rested on his chest and his chest hairs tickled her nose, but she didn't move. She wanted to stay like that forever. Hidden and safe.

Lee spoke first. "What's her name?"

Sam drew a long, shuddering breath. She was torn between the need to hide the scabbed and shameful wounds of her past and the desire to give him that same secret history, as if it were a gift. "Libby," she said. "Short for Elizabeth. Elizabeth Faye."

"Libby," he said.

At the sound of her sister's name on his lips, in his mouth, she felt the tickle of panic in her stomach. She willed it away. This was Lee. Her Lee. A man she could trust, a man who salvaged boats, rescued cats. A man who knew celestial navigation.

He drew his finger along her cheek, lifted back a strand of hair.

"Is she older or younger?

"Older. By two years."

"And how long has it been since you've talked?"

How could she make him understand? His older brother Jim was an organic farmer out on the far end of Long Island, and when they got together it was easy to picture them as boys, playing basketball together, horsing around. She could never envision Lee and his brother lashed together playing Siamese twins. Each of them stood alone. There was affection and brotherly love between them, but none of the passion she had shared with Libby. Was that kind of passion—the kind that could change into hate—possible only between sisters?

"Six years."

A look of puzzlement passed over his face, and something else, too, something she couldn't identify—disappointment?—just a flash, but she felt a thrill of panic, as she had when he spoke her sister's name.

"You're kidding," he said. "You haven't spoken to your sister for six years? What the hell happened? A fight?"

She wasn't ready to talk about the fight. Nor was she prepared to talk about the recent past, the woman Libby had somehow turned into—the wife, the mother of twins, living in a home of false abundance, in a wealthy midwestern suburb, capable of deceit. If she was going to tell him anything about Libby, she would have to go back to a less emotional time, back before everything went wrong, back when Libby was the bold and rebellious one, the rule breaker, afraid of nothing, when Libby was her idol. She rolled over onto her back and stared up at the ceiling. He laid his hand on her stomach.

"When we were teenagers," she began, "Lib used to drive my mother mad."

"How?"

"You name it, they fought about it. There was always a running battle between them, a contest of wills. Makeup and music, curfews and clothes, the fact that Libby refused to wear a bra. The truth is, I think what my mother saw as caring, Libby saw as control."

"And you?"

"I didn't draw my mother's wrath the way Libby did. Partly because I wasn't rebellious by nature and partly because I was invisible in Lib's shadow."

"Hard to imagine you invisible." He stroked her belly.

"You didn't know Lib back then. She was the kind of person that made a roomful of people pay attention when she walked in. But she didn't care about that. She never cared what people thought. That's what made her so powerful. And it's what made my mother so afraid of her. People in town were always going on about something or other that she'd done."

"Like what?"

Sam thought back over the Libby stories. What she most remembered about those years was the tension between her mother and Libby. She had felt like a sponge wedged between them, absorbing and deflecting anger, lying low and listening to them battle.

"Well, there was the time she pretended she was a mannequin," she said. His body shifted, she felt his interest—his interest in Libby—but there was no way out now. And so she began.

It is August, the steamy part of summer when, beyond the sweeping arc of the sprinklers, brittle patches of brown spread across the yard like disease. The first thrill of vacation freedom has long worn off and the shadow of school looms ahead. It is 1979, the year Libby turns sixteen. In September she will be a junior and already the conversation at meals centers on which colleges they will be visiting in the fall, on the PSATs and the need for a tutor. It is this conversation that is going on now.

"No tutor," Libby says. "Forget it."

"You think you can get by on the verbal part," their mother says. (This is true. Libby is straight A in English, a subject Sam struggles to get Cs in.) "But math counts, too. Sue Drummond's mother gave me the name of an excellent math tutor. I'm calling him today and that's all there is to it."

"Who died and made you God?" Libby says, pushing away from the table. She escapes before their mother can ground her for being mouthy. Sam is astounded by her sister's audacity. She risks a glance at their mother, who beneath her anger seems tired and sad. Sam finishes her breakfast and clears the table, conscious of being good to make up for Libby. She takes the morning paper out to the porch and settles in on a wicker rocker. Every morning, she reads the front page so at dinner she can talk with her father. In Detroit, Chrysler has laid off forty-six hundred workers. In Alabama, Klansmen are beginning a fifty-mile "white rights" march from Selma to Montgomery. Sam looks at the accompany-

ing photo of men concealed in white hoods and robes, and shivers. They seem spooky. Evil. She knows bigotry is one of the few things that make her father absolutely incensed.

The paper is suddenly snatched from her hands. Libby grins down at her.

"Cut it out," Sam says, grabbing at the paper.

"I'm sure you've read enough to impress Dad with your knowledge."

"Unlike some people I might name," Sam says tightly, "I find the news interesting." Her cheeks redden. As usual, Libby has seen right through her.

Libby looks down at the page she holds. "What," she says, "is so interesting about people getting the axe in Michigan? What difference does it make?"

Sam turns away, refusing to answer. She wants to stay mad at Libby, but when her sister mentions heading downtown and getting a Dairy Queen, she can't resist. Just like everyone else in the world, she thinks. She can never resist Libby.

After the DQ, they decide to visit Libby's best friend, Jeannie. Jeannie's mother owns a dress shop on Main Street, a store that carries shapeless dresses with buttons down the bodice and Orlon pants suits, clothes designed for middle-aged women who want to conceal their bodies, clothes Libby says she'd rather eat a rat than be caught wearing. If getting old means having to wear a pants suit, Libby says, she would rather die.

In a week, on August 24, Libby will turn sixteen. (The birthday is the cause of another quarrel. Their mother wants to give Libby a Sweet Sixteen party. She has it all planned, a dinner party complete with china and crystal and the good silver service. Libby hates the idea. There is nothing sweet about sixteen, she shouts. She tells Sam she can just picture the party. Their mother will probably use the lace cloth and set out finger bowls and napkin rings. She says this with disdain, but to tell the truth this doesn't sound so awful to Sam.) Libby can't wait to be eighteen. Can't wait to be legal. Out from under their mother's thumb.

When they arrive at the store, Jeannie is in the display window. Libby climbs in with her and Sam follows, picking her way carefully to avoid stepping on the corpses of black flies that litter the floor. Jeannie is in the midst of replacing one bland, baggy outfit on the mannequin with another. Libby says she doesn't know why she bothers. No one could tell the difference.

The mannequin is already stripped. A metal frame holds the torso—the nude torso—upright, and Jeannie lifts the body free from the frame. The body is composed of some kind of plastic, the surface smooth as water. It has toeless *feet, long legs, a narrow waist that rises to perfect breasts*, nude, *nipple-less breasts that cause Sam to flush furiously. She wishes Jeannie would hurry and cover them up before someone walks by the window.*

Jeannie detaches the top of the figure from the bottom and starts shoving the legs into a pair of navy blue trousers. Libby picks up an amputated arm and fans herself with it.

"Don't let my mother catch you with that," Jeannie says. "I'm not kidding. These things cost an arm and a leg." The unintended pun makes them giggle.

Libby puts down the arm and picks up a spare leg. She props it in her armpit and limps around the display window, as if she had a crutch.

"Come on," Jeannie says. "I'm not fooling. She'll kill you."

Libby faces one of the other mannequins and begins mirroring its stance, an artificial pose with one hip jutted out and an arm akimbo, fist perched low at the waist, head thrown back, chin raised. Libby's tanned legs look even darker in contrast to those of the pale plastic figure. She is wearing a pair of denim cut-offs and a white pleated chemise with narrow bands over the shoulders, a piece of clothing she found in a vintage clothing store in Northampton. No bra, of course. Her honey-colored, sun-streaked hair is gathered loosely at the nape of her neck. She is wearing blue-and-yellow feather earrings she made herself. She stole the feathers from the material their father uses to fashion trout flies.

Jeannie glances nervously back toward the shop interior.

Libby moves from pose to pose, imitating ones she has seen in the pages of Seventeen. *She stares out through the plate glass, head tilted to one side, face devoid of expression. A perfect blank. Sam can't believe Libby can stand and pose like this, right in the window, right there on Main Street where anyone could see her. Sam is so self-conscious that she gets absolutely ill when she has to read in front of her class.*

On the sidewalk, two women walk by. They glance in the window and, seeing Jeannie, smile and wave, then, at the sight of Libby, do a perfect double take. Libby does not move.

Sam recognizes the women. Mrs. Parker and Mrs. Burgess. Friends of her mother's.

"Shit city," Jeannie says.

The women have stopped dead in front of the window. They squint in at Libby. Their lips are moving, and Sam can just imagine what they are saying. Libby does not breathe. She does not blink. Her blank face is stripped of life. Sam does not know how she does this.

On the street, a car slows as it passes, the driver stares.

Finally the women, still talking, move on. Jeannie finishes dressing the legs and now starts buttoning the jacket around the mannequin's torso, covering the breasts. Thank God. Now if Libby would just stop fooling around. Sam doesn't know exactly what's wrong with what her sister is doing, only that their mother definitely wouldn't approve. It would probably come under the heading of "making a spectacle of yourself."

Now Libby changes the pose. She angles her body toward the window and lifts her hand to her shoulder, dips the strap on the chemise to bare her shoulder.

At that moment Old Man Crowley walks by. Mr. Crowley is not really old, the same age as their father really, but that's what Libby always calls him. She says he gives her the willies. He lives off the desperation of widows, she once told Sam, who has no idea what that means. Now he looks up, smiles at Libby, not mistaking her for a mannequin at all. Libby drops the blank stare and looks straight at him, then so fast Sam can't believe it, she pulls the chemise strap lower and flashes her tit, just bares her breast for Old Man Crowley to get a good look at.

"Young lady," Jeannie's mother's shouts, so loud they all jump, all except Libby. "Get out of that window this instant."

"Shit," Jeannie says.

Sam scrambles out of the window and slithers by Mrs. Gault. For a minute, Libby stays just as she is and then—slowly—she shrugs the strap back over her shoulder. Then, as if she were royalty, as if just the minute before she hadn't bared her breast to Old Man Crowley and anyone else who happened to be look-ing, she climbs out of the display window.

Naturally it takes the buzz no more than an hour to reach their parents. People can't wait to tell their mother how Mr. Crowley said Libby stood there brazen as you please and flashed her tit.

Libby denies it.

"Why would he make it up?" their mother says. "The man saw what he saw."

"He wishes," Libby said, her tone dripping with derision.

Denial was always Libby's first line of defense. Even in the face of in-controvertible proof, her modus operandi was Just Deny. Unless someone saw what she'd done with his or her own eyes. Then, of course, she couldn't refute it.

Next to Sam, Lee was chuckling. "It sounds like she gave your parents a run for their money."

"You could say that," Sam said in a dry voice. Of all the stories she might have told Lee, why had she picked that one? To show him her sister's beauty, her defiance? But what else was she revealing?

"Did she want to be a model?" Lee asked.

"No. She was going to be a poet and live in Paris, a stone's throw from the Seine."

"Did she? Become a poet?"

"No. She got married her senior year of college."

"Eloped, I bet," Lee said.

"Why would you think that?"

"The story you just told me. How she didn't want the Sweet Sixteen party. A big wedding doesn't seem her style."

Sam bit her lip. So now he knows Libby's style? "She had one of the biggest weddings ever seen in Amherst." She wondered what he'd say if she told him that she had been the one who eloped. Would he think that was *her* style?

"Where does she live now?"

"Illinois," she said. He would press her for more, she knew. He would not be content now to hear only stories from the distant past. Now he would want her to tell him why she and Libby hadn't spoken for six years.

She rolled on her side, pushed herself against him, tried to draw his warmth to her newly chilled skin.

Libby had entered their lives.

Libby

. . . .

Rain was predicted, but the gentian sky belied the forecast.

"Shall I put on a CD?" Richard asked. He was reaching toward the dash when she stopped him.

"No," she said. "No music."

"Are you sure? It might help. I could choose something calming."

"I'm calm," she said, unable to control the edge that crept into her voice. "I'm fine."

"I'm just trying to help, Lib." He darted a glance over at her.

A bout of nausea swept over her and she dropped her face to her palms, took several deep breaths, swallowed against the queasiness that grew in her stomach.

"Are you all right?"

"Yes."

"Are you sure?"

She straightened her head. "I'm just a little nauseous."

"Do you want me to pull over?"

"No. I'll be okay."

"Are you sure? I can pull over."

"I said I'd be okay." They had advised her to eat breakfast. It was important, they said, that she have something in her stomach, a small meal, not much, but the eggs had been a mistake. Next time she'd have toast. *Next time.* She wasn't sure she was going to make it through this time.

"It's no problem to pull over," he said. He looked at her, his brow furrowed with concern. Ahead, a car swerved into their lane, cutting them off.

"Look out," she shouted.

"Christ," he said. He jammed on the brakes, tires squealed.

"Great," she said. "That's all we need."

"Sorry," he said.

They rode in thick silence the rest of the way.

The Oak Hill Dialysis Center was housed in a long, windowless brick building, so lacking in character it might as well have been attached to a strip mall. In front of the entrance there were twenty parking spaces marked with the universal yellow sign depicting a wheelchair. Every slot was taken.

"Want me to drop you off in front?" he asked.

"No. Just find a place to park."

"It's no problem to drop you off."

"Just park, okay?" She'd become a shrew, she knew, and she hated it but couldn't seem to stop.

He spotted a vacant space four rows over, pulled in, and switched off the engine. He turned to her and took her hands in his. His fingertips, skin thickened from years of playing the cello, stroked the backs of her hands. "It's going to be all right, Lib," he said. "We'll get through this."

She leaned against him for a moment, let him hold her, as if it really was possible to draw strength from him, then straightened up. "We'd better go in."

He reached over to the rear seat and retrieved the tote bag that contained her things. They had told her to bring a book or magazines or knitting, something to pass the hours while she was attached to the machine. She'd need a blanket, as well, and a change of clothing. According to the "Patient's Handbook," the clothes were in the event hers became "soiled due to complications." Access bleeding. Vomiting. Another wave of dizziness overtook her. She waited while Richard came around and opened her door. This couldn't be happening, she thought. There had been a mistake. She slipped her hand in his as they crossed the lot.

Although it was only six thirty in the morning, the waiting room was already crowded. A roomful of sick people. There were two men in wheelchairs, one missing a leg. *She was not one of them.* She was *not. Not. One. Of. Them.* She allowed Richard to take over, surrendered to his care. He got her settled, then headed off to sign her in. She watched him cross the room. Although he never tanned and seldom exercised, in this room he looked fit and aglow with health.

The woman to her right shifted slightly to make more room for Libby. "Your first time?" she asked.

"Yes." Libby hugged the tote tight to her chest.

"I thought so. You can always tell."

Libby set the bag at her feet and reached for a magazine. She flipped though the pages without looking.

The woman patted her knee. "You'll do fine. The staff here is wonderful. Wonderful."

Blah, blah, blah. "I'm sure." Libby pretended to be engrossed in an article on how to construct wreaths out of wild grapevines. Finally Richard returned. He handed her a clipboard bearing a half-dozen forms. "They need you to fill these out."

"You must be her husband," the woman said to him.

"Yes," he said. Without even looking, Libby knew he was smiling at the woman.

"I'm Eleanor Brooks." She thrust out a hand for him to shake.

"Richard Barnett. This is my wife Libby."

Trapped, Libby shook the woman's hand and gave her a social smile.

"I know you're both probably nervous," Eleanor said. "I know I was, my first time."

"How long have you been coming?" Richard asked.

"Three years."

Three years. Oh, God. Three years.

"Lord, I was so nervous my first time," the woman on Libby's left chimed in. "For once I was grateful I couldn't pee or I'd have wet myself."

Everyone laughed except Libby. She was *not* one of them and she didn't belong here. This was a nightmare, a horrible, depressing nightmare.

"Diabetes?" Eleanor asked. "That's what most of us have."

"FSGS," Richard said. "Focal scelerosing glomerulonephritis."

As if it were any business of theirs what she had. Libby shot him a Be Quiet look.

"FSGS," Eleanor Brooks said. "I've never heard of it."

"It's fairly uncommon," Richard said.

Eleanor chatted on. She was from Great Lakes and had been a civilian worker at the naval station until she got sick. Richard, ignoring Libby's signal, told her they lived in Lake Forest and had two children who were both away at college. He said FSGS was not inherited, so they didn't have to worry about that. Libby glared at him. Why didn't he just reveal their entire history while he was at it?

At last he bent toward Libby and asked if she'd be all right for a minute while he went to the men's room.

"Sure," she said.

As soon as he'd gone, the woman to her left leaned closer, her tone that of a conspirator, as if she was to impart a grave secret. "Don't you worry about the pain, dear," she said. "It only hurts for a minute."

"What?" Libby was not sure she had understood.

"When they put the needles in. Don't look. That's my advice. Those things look like they're for hippopotamuses. I think the same people that make them, make the nozzles for fire hoses. Anyway, it only hurts for a minute."

Fire hoses. "It hurts?"

"I bet they didn't tell you about that. They never do." The woman's lips were tight.

Pain? Why hadn't Carlotta warned her?

"That's why I'm telling you," the woman continued as if reading her mind. "It's better to be prepared."

Libby pulled back from the woman and busied herself filling out the information forms, although it took a moment to steady her hand enough to print out her name and address, Richard's name, their phone number. She dug through her billfold until she found their insurance card and copied the information down. She completed the Health Profile (another two pages) and signed a paper authorizing treatment and the form acknowledging that she fully understood the "risks of unforeseen complications."

"Elizabeth Barnett?" A girl in a white smock stood in front of her, smiling. A badge on her lapel identified her as Kelly. She looked like she should have been in school. Her lipstick was the color of cherry Popsicles and she wore three earrings in her left ear, one a fake diamond. "I need you to come with me."

Oh, God. Oh, God. Where was Richard? "Can I wait for my husband?"

"The receptionist will tell him where you are," Kelly said.

"Good luck," Eleanor Brooks said.

"You'll do fine, dear" said the woman who had told her about the needles. *Fire hoses.*

Somehow she found herself in a small room; she couldn't remember walking there.

Kelly instructed her to stand on the scale so she could be weighed and then took her blood pressure and her temperature, inspected the catheter in her chest, the shunt in her arm.

"Looking good," she pronounced cheerfully. "No sign of infection." She went over things Carlotta had already told Libby about how important it was to not wear anything—constricting clothing or watchbands—that would put pressure on the shunt, and to avoid sleeping on it. She showed her how to check for clots and infection. Next, Kelly examined Libby's legs and back, her eyes, the veins in her neck. "Checking for pooled fluids," she said in the bright voice. Libby kept her eyes fixed on the Popsicle lips as they informed her that she would need to restrict phosphorus in her diet and take pills for bone health, and that her blood count would be checked weekly to monitor for anemia, and once a month for chemistry levels.

"This afternoon we've set up an appointment for you with the dietician. She'll go over all this again," Kelly said. "And I've given your husband a folder that contains all of our rules and regulations and procedures."

"Regulations?"

"What to do in case of inclement weather. How to file a griev-
ance. That kind of thing."

Libby's body sat in the chair, disconnected from her mind, which
had escaped the room. Later, she wouldn't remember one word those
pink lips had said.

The treatment area was as large as a high school gym and had been
divided into three bays. Each bay had ten stations and a television
set, each set tuned to the same channel, the Food Network, where a
chef was slicing beets the color of blood. Kelly led her to a vacant
chair in the middle bay. The green leather chaise was next to an
oblong machine with a monitor attached and tubes snaking in and
out. A rod on the side ran up the frame of the box to a small tricolor
bulb divided into green, red, and yellow sections. A traffic light, she
thought.

Richard, sheathed in a protective plastic smock, found her there.
He gave her a half smile. "How are you doing?"

"Okay," she said.

"You just relax," Kelly said. "Get comfortable."

A black woman watched from the next chaise. "I cried my first
time," she told Libby. "My daughter was with me and we both cried
like babies."

Libby nodded. She was *not* going to cry.

"But I got through it," the black woman said. "With the help of
my Lord and Savior, Jesus Christ, I got through it."

Oh, Lord, Libby thought. It was not a prayer. She rolled her eyes
at Richard. He squeezed her hand. For a moment she felt warmth
toward him, connection, and was grateful he was there.

Kelly slid a blood pressure cuff over Libby's right arm, made ad-
justments. She turned to Richard. "You might want to wait outside
while I get her started. We'll come get you when we've got the treatment going."

Richard bent and kissed her. "I'll be right back," he promised.

"Here we go," Kelly said, unbuttoning Libby's blouse.

Libby's hand rose, touched the catheter on her chest, felt the twin channels that hung from it. She closed her eyes, bracing herself for pain, tensing every muscle, curling her toes.

"I'm going to attach the A line first," Kelly said. "That's A for arterial, and then the V or venous line. Once we've got the tubes in, you'll be good to go." She hummed under her breath, a tune Libby knew but couldn't identify. Libby waited and waited for the pain, felt a slight tugging sensation in her chest, and then heard Kelly say, "Okay. You're home free now."

She opened her eyes. Tubes ran from her chest to the machine. Her blood flowed through them. Overhead, the green section of the tricolor bulb was lit.

Kelly pulled a sheet up over her chest, covering the tubes and the catheter. She wiped the sheen of perspiration off Libby's brow. "How are you doing?" she asked.

"It didn't hurt," Libby said.

"No. Did you think it would?"

Libby felt both relief that there was no pain and anger at the woman in the waiting room. Why would she have told such a lie? "Someone told me it would."

"Not the catheters. That's one of the blessings of them. The downside is, you've got to be real careful of infections."

"What about the shunt? Does it hurt when you use that?" The shunt in her arm wouldn't be healed and ready for use for another three weeks.

"Sometimes there's a little discomfort with that," Kelly said. "Nothing to worry about now. We rub a local anaesthetic on the site, before we needle."

Discomfort. Libby knew what that meant. Pain. Just get through today. One day at a time.

A technician rolled one of the wheelchair men in from the waiting room. Libby averted her eyes while he was attached to his machine. She couldn't bear to think of what might be in her future, couldn't imagine herself in a wheelchair, but then there had been a time in the not too distant past when she couldn't have imagined herself here, hitched up to this machine.

Richard returned, carrying the blanket. "They told me you might want this," he said. "They said you might feel chilled." He gave a glance at the machine, paled, and turned away. She hoped to hell he wasn't going to faint.

He sat in a chair by her side, took her hand. "Can I get you any-thing, Lib?" he asked. "Anything you want?"

Was there anything she wanted? She ran over her laundry list of desires. "Yes."

He leaned forward, eager for the chance to do something, to help. "What?"

"A new kidney," she said.

He laughed so loud the woman in the next station looked over. "A new kidney," he said. He thought she was joking. He tucked the blanket around her, hovered over her.

"Listen," she said. "There's no sense in you hanging around here."

"Don't you want me to keep you company? It's four hours," he said, as if by some miracle this pertinent fact had escaped her notice.

She nodded toward several of the other patients, who were sleep-ing. "I think I'll try and sleep," she said.

Kelly, returning to check the monitor, overheard. She nodded ap-provingly. "Lots of people nap. It helps pass the time."

"I could sit here while you're sleeping," Richard offered.

"No, really. Please. Why don't you go to your office? Get some work done and come back later. There's no sense in hanging around here for half the day."

"Are you sure?"

"Yes. I think I'll try and sleep."

She wouldn't. Sleep was out of the question. After he left, she looked around at the other patients, each tethered to a machine, blood flowing in and out. The TV chef was taking a casserole out of the oven but Libby noted he was not wearing hot mitts. Did they think viewers wouldn't notice? Did they think people were stupid?

She closed her eyes. She would just pretend she was somewhere else. Somewhere far away. Somewhere pleasant. A chaise on a cruise ship, she decided, although she had never been on one. She tried to imagine sea breezes brushing her face. She imagined a deck, swim-ming pools, shuffleboard courts, courteous staff in white coats waiting on her. She pictured a cabin with crisp linens on the bed and a port-hole looking out to the sea. Finally, when she guessed that at least a half hour had passed, she opened her eyes. She checked the clock. Five minutes had gone by. Five minutes. She didn't know if she would be able to get through this. She scanned the room, the other patients. How did they stand it? She felt cornered. Claustrophobic.

Libby shifted her gaze, scanned the room. Her attention was caught by a girl at the station across from hers. The girl looked vaguely familiar, like someone Libby had once known. She had cropped blond hair and was thin. Beyond thin. Skeletal. So gaunt her body didn't appear capable of holding organs inside its frame. Libby couldn't shake the feeling that she knew the girl, had seen her some-where, not like this—this creature of bones and sinew—but a health-ier version.

The girl was not sleeping or reading or knitting, but stared straight ahead. She had the inward-focused look of a monk. Her lips curved in a smile, so eerily tranquil Libby wondered if she was blind. She knew that diabetes sometimes caused loss of vision. Or maybe she had been drugged, which wasn't such a bad idea, come to think of it. Why hadn't she asked Carlotta about that? Some magical pill that would put her beyond anxiety or fear.

Who did the girl look like? Why did she seem familiar? It nagged at Libby and she studied the girl's thin face. It was utterly without expression, yet there was about her an aura of peacefulness. The ter-rible frailness and halo of hair reminded Libby of a medieval martyr. As she studied her, Libby felt the unearthly serenity flow from the girl across the bay to where she lay. It bathed her, calmed her. For the first time that morning, her breath came normally. When she finally pulled her gaze away from the girl and checked the clock, a full forty minutes had passed. Maybe she would be able to get through this after all.

The man in the wheelchair was sleeping. So was the Jesus Christ woman in the next chaise, her eyes flickering beneath their lids, as if in her dreams someone were chasing her. Her knitting lay in her lap. Turquoise and purple yarns, so bright they were practically neon. Colors only a child would wear. A memory stirred. Colors. Bands of color. Green, red, purple, turquoise, yellow, and pink. With ivory bone heart-shaped buttons. The sweater her grandmother made for her the Christmas she was twelve. It had been years since Libby thought of that sweater. Sam had a matching one. *Sam.* It took her by surprise, this longing for her sister. It lodged in her chest, beneath her heart, her heart that beat on and on, pumping blood out of her body and into the machine.

The peace she had felt moments before evaporated. She wanted to get up, rip the tubes from her chest. She wanted to go home.

Her mother's voice spoke out. *You think you're so smart, young lady. You think you're getting away with something, but sooner or later you'll have to pay the piper.* Pay the piper. As Matthew would say, life bites you in the ass.

I've done nothing to deserve this, she whispered, but the protest was weak.

Was this the price she had to pay for her sins? For the harm she had caused.

Over the machine, the green light flicked off and the yellow light flashed. Kelly was there at once.

"What's wrong?" Libby asked.

"Not to worry," Kelly said, checking the monitor. "Your blood pressure elevated." She adjusted a dial on the machine. "It's not unusual the first time. Just try and relax."

Libby concentrated on slowing her breath. She looked across at the saintly girl, concentrated on the serene face, tried to feel again the girl's peace flow across to her. On the machine, the yellow light blinked off. The green light glowed on.

"There you go," Kelly said. "Like I said, you're just a little nervous. It's not unusual the first time."

"Yes," Libby said.

"Your husband said to let you know he's out in the waiting room. He'll be there reading. He said to let him know if you can't sleep and want him to come back."

She felt a weight beneath her breast, a burden she knew was guilt. And grief. She didn't want Richard.

She wanted . . .

She wanted to be forgiven.

She wanted Sam.

Sam

. . . .

*J*ust before four, Sam woke. The room held the soft lavender shadows of predawn. Lee was still asleep and she snuggled closer, inhaled the scent of him. He smelled to her of the sea. The distinctive smell of ocean air. Of salt.

Salt preserves and cures.

She had learned this from a baking instructor when she was enrolled at Johnson & Wales. The instructor had also told their class that ages ago salt had been so valuable it had been used for currency, that its Latin name was, in fact, the root of "salary." He said salt had caused wars, had been used to preserve Egyptian mummies, and was an essential element in the human diet. There were more than fourteen thousand known uses for salt, he told them. He then explained how one of those uses was in bread making. Salt provided uniform grain and texture, he said, and strengthened the gluten in the dough, allowing it to expand without breaking.

Salt, the instructor had told them, was the only rock that was eaten by humans.

She inhaled Lee's sea smell again. Still half awake, her mind circled around in languid word association. Pillar of salt. Salt of the earth. To ward off bad luck, throw a pinch over your shoulder. To protect a newborn, bathe him in salt water. Salt water. Salt marsh. Saltworks.

She recalled how, when Alice was showing her real estate properties, she had told her that two hundred years ago saltworks had been a mainstay of Sippican's economy. Alice had driven by the sites where windmills had once pumped seawater upland through hollowed logs to vats. She'd explained how it had been moved from vat to vat until the sun evaporated the water and left salt deposits at the bottom. Wooden roofs, swung on cranes, covered the vats at night or when it rained. The salt produced in this way, she said, was pure, strong, and free from lime.

Sam wondered if the tears of all the women widowed by the sea were pure and strong. Did the salt they wept make their hearts expand but not break? Had it warded off spirits? Had it preserved? Worked cures?

"Hey." Lee, awake now, lifted his arm and wrapped it around her shoulders, drew her to him.

"Hey, yourself."

"You looked like you were pretty far off."

"Just thinking."

He kissed her temple. "About what?"

She smiled. "You'll never guess."

"Tell me." He kissed her nose, the curve at the corner of her lips.

"Salt."

"Really?"

"Uh-huh."

"What about it?"

She closed her eyes, ran though her thoughts. "Did you know that it is the only rock that humans eat?"

"Is that a fact?" He lifted her arm and brought it to his mouth. His brown eyes were steady on hers. He licked the inner crease of her elbow. "Salt," he said. She trembled. He ran his tongue up the tender, white underpart of her arm. "Salt," he said. She felt the deep, hot bolt of desire. He continued, licking around her breasts, up the curve of her neck to the hollow of her throat. "Salt," he said.

She knew there were women he had loved before. She had seen them around town and knew their names. Alison. Kerry. Carolyn. They were friendly with him, cordial to her. One, Carolyn, still gave him birthday gifts: bottles of good wine, expensive books.

"If you leave me—," she began.

He traced his tongue back down between her breasts, then lower. Her back arched and she caught her breath. "If you leave me," she whispered, "we couldn't stay friends."

He burrowed his face in her belly, murmured something.

"What?" she said.

"I will never leave you," he said.

She allowed herself to believe this. Her body opened to him.

He ran his tongue lower, dipped into the salt of her hidden places.

Their bodies, warm and open and not yet inhabiting the day's defenses, coupled, melded, merged, swam, dove deep, grew salt.

"Tell me something," Lee said. His voice was sleepy, postcoital.

She curled her body closer to his. Happiness this deep should be outlawed. Taboo. Illegal. Or bottled and sold. At prohibitive prices. Taxed like a luxury item. New brides with costly weddings and elaborate cakes, brides with Cartier rings that cost more than her home, these brides had nothing on her. "Tell you what?"

"Something about you," he said.

"About me?"

"Tell me a story about you." His hand settled on her hip. "About when you were a girl."

"I told you one last night. Remember?" She slung her leg over his thigh. "About the time I was fourteen and Libby pretended she was a mannequin."

"Tell me another one."

Through the window, the first streaks of rose lit the eastern sky. They should get up. She had the three weddings on Saturday and there was a ton of work ahead. She didn't move. "You go first. Tell me something about when you were a boy. Something you haven't told any of your other girlfriends."

"Like there's been so many," he said.

"Come on," she pressed. "Just one thing. One thing you haven't told anyone else."

He thought for a minute. "Well, when I was ten I had a crow."

"You mean like a pet?"

"Not really. It was wild."

"You had a wild crow?"

"I found it in the parking lot by the Yacht Club. It had a broken wing. I put it in a carton and my mom drove me over to Doc Osborne's. Doc said once a bird's wing is broken, it can't be healed. He said it would be cruel to keep it and it should be put down."

"But you kept it." She was thinking about the stray cats at the boatyard, about his way with the broken ribs of sloops.

"I talked my mom into it. She agreed but said I'd have to keep it out on the sunporch."

A fondness for Alice washed over Sam. "Did you name it?"

"No."

"You didn't? Why?"

"I don't know. I guess because it wasn't mine to name. I just called it Crow."

"What happened to it?"

"It stayed there six months. It about drove Mom crazy." He laughed at the memory. "When I let it go, we had to take a chisel to clean the bird shit off the floor."

"And did it fly again?"

"Yeah," he said. "It did." There was still joy in his voice at the memory. She wondered if it was possible to love a person more.

"What about you?" he asked. "Did you have a pet?"

She shook her head. "My mother was allergic." She couldn't imagine her mother allowing them to keep a chickadee, much less a crow.

"Not even a goldfish?"

"We had a snapping turtle for a couple of days once. My sister found him. She wrapped him up in our sweatshirts and I helped her carry him home." Even now Sam could remember how afraid of the snapper she'd been, her terror so different from Libby's fearlessness. "When we got home, Libby put him in the upstairs bathtub. Then she charged the neighborhood kids admission to come and look at him, until my mother found out. She made her give them back all their money."

She lifted her knees and made a tent of the bedclothes. "Now tell me something else about you," she said.

"What do you want to know?"

She imagined him young. A boy. A teenager. "Who was your first love?"

"Very first?"

"Uh-huh."

"Mrs. McIntire."

"Mrs.? A married woman?"

"Very."

"How old were you?"

"Seven." She smiled, picturing him at seven. "She was my second-grade teacher."

"Did she know you had this crush on her?"

"It was hard to miss. I used to leave candy kisses on her desk. I cut her picture out of the class photo and slept with it. I think I was in high school before I could even look at her without blushing."

"You should have had our second-grade teacher. On second thought, I'm glad you didn't. Miss Granger would have cooled you on women forever."

"I can't imagine."

"Miss Granger was older than my grandmother and smelled funny. And crabby. God, she was mean. Beats me why she wanted to teach. I think she hated kids." She felt the heat of old anger rising in her cheeks, surprising her.

"You are to draw a self-portrait," Miss Granger says. "A picture of yourself." She passes out sheets of heavy paper the color of oatmeal.

Sam wants a purple crayon. It is her favorite color and the one she always uses from her big box at home, but the box Miss Granger hands out for art has only eight colors. She chooses the blue since it is the closest she can find to purple. She begins with the head, carefully drawing a round balloon. She concentrates, her tongue tucked in her cheek, wanting to get it right. She adds eyes and a mouth, five corkscrew curls for hair. She draws a line down from the balloon, adds stick arms and legs, pitchfork hands, a bell skirt. The figure floats, unteth-

ered to the ground. When she is done, she draws a second figure, identical to the first except taller. She smiles, pleased with the portrait.

When Miss Granger sees it, she frowns. Sam has done something wrong. She looks at the picture, unable to see her mistake.

"Who is this?" Miss Granger points to the smaller figure.

"Me," Sam says in a small voice. What has she done wrong?

"And this?" Miss Granger's finger lands on Libby.

"My sister."

Miss Granger snaps the paper up and takes it to her desk, snips off the part with Libby.

"You were to draw a self-portrait, Samantha," she says. "Not a family picture."

Sam cries and won't stop, even when Miss Granger sends her to the principal, who calls for the school nurse. They send Sam home. She cries all night. Makes herself ill. Actually has a fever. She refuses to go to school the next day. Or the next. There are whispered phone calls, consultations with the principal.

When she returns to class, all the self-portrait drawings have been taken down from where they were clipped to a string above the chalkboard.

"Miss Granger never mentioned them again," Sam said.

"Funny . . ." Lee's voice was lazy; he was drifting off to sleep.

"What?"

"Your stories," he said. "They're not about you."

"Yes, they are."

"Partly. But they're really about your sister."

She felt chilled. The intense feeling of pleasure that had enveloped her earlier faded.

They overslept, then woke to the aroma of coffee. Downstairs, Stacy banged around in the kitchen. Lee got up first, headed for the shower. Moments later she joined him. He kissed her beneath the water flow and grinned. "My lucky day."

She took the soap from him and lathered his chest. He was muscular and still summer-tan. A song fragment floated through her head. *Somewhere in my wicked, miserable past, I must have done something good.*

She washed his belly, tried to picture what he would look like in ten years, or twenty, the person he would become—thicker through the waist perhaps, gray hair—but she couldn't imagine. She had nothing to go by. In Alice's home there were no photographs of his father, a man who deserted the family when Lee was five.

She soaped his pubic hair, felt him quicken beneath her hand.

He ran his palm over her back, down over her buttocks. "I thought you were in a hurry?"

She grinned and handed him back the soap. "I am. Do you take rain checks?"

"Count on it."

He turned off the shower, stepped outside and grabbed two towels, handed one to her.

She watched him dry off.

Their eyes met in the vanity mirror. She noticed faint lines fanning out from the corners of his eyes and this reminded her of something Stacy had told her months before. "Lee's a Sagittarius," she had said. "What does that mean?" Sam asked, even though she did not believe in that stuff. "A good catch," Stacy said. "Sagittarians are loving, wise, and capable of great understanding."

"Lee?" She wrapped the towel tighter around her torso and sat on the edge of the bed. He was dressing.

"Yeah?"

"Can I ask you something?"

"Ask away."

She swallowed. "Have you forgiven your father?"

He stopped in the middle of pulling on his shirt and looked at her. "Forgiven him for what?"

"For abandoning you. You and your brother. And Alice."

"My father did what he had to do. It wasn't about me."

"You were only five, Lee. What kind of man walks out on a five-year-old son?"

He crossed to the bed, sat at her side and reached for her hand. He knew she wasn't asking only about his father.

"He did what he had to do," he said again. "The things we do, they make some kind of sense to us when we do them, even if they don't to anyone else."

"But it doesn't make you angry, the way he abandoned you?"

"I can't carry that weight with me." He said this like it was a simple thing. And maybe it was, for him. Lee thought relationships were like boats, that no matter what damage had been done, things could be salvaged.

Why did people think it was so easy to forgive? That forgiveness could be bestowed so lightly. That it didn't have to be earned.

Libby

. . . .

As she pumped the blood pressure bulb, Carlotta bent over Libby. There was, on her breath, the rich whiff of coffee. Libby would have killed for a cup of coffee, a double latte with a free refill. *Killed* for it. Well, that was a privilege disappeared. Now all she allowed herself was a half cup each morning. She saved her liquids—her four cups of allowed fluids—for afternoons, when thirst hit the hardest. She portioned her fluids out, a half Dixie cup at a time. She had seriously contemplated drinking more than the amount set by the nutritionist, but so far had resisted the urge. Some of the other patients cheated on their diets. They talked about it in the waiting room. The Jesus Christ woman—whose name she had learned was Jesse—said she just couldn't give up her country ham. She truly didn't see how an occasional slice now and then would harm her. Like she was exempt from the rules. But Libby sympathized. She fully understood now why alcoholics soaked up booze, why emphysema and lung cancer patients sucked on cigarettes. The body wants what it wants.

Carlotta released the bulb, the cuff deflated. "Blood pressure's down," she said, smiling.

"That's good," Libby said. It should be down, the amount of salt she'd been reduced to. She wasn't even allowed commercial substitutes because they were almost all potassium salts. Two nights ago she'd had a dream about pigging out on junk food. Pretzels. Potato chips. Cheez Doodles. Stuff she hadn't allowed herself in years.

Carlotta unstrapped the cuff from Libby's arm, made a notation in her file.

Libby shivered and wrapped her arms close.

"Chilled?"

"A little." She was always cold now, and hungry. Before she began dialysis, her appetite had diminished. Now it was back in full force, but there was so little that she was permitted. Her diet had gone from not bad to pretty dismal. The irony would make her laugh if she had a scrap of humor left.

"We're almost done here," Carlotta said. "Then you can get dressed and we'll talk." She finished the exam, taking Libby's temperature, pressing her abdomen, checking for excess fluid. Libby was used to the drill.

Carlotta lifted Libby's left arm, ran a thumb over the shunt. "Swelling's gone down and it looks clean," she noted with satisfaction. "And you're checking it three or four times a day to make sure there's no clot?"

Libby nodded. She looked down at Carlotta's hand, noted for the first time her ringless fingers. To date, she'd had no more curiosity about Carlotta's personal life than she would have had about a plumber's, but now she found herself wondering if she was married, perhaps to a fellow doctor. Who else would put up with the hours? But there were no children, Libby thought. Carlotta had the boyish build of a woman who had never given birth.

"The graft is looking good," Carlotta said. "It won't be long before we can switch and get rid of the catheter. Bet you won't be sorry to see that go."

"No." Once she had been worried that she would have a scar on her chest from the catheter, but now that seemed an insignificant concern.

"And no catheter means . . ." Carlotta beamed at her.

"What?"

"You can take showers again."

For the first time, Libby smiled.

"With that good news, I'll leave you to get dressed. I'll be back in a minute."

After Carlotta left, Libby shrugged off the thin gown and pulled on her sweater and a pair of gray trousers, glad for the warmth. If she was this cold in October, she could only imagine how she'd be come winter. She'd be wearing so many layers she'd look like the Michelin Man. Her charts lay on the stool by the examining table and she looked over at them, wondered what was written there. Were there things noted there that Carlotta had kept from her? She reached out, then hesitated, worried that Carlotta would return and catch her in the act. Well, what of it? They were her charts, after all. She had a right. Before she could pick them up, there was a soft rap on the door and it opened.

"All set?" Carlotta entered, picked up the folder, sat on the stool. She leafed through the pages, picked out the chemistry-levels report. "Your numbers are good," she said. "Your iron is getting better. I don't think we're going to be looking at iron IV for a while." Libby was on a supplement to prevent anemia and still had occasional EPO—erythropoietin—injections. She was on another supplement for bone health, an evil-tasting pill she choked down with a table-spoon of applesauce, heavy on the cinnamon.

Carlotta ran a finger down the chart. "Your potassium levels are fine. Creatinine and BUN are higher than I'd like, but nothing we need to be terribly concerned about at this point. Protein levels are a little elevated. You're watching that?"

Libby nodded. What wasn't she watching?

"Any dizziness, nausea?"

"No."

"Fatigue?"

"No." In fact, she was feeling better than she had expected to. She had energy again, energy she hadn't had in nearly a year. Over the past months, the loss had been so slow, so insidious; she hadn't realized how weak she had become.

"Any problems at all?"

Libby reddened. She absolutely hated talking about this. Disease stripped dignity away, one shred at a time. "One thing . . ."

"Yes?"

"Well, I've been a little—a little constipated."

"That's not unusual. Nothing to worry about." Carlotta picked up a prescription pad, jotted down a few words, and handed the slip to Libby. "A stool softener," she said. "That should help. Let me know if it doesn't, or if it causes diarrhea. We don't want that either."

"Okay." Everything was such a fucking balancing act.

"How's your sex life?"

"Fine," she said, thinking, What sex life?

"Some patients report a lessening of desire. It's not unexpected."

Please, she thought, drawing the word out like Mercedes would have. Pulleeze. She managed a smile. "No. Really. We're fine in that department."

Carlotta checked a page. "Let's see. You've had two sessions now. How is it going? You doing okay with it?"

"I'm managing." She dreaded the dialysis, but what choice did she have? What was it one of the techs there told her? It's a part-time job you take to stay alive.

Carlotta closed the file. "You've met some of the other patients by now, I'm sure," she said.

"Yes." Barely. She had to go to the center for her part-time job of staying alive, but there was no rule that said she had to socialize. Mostly the other patients irritated her. The one-legged man wanted the TV volume so loud people up in Alberta could hear it.

"There's a support group that meets once or twice a week," Carlotta said. "Shall I set it up for you to attend?"

"I don't think so."

"Some people find it helpful."

"Maybe later." Fat chance. The last thing in the world she wanted to do was sit around with the other patients and talk about it. *And how are your creatinine levels, Mrs. Lincoln?* She had nothing in common with those people. Certainly not with the Jesus freak who told her at the last session that in the beginning she was fighting to survive and now she *wanted* to survive—wanted to survive for Jesus, was what she said. Nor with Eleanor Brooks, who told anyone who would listen how important it was to maintain a positive frame of mind, an upbeat attitude, and was always handing out little square cards with affirmations written on them. "Faith is daring the soul to go beyond what the eyes can see." " If there is no wind, row." "Nothing is impossible." A virtual pep squad of positive thinking, that woman. "If you can't plant a garden, be one." Honestly, it made Libby ill. She wished they would all keep quiet, that they would keep things to themselves. The only one she found even remotely interesting was Hannah, the gaunt, blond Saint Joan creature. Richard was the one who eventually recognized her. Hannah Rose, whose husband, Gabriel, worked for the Open Lands Association. In the past, Libby and Richard had seen them several times around town. Libby was saddened by Hannah's transformation from a lovely woman to this wraith, but she also found the girl's presence deeply calming, soothing in a way she couldn't explain.

Carlotta absently tapped the file against her knee. "The other thing I want to talk about," she said, "is that I've put you on the list."

"The list?"

"For a transplant."

Libby was stunned into silence.

"Right now there are sixty thousand names on the national list for prospective transplants," Carlotta said. Libby knew this. Richard had done the research. "The average wait time is anywhere from two to five years." Richard had told her this, too. "So the sooner we get you listed, the better. That said, I think it's time we set things in motion for your evaluation."

"Evaluation?"

"Preselection testing. To make sure you're deemed an acceptable candidate."

This was going too fast. Carlotta had brought up the subject in the past, and Libby had, at her urging, called Josh and asked him about the possibility of his being a donor. But the actual transplantation was to have been "at some future time," and Libby was not ready to explore it now. "What's the rush?"

"The truth is, the earlier in dialysis treatment you have a transplant, the better it is. There are fewer complications. The body's in better shape. Systems aren't broken down."

Libby had just *started* dialysis. She was not ready to talk seriously about transplants, not by a long shot.

"In the meantime," Carlotta went on, "be thinking about whether or not you have friends or coworkers who might be willing to be a donor. Someone your husband knows at the college."

"How would you ask someone that?" She couldn't control the sarcasm that crept into her voice. "Do I just walk up to them? Say, 'Excuse me, but would you be interested in giving me a kidney?' "

"You'd be surprised."

I bet, Libby thought.

"Have you thought again about asking your children?"

"No. Absolutely not. I thought I made it clear that they are not to be asked." Libby would not even consider this. Carlotta had told her that, with regard to their ages, they were both over eighteen and there was no reason they couldn't be donors. She'd had several patients who had received kidneys from their children and she said she would be happy to put Libby in touch with them. Wouldn't you want to give a kidney to one of your children if they needed it? she'd asked Libby. Well, naturally Libby would. No question. But it wasn't the same. Matthew and Mercedes had their whole lives in front of them. She wouldn't think of asking them to make this sacrifice and refused to discuss it further. Of course, they had known from the beginning that Richard was out of the running since his blood type was incompatible with hers.

"You might give your brother another call," Carlotta said.

"I told you. He's not interested." One call had been enough there. Josh, the Switzerland of relatives, stayed true to his policy of noninvolvement and nonintervention. Just as he had refused to take sides in her estrangement from Sam. "Keep me out of it," he'd said to her, and that was pretty much his reaction when she'd asked him if he'd consider being an organ donor, although he'd used kinder language.

"That's not an unusual response," Carlotta said. "You caught him off guard. Now that he's had time to get used to the idea he might be more receptive. He might at least be willing to be tested. I'd be happy to talk with him if you'd like." She reopened the folder, removed two booklets from the back. "Here," she said. "Take these home and look them over."

"What are they?"

"Some material on transplantation. I think you'll find them interesting. The first contains information for potential donors. The other is intended for transplant patients. In the back there are some letters and essays from people who have donated organs. There are even a couple of poems; some of them are quite moving."

Libby didn't reach for the booklets. Panic stirred beneath her heart.

Carlotta reached over and took her hand. "You're doing fine," she said.

Libby looked at the booklets Carlotta held, read the quote on the cover of the one for patients. "Gifts make their way through stone walls." Well, there was another quote for Eleanor Brooks.

Carlotta handed her the booklets. "Look them over," she said. "Then we'll talk some more."

It was after eleven when Libby returned to the house. It was Tuesday, her day for dusting and vacuuming. Once, she would have done it earlier, before she went out for the appointment, but these days she found it difficult to dredge up interest in the house. Her mornings at the center had completely thrown her schedule awry anyway. She hadn't even changed the sheets this week. She supposed she should vacuum, but right now she was hungry.

In the kitchen, she fixed up a plate—hard-boiled egg, sliced cucumber, cold asparagus, a half cup of applesauce—and took it onto the back porch, along with a copy of the *Tribune*. She stretched her legs out on the wicker ottoman and ate her lunch, drinking in the warmth of the noonday sun. She opened the paper, but must have dozed off almost at once. When she woke, the *Trib* was on the floor and the sun had moved across the sky. Her legs were in shadow. She got up and took her plate to the kitchen. She heated up the teakettle, permitted herself a half cup of mint tea. The booklets Carlotta had given her lay on the counter next to her handbag. She picked one up.

"Your Kidney Transplant—Every Step of the Way," she read. "A Patient's Guide to Transplantation." There was a photo of a man on the cover. He held a brown dachshund in his lap. "Now I know that dreams do come true," proclaimed the quote beneath the picture. The deliberately upbeat tone infuriated her. Why did everyone act so cheerful?

She opened the booklet and scanned the first three entries in the table of contents: "Learning the Facts," "Understanding How a Healthy Kidney Works," "Getting to Know Your Transplant Team." Panic pinched at her throat and she closed the booklet. She couldn't imagine this was what really lay ahead for her. She knew for sure that she wouldn't tell Richard what Carlotta had said about putting her on the list. Not yet. He would just start on her again to call her brother. And Sam. The best thing was to hide the booklets before he saw them.

She carried them upstairs, to the guest bedroom. She changed the linens regularly here and they were always clean, fresh, although the room hadn't been used for years, not since her parents died. It was ridiculous, really. Pointless, like so much in her life. She crossed to a pine dresser (an antique she had refinished the first year of her marriage) and knelt, then opened the bottom drawer. Her flute case lay in the center. She had completely forgotten it was there. She stared at it a moment, then opened the lid. A faint smell of must drifted up from the plush lining. She reached for the head joint; the silver metal was cool to her touch. She twisted it onto the body and then attached the foot joint and, without thinking, lifted the flute to her mouth. It had been years—fifteen at least—since she had played, but her fingers had not forgotten the placement. She wet her lips, drew her bottom lip taut, blew. The tone was flat. She had lost control of her mouth muscles; the flute pads were dry. She disassembled the flute and settled it back in the case. She probably should sell it. She'd certainly never play again, and Mercedes had never shown an interest. Someone might as well get some use out of it. She scanned the other contents of the drawer. Good God, the things she had forgotten about, things that at one time she had thought were treasures important enough to save. A white tassel from her high school graduation, a slender photo album. She flipped open the album and studied the pictures inside the plastic sleeves, photos of her high school classmates: Sue Drummond and Jeannie Gault, once her best friends, although it had been years and years since she had seen them. She didn't even know their married names. She'd never been good at keeping in touch; when her mother was still alive she would give Libby periodic updates. She studied their faces. Had they ever been so young? She turned a page and saw a photo of herself. She was on horseback, riding down a narrow lane. At her side, astride an Appaloosa, was Russell, the first boy she had been serious about and the first boy to break her heart, or at least bruise her ego. On the last page of the album, there was a photo of her and Sam. She remembered the day it was taken. Both of them wore white sundresses. They were end-of-summer tan, their hair sun-streaked. She stood behind Sam, her arms wrapped protectively around her younger sister.

Deep in her chest, beneath the place where the catheter had been inserted, Libby felt a twist of pain. She shut the album.

There were other books in the drawer as well. Three volumes of poetry. Anne Sexton. Sharon Olds. Adrienne Rich. Why had she set them aside in this drawer instead of putting them on the bookshelves in the study? She opened the Olds book, saw notations in the margins, in her own handwriting. The ink—green—had faded so badly she could barely make out the words. Once she had known these poems by heart.

Beneath these books she found another slender volume. Its cover was beige and textured, with pieces of grass and flower petals pressed into it. Instantly, as if it had been last week instead of more than two decades ago, she remembered the day she bought the book. She had found it in a stationery store in Northampton the summer before she'd left for Oberlin. It had been costly, and the shop owner had told her it had been made entirely by hand: cover, pages inside, everything. In spite of the price—she could have bought a skirt for what it cost—she hadn't been able to resist. Now she opened it. Her name—her maiden name, Elizabeth Lewis—was penned neatly on the first page. She turned to the next page, read the poem she had written there.

The History of Water

Waterfalls.
Water falls

in slippery flow, motion
like music, invading
sculpted rock.

Silver-swift crystal
fills stone-pocked memories
Then spills

And falls, water.

She remembered now. The poem had been inspired by an oil painting she had seen at the Museum of Fine Arts in Boston. She had been mesmerized by the way the painter had captured the light, the motion of water. The poem had pleased her, but now, looking critically, she saw its faults, although the "stone-pocked" was nice.

With an odd, mingled sense of loss and affection, she recalled the years held in this drawer. High school. College. A perfect blending of friendship and music, poetry and freedom. Drinking bargain-shelf merlot, sitting up with friends until dawn, talking about sex and politics, love and obsessions, struggles with desire and hope. She remembered curling up on the floor in the corner of Richard's cheap apartment, sublet for the semester, and listening to his cello, his playing a kind of foreplay. She recalled desire and the lovemaking it kindled.

It had been a long time since she'd felt desire, or written a poem, or even read one, so long she could barely remember, although back then she read poetry constantly. Olds and the others. Volumes and volumes, lines written with strength and pity and tenderness and, sometimes, terror. She remembered what a teacher had once told her and how she had believed it absolutely: *What we create may save us.*

Futile words. Not true. Not true. On the page in her hands, the lines blurred. Nothing could save her. Certainly not the poetry of a girl who still believed in hope, before she became the wasted shell of a woman.

But there she went, getting maudlin again. She shook off the memories.

But the grief. Oh, the grief. What was she to do with the grief?

Sam

. . . .

*N*ever again, Sam vowed. Never again would she schedule three weddings for the same day, not when one of the orders included a smaller, individual cake for each table at the reception. It was well after ten and she'd been up before dawn, and working—under pressure and without a break—ever since. Now she was exhausted. Totally wiped out. She closed her eyes; cakes floated behind her lids. The Hawkins cake: three tiers. Yellow cake with raspberry preserves and buttercream filling, decorated with white roses and edible pearls, and iced a hydrangea blue that matched the bridesmaids' gowns. The Weaver cake: three tiers. Seashore motif. White cake with a chocolate mousse filling, set on a bed of sugar tinted to look like sand. White chocolate shells. The Van Horn cake: six tiers. Lemon cake with white chocolate mousse, emerald fondant ribbons edged in gold foil at the base of each tier, fluttery sweet peas growing up the sides. Topped with a nosegay of emerald-striped lady slipper orchids. For certain, that cake cost nearly as much as the bride's gown. And that wasn't counting the twenty table cakes or the groom's cake, which was an exact replica of Fenway Park. In chocolate. (Emily Van Horn and her new husband were spending the first night of their marriage in Boston so they could catch the Red Sox the next afternoon. Then, before leaving for St. Bart's, they were taking a week to see games at a half-dozen other major league parks.) And good luck to her, Sam thought.

"I swear," Stacy said. Her feet were swollen and she had them propped up on a stool. "If I have to listen to 'The Wind Beneath My Wings' one more time, I'm going to shoot the bride."

They had stayed through each reception, at least until the wedding cake was cut—a service few pastry chefs provided; most just assembled the cake and took off—and now they were both slightly tipsy. They'd gone through nearly a bottle of champagne, one of two thrust on them by the caterer and charged to Howard Van Horn, a man who could certainly afford it.

"Or 'True Love,'" Sam said, laughing. "I could sing that in my sleep."

"'I Love You Truly,'" Stacy said. She stuck out her tongue and jabbed her finger toward her throat.

"'You Are the Sunshine of My Life.'" Sam poured the last of the champagne into the coffee mugs they were using for glasses.

"'Sunrise, Sunset.'" Although more wine was the last thing they needed—they hadn't had more than two bites to eat all day—Sam thought there was a better-than-even chance they'd open the second bottle before they closed up shop.

"'Chapel of Love,'" Stacy said.

"'True Love Waits.'"

"'When I'm Sixty-Four.'" Stacy fired a gun-barrel finger at her temple.

"'Always.'"

"'Always and Forever.'" Stacy drained her champagne. "And the soloist thinks he's Lionel Richie."

"You win," Sam said, refilling her assistant's mug. She swung her feet up next to Stacy's. "God, but I'm way too young to feel this old."

"Okay," Stacy said. "True-confession time. What'd they play at your wedding?'

"They didn't."

"You didn't have music?"

"I didn't have a wedding."

"What?"

"I eloped."

"Get outta town."

"A justice of the peace in Cape May, New Jersey."

"Wow. I figured you'd have had a big wedding."

"Nope. One production in the family was about all my mother could stand." Their mother had spent the months leading up to Libby's wedding moaning and bitching about the expense, making it sound like they were going to have to remortgage the house or something. No way was Sam going to go through that.

She got up, steadied herself, and crossed to the refrigerator. She took out the second bottle of champagne, held it toward Stacy and raised an eyebrow in question.

"Better not," Stacy said. "I'm already as wasted as a sailor on shore leave."

"Say *that* three times quick," Sam said.

"I'm lucky I could say it once."

Sam tilted the bottle toward Stacy. "You sure? I'm going to."

"WTF," Stacy said—her shorthand for what-the-fuck. "Twist my arm."

Sam stripped the foil, twisted out the cork, refilled their mugs. The champagne was good. The sixty-dollars-a-bottle-wholesale kind of good.

"To Howard Van Horn," Sam said, raising her mug overhead.

Stacy lifted hers, sloshed a little of the champagne over the rim, drank. "To the father of the bride," she said. "So whaddaya think that wedding cost him?"

"Plenty." The Van Horn wedding, a Great Gatsby extravaganza, had gone on for four days. Golf tournaments. A whale watch charter for the entire bridal party. Brunch for their closest friends at the yacht club. Clam-and-lobster-bake rehearsal dinner. All overseen by a fidgety little wedding planner from Boston who charged by the hour and acted like everyone had signed on as her own personal staff, including Sam and Stacy and a couple of high school boys who parked cars. "Plenty," she repeated. Sometimes it stunned her how much people were willing to spend on an event that was ancient history within months.

"Well, Old Lucy Van Horn was in her glory," Stacy said. "Didja know she and my mom were kids together? Mom remembers back before she was Mrs. Howard Van Horn and her father was the school janitor. She said back then Lucy didn't own two socks that matched."

"Well, she sure does now." Matching hosiery might not be one of Lucy Van Horn's problems, but Sam bet that she had more than her share. An anorexic daughter and a son with suspiciously dilated pupils and a runny nose, for starters.

"I can't believe you eloped," Stacy said, returning to the earlier subject. "Didja ever regret it? Not having a wedding, I mean."

"God," Sam said. "If we're going to talk about this, I'm going to need more in my stomach than champagne." She poked around until she found a bag of potato chips in the cupboard and some leftover buttercream icing in the refrigerator. She dragged a chip through the icing. "Mmmmm. Salt, fat, and sugar. God's perfect combo."

Stacy took a handful of chips. "Didja?"

"Did I what?"

"Regret it."

"Not the wedding part. Not having one, I mean." Stone-cold sober, she would not be sharing this with Stacy. But then she was a long way from sober. "The marriage, now that I lived to regret."

"How long'd it last?"

"What? The marriage?"

"Yeah."

"Four years. Which was just about three too many." She poured them more champagne.

"What was his name?"

"Jay. Jay Trumbel."

"What was his sign?"

"Good God, I don't know."

"When was his birthday?"

"March. March twenty-eighth."

"Aries. Fire sign. Impulsive. Born leaders and born fighters."

Sam couldn't argue with that. She was an Aries, too.

"So was he good-looking?"

"Only if you count tall, dark, and handsome."

"So what happened?"

Sam yawned, stretched, feigned indifference. "A boring story. Not worth relating." She'd have had to be a lot drunker than she was to share that part with Stacy. "What about you? Did you have a wedding each time?"

"The first time, I was only sixteen and we eloped. My period was late and we panicked." Stacy licked salt from her fingers, then leaned forward and kneaded the arch of her foot. "False alarm, as it turned out. Big whoop. My parents got it annulled and I went back to school. The second time I did it up right. Church, flower girl, the whole nine yards. The next time—with Carl—it didn't seem worth the bother. New Bedford City Hall seemed good enough." She shoved her foot into her shoe, wriggling it to get it in. "God, speaking of Carl, I'd better get going. He'll be pitching a fit, wondering what the hell happened to me."

Sam held the bottle high. "This one's not dead yet."

Stacy shook her head. "I'll be lucky if I can walk as it is."

Although they both should have known better—they'd polished off nearly two bottles of champagne between them—Sam drove her home, holding it steady at thirty the whole way.

When they pulled up to Stacy's cottage, the porch light was on. Sam saw a shadow behind the front window. "Carl's still up," she said.

"Shit," Stacy said. "I told him not to wait. I told him I'd be late." She swiveled toward Sam. "Can ya tell I'm blasted?"

Sam cocked her head and studied her assistant. "Not a hint," she said. "Except for the bloodshot eyes."

"Oh, shit." Stacy grabbed for the visor mirror. "You're kidding."

"Yeah," Sam said. "I'm kidding."

"Not funny." Stacy ran her fingers through her spiked hair, then climbed out of the car. "Wish me luck."

"Always." Sam watched her walk up the steps, weaving only slightly.

———

Without Stacy, the kitchen felt empty. Sam tossed her handbag on the table. On her desk, the phone message light blinked insistently. A call must have come through while she was driving Stacy home. Sam knew at once who it was, and although she'd been expecting it every day since the first call, she was no more prepared to hear Libby's voice now than she had been then. She wiped up the counters, carried the coffee mugs to the sink, buying time. Finally she crossed to the desk and punched PLAY.

"Hey, have I reached the cake goddess of Sippican?"

Lee. She let out a breath, relaxed her shoulders. She leaned toward the machine, as if that could bring him closer. He'd driven up to Maine that morning, an unexpected trip up to Camden to survey a sloop and give an estimate on its restoration.

"So where are you?" he said. "Should I be worried? Have you run off with an usher? The drummer in the band?"

She loved the sound of his voice. Every modulation. The way you could hear a smile behind the words.

He asked how the weddings had gone and told her that he expected he'd be back sometime on Monday. He said that he missed her and that she'd better stock up on whipped cream for his return. He'd hung up without leaving a callback number.

There was still an inch of champagne in the bottle and she poured it into her cup. She finished the potato chips. She wanted to tell him about the weddings and ask about the sloop. She wanted to hear that he loved her and find out what he planned to do with the whipped cream. Okay, she wanted to have phone sex. God, but she missed him. Feeling like a teenager, she replayed the message. His voice had the expected effect. She couldn't wait to have him in her bed.

She thought of Emily Van Horn and Sally Weaver and Lisa Hawkins, brides who were at that very moment abed in hotel rooms with their new husbands. "To your happiness," she said aloud, meaning it. In spite of the insane extravagance of their weddings, the trite, predictable songs she and Stacy had poked fun at, she admired the brides. It was a courageous thing to trust in love. To stand before family and friends and declare this love. To accept public blessings.

Would things have turned out differently if she and Jay had had a wedding?

Sam arrived in Illinois the day before and finally she and Libby have managed to catch some time alone. Richard is at the college. Matthew and Mercedes are playing a video game downstairs. The sounds of their voices and electronic pings and buzzes filter up the stairs.

They are in Libby's bedroom, ostensibly to find something in her closet for Sam to get married in, but it's quickly apparent that Libby has something else on her mind. She closes the door and turns to Sam, cups her face in her hands. "Listen," she says, her voice serious.

"What?" Sam says, although she knows what's coming. They have been through this earlier, when Libby asked if Sam wanted her to go with them. "To be your maid of honor," Libby said. "Matron," Sam said. "You're married. So you'd be my matron of honor." "So do you want me to come?" Libby asked. "No," Sam said. She'd already thought this through. If Libby went, then Jay's sister would be hurt if they didn't ask her, and she'd want her husband to go, too, and then both sets of parents would have to be included and pretty soon it would turn into a big production. Exactly what Sam wants to avoid.

Libby draws her toward the bed, sits down next to her. "Listen," she says again. She has what Sam calls her "responsible big sister" expression, a look she'd developed sometime in the past two years.

"What?"

"Are you sure you want to do this?"

"Do what? Elope?"

"Not just elope. Marry Jay. Are you absolutely sure you want to marry Jay?"

Sam sighs. She's twenty-eight. She's not a child.

"I mean, maybe you should live with him for a while. Try it out. Make sure he's the one."

"Oh, right, like shacking up with him would make Mother and Dad a lot happier than if I eloped."

"I'm not thinking about them."

"Well, what are you thinking about?"

"You. I'm just trying to protect you."

"Protect me?" Sam is taken aback. This isn't what she wants from Libby. She wants her sister to be excited for her, happy for her, not worrying about protecting her.

Libby studies Sam, decides to continue. "How long have you known Jay, anyway? Three months?"

"What's that got to do with anything? If I remember, you didn't know Richard very long before you two got married."

"That was different."

"What made it so all-fired different, Lib? That it was you, not me?"

"That's not what I'm saying, honey. I just think you should wait, get to know each other better, be sure this is what you want to do."

"What, are you in some way smarter than me when it comes to picking a husband? Do you have some special gene?" Libby puts her arm over her shoulder, but Sam shrugs it off. "I mean it, Lib. Back off."

"Sam, baby. I don't want to fight. I love you."

Sam swallows her tears.

"I am just asking what you know about Jay. I mean, it seems like he blew into your life from nowhere and swept you up."

"I know I love him and he loves me. That's enough."

"I only want what's best for you."

"Well, this is best."

"And you're sure?"

"Yes."

"I mean, you don't have to——" Libby stops and looks at Sam. "Oh, God. You're not pregnant, are you?"

"Christ, Libby."

"Well, are you?"

"No. I'm not. If it's any of your business."

"Well, it's not a completely ridiculous question, Sam. I mean, girls do get pregnant, you know."

"Jesus, Lib. You think I'm a complete fuckup, don't you?"

"No, Sam. I know you are not a complete fuckup."

"What then? A partial one?"

"I just want you to be sure." Libby pauses, catches her bottom lip between her teeth, a dead giveaway that she's worried.

"I'm sure. So let's just drop it, okay?"

Libby nods. "Okay," she says after a minute. "Let's see about finding you a wedding dress."

Wedding dress. For the first time, it hits Sam that she is really getting married.

Libby flicks through the hangers, rejecting one outfit after another. "You know Mother's going to be hurt," *she says.* "And disappointed."

"Who are you kidding?" *Sam says.* "The only thing she'll feel is relieved."

"Don't fool yourself. She's been planning your wedding since you turned twenty."

"Oh, right. The Wedding. And then I get to spend the next six months listening to her complain about how much it cost."

"She wouldn't complain." *Libby pulls out a pastel linen dress. The color is the watery blue of a sky before rain. She holds it up to Sam.* "What about this? It will be the 'something borrowed and something blue' all in one."

Sam shrugs. The dress won't fit right. Libby is thinner and taller then she is.

"At least try it on," *Libby says.*

Sam pulls off her jeans, slips on the dress, waits while Libby zips the back. She studies her reflection in the mirror and sees in her face the disappointment of someone who was hoping for a transformation.

"The color's great," *Libby says.*

"You think?" *Sam tugs at the material stretched over her hips.*

"It's perfect." *Libby disappears into the closet, searching for shoes. She decides on sandals, straps crossed at the ankle and drop-dead heels.* "Now, what about jewelry?"

"Something simple," *Sam says.*

Libby selects a thin silver necklace and Sam holds still while she catches the clasp at her neck.

Downstairs a door slams, a television is turned on.

"You know Mother's going to blame me for this," *Libby says.*

"That's silly. You have nothing to do with it."

"Right. Like she doesn't always blame me for whatever goes wrong. Besides, you're her favorite."

"No, I'm not." Whatever goes wrong? *Is Libby going to start up again about Sam waiting?*

Libby lifts an eyebrow. "You know it's true."

Sam doesn't want to be the favorite. It fills her with a responsibility she does not want. "Well, you're Dad's."

Libby ignores this. She stands back to survey the work.

"Do you think this is okay?" *Sam asks.*

"Better than okay. You look beautiful."

"Honest?" Sam's cheeks warm. "Thanks."

"Okay. Now the hair." Libby scoops Sam's hair up off her neck. "How are you thinking about wearing it?"

"I don't know. What do you think? French braid?"

"Down, I think," Libby says. She reaches for a brush and strokes Sam's hair. "Guaranteed, Mother's going to blame me for letting you go off this way."

"Just tell her you had nothing to do with it."

"She'll still find some way to blame me."

Here they are, twenty-eight and thirty, and they still bear the weight of their parents' expectations.

Anyway, at twenty-eight, is Sam really eloping or just performing a legal technicality, like getting a driver's license? Eloping. It has an adventuresome, middle-of-the-night sound to it but it turns out to be a lot less romantic than Sam had imagined.

Sam and Jay. Sam and Jay. She runs their names through her mind as the two of them drive into Cape May, following the directions the wife of the justice of the peace has given them over the phone. Their linked names sound ridiculous to her ears, like a cheap chain store. Or a songbird found only in the South. Samandjay. Jay's car—a gold Plymouth Duster—lost its tailpipe somewhere back in Connecticut and now people turn to look as they roar through the resort town. The day is cool, even for Cape May in September. Sam's feet hurt from the sandals. The blue dress, still holding the scent of Libby's perfume, is already wrinkled. Jay wears pleated-front chinos and a faded chambray shirt. The color matches the borrowed dress.

The broken tailpipe. The shoes that pinch, Libby's perfume. The ludicrous sound of their linked names. Later Sam will see these as signs she was not smart enough to read.

Now Sam understood that she had married Jay simply because he asked her, and at the time saying yes had seemed somehow a lot easier than saying no. Not a good reason by anyone's reckoning. Well, you couldn't expect to behave stupidly at no cost to yourself.

She replayed Lee's message, overtaken by the need to talk with him. Maybe Alice would know how to reach him. Sam started to punch the number in, then realized it was after eleven, too late to be waking Alice. If she hadn't been a little drunk, she would have re-placed the receiver. Instead, before she could stop herself, she punched in another number, one she knew by heart.

She got cold feet and hung up on the second ring. Before her sister could answer.

Libby

. . . .

Earlier, when Libby arrived at the center, Eleanor Brooks had handed her a pink-edged card that said: "Each day comes bearing its gift. Untie the ribbons." What this day was handing her certainly wasn't coming gift-wrapped. Coolly, she'd tried to refuse the card, but Eleanor wouldn't take the hint and so it sat on the tray table at Libby's station. Just the sight of it irritated Libby. Untie the ribbons indeed. The gift she'd settle for right now was for someone to come in and turn down the damn TV, which the one-legged man had tuned to one decibel below shatter-your-eardrums. His name was Harold Lenehy and he had diabetes, according to Eleanor, who apparently knew everything about the other patients. Names, diseases, history. Mrs. Fitzpatrick, the old woman who always came dressed in a pink nylon sweatsuit, was on her second round of dialysis. Earlier she'd had a transplant but she had rejected it last summer. Jesse, the black woman who praised Jesus, had diabetes. Hannah Rose, whom Libby always thought of as Joan, as in Joan of Arc, had cancer of the kidneys.

"You'll get to know everyone," Eleanor had told Libby. "We're all family here."

Not me, Libby had thought. She struggled to feel empathy toward the others, something other than irritation. She knew she *should*, but her heart felt closed to them. She had considered switching her schedule to other days, but then she supposed there would just be another set of people who would annoy her as badly as the one-legged man, and Eleanor with her positive affirmations, and Jesse with her faith in Jesus.

Today Jesse again occupied the station to Libby's immediate left. She was busy playing a variation of gin rummy with her daughter, Lorraine, a seriously overweight woman Libby guessed could be anywhere from twenty-nine to forty-five. It was so hard to tell with fat people. As Jesse dealt, Libby noticed that the woman's faith in Jesus didn't appear to hold her back from playing fast and loose with the rules, though the daughter didn't seem to mind her cheating. They'd been playing steadily for half an hour, but for the past fifteen minutes Lorraine had been fidgeting. All the nerves in that massive body seemed to have settled in her right foot, which tapped and twitched, jiggled and swung. Finally she shifted her weight and, bracing her hands against the chair seat, lurched upright. "Be right back," she announced. "Gonna get a Pepsi."

Jesse nodded and continued to shuffle the cards, then laid out a hand of solitaire. "She's going out for a cigarette," she said to Libby. Disapproval radiated off her like heat. "She thinks I don't know. You wait and see, she'll come back here sucking on a mint and reeking of that stuff. What's its name? You know what I mean. The stuff you spray on rugs to hide the smell of dogs."

Libby gave an I-haven't-a-clue shrug. She had never had to resort to covering up odors in her home.

"Febreze." Jesse seized on the name. "That's it. Lorraine's always got a spray bottle in her purse to cover the stink of tobacco smoke. Thinks she's got everyone fooled."

Libby nodded noncommittally, watched her shift a card. The woman cheated even when she was playing solitaire.

"Though she'll deny it right to your face, that girl's been smoking since she was fourteen," Jesse said. "And drinking since she was sixteen. Me, I've never touched a cigarette in my life. Or a drop of liquor. And yet here I am lying here and she's out front having a smoke. It don't make sense."

Nothing made sense to Libby. She didn't know how much longer she could keep coming here. She looked over at Eleanor. How long had she said she'd been coming? Three years. Libby knew she couldn't do that. She honestly thought she'd rather die.

"You got children?" Jesse said as she put the ace of diamonds at the head of a column.

Libby nodded.

"How many?"

What was it with the people in this place? Hadn't they grasped the concept of privacy? "Two."

"Girls or boys?"

"One of each. Twins."

"Twins." Eleanor joined the conversation. "How sweet."

What exactly did she think was so sweet about it, Libby would have liked to know.

"What're their names?"

"Matthew and Mercedes."

"Mercedes," Jesse said. "After the car?"

Good Lord. "No, after her grandmother."

"Well, I hope she don't smoke."

Did Libby know any more about what Mercy did than her mother had known about what she used to do? In spite of her spying and prying through Libby's things, her mother hadn't known the half of what she'd done. All through high school, Libby had barely escaped serious trouble, mostly getting grounded for sneaking out at night. Her mother knew nothing about the pot she smoked or the times she pocketed lipstick from the drugstore. One night Libby had cut through a porch screen at Russ Fuller's house, climbed right through the window, and gone up to his room and super-glued the zipper on every single pair of pants the cheating son of a bitch owned. Remembering, she nearly laughed out loud.

She couldn't picture Mercy doing a thing like that. But what did she know? She had strived for a connection with her daughter, for communication, but in the end she couldn't really know what Mercy did.

Over the weekend, at Richard's insistence—"You can't hide it from them forever. It's not fair to them"—they had phoned the twins to tell them about the dialysis. Mercy had been angry that they hadn't been told earlier. There was something else in her daughter's voice, too, a note of distraction that normally Libby would have picked right up on had she not been so concerned with reassuring Mercy that everything would be fine. Matt was another story. Ever the scientist, he'd wanted details, had asked if there was talk of a kidney transplant. If so, he wanted to be tested. He had wanted to come straight home, as if Libby would even *consider* such a thing. Eventually Libby had calmed him down, reassured him, told him she was really doing fine and was looking forward to seeing him over Thanksgiving. To both of them, she made dialysis sound no more difficult that donating a pint of blood. Well, wasn't that what she herself had once believed?

Jesse tapped a card on the tray table, trying to get Libby's attention.

Libby looked over.

Jesse leaned toward her, lowered her voice. "My church group is working on my healing," she said. Jesse's eyes took on a hot intensity that Libby associated with door-to-door proselytizers.

Libby gritted her teeth.

"Do you believe in the power of prayer?"

"I . . ." Of course she didn't. If she believed in anything she believed in . . . what? She searched her mind for a word. "Mystery" came to mind. Okay, she'd agree to that. There was a mystery beyond explanation. Yes, she believed in that. Mystery. Why couldn't people leave it at that? Wasn't that enough? She looked across at Hannah Rose sitting in the station opposite, her body as translucent as skin. The circles beneath her eyes were so dark that Libby could see the shadows from where she lay. As far as Libby had noticed, the girl seldom talked to anyone. She never had company during the treatments. Yet she radiated peace. Libby thought Hannah would understand the concept of Mystery, that it would be enough for her without attaching titles or dogma to it.

"If you want," Jesse was saying, "I can ask them to include you."

"What?" Libby pulled her attention away from the girl.

"In their prayers. They have a list. If you want, I can put you on it."

Libby *didn't* want. What she *wanted* was to be left alone. She turned pointedly away, as if she was going to try to get some sleep.

Jesse was not about to give up. "It's a fact, you know. They've proven it. People who are prayed for heal quicker. Why, they are even proving the power of prayer can cure cancer. Cancer!"

Fascinating, Libby thought. I'll be sure to tell my doctor. She looked over at Hannah Rose and thought maybe she would like to know about Jesse's belief in the power of prayer to cure cancer.

Kelly came over and checked Libby's monitor. "Your blood pressure is holding fine," she said.

Too bad they couldn't measure irritation, Libby thought. Her levels would shoot right off the charts, set off alarms.

She had tried to talk to Richard about how irritating she found the people here, but he had told her she should work at trying to develop a better outlook. "Attitude is important," he told her, "it creates positive energy." Like he was suddenly Mr. New Age Guru. Maybe he should have married Eleanor of the Positive Affirmations.

She pulled her blanket up over her chest and considered the futility of asking if the TV could be turned down. Katie Couric was interviewing an actress whose smile was the too-wide, false kind, someone Libby had never heard of, someone who probably knew all about the power of positive energy. She sighed and reached for her tote bag. On an impulse, she'd brought *The Will to Change*, the volume of poetry by Adrienne Rich that she'd found in the guest room dresser. Jesse had Jesus. Richard had the prairie. And Libby had poetry. In truth, it always had been her connection to something larger than herself.

Shielding the cover from Eleanor, who would no doubt think it was some kind of self-help book, she flipped it open. An envelope was glued inside the back cover. "Property of Northampton Public Library," she read. She slipped the card out, read the last Due Dates: APR 10, 1977; DEC 18, 1977; NOV 19, 1978. She pictured the librarian stamping the card, using the date stamp affixed to the end of her pencil. When Libby was a child she had coveted one of those pencils. If she could have figured out a way, she would have swiped one from the librarian's desk. She turned the card over. The final date stamped was FEB 5, 1979. The year she turned sixteen.

Why hadn't she returned the book to the library? Had she thought she'd lost it? Had she had to pay for the book? She couldn't remember. She thought she would remember if she had stolen it, but it was possible. In those days she shoplifted regularly. She opened to the contents page, scanned the titles: "Planetarium," "The Blue Ghazals," "Our Whole Life." Once she had known many of these poems by heart but now she couldn't remember them. "The Stelae," "A Valediction Forbidding Mourning."

Well, that one she did recall. Words of the opening line floated up out of deep memory. "My swirling wants," it began. How she had loved that line. *My swirling wants.* It had spoken directly to her, captured precisely the longings that eddied deep inside her at sixteen. She checked the page number for the poem. When she turned to the page, a slip of paper fell out of the book onto her lap. It was the thin kind used for airmail. Onionskin. The handwriting was hers. Two lines.

Birds are language
words written on the sky.

She read it again, held the syllables in her mouth.

Birds are language
words written on the sky.

She remembered then, could see the birds overhead, could recall the thrill of transforming feelings into language.

She is walking home from school, book bag slung over her shoulder. It is winter, cold, and then, unexpectedly, overhead, a pair of larks. They circle in flight, their white underparts brilliant against the blue sky, and sing out their bell-like pit-wit call. She stops right there—right in the middle of the sidewalk—plops her book bag down in the middle of the sidewalk, mindless of the slush from a snow the night before. She pulls off her mittens, flings them down on top of the bag, and tears a piece of paper from a pad of airmail stationery she'd bought that morning at the drugstore on her way to school so she could write to her Swedish pen pal. A car drives by, a horn beeps, but she does not look over. Nothing else exists. Birds are language . . . She knows from experience that if she waits until she gets home, this fragment of a poem will vanish, go as swiftly as it had come. She scribbles down the words.

Libby looked down at the paper, at the words written more than twenty years ago. She began to turn the lines over in her mind, wondering why she had never finished the poem. That long-ago day was suddenly perfectly clear to her, clearer than anything that had happened in weeks. Once she'd had more important things to do than polish silver and launder sheets. Once she had been a girl who looked up and saw not larks but hands signing against the sky. Once, she thought, once she had been a girl daring enough to write poetry, a girl bold enough to break into the house of a cheating boy and glue shut the flies on his pants.

A picture—as vivid as a scene from a video she and Richard had watched last weekend—flashed in her mind. A girl—herself—in a convertible, hair flying in the wind, foot propped on the dashboard, knee bent like the wing of a bird. There is a bottle of beer in her hand, held low so it is concealed from sight, and she is laughing, filled with the joy of summer, the exultation of being free.

The image faded. Sorrow and loss weighed on her. When had she lost the girl she had once been? When had she lost herself?

The pain hit then, knifing through her, erasing memory. It took her hard, robbed her of breath. She heard a sob—half scream—knew it was her own.

As if from a distance, she heard Eleanor call for Kelly, but the nurse was already there, bending over her, talking to her, fiddling with the machine. One of the technicians was clearing the bay of visitors.

Voices floated in from afar. She tried to brace herself against the pain, but it was immense, like nothing she had known, worse than childbirth. Her body was honeycombed with pain. She wondered if she was dying. Her legs contorted with spasm. Her fingers twisted, became crone's hands.

Dimly, she heard Kelly talking to her, telling her she would be okay, stroking her arm, telling her to breathe, telling her to hang on, hang in, promising her the pain would go away. Someone brought warm pads and laid them on her legs. Later they would explain to her how the cramps were caused by an imbalance, a too-quick shift of sodium and fluid in her body. But for now she knew only the pain.

"It will ease up soon," Kelly promised.

"Happened to me once, too," Eleanor said.

"You just be like a Timex, honey," Jesse was saying. "That's what you got to do. You just take a licking and keep on ticking, that's what you got to do."

Libby tuned them all out. She wondered again if she was dying, if *this*, this sweeping, paralyzing pain that made thought and breath impossible, if this was what death felt like.

Then, suddenly, warmth brushed over her, flowed through her, surrounded her as if she had been submerged in a bath. She did not open her eyes but knew the source of the heat, felt it flow from the station opposite hers. Finally she managed to lift her eyelids. Hannah Rose was staring at her. Libby blocked out everything—Eleanor's words, Jesse's chattering, the weight of Kelly's hand on her shoulder—everything but the girl's eyes.

I'm with you. The words floated silently across the space that separated them. And then again: *I'm with you. You're not alone.*

Libby closed her eyes, surrendered to the warmth, allowed the incandescence to enclose her. She concentrated on the soft syllables of the girl's name. Han-nah.

Slowly, the pain receded. The cramps eased and her legs straightened, relaxed. Libby could bear to return to her body.

When Libby opened her eyes, she looked over at the girl in the opposite chaise. Then her gaze fell on her tray table, on the pink-edged card. *Each day comes bearing a gift. Untie the ribbons.*

Hannah, she thought. She raised her eyes, looked again at the girl.

Across the bay, the girl's mouth curved in a gentle smile and she nodded.

Sam

. . . .

Earlier a V of geese had flown over, called south by some instinct that defied imagination. Sam wondered what it would be like to live an existence governed solely by instincts.

In the boatyard, the majority of the yachts were settled in cradles, like ghosts shrink-wrapped against the weather to come. A handful were still moored at their slips, kept there by sailors who prolonged the season as long as they could.

There was a slight chop in the harbor and Sam's fingers whitened on the gunwale. She was already regretting this. She'd been fourteen the last time she had tried sailing and had been intimidated by the instructor, a cool Dartmouth boy far more interested in flirting with Libby than he'd been in teaching an awkward high school freshman her way around a boat. He'd seen at once how nervous Sam was, but instead of reassuring her, he'd thrown directions and nautical terms at her so rapidly (windward, leeward, main sheet, jibe, tack, and center of effort) that she'd become completely rattled. Within minutes, while he'd yelled at her from the raft where Libby was sunbathing in a bikini, she had managed to capsize the dinghy. With no desire ever to repeat the humiliating experience, she had stayed away from sailboats for years. Until today.

Lee had been trying to talk her into this since their first date, and she had finally succumbed. They were in the smaller of his two boats, a Herreshoff 12½, a sixteen-foot gaff-rigged sloop. She focused on him, trying to draw a measure of confidence from his sure movements, his attunement with sea and boat. He looked as if he had been born to this.

"The first step," he said, "is to determine wind direction."

Her stomach began to knot.

He pointed to the flagpole in the yard. "It's blowing northwest," he said.

She nodded, as if that meant something to her. Okay, she told herself, a child can do this. She'd seen kids no more than ten ripping around the harbor in Optimist dinghies. In the distance she heard the clanging of halyards snapping against masts.

Lee started letting out the sail. "It's simple," he told her. "Get on course, then let the sail out until it luffs, then pull it in a bit until the luffing stops."

She nodded again, her mouth drawn tight. *Luffs?* She had *told* him she didn't want to do this.

"With this boat, because it was so well designed, we're aiming to balance the sails so that you can let go of the tiller and still have the boat track in the same direction."

Track? Above her, the sail curved out, then tightened. The boat slipped through the harbor. It looked so easy when he did it.

"Sailing is all a matter of balance."

She tightened her grip, braced her feet against the floorboards.

"Here. You try it."

She froze. "I can't." She felt fourteen again, stupid and inept.

"Sure you can."

She shook her head. Her fingers curled over the deck coaming.

He gave her a steady look, then reached over and pulled her to his side. He placed her hand on the tiller and covered it with his own. "You can do this, Sam. I know you can."

She gripped the helm, felt the tension run up her forearm, through her biceps. She did not want to be doing this.

"Relax," Lee said. "The trick is, stay cool. Don't oversteer."

"I'm not," she said. Why had she let him talk her into this? She *hated* sailing.

"Lean back against me," he said. "And relax. I won't let anything happen. Promise."

"Right," she said, still mad.

He laughed. "Come on, Sam. Don't be stubborn." They skimmed past Ram Island. "Give it half a chance. Trust me, you're going to fall in love with sailing."

Fat chance. Her hand tightened on the tiller. "Which way do I tack?" She remembered that from the Dartmouth boy. You were supposed to tack.

"Forget about all that for now," Lee said. "Just try and feel what it's like. Imagine being one with everything around you. The boat, the water, the wind."

One with everything. Right. "I can't."

"Sure you can."

"Oh, God." They were leaving Sippican Harbor, heading out beyond the jetty into Buzzards Bay.

"Take a deep breath," he said, drawing her tighter against him. "Close your eyes."

"What?"

"Come on. Just close your eyes."

Close her eyes? Was he crazy? "Not on your life."

"I've got the helm with you. Nothing will happen."

She scanned the horizon. There were no other boats in sight. "Why?"

"Just try it."

She squeezed her eyes shut.

"That's it," he said. "Relax."

Right, she thought. But, surprisingly, it *was* easier with her eyes closed. It calmed her nerves. The boat did not capsize. Gradually her irritation and anxiety ratcheted down.

He pressed his head to hers. "What we want to do," he said, "is keep the boat steady. Feel the groove."

Her eyes popped open.

"Eyes closed," he said.

"What's the groove?" she asked after a minute, eyes again shut.

"It's hard to describe," he said. "It's like a slot you and the boat find together, heading upwind. Don't think about it, just feel it."

She chewed at her lip. What *exactly* was she supposed to feel?

"Listen to the wake slap against the chop, water against water. Smell the air. The salt of seaweed and salt and pine tar." He laughed. "My brother used to say it smelled like watermelon."

"Watermelon doesn't smell."

"That's what most people think. But it does. And it's close to this. A combo of salt air and must," he said. "Do you feel the boat heel, the acceleration?"

She nodded.

"That's it," he said. "The sounds and smells and the feel of the boat and the water. Take it all in. That's the groove."

She lifted her face to the wind, felt salt spray mist her cheeks. She felt, at her back, the heat of Lee's body. Her grip—beneath his—eased.

They picked up speed and the breeze lifted Sam's hair away from her face. Beneath her feet, through the planks, she felt the rush of the sea. Adrenaline coursed through her. She surprised herself by laughing.

"Attagirl," he said. "Do you feel it?"

"The groove?"

"Freedom. Do you feel the freedom?"

She smiled into the wind, laughed again. "Yes," she said. "Yes." She was beginning to understand. This was why he loved to sail. This was what he could teach her.

Lee opened a couple of beers. Sam prepared lunch—westerns, although since he didn't eat red meat she made them without the ham and so technically they were not westerns. She diced onions, added them to the eggs, and poured the mixture into the skillet. He came over and handed her a beer, kissed her cheek. She turned her face so the kiss slid to her lips.

"We could get seriously derailed here," he said minutes later.

She laughed. "Lunch first," she said.

"You're kidding?"

"Your crew's beyond hungry. Perishing." She felt so alive, energized. They had sailed for more than an hour and by the time they returned to the harbor, she had actually been trimming the sails by herself. And once or twice, she had thought she felt the groove Lee spoke of. She adjusted the flame to low.

"You're telling me you want lunch before love?" He nuzzled her neck, cupped the small of her back, pulled her to him. "Bet I could make you change your mind."

"You'd lose."

"You're tough." His hand slid over her buttocks.

She slipped her hands beneath his shirt and felt his flat belly. "Not so tough," she said. "Just starving." But it wasn't that. Not at all. It was the idea of delaying that moment when they would go up to the bedroom. She loved the anticipation, the way it made her whole body ache for him, made the air hum with the intensity of their desire. The heat she was feeling now, they'd be lucky if they got to finish half a sandwich.

He kissed her again, a long, deep kiss that held the passion and promise of what was to come. She could feel the heat of desire in the hollow of her ankle, the arch of her foot, the pulse point at her wrist. When he let her go, her legs nearly gave way.

He crossed to the table, pulled out a chair. She gave him a wide grin. She loved being in love. Days like today, the dread that lay beneath—the fear that something would happen to destroy it—actually eased.

"Will you do something for me?" Lee asked.

"What do you have in mind?" She flipped the omelet. "Does it involve whips? High heels? Handcuffs?"

"Seriously."

"What?" Anything, she thought. Just ask. She was madly in love with him, the scary kind of deep, nothing-held-back, for-a-lifetime love.

He set the bottle down. "Will you tell me why it's been six years since you talked to your sister?"

She shivered, as if a sea breeze had suddenly swept through the kitchen. They hadn't talked about Libby for a couple of days. She had hoped he wouldn't bring it up again, but of course had known that he would. "What does it matter?"

He rose, took the spatula from her, turned off the flame beneath the skillet, forced her to look at him. "It matters, Sam."

"Why?"

He stroked her cheek with his thumb. "Because I love you."

"And I love you." Why couldn't he let this alone?

"And I want to spend the rest of my life with you."

She closed her eyes and took in his words.

The rest of their lives. Forever. She wanted that, too, and for that moment, allowed herself to believe that such a thing was possible, believing it just as innocently as did the brides who came into her shop.

"And I just can't ignore the fact that you have a sister," Lee said. "A sister you haven't spoken to in six years. I need to know what happened."

"It's got nothing to do with us," she said. She wanted to return to the magic of that moment when he'd said he wanted to spend the rest of his life with her. She didn't want that ruined.

"Of course it does."

"I don't think so." She wished he'd stop pushing, just let it go.

"Don't you see? It's about trust. When you keep something like that from me, it feels like you don't trust me."

"I trust you." She thought back to the morning, when they were on the boat—how she'd closed her eyes, let him guide her. She had trusted him completely. Or as much as she had anyone in a long, long time, as much as she was capable of.

"So why won't you tell me what happened?"

"You won't understand. Can't we just drop it? I'm sorry I ever told you that I have a sister."

"Sam," he said. "Do you think something disappears just because you don't talk about it?"

She didn't answer.

He took her hands, forced her to look at him.

"Try me," he pressed. "Please."

"You want to know what happened?"

"Yes."

It had always been easier for her to feel mad than sad and she swallowed against the anger that closed her throat. "Okay," she said. "My sister stole everything from me. Satisfied? Now can you let it go?"

"Stole what?"

"Everything."

He considered that for a moment. "Whatever she took, Sam, it wasn't everything."

She sighed. "It was close enough."

"And you can't forgive her?"

She pulled her hands from his. "I knew you wouldn't understand."

"I'm trying to, Sam. I want to. But you're right. I don't. It just doesn't make sense. Whatever happened between you, how can you cut off love like it never happened?"

Libby calls from the road, less than an hour away. Although the visit is completely unexpected, taking her by surprise, Sam doesn't question it. Before she even hangs up the phone, she starts making plans. That afternoon they will head over to Tiverton and pick wild strawberries, just as they had when they were girls. On the way home, they will stop for ice cream. For dinner they will have the salad Libby loves: grilled bluefish and field greens tossed with the strawberries. They will drink white wine until they're tipsy and then they'll talk into the night. And maybe then Sam will share the things she has not dared tell anyone. If anyone can understand what she has to say, it is her sister.

When Libby's car finally pulls into the drive, Sam races to meet her, hugging her until they are both breathless. She fights tears. The missing has been marrow deep.

Libby plans to stay for a week. Maybe two. Sam delights in the stretch of days they will have and does not stop to question the suddenness of the visit, or the length, although her sister has never before left the twins for more than a weekend. All she can think about is her own need for Libby. Two weeks. Two glorious weeks. Time to talk and laugh, to get caught up, to get advice. Sam is blinded by joy at having her sister there. Is that why at first she does not see the sorrow in Libby's eyes?

The third day, they have a small argument when Libby says she thinks Sam

*is wasting her talents by becoming a cook. The way she says it, it sounds like Sam
plans to spend her life flipping burgers at a diner. Sam explains she's studying
to be a pastry chef. You can do better, Libby says. The moment passes. Soon they
have found something to laugh at. But the small conflict unnerves Sam, and
that night she turns around in the parking lot at Johnson & Wales and ducks
out of her evening class. She imagines another night of conversation ahead,
making popcorn. Maybe tonight she'll confide in Libby, tell her some of the
things that have been bothering her. She knows every couple hits rocky spots,
marriage isn't Eden, after all, everyone knows that, but it will feel good to talk
to Libby about it. And maybe Libby will tell Sam her own problems, whatever it
is that makes her stare off into space with sad eyes.*

*Tonight, Sam thinks, she will ask Libby's advice about the things she has
been too proud to talk to anyone else about. She rushes into the house, calls out
for Libby. (Later, she remembers those last moments of innocence and trust and
how she stood in the front hall of the apartment and called out to her sister.)
There is no answer, and then she hears voices. And music. Carly Simon. (To this
day Sam cannot bear to hear the singer.) She runs up the stairs, toward the
music. Toward the voices. Libby's. And Jay's. Even then, as she follows their voices
to her bedroom, she is unprepared, does not suspect.*

"Sam, look at me."

Her body was rigid.

"I've never seen you like this," he said. "It's like I don't know
you at all."

She shrugged.

She opens the door, sees them, although they do not see her.

*"You're the best I've ever had," she hears Jay say. "You should give your sis-
ter lessons."*

"I've never seen you like this. So cold."

She closed her eyes against remembered pain.

"Talk to me, Sam," Lee said. "You're behaving like—like you
have the heart of a terrorist."

"You want to know?" She turned back to him. "You want to know
who the terrorist is?"

"Yes. Because it's about you. And because I need you to trust me enough to tell me."

She turns to flee, but before she can escape she hears Libby. Hears her laugh.

"She fucked my husband." The words were torn from her, burned in her throat. "My sister fucked my husband. And then she laughed."

The laugh. Harsh as a side of beef slapped on a table. The laugh. Libby. So pleased to have bested Sam.

Libby

. . . .

*L*aughter floated toward her. It intruded on her need for solitude.

Last night, anxious about the day ahead, Libby had barely slept, despite Kelly's promise that today she'd stay right beside her the entire time and monitor her saline levels. The nurse had said a "pain episode" probably wouldn't occur again. *Probably.* No ironclad promise there. Probably.

At dawn Libby had left the house and driven to the lake instead of heading directly for the dialysis center. This early in the day, this late in the season, she had thought she'd be alone, but several joggers were running along the shore. And out on Michigan, a couple sailed. Theirs was the laughter that echoed across the water. The mainsail and jib of their sloop formed chalk-white silhouettes against the rose-streaked October sky.

Red sky in the morning, sailors take warning. The saying popped into her head. It was one she had learned back when she and Richard sailed, one of those old maxims crews used to forecast weather in the days before electronics. Wind before rain, the sun will shine again.

Rain before wind, take tops'ls in. Even now she relied on them for a forecast as much as she did on the weatherman.

Again, laughter reached her from across the lake, pulling her attention to the hull slipping through the water. Watching, she remembered the exhilaration of sailing and felt the sharp pang of regret and loss. She supposed boating was something she would never do again.

She glanced at the dashboard clock. If she left right then, she would just about make it to the center in time. The staff stressed the importance of promptness. If a patient was late, it set the schedule off for the entire day. What would happen, she wondered, if she didn't show up at all, if she missed a session?

She was tempted, just this once. Since waking, she'd dreaded the treatment and the possibility that she would again experience the pain. The memory of it was so fresh, so immediate—the way it had seized her body, shutting out everything. She didn't think she could tolerate such anguish again. The prospect of continuing treatments for another month, never mind a year, was unthinkable. Even a transplant, once an inconceivable resort, now seemed preferable.

Yesterday, she had gone to the guest bedroom and dug out the booklets Carlotta had given her. She had read them through. Then, marshaling strength, she had called her brother, the neutral country. Cynthia, the Swiss Guard, answered the phone.

"How are you doing?" her sister-in-law asked.

"I've started dialysis."

"Josh will be so sorry he missed you." Cynthia rushed right on, as if Libby had said she'd started painting the dining room walls.

"I go for treatment three times a week."

"That's good. It's amazing what they can do nowadays. We have a friend who just got new lenses implanted in her eyes. She swears her eyesight is better than ever." Cynthia prattled on. "So how are the twins? And Richard?"

"They're fine." Libby couldn't do small talk. "I really need to talk to Josh. When would be a good time to catch him?"

"These days his schedule is pretty erratic. It's the middle of the hockey season."

"Could you have him call me?"

The wire hummed. Libby could almost hear electricity flow over wires.

"What about?"

If she could just talk to Josh without Cynthia running interference. "My doctor suggested he be tested."

"Tested? What for?"

"To see if he's even a possible match."

Another moment of humming electricity.

Cynthia finally spoke. "What about Richard? Has he been tested?"

Libby held back a sigh. "Of course he's been tested. I told you." During their last conversation, Libby had explained to both Josh and Cynthia why Richard couldn't be a donor, how he was AB-positive and she was A-negative. Did Cynthia honestly think she'd be calling them if he could?

"Listen, Elizabeth. Josh can't do this."

"What are you saying? That he won't even be tested?"

"Yes."

"Is that what he said?"

"You're putting him in a terrible position. You're making him feel guilty for saying no. It isn't fair of you to ask."

Fair. What did fair ever have to do with anything?

"He has responsibilities here. To his own children."

"Yes," Libby said. "Of course he does."

"And even if he didn't, think about what you're asking him to go through. I mean, how can you ask him to do that? He's a coach. He relies on his body."

Libby called up the facts and figures she'd read in the booklet Carlotta gave her. "They've done studies. Ninety-two percent of donors haven't had one bad side effect."

"That still leaves eight percent. And what if he does get this disease? I mean, have they guaranteed that this disease you have—what is it?"

"Focal sclerosing glomerulonephritis," Libby said. "FSGS."

"Well, have they guaranteed it isn't hereditary?"

"Yes, they have. They're pretty certain of that."

"Pretty certain." Cynthia jumped on the qualifier. "And what if he gets it? Or something else? Diabetes? Or what if someday one of our boys ever needed a transplant?"

Libby had no answer for this. What would she do if the circumstances were reversed, if Josh needed a kidney? She knew without question she would want to be a donor. How could she not? "Could I at least send him some donor information? It doesn't commit him to anything."

"Really, Elizabeth, Josh can't do this. I don't know if you've thought this through, if you understand the implications of what you're asking of him. It's a sacrifice I don't think you have a right to ask of him. He has his family, his career."

And what of her family, her life?

"Has your doctor put you on a list yet?" Cynthia continued.

"A list?"

"Isn't there a national register or something for people who need organs?"

"Yes."

"Are you listed?"

"Yes."

"Well, you're all set then." *All set.* "But keep in touch. Let us know how you're doing. Promise."

"Promise."

Libby had hung up, wondering if Cynthia would even tell Josh she'd called.

She was really going to be late. If only someone could promise her that today there would be no pain.

Here was a question: If it were possible to know the future, to absolutely know what lay ahead, would you want to? She couldn't imagine. It would be a curse. To know what lay in wait and not be able to change it? Far better not to know. For if it *were* truly possible to see the future, a person would be forewarned of not only joy and success but of illness, betrayal, loss, and of unbearable pain. And what then? How could a person bear to go on? No, it was just as well not to know. It was bad enough knowing the past, to have to live with that, with memories.

She never had understood why anyone wanted to go to fortune-tellers or palm readers. (Several years ago Mary Hudson had had a tarot card reading, for all the good it had done her. Like most people, Mary had gone hoping—expecting—to receive promises of long life, success, wealth, love, health. As Libby remembered it, the reader hadn't promised Mary riches, but neither had she said one thing about Larry running off with a girl nearly the age of their daughters.)

On the dash, the clock ticked off minutes. Time was running out. Well, that was all time did. Run out. Minute by minute.

And what had she done with the time allotted her, all the months and weeks and days and hours of her life? All those days she had been cleaning when she should have been celebrating. All the time wasted, thinking there was plenty of it, as if there were an endless supply of days. The arrogance.

There were a lot of things she had dreamed of doing, things she had tucked away in her mind, thinking, *someday*. Seeds planted over a lifetime, like wanting to see the northern lights ever since the sixth-grade geography book told them about the aurora borealis. Just saying those words, "aurora borealis"—so full in your mouth, a magic incantation—you could just imagine what kind of lights would bear such a name. She wanted to do those silly, romantic things that sounded so appealing, like swimming with dolphins. (Just thinking about it, she could almost feel the sting of salt water, the heft of a buoyant body at her side. Was it only women who longed for this, found in it both sensuality and freedom? She had never heard a man say he wanted to backstroke with Flipper.) Important things, too, like seeing Mercedes get married, and holding her first grandchild. (The first time she'd breast-fed the twins, she'd felt a near-sexual twisting in her womb, as if it was remembering how, for nine months, it had cradled those bodies. Now, at the thought of holding a grandchild, she felt deep in her belly the same sweet spasm.)

She wanted to learn Latin, the parent tongue of so many ordinary words she spoke every day. She had always thought someday in the future she would master the real thing, not the *veni, vidi, vici* of high school freshmen. And then she'd travel to Italy and sit in a *pensione* and read the *Aeneid* in the language in which it was written.

And while she was traveling—Portugal. She dreamed of walking through country vineyards and later, at night, drinking wine and dining from glazed pottery the colors of the sky and sun, plates formed from the same earth that had produced the grapes in her wine.

And England. Her grandparents and Richard's, too, had come from Great Britain. Somewhere in her papers, she had the deed for the cemetery lot where her maternal great-grandparents were interred.

She wanted to play tourist in London. A funny thing, but over the years, as she had listened on the local NPR station to concerts broadcast from St. Martin-in-the-Fields, she had dreamed of going there, had even found the church's Web site. The church was in the West End, on Trafalgar Square, directly across from the National Portrait Gallery. There were free concerts at lunchtime and candlelight concerts in the evening. She imagined sitting there and listening to a Bach oboe concerto or a Haydn symphony. She had told no one of this dream, not even Richard, but she had always believed they would go there someday.

And once, long ago, she had thought she would write poetry, even publish a collection.

In that long-ago time, everything had seemed possible, but life narrowed one's choices and possibilities, and existence grew narrower and narrower, marked with the regrets and longings of all the things one would never do. Countries never seen. Adventures never had. Music never heard. Poems lost, never written.

She felt robbed. Ripped off. She wanted to have lived before she died.

"Am I going to die?" She had asked Carlotta the question during her last visit.

"We're all going to die," Carlotta had answered. "We just don't know the date and time."

"That's not what I mean."

Carlotta had hugged her. "We're all dying," she said again. "The trick is to really live while we are dying."

The answer—so facile, so like one of the sayings on Eleanor's affirmation cards—had irritated Libby, but now Carlotta's words echoed. *To really live while we are dying.* Suddenly it seemed important to write down all the things she had dreamed of doing.

Usually she kept a notepad in the glove compartment, but now it wasn't there. She pawed through her tote but couldn't find one piece of paper, not even a bank deposit slip or supermarket register print-out. The only paper in her bag was Adrienne Rich's book of poetry. She opened the book to inside the back cover and began. Slowly she penciled in the list of all the things she had once believed there would be more than enough time for.

When she had finished, the dash clock said it was nearly seven. Now she really was going to be late. She supposed the staff would be angry with her. Once, that thought would have paralyzed her. Once, it wouldn't have occurred to her to show up late for an appointment because although a maverick as a teenager, it seemed to her that she had lived her entire adult life trying to please others. Richard. The twins. Her friends. Her mother. Wasn't that why she had turned into the perfect wife? Wasn't all the cleaning, cooking, baking, gardening nothing more than an attempt to please her mother? To make up for all the ways Libby had disappointed her? To show her mother that she was not a screwup? Well, the plane crash that had taken her parents had also taken any possibility of fixing that part of her past. The past. What was that line of Faulkner's? She stared out at the lake and pulled the quote from memory: "The past is never dead. It's not even past." That line had always haunted her, the idea that a person could never walk away from her history. Certainly she couldn't separate her present from her past when it came to Sam.

And this was the truth of her life: She and Sam were hopelessly estranged. Time was running out and she was left with recrimina-tions and wizened dreams.

Sam

. . . .

o we're watching this old movie on AMC," Stacy said. "The one with—what's her name? The swimmer?" She shouted to be heard over the roar of the Hobart.

"Mmmm." Sam was bent over the sketch for the Sanderson cake, tweaking the final details.

"Williams. That's it. Esther Williams. So Carl says, 'If one synchronized swimmer drowns, do the others have to, too?'" Stacy switched off the mixer and looked over at Sam. "And then he laughs like that's the funniest thing anyone's ever said. *If one drowns, do the others have to, too?* That man's living on borrowed time. Skating on thin ice. I swear, between his sorry jokes and his toe fungus, we'll be lucky to last the year."

Sam frowned, debating whether to set a couple of roses at the base of the cake, an echo of the spray on the top, or to stay with the double row of seed pearls that trimmed each layer. Normally she could have made this kind of decision in an instant, but this morning her brain felt foggy. It was hard to focus. All she could think about was Lee.

"Hello? Earth calling Pluto. Anybody home?" Stacy cupped her hands around her mouth. "Helloooo."

Sam gave her a blank look. "What?"

"Okay, so maybe I'm not *Entertainment Tonight*, but you could at least pretend to listen." Stacy lifted the beaters from the batter.

"I'm listening."

"Really? I don't think you've heard anything I've said in the past fifteen minutes."

"Yes, I have." Sam closed her eyes, pulled the words from somewhere. "You said that between Carl's humor and his foot fungus, you don't think you're going to last."

"I know you can recite the *words*." Stacy swirled a rubber spatula around the rim of the Hobart's bowl, then dipped a finger in the mixture and tasted it. "I'm just saying I don't think you *heard*."

Stacy was right, of course. "I'm sorry," Sam said. "I was concentrating on this."

Stacy looked straight at her, narrowed her eyes. "Okay. Spill it."

"Spill what?"

"What's wrong?"

"Nothing's wrong. I told you. I'm just preoccupied with this cake." Sam reversed the drawing so Stacy could take a look. "Whaddaya think? Should I put a couple of the roses at the base?"

Stacy ignored the sketch. "Try again."

"What?"

"Listen, it's plain as sugar on powdered doughnuts that something's flying up your ass a million miles an hour."

"What do you mean?"

"You haven't smiled once since I walked in. Not once."

Sam sighed, then flashed a toothy fake grin. "There. Better?"

Stacy carried the beaters to the sink and rinsed them. Then she leaned back against the sink and crossed her arms. "Just tell me straight out. Is it me?"

"Meaning?"

"Are you mad at me?"

"Why in the world would I be mad at you?"

"You know. 'Cause I got drunk Saturday night."

"Good God, no. If memory serves me, I was as drunk as you. No, of course I'm not mad at you."

"Well, who then? Because you're sure pissed at something or someone." Stacy cut parchment paper for the bottoms of four cake tins, brushed the sides of the tins with oil, and spooned batter in.

Sam paused. If she told Stacy about the argument with Lee, she'd have to explain about Libby and the whole story and she wasn't sure she was ready to have her history exposed. It was hard enough to keep some semblance of an employer/employee boundary with Stacy without opening up that mess.

"What'd you have a fight with the Hunk?"

So much for boundaries. The word wasn't even in Stacy's lexicon. "Not exactly."

"Whoa. Wait a minute, here. 'Not exactly'?"

Sam bit her lip, fiddled with a detail at the base of the cake drawing. "All right. We had a disagreement. Let's just leave it at that."

Stacy left the tins half filled and plopped down at the desk next to Sam. "Jeez."

"What?"

"You had a fight with the Hottie? Is that crazy or what? Half the women in town say a prayer every night that you two will split up. Believe me, they're waiting in the wings."

Sam didn't doubt that for one second. "Not a fight. Okay? A disagreement."

"Whatever." Stacy paused. "Let's see. He's what? A Sagittarius, right?"

"I guess. December fifteenth."

"Fire sign."

In spite of herself, Sam's interest was captured. "Which means what?"

"Slow to anger." That was Lee all right. "And idealistic."

"So where's the bad part?"

"Carried to an extreme, Sagittarians can be condescending or dogmatic."

Try self-righteous, Sam thought.

"So what happened?"

"It's ridiculous, really." Sam pushed aside the sketch and fought back the tears that suddenly threatened.

Stacy gave her a quick look and rose. "Wait a minute. This *is* serious."

"Let's forget it." Sam focused again on the sketch. "I'm okay. Really."

"Really, you're not," Stacy said. "Believe me. I know the signs, and I'm not talking zodiac."

"What signs?"

"The trouble-in-paradise signs. God knows I've been there often enough."

"We've had a disagreement, that's all. We'll work it out." Sam prayed this was true.

Stacy crossed the kitchen and rooted through the cupboard.

"What are you looking for?"

"Coffee. This conversation definitely calls for coffee."

What it called for, in Sam's mind, was a reestablishment of boundaries. "I think there's some on the bottom shelf."

"I opened that last week."

"Then I'm out."

"No prob. I'll just hop over to the General Store and get us fresh-brewed to go."

"Please, don't bother. Really, there's no need."

"Regular or Irish cream?"

Sam surrendered. "Hazelnut. If they have it. If not, regular. Tall. With skim." As if problems could be resolved with a jolt of caffeine. "Take some money out of the drawer."

"This one's on me. Anything else? Bagel or Danish?"

"Just coffee's fine."

"Be back in twenty."

Sam left the desk and finished up with the cake tins Stacy had left half filled. She put them in the convection oven and set the timer. *We'll work it out.* She wanted to believe this, but her heart felt stone-heavy. She pictured the hurt look on Lee's face, the stubborn set of his mouth when he left. She would have given her left foot to be able to retract some of the words she'd flung at him.

———

"After you came home and found them, what did she say?" Lee had asked. They were lying on her bed.

"I don't know. I never spoke to her again," she said.

"You didn't give her a chance to explain?"

Sam looked at him. "Explain? How could you explain something like that? I never wanted to see her again."

"I can understand that. But didn't she want to talk to you?"

"I wouldn't take her calls."

"Jesus, Sam."

He raised himself on one elbow and looked down at her. "You have to call her, Sam."

"No way. Forget it."

"Why?"

"I can't."

"Why not?"

"I just can't, that's all."

He fell back against the pillow. "Just tell me what's so difficult about picking up the phone."

"Look, Lee. I don't want to talk about this."

"My God, Sam, it's been six years. When will you want to talk about it?"

Try never.

"She's your sister. Your only sister."

When she didn't respond, he stared at the ceiling, considering. "Is it about punishing Libby?" he said after a few minutes.

She could not believe he was asking her that. "Wrong question, Lee. The question here is, why are you acting like it's my fault? I'm not the one in the wrong."

He reached over and stroked her cheek. "It's not about who's at fault, hon."

She pushed his hand away. "The hell it isn't. That's exactly what it's about."

"No, it isn't, Sam."

"Then what is it about?"

He drew her to him, held her. She could feel his heart beat against her skin.

"I'd say it's about being hurt," he said. "It's about pride."

"Pride?" She pulled away. "How can you even say that? Shit, I just finished telling you what she did to me and you think I'm not calling her because my pride is hurt? Jesus. I can't believe you think that. She *betrayed* me, Lee."

"Sam?" He cupped her face in his palms. "Listen to me. It's true. She did betray you."

"In the worst way."

"Okay, okay. But sometimes people who love each other do that."

"Well, they shouldn't."

"Maybe so, but they do."

"Oh, please."

"They do, Sam. It's called being human."

"Spare me the platitudes."

He fell silent, then, after a moment, stood up and started to dress.

"What are you doing?" Fingers of panic brushed her chest.

He buttoned his shirt, found his shoes. "Just tell me this, Sam. Don't you think you've punished her enough?"

She sat upright, her back rigid. "You think that's what it's about? Punishing her? Christ, whose side are you on?"

"I'm not taking sides here."

"The hell you're not."

He sat on the edge of the mattress. "Forgive her, Sam," he said.

"I can't."

"You can. Forgiveness is a choice we make. You won't. That's the choice you've made. So don't say you can't."

"Don't you understand, Lee? There are some things you can't forgive."

His brown eyes were steady on hers. "There's nothing that can't be forgiven."

"Well, thank you, Mother Teresa."

"Jesus, Sam. Don't let's do this."

"Do what?"

"I don't want to fight with you, Sam. I just want you to call your sister. It's been too long. You know I'm right."

"You're not right. You're self-righteous."

"Sam—" Lee's voice was low and it held a warning she was too angry to heed.

"You're self-righteous and smug and just because you found it so goddamn easy to forgive the father who walked out on you, that doesn't make you the authority on forgiveness. For sure, it doesn't give you the right to tell me what I should or shouldn't be doing."

"Okay," Lee said. "I'm getting the message." He crossed the room, turned to her at the door.

"Where are you going?"

"I'll be at the yard. Call me when you're ready."

"Ready for what?" she said.

"To grow up."

Her hands clutched the pillow, but by the time she threw it, he had left the room.

"Here we go." Stacy set the bag on the counter. "Two hazelnuts, one skim regular and one with the works." She passed a coffee to Sam.

"Thanks." Sam pried the lid off her cup.

Stacy reached back into the bag and took out a paper-wrapped pastry. "And one Danish. Cream cheese and cherry. To split."

"I'll pass."

"Oh, come on. How bad can half be?" Stacy broke the pastry in two and handed Sam one half. "So I was thinking," she said. "I don't know what happened with you and the Hunk, but I think you should just pick up the phone and call him." She took a bite of the Danish.

"Wait a minute. Why should I call Lee?"

"To apologize." Stacy finished the pastry, licked her fingers.

"I should apologize? You don't even know what we argued about."

"Listen, you're both stubborn. Right? So the question is, do you love him?" Stacy plowed right on without waiting for Sam to answer. "Of course you do. Anyone who's been around the two of you can see that. You're crazy about him and he's mad for you. So don't screw it up. Are you going to eat that or not?"

Sam slid her Danish across the counter.

Stacy took a bite. "Or go over and see him."

Sam sipped her coffee. "I think we need some cooling-off time."

The telephone cut off Stacy's response. "Want me to get that?"

Sam nodded. She hoped it was Lee.

"Golliwog's Cakewalk," Stacy said. "Yes. May I tell her who's calling?"

Sam blew out a breath of disappointment.

"Sure," Stacy said to the caller. She held the phone toward Sam. "It's for you."

"Who is it?" Sam mouthed the words.

Stacy cupped her hand over the receiver. "Cynthia," she said. "She says she's your sister-in-law."

Sam's hand rose to her throat and she automatically noted the time. Eleven o'clock. Nine o'clock in Denver. Even now, after all these years, whenever Cynthia called, Sam's first reaction was to check the time. It had been Cynthia, not Josh, who had phoned with the news about the plane crash and her parents' deaths.

"Hi," Cynthia said.

"Hi," Sam said. "What's happening? How are the kids?"

"They're fine. Both on varsity again," Cynthia said. "Jeffrey's playing goalie this year. Robert's still at center."

"That's great." Would she even recognize her nephews? Cynthia sent a picture every Christmas, but Sam hadn't actually seen them since her parents' funeral. She did a quick calculation. They were eight and nine then, so they had to be sixteen and seventeen now. "How's Josh?" It had been weeks and weeks since she'd spoken with her brother.

"Crazy," Cynthia said. "Training like a madman."

"Another marathon?" Josh had started running after their parents died. He'd done Boston four years ago and Sam had been in the crowd at Chestnut Hill to cheer him on for the final miles.

"No. He's training for an Ironman. I wrote about it in our Christmas letter. Remember?"

Ah, yes. Cynthia's annual letter detailing her family's many successes. "That's right," Sam said. "Hawaii, is it? The one in Maui?"

"San Diego," Cynthia said. "Next August."

"Good for him," Sam said. She took a sip of coffee, wondered if it was the difference in their ages or geography that distanced her from her brother and his family.

"He's training twenty to twenty-five hours a week. This competition is very important to him."

"I can imagine," Sam said. She drank more coffee and rolled her eyes at Stacy, a just-get-me-off-the-phone look.

"That's why I think it's so unfair of Libby."

The name shot through Sam. "Libby?"

"Naturally, I feel sorry for her," Cynthia said. "You know I do. But I don't think she has any right to keep after Josh like this. He's already told her he can't do it, but she keeps at him. Then he feels guilty for saying no. She called again yesterday. This time she said all she wants is for him to be tested, to see if he is a match, but then what? I mean, why even be tested if you're not going to be a donor?"

Sam had to sit down. A donor?

"And what if the disease is inherited?" Cynthia went on. "She says it isn't, but how can they be certain? And God forbid, what if Jeffrey or Robert ever needed a kidney? What then?"

"A kidney?" Sam said. Stacy looked over at her.

"Exactly. Josh would want to be able to give one to his own sons. Besides, it's not like it's a huge emergency. They've got her on dialysis. From what I understand, people can stay on that for years."

Sam swallowed against the coffee that rose to her throat. She felt suddenly light-headed.

"I mean, if she wanted money, that would be one thing, although with Richard's trust money they have more than God. But body parts are quite something else. Anyway," Cynthia went on, "I thought maybe you could give Josh a call. Support him in his decision." She drew a breath. "Wait a minute. Wait a minute. You're not going to be tested, are you? She hasn't guilted you into it, has she?"

"No," Sam said, barely able to get the words out. "I'm not getting tested."

"Well, give Josh a call, will you? You two need to stick together on this."

"Bad news?" Stacy said after Sam hung up.

Sam nodded, unable to speak. She stared up at the bulletin board over her workstation, stared at the dozens of couples posed by their cakes, preparing for the ritual cutting.

"Are you all right?" Stacy said. "You're as white as a cup of Crisco."

Libby needs a kidney. The photos on the board blurred and she blinked away tears, stared at the cakes. They were four and five layers, their height a tradition from the middle ages. *Libby needs a kidney.* A couple would kiss over a tower of cakes, trying not to knock them down. If they succeeded, it meant a lifetime of prosperity.

"Sam?"

Why would anyone believe it was possible to protect against the future?

Stacy crossed to Sam. "You're shaking," she said. "What's happened?"

Sam looked away from the bridal couples, so certain of the happiness that awaited them. "It's my sister." She remembered the message Libby had left on her machine. *Please,* Libby had said. *Please call me.*

Six years. Sam had thought she was free. But love was never free, she realized now. It bound you.

"Will it hurt?" Sam asks in a baby voice.

Libby does not answer. She concentrates on the match flame at the tip of the safety pin.

"Why are you doing that?" Sam whispers. They are not supposed to have matches. They will be in big trouble if their mother catches them.

"So the pin will be sterile," Libby says, "and we won't get infected." She is eleven and knows a lot more about things than Sam.

"Oh," Sam says. Her hands are still sticky from the peach they had eaten earlier and she thinks maybe she should have washed before they began.

Libby goes first. Sam watches, mesmerized, as her sister pricks her finger and, immediately, a drop of blood appears. Sam wants to stop now. When Libby told her all about the Three Musketeers and about vows for life, it had sounded exciting, but now she isn't sure. Libby reaches for her hand.

It does hurt. Tears fill Sam's eyes, but she does not cry out.

"Good girl," Libby says. She lifts Sam's finger to her mouth, licks off the blood. Her tongue is warm on Sam's skin.

"Now you," Libby says. She holds her finger for Sam to lick.

Blood always, always makes Sam feel funny in her stomach.

"Go on," Libby says. "We both have to do it, or it won't work."

Sam closes her eyes and licks Libby's finger.

"*Forever and ever,*" Libby says, using her grown-up voice. "*Me for you and you for me. Now it's your turn.*"

"*Forever and ever,*" Sam says.

"*Me for you and you for me,*" Libby says.

"*Me for you and you for me,*" Sam echoes.

Libby hugs her. "*I love you, Sam-I-Am.*"

"*I love you back,*" Sam says. Her tears have dried. She tastes the sweetness of peach juice, the salt of Libby's blood.

Libby

. . . .

*L*ibby took the entire drive from the lake to the center at a good ten miles over the limit, risking a stop by the local traffic cops, who were notorious for ticketing speeders. Even so, she was thirty minutes late for her appointment.

Dodi, the receptionist, looked pointedly at the wall clock and then back at Libby. "You're late," she said.

"I'm sorry." Several people in the waiting room looked over at her. Libby's cheeks flushed. What was this? Grammar school? A reprimand for a rule infraction?

Behind Dodi, in a separate cubicle, several nurses had gathered. They talked softly.

Dodi tapped her pencil on the appointment book. "It's important that you be on time for your treatment."

"Yes." Libby considered excuses. An emergency in the family, car trouble, flat tire.

"Otherwise," Dodi continued, "you set everything back for the entire day."

"I understand." Forget the excuses, Libby decided. She'd be damned if she was going to lie just to avoid this lecture. Maybe she'd just blurt out the truth, how she'd been sitting in a parking lot on the edge of Lake Michigan trying to build up courage to face another session. Did these people understand what it was like, coming here?

Libby was rescued by Kelly. She followed the nurse to an exam room and was weighed, her legs and abdomen checked for fluid retention. The checkup was perfunctory, almost abrupt, performed without Kelly's usual chatter. Libby assumed the nurse, like Dodi, was upset because she'd been late.

"I'm sorry to set the schedule back," she said.

"Don't worry about it," Kelly said. She led Libby out to the treatment bay.

It took Libby a moment to notice how quiet the area was. Conversation was subdued. The television was nearly inaudible.

Libby barely had time to sit down when Jesse leaned over. "Lord, I'm glad to see you, girl."

"You had us worried," Eleanor said from Libby's other side. "Is everything all right? Did you have car trouble?"

"No. The car's fine." The women's concern took her by surprise. She settled back, unbuttoned her shirt. Kelly slid the tubes into her catheter. The nurse stayed until the machine began pumping blood.

"I don't think you'll have to worry about any saline imbalance today," Kelly said. "Your numbers are textbook, but I'll keep checking anyway. Right now I've got to go get Mr. Waters off his monitor. I'll be back. Okay?"

"She'll be fine," Eleanor said. She turned to Libby. "I tried to call you," she said. "Monday afternoon."

"You tried to call me?"

"To see how you were doing," Eleanor said. "I know it was pretty rough on you last time. I wanted to check and see that you were all right."

"We put you in our prayer circle," Jesse said. "The one I told you about."

Disconcerted by this show of concern, Libby fell silent.

"I remembered your husband said you lived in Lake Forest,"

Eleanor continued, "but I couldn't remember your last name. I called the office here but they won't give out that information. A privacy policy, they said. If you can imagine."

"Yes."

"As if any of us had any privacy here."

That, at least, Libby agreed with.

Eleanor reached for a small notebook and pencil. "So what is it?"

"What?"

"Your last name."

Short of being rude, there was no way out of it. "Barnett," Libby said. "Elizabeth Barnett."

"You might as well give me the number, too," Eleanor said. "That'll save me the trouble of having to look it up."

Libby recited her number. Out of the corner of her eye, she saw Jesse jotting it down as well. She could just imagine what she was letting herself in for. The next thing she knew, Jesse'd be showing up at her door trailing her entire prayer circle.

Kelly returned and checked Libby's monitor. "Looking good," she said and then rushed off again.

"She's mad." Libby surprised herself by confiding this to Eleanor.

"Who?"

"Kelly. I guess because I showed up late."

"She's not mad," Jesse said. "She's just upset."

"I guess everyone is," Eleanor said.

Libby could not believe it. "I can just imagine what happens if you miss an appointment. You probably have to make a confession."

"Oh, they're not upset about you," Jesse said. "It's Harold."

"Who's Harold?"

"Mr. Lenehy," Eleanor said.

"You know," Jesse said. "The wheelchair. Deaf as a brick."

"What about him?"

Eleanor pointed to the empty chaise on the other side of the bay. No wonder the television was turned so low.

"The poor man's in the hospital," Jesse said.

"Oh, no," Libby said. "What happened?"

"We don't know for sure," Eleanor said.

"*They* know," Jesse said, tilting her head toward the nurses' station, "but of course they won't say a word to us."

"I heard it was a heart attack," Eleanor said.

"Heart attack?"

"It's not that unusual," Eleanor said. "Half the people in here are at cardiovascular risk. It goes with the territory."

This was news to Libby and she made a mental note to ask Carlotta about that. "Will he be all right?"

Eleanor shrugged. "My guess is, it isn't good."

"Here you go, dear," Jesse said. She handed a tissue to Libby. It was only then that Libby realized she was weeping. Ridiculous. Weeping over a man who had done nothing but irritate her with his insistence on having the TV volume high, a man she barely knew.

When she came out of the center, the air had turned heavy, forewarning of a storm. The dense atmosphere matched Libby's mood. She couldn't believe how sad she felt. It was ridiculous, really, how disturbed she was about Harold Lenehy. It was the cruelty of it that got to her. First he lost the use of his kidneys, then he lost a leg. Now, after all he'd gone through, to have a heart attack. It made existence seem so pointless, a mean joke, as if life were no more than a series of wrong turns and disappointments, more than one could bear. It was so *unfair.*

Of course, it was foolish to rail against the injustice of it. If she knew anything it was that the universe didn't concern itself with being fair. Good people died every day. Parents were plucked from the sky, pulled from one's life with no warning, dashed to earth in an eruption of fiery steel. Lumps appeared in breasts. Organs stopped functioning. Husbands walked away from wives they'd loved for twenty years, or betrayed them. The only surprise was that she could still be astounded—taken out at the knees—by the capriciousness of life. People like Jesse—those who believed in some power or god, people who had faith—were lucky. Libby supposed it was easier to have an answer for unanswerable questions.

She switched on the car ignition, but sat a moment before shifting into gear. She couldn't face the idea of going home, of spending the afternoon alone. She considered driving to the college and finding Richard, but she was almost positive he had a class. Then, too, it was an unspoken rule that she would never bother him at work. She thought about calling someone on her cell phone. Sally Cummings or Jenny Cartwright. But she hadn't spoken with either of them in weeks. She wasn't ready to face the explanations required of her.

When she pulled off the highway and onto North Green Bay, she thought about returning to the lakeshore, but changed direction at the last minute. For the second time that fall, she drove to the nature preserve, following an impulse she couldn't explain any more this time than before.

The parking lot was half full and she edged past a school bus and a handful of cars. She parked and opened the car door, inhaled deeply the slightly acrid air of dead leaves. The maples at the perimeter of the lot were in their last collapse of color.

It felt good to be outside. She crossed the meadow, circling a towering pile of brush and tree limbs, preparations for the annual bonfire. She and Richard always attended this autumn event, along with half the populace of Lake Forest. In the past she had enjoyed the ritual, weaving her way in darkness with Richard's flashlight, standing with him in the dark, waiting for the pile to be torched. And then the hungry roar, the leap of flames stretching up into the night sky, and in the distance the sound of the bagpipes. Julia Plumb's husband was one of the pipers.

You have to pay the piper.

She quickened her step, as if she could outrun her past, outdistance a history she would give anything to be able to change. She hurried past woolly mats of prairie catsfoot and dried stalks of coreopsis and loosestrife. She settled onto a bench. "Let Nature Be Your Teacher," the brass plaque on the back instructed her. Honestly, why couldn't someone just give a memorial bench without attaching some preachy sentiment? She sat, placed her tote by her side.

You have to pay the piper. Her mother's voice again.

Well, she didn't need any maternal echo to engage her sense of guilt. Guilt, anger, and fear were pretty much the extent of her emotional range lately. And remorse, she thought, let's not forget remorse. At that, she reached into her bag for the book of poetry. She flipped to the back and read the list she had written by the lake. Had it been only that morning?

Northern lights
Learn Latin
Swim with the dolphins
Italy
Portugal
Attend a concert at St. Martin-in-the-Fields
Hold my first grandchild
Write a book of poetry

She studied these items, these delayed dreams, her goals of a lifetime. Only hours before, they had seemed so consequential, significant enough to write down, to mourn the thought of their loss. But now? Harold Lenehy's attack had disturbed her. She stared out over the prairie for long minutes. Say she was given one week. One day. Say she could be granted anything. What really held significance? She looked out over the champagne-colored land, watched a woodcock swoop by. What did she desire with all her heart? The answers came swiftly. She dug a pen out from the depths of her tote and added two more items to her list.

Forgive Richard
Reconcile with Sam

"Hello, Elizabeth."
The greeting startled her.
"Sorry," Gabe said. "I thought you saw me coming."
"No," she said. "I didn't." She thought at once of Hannah, wondered how Gabriel Rose was coping with his wife's illness. Not too well, she thought, judging by how he had aged since she'd last seen him.
She and Richard had met Gabe about two years ago. He had been

collecting seeds from the prairie grasses, part of his job at the Open Lands Association. Richard had struck up a conversation with him, and soon they were deep in the middle of a discussion about ecology and the history of the prairie. Gabe had told them that this acreage was virgin land, never plowed or tilled for crops. She remembered how she had watched his hands, moved by how gently he shook seeds from the stalks of grass into the pockets of his canvas apron. She had seen him around town occasionally after that and he always called her by name, although they'd been introduced only that once.

She wanted to tell him how Hannah's presence at the center eased her sessions, helped in some nearly mystical way, but then decided to let him bring up the subject if he wanted. "Collecting seeds again?" she asked. She slid the volume of poetry back into her bag.

He nodded. He was dressed in his orangy-tan Carhartt overalls, double cloth at the knees. He cupped a handful from the pocket of his apron. "Big bluestem," he said.

She nodded, as if she actually knew the difference between big bluestem and Kentucky blue.

He sifted the seeds from palm to palm. "The poetry of reproduction," he said.

She looked up at him, surprised. "What a lovely phrase."

"But not mine," he said. "Jean Giraudoux. He was talking about flowers. 'The flower is the poetry of reproduction. . . . an example of the eternal seductiveness of life.' "

"Lovely," she said again.

"It's from *The Enchanted*." He dumped the seeds back into his apron pocket. "Have you read it?"

"No." Gabe reciting poetry? Wasn't the world a hotbed of surprise? She nodded toward his hand. "What do you do with the seeds?"

"Use them to restore other preserves." He pushed back his hat and wiped his shirtsleeve across his brow. "Mind if I join you?"

She scooted over on the bench. When he sat down, the muscles of his thighs bunched. She looked away, stared out at the grasses. The wind had come up and the blades bent and heaved in waves. He took an apple out of the apron, produced a pocketknife. He bisected the fruit and handed her half. She nibbled at hers. He ate his half with relish, swallowing even the seeds and core, wasting nothing.

"Willa Cather had a line about the prairie," he said. "About times when the winds come up like this. She wrote: 'The whole country seemed, somehow, to be running.' "

His hands looked rough with calluses and he could have used a decent haircut. When she was twenty, Libby wouldn't have bothered to speak to him, never mind share an apple, but now she could understand why a girl like Hannah would go for him. He was exactly the kind of man Libby would wish for Mercedes. Of course, Mercy wouldn't give him a second look, would dismiss him as not her type. Not *edgy* enough. The last boy she'd brought home had red spiked hair and a stud in his tongue. Richard could barely eat dinner at the table with him. Libby wondered if it was age that made one recognize goodness. Appreciate kindness. And she wondered how someone like Hannah had recognized it so young. She hoped to hell Mercedes would outgrow the "edgy" stage quickly.

"Are you and Richard coming Sunday?" Gabe asked.

She pulled her mind back from thoughts of Mercedes. "Sunday?"

"The bonfire."

"Oh. That's on Sunday? I don't know. We haven't talked about it."

Gabe leaned back, lifted his face to the sun. "The Indians used to call prairie fire the Red Buffalo," he said.

She remembered hearing this.

"Whatever it's called," he said, "fire is essential for the prairie."

Richard had told her this, but she nodded, letting him continue, lulled by his voice.

"The upper parts of the grasses are tinder dry. A hundred years ago, lightning strikes used to kindle them, set off fires."

She shuddered, just a brief shiver, but he noticed.

"Cold?"

"No." Then, "It's just the mention of lightning. My mother was struck by lightning once."

He turned toward her. "You're kidding."

"No. When I was ten. Right in our backyard. She was taking in a load of laundry. Trying to get it all in before the rains came. She said the first thing was she smelled a peculiar odor—just a hint of something that was vaguely familiar, ozone, she thought after—and then she was hit."

"So was my father."

"What?"

"Hit by lightning."

She stared at him. "You're not serious?"

He raised his palm as if taking an oath. "God's honest truth. One minute he was talking on the phone and the next he was laid flat on the floor on the opposite side of the room. He couldn't hear right for weeks."

"God, your father and my mother. I mean, what're the chances of that?"

"Pretty damn slim, I'd say."

"Very." She shook her head. "I've never met anyone else who actually knew someone who'd been hit."

"After your mother was struck," Gabe asked, "could she wear a watch?"

Her eyes widened. "No. Never. Any watch she wore couldn't keep correct time. It would gain or lose hours overnight. Your father, too?"

"Not even a pocket watch."

She finished her apple. "Amazing," she said.

"Amazing," he agreed.

They sat in silence, neither in a hurry to talk. It was funny, Libby thought, that Gabe possessed the same deep, soul calm that Hannah had.

"Do you know about the bonesetters?" he asked.

"Bonesetters? No."

"There's this tribe out in Santa Fe," he said. "And there are healers in it called bonesetters. They lay a hand on wherever a bone is broken, and just by their touch, the bone is knit."

"I've never heard of that. Do you believe it? That they can really heal by touch?"

"I don't disbelieve it. The thing is, the bonesetters are those who have been hit by lightning and survive."

He lifted a finger, pointed to the shunt on her forearm. "Hannah told me she's seen you at the center."

"Yes."

"Diabetes?" His voice was clear, his expression devoid of the pity she had expected and feared.

"No. I've got something else." She told him about her disease and what Carlotta had said about the three causes of disease.

"Bad genes, bad habits, and bad luck," he repeated. "That about covers it all."

"Yes."

They sat for a moment staring out at the prairie. Gabe broke the silence.

"It took Hannah a while to get used to the treatments," he said. "How're you doing with it?"

"It's not my favorite part of the day."

"I can imagine."

"Actually, I hate it." She blurted it out, relieved to be honest.

He surprised her by laughing. "Tell it like it is," he said.

She laughed, felt her shoulders relax. "How's Hannah doing?" she asked.

"Some days are better than others. She's trying to get well enough to be considered for a transplant. She's had one already and it's harder to get a second one."

"Did she know the donor?"

Gabe nodded. "I gave her one of mine. I swear I'd give her the other one if they'd let me." A spasm of pain crossed his face, so pure Libby had to look away. "She refuses to let me get down. She says we don't have that luxury. She says every day must be one of the good ones. The hardest thing for me is knowing that she's had to let go of some of her dreams."

Libby knew about lost dreams.

"She always wanted children," Gabe said. "I swear if any woman was born to be a mother and raise kids it's Hannah. It about breaks my heart, but you know what she says?"

"What?" Libby tried to envision what it would be like not to have Matthew or Mercedes, to be robbed of the riches they brought to her life.

"She says she'll just help other mothers with their kids. As soon as she can, she's going back to school. She wants to get certified so she can open a nursery."

Libby fell silent. She pictured Hannah—so thin and worn, skeletal, really—holding on to her dream, refusing to let it go.

"If anyone can do it," Gabe went on, "it's Hannah. She's my miracle."

Libby felt something stir in her breast, beneath the rise of the catheter, a sensation it took a moment to recognize as hope. She willed it away. Hope was as much a phantom as faith and she knew better than to trust it. She raised a hand to her chest, let her fingers brush over the catheter.

"Look," Gabe said, his voice so hushed she barely heard.

"What?"

"Over there." He nodded toward the edge of the prairie, beyond a clutch of hawthorns, to the opening by a stand of sycamores.

A buck stood just free of the trees. If Gabe hadn't pointed him out, Libby would have missed him. She caught her breath at the majesty of the deer.

"Six point," Gabe whispered. Then, as if he knew what was coming, "Watch."

The animal turned his head back toward the sycamores. A doe emerged from the shadow of the trees.

"Beautiful," Libby said. The word seemed insignificant. This was more than beauty. It was power and grace beyond language.

"It's their mating season," Gabe said.

She stared, transfixed.

"You know what hunters say?" Gabe asked.

She shook her head.

"They say for every deer you see, a hundred have seen you."

The buck lifted his head, turned toward them.

"We're upwind," Gabe said. "He's caught our scent."

Libby longed to freeze this moment, to capture it. Then, in the distance, a dog yapped. In one fluid motion, the buck and his doe were gone, swallowed by the sycamores.

For one moment, one still moment, she understood the miracle of it all. The buck and his doe, the prairie and sky and the gathering clouds. The grasses, and the snakes and voles that hid in their depths. She felt the magnificence of wind and fire, of love and beauty. Of connection. Even—in that one flash of understanding—of pain and grief and loss. Of bonesetters and those who were broken. In the time it took to draw a single breath, she grasped it all. She felt it in her heart and in her diseased body. For that one moment, she *felt* it, and she knew absolutely that she had a place in it, was part of it all, the mystery and miracle of life.

Sam

. . . .

Forever and ever. Me for you and you for me.

Forever and ever. Her and Libby.

Why was it so easy to make a promise, swear an oath? And, why did anyone, having made a pledge, think it possible to keep it for a lifetime? Intentions weren't enough, Sam thought. What else did it take? Was it even realistic? Did it all come down to luck?

"Here you go." The waitress placed a glass of wine in front of her. A red. Merlot or a cab, probably. Sam couldn't even remember ordering it. She could barely recall phoning Lee or walking to the Moonfish. She stared out through the front window of the café, lost for a moment in her imaginings of Libby hitched up to a dialysis machine. She tried to picture how her sister, always the healthiest in the family, would react to serious illness. Would she be afraid? Stoic? Resigned? Philosophical?

People liked to believe they knew absolutely how they would respond in a particular situation, but they didn't. Their father had been a pacifist who marched against war and racism, but he'd once struck a man he'd seen beating a dog. Later, he had nearly wept at how, when tested, and in spite of his firmest, deepest beliefs, he had met violence with violence. And Josh? Her brother had always thought of himself as strong, heroic in the John Wayne, do-the-right-thing sense, but now, when Libby needed him, he wouldn't even agree to be tested to see if he was a match.

Sam knew she was no different. Once, she believed that at news of Libby's illness she would have flown to her sister's side, done anything for her. But her immediate reaction when Cynthia phoned— one she could confess to no one, could barely admit to herself—had been a grim flash of satisfaction. *She got what she deserved.* The thought had lasted just a moment, but she could not deny it. *She got what she deserved.* Sam was shamed to find herself capable of such vindictiveness.

"Sam?" Lee stood by the table.

"Hi," she said. When she phoned him earlier he had agreed to meet, but some part of her had been afraid that, still upset, he would not show.

He hadn't changed after work. There were spatters of white paint on his shirt and a smudge of grease on his forearm. She reached over and traced a finger over the dirt. He bent and kissed her cheek.

"Thanks for coming," she said.

"No prob." He slid into the chair opposite her. He looked exhausted. He seemed reserved.

"Are you okay?" she asked.

"A little tired," he said. "It's been a pretty full day."

She wanted to believe that this was all that was wrong, but their last argument echoed. "Lee," she began, "about the other night . . ." She wished it were possible to take back words, to erase them from a person's memory bank. Why did she find it hard to apologize? "I'm sorry," she finally managed.

He nodded. "I'm sorry, too, Sam." He did not smile or take her hand.

Pain overtook her. She didn't think she could bear it if he stayed angry. Not on top of hearing about Libby.

"What's going on?" he asked. "You sounded upset when you called."

"It's Libby. She's sick." She toyed with the place setting. "She has some kind of kidney disease and is on dialysis."

Lee absorbed the news. "How did you find out?" he asked. "Did you phone her?"

She shook her head, told him about Cynthia's call.

He reached for her hand. "How bad is she?"

She shrugged. "Cynthia didn't have a whole lot of information. All she said was that she was on dialysis and she is on a list for—" The reality of it hit her, robbed her of breath.

"Sam?"

She shook her head, swallowed, blinked back tears. The words would not come.

"Come on," he said. "Let's get you out of here." He threw a bill on the table to cover the wine, still untouched.

Outside, the air was sultry, so thick moisture practically hung from it, the kind of heaviness that left a person praying for a storm to roll through and clear things up. He led her to his pickup and headed toward Sprague Cove, driving with one hand, the other curved over the seat back. His fingers brushed her shoulder. At the Silvershell Beach parking lot, he cut the engine and opened the truck door.

"Come on," he said. "Let's take a walk."

They went to the water's edge, where the sand was firm underfoot. Overhead a gull screamed. There was a beer can on the shore. Lee stooped and picked it up. Sam waited while he carried it to the trash barrel. Lee had told her that it took two months for an apple core to disintegrate in the sea. A tin can took fifty years, a disposable diaper four hundred and fifty. He'd railed against the disposable culture and the men who came to his yard with more money than they had love for boats. "These people think you buy a boat, hop in, and go," he'd said. "They think there's no payback, they just go on to the next. But to sustain a boat you have to put in time, energy, thought. You need commitment. It's true of life, too."

They walked along the shore toward the far jetty. Lee stopped to pick up a stone. Gray granite and worn smooth by water, the stone was bisected with a narrow band of white. He slipped it in his pocket. For Alice, Sam thought. Alice had a wooden bowl on her coffee table filled with stones, each bearing a perfect line through it. Alice believed they were good luck and collected them the way another person might pick four-leaf clovers and press them between the pages of a book.

"It feels so funny," Sam said.

"What's that?"

"That Libby has been seriously ill and I didn't know."

"Did your sister-in-law tell you how long she's been sick?"

"No. She didn't say much except that Libby wanted Josh to get tested to see if he was a match. She said Libby has been put on a list." She thought of the message her sister had left on her machine. "I guess that was why Libby was calling me."

"So what are you going to do?"

"I don't know. Call her, I guess." She could not think beyond that.

"Any thoughts of going out to see her?"

"Out to Illinois?"

Lee nodded.

"I can't. I mean, there's no way I can leave now."

He looked at her carefully. "Why not?"

"For one thing, I've got two weddings coming up."

"Can't Stacy do those?"

"I don't think so."

He put his arm around her. "How are you doing with this?"

"All right, I guess. I don't know. It's so mixed up."

"What do you mean?"

"I'm still so angry with her, Lee." She looked up at him. "Maybe I shouldn't be now, but I'm still so mad."

"What are you afraid of, Sam?" he asked.

"I didn't say I'm afraid. I said I'm angry."

He studied her.

"What?" she said. "You think I'm afraid?"

He picked up another stone, juggled it a moment and then skipped it out over the water. They watched it hit, once, twice, three times, before it sank below the surface.

"You think I'm *afraid*," she said again.

"Anger is just another face of fear," he said.

"That's ridiculous."

The rain began then, sharp drops that pitted the sand, and they headed back.

"What you said back there," she said when they were in the pickup. "That's completely ridiculous. Anger and fear are two separate things. Totally unrelated."

He shrugged.

"I'm sorry Libby's sick and of course I'm worried about her. And I'm still angry at her for how she betrayed me," Sam said. "But I'm not afraid. What would I be afraid of?"

"I don't know, Sam." Lee's voice was even, calm. "You tell me."

"Well, I'm not."

"Okay," he said. "You say you're not afraid, you're not afraid." He shifted into reverse, backed out of the lot.

Her hands lay clenched in her lap. Her stomach ached. *Anger is another face of fear.*

Admit it, she thought. There's a lot you are afraid of. Losing Lee, for one thing. Being hurt.

Being betrayed.

There it was. As irrational as it was, she was afraid that somehow, given another chance, Libby would once again betray her.

Libby

. . . .

*W*hen Libby got home, there were three hang-ups on the answering machine and a message from Richard, calling to say he'd slated a private session with one of the students and reminding her, too, that he had the full rehearsal for the Music Department's fall concert. He told her not to hold dinner. It was the first time in months that he'd stayed at school late, a sign that he was returning to his normal schedule. She supposed she should be glad, but she wasn't. It was perverse of her, she knew. Hadn't she been urging him for months not to worry about her, not to alter his schedule to tend to her, not to pass off all his duties to his teaching associate? But his message left her off balance, as if he had, in some way, gone on with life without her.

In the kitchen, the dishes were still in the sink from breakfast and she filled a pan full with soapy water. She could have put them in the dishwasher, but the ritual of doing them by hand calmed her. There was something almost meditative about immersing her hands in the warm water, wiping each dish with the sponge, and then rinsing the piece free of suds.

When she finished, it was a little after three o'clock, with the remainder of the afternoon to get through. There was always television, but she hadn't the least interest in watching talk shows or soap operas or, God help her, reruns of situation comedies.

The wide gray stillness of the house encased her. She missed Richard. She missed the twins. She thought about how Hannah Rose could no longer have children, and she tried to imagine how bereft her own life would be without them. All her memories were wrapped up in them. Big moments, of course, the ones every mother keeps in her memory bank (all the firsts: tooth, step, school), but small, cherished ones, too, individual to her children. The time at the aquarium when Matt stroked the silken back of a moray and said, "I wish I had a pillow just like this." The day she'd looked out the window to see him sitting on the porch, eyes determined, chin slick, as he tried to learn how to spit. Or Matt at seven, when his hamster died and he refused to allow anyone else to bury it and she had watched from afar as he laid the stiff little body in the ground. She remembered the glee on Mercedes' face the day she mastered layups in basketball, and her Christmas list the year she turned twelve: a soccer ball and pink lipstick. And her rage when she learned about the cruelty that turned calves into veal, and her subsequent, stubborn refusal to eat meat.

Motherhood, she realized, was a series of memories and a gradual progression of loss. Each day, with each new step of independence, children grew farther away until they left, claimed by their own life.

Mercedes was better than Matt about keeping in touch. She e-mailed regularly, giving Libby news of campus life, her take on her professors, and, after she learned about the dialysis, cheery "be well" messages. But the last three times Libby had called Mercy's dorm, her daughter hadn't been there. Nor had she returned the calls.

She knew it was trite—that all mothers said this—but it *did* seem like only yesterday that her life had revolved around the twins' activities. This time of day, they would both be home: Mercy studying at the kitchen table, or in the den curled up in the leather chair that had once belonged to Libby's father, engaged in one of her endless girlfriend conversations; Matt planted in front of the refrigerator, disarming her with his grin, or zigzagging across the backyard, weaving a soccer ball between his feet with an agility that astonished her. She wouldn't have thought it possible, but she missed the detritus of their daily lives strewn about her home. Gym bags and backpacks, discarded jackets and ball caps, empty Diet Coke cans, pizza boxes and orange peels on the den coffee table, grimy sweat socks on the bathroom floor.

She and Sally Cummings were the only two in their group of friends who hadn't filled the postchildren years with employment or volunteer activities. Richard used to encourage her to get a job, even part-time. But what could she do? Work sales at Williams-Sonoma or B. Dalton? She couldn't imagine. Before her illness, she and Sally used to meet for lunch and trade news of their children, and she missed that, too, even if it had only been surface chat, for the most part, not touching on the secret longings and linkages of motherhood: how one could be torn almost in half by fear or brought to one's knees with love.

Libby was overcome suddenly by a simplicity of sorrow, by all the losses of her life—her parents' deaths, her health gone, her children out in the world, Richard lost in his work, Sam estranged from her—all one great symphony of sadness. She felt weighted with forty years of accumulated disappointments and grief and loss. But she also knew that if someone walked into her home at that minute and asked her if the worst had already happened to her, she could not have said yes. Somehow she knew the worst was yet to come.

She thought back to the moment on the prairie earlier that afternoon when she and Gabe had seen the deer. She closed her eyes and tried to call up the momentary hushed certainty when she had felt on the verge of some tremendous understanding, the sense that all was well and that she was connected to everything. Now that moment of pure peace seemed elusive, imagined.

A memory, triggered perhaps by her prairie reflections, arose in her mind. She suddenly thought of her poetry professor at Oberlin. Libby could picture her clearly, even after twenty years. Anna Rauh was a strikingly dramatic woman, nearly six foot four, with silver-streaked auburn hair and hazel-green eyes. She dressed in long skirts with vibrantly colored overblouses, turquoise and purple and deep blues, and, around her neck, ropes and ropes of beads. Her voice, Libby recalled, was so low it could have been mistaken for a man's.

Funny to think of her now. Libby remembered how Anna would stand in front of the class and make pronouncements that carried the weight of truth and that Libby would dutifully copy down in her notebook as gospel. Even now, she could recall these declarations. "Some things are unfixable," Anna Rauh had said, urging them to have the courage to toss poems that were not working. "Notice all things," she had told them. And this: "When the heart opens, everything matters. Everything."

Libby thought again of the prairie. Was that what had happened to her in that moment when she saw the buck and his doe? Had her heart opened? Well, it was dangerous to unseal your heart. If Libby knew anything it was that. It opened one to loss and disappointment. It was better not to chance it.

There was something else that Anna Rauh used to tell them: "Follow love whatever the consequences." She had made it sound easy, but another thing Libby knew was that love was never easy and consequences were often more than a person could endure.

The phone rang, interrupting her thoughts. Richard calling to check in, to find out how the morning's treatment had gone, she assumed, and she reached eagerly for the receiver. In the past days, she had softened toward him. She had come to appreciate the depth of his concern, had allowed it to heal the rift that lay between them, unspoken, but not forgotten. Nor forgiven, if Libby was honest about it.

"Elizabeth?"

"Yes?" Not Richard. Foolish to feel this disappointment, she told herself.

"I'm so glad I got hold of you."

"Yes?" She tried to place the voice. It was vaguely familiar.

"It's Eleanor."

"Eleanor?"

"Eleanor Brooks. From dialysis."

"Oh, yes. Hello." Libby's tone was polite. It had been a mistake to give out her number.

"I'm so glad I got you. I called earlier but there was no answer and I didn't want to leave a message."

"I just got home." She envisioned daily phone calls, attempts at friendship.

"Well, I'm glad I reached you. I only now heard and I thought you'd want to know about Hannah."

"What about her?" Libby exhaled, more sigh than breath, already dreading what was to come. Every piece of bad news that she'd ever received had come in a phone call.

"Her husband told me. I called Hannah's house to see if she wanted to contribute to the flowers we're sending to Harold, and her husband answered."

"What about Hannah?" Libby said again.

"Well, that's what her husband told me. He was on his way back to the hospital when I called. Hannah's in a coma."

She says every day must be one of the good ones. "Is she all right?" Stupid question. Of course she couldn't be all right.

Eleanor said. "I don't think it's good. Her husband asked me to pray for her."

The line fell silent. Libby thought of Gabe, the fierceness of his love for Hannah. *I swear I'd give her the other one if they'd let me.*

"Some of us are getting together on flowers," Eleanor said.

For the second time that day, Libby railed at the unfairness of life. Her body felt pocked with pain, her head ached with the intensity of tears held in. After a while it became impossible to stay in the claustrophobic solitude of the house. The need for escape, for consolation, drove her to Richard. She needed him as she hadn't in a long, long time, needed the comfort of his arms.

She parked in the visitors' lot by North Hall—Richard had never gotten around to picking up a faculty sticker for her car—and crossed to Reid. Classes were over for the day and the building was deserted. Richard's office was locked, but an adjacent office was open and Libby knocked on the door. A woman sat at the desk, a professor Libby had been introduced to at a faculty party but whose name she couldn't now recall.

"Hello," Libby said. "I'm Elizabeth Barnett. I'm looking for Richard. Have you seen him?"

A frown that could be taken for either concentration or irritation crossed the woman's features. "You might find him in the chapel," she said.

Libby should have thought of that. Richard liked to give his private lessons in Hoyt Chapel. Something about the acoustics, he'd told her. It was the quality of the acoustics that made it the perfect venue for strings.

"Thank you," she said, but Richard's colleague had already dismissed her.

When she opened the chapel door, she stood for a moment, absorbing the peace the place always brought her. This was her favorite building on the entire campus. Its lines were graceful—the ceiling vaulted and beamed. She loved the Tiffany windows and the hanging lights of stained glass. She lingered in the entry, listening to the lesson already under way. The playing was accomplished. This was no first-year student, tentative and weak. The choice of music, too, was more sophisticated than she would have imagined. Vivaldi. Music that breached defenses.

She entered the sanctuary. Richard was in front with the student, by the chancel rail. The girl was lovely; even from the back of the chapel Libby could see that. Richard stood behind the girl, his arms over hers, guiding her as she pulled the bow across the strings. His cheek rested on the girl's temple. His eyes were closed.

Sarah James. The girl's name came to her instantly, although she had never seen her before. She remembered how Richard's voice softened when he talked about her. The gifted Sarah James.

"Richard," she said, her voice shaking.

They both looked up at her, startled. It was the look in his eyes that told her everything. A flash of guilt, then shame.

She did not wait for explanations. She fled.

"Elizabeth." Richard called out her name but she did not stop, did not turn. "Libby, wait," he cried.

She raced to the car, slammed it into reverse and pulled away. He ran toward the car, but she did not slow. He had to jump back to avoid being hit.

She did not look back. She heard him shouting her name even after he was no longer in view.

Sam

. . . .

Sam carefully placed the 5 × 7-inch card next to the phone and read the notes she had made.

Sorry to hear about illness
Ask about Richard and twins
Don't blame
Don't get angry
Don't be defensive
Don't go over old history

The last item was underlined twice.

Sam had jotted down the list the night before, hoping it would keep her on track during this first contact, but there was really no way of preparing. Her stomach was tight, her hands were clammy. Keep it simple, she counseled herself. Let Libby do the talking. Just start with hello and take it from there. She hadn't been this nervous in years. She could have used a—what did they call them?—an intermediary. She considered waiting to make the call. Late afternoon or evening, a time when Richard might answer.

She stared at the phone and tried to imagine a conversation with her sister. "Hello, Libby," she said aloud, testing her voice, which, while faint, did not shake, as she had feared. She read over the list a third time. Just do it, she thought. She punched in the number, pulse racing.

On the fourth ring, Libby answered. Sam's breath caught. "Hello," Libby said. But not Libby, Sam realized. Libby's voice on an answering machine. Sam listened to her sister instructing the caller to please leave a message. And then the beep sounded.

"It's Samantha," Sam said in a rusty voice. "Your sister. Give me a call. I'll be here all day." She hung up abruptly, as if anything she said might be used against her, and then she regretted it almost immediately. She must have sounded uncaring. She should have said something about learning about Libby's illness from Cynthia. She debated whether to call back and leave another message, but finally decided to let it go. She had made the call. That was enough. She headed downstairs to the kitchen.

"So you and the Hunk are still on the outs, huh?" Stacy said when Sam entered the room.

"Why do you say that?"

"Like I can't see the clues?"

"Clues?" Sam was replaying in her mind the message she'd left on Libby's machine. She couldn't remember if she'd given her name. She wondered if Libby would recognize her voice.

She thought about calling Josh. There was so much she needed to know, like what exactly was wrong with Libby, and were they really sure it wasn't hereditary. But Josh would be at school and Cynthia was a dead end.

"Have you checked out a mirror this morning? You look like you spent the night sleepless in Somalia. Sucking lemons."

Without bothering to answer—she knew she must look like roadkill, she certainly felt like it—Sam crossed to the coffee machine and poured a mug. She considered asking Stacy if *she* had seen a mirror yet. Today, her assistant's gel-spiked hair was tipped with blue, not the most attractive look Stacy had ever sported. But she kept the thought to herself. No sense taking her edginess out on Stacy. She settled in at the desk and went over the work sheet, glad for the distraction.

Three days until the Chaney wedding and no problems that she could foresee. The couple—the two architects—had been charmed with her design. Narrow, silver-edged stripes in apple green and hyacinth, overlaid with gold and silver gilded ropes. The actual baking she'd leave to Stacy. The necessary supplies—food coloring, silver dust and pearl dust, sugar-paste dough—were all on hand. Tomorrow Sam would finish the sugar-paste tassels that would adorn the bottom layer and the sugar-paste roping that looped over alternate tiers. And Saturday morning she would decorate and assemble the cake, transport it to the wedding, where, after exchanging vows, the couple would slice into it and feed each other the first piece. Gently, Sam hoped. Respectfully. She absolutely hated it when the groom smeared the cake on his bride's face and then she returned the favor while people laughed and applauded. In spite of researching this, Sam had never learned where that particular custom had started or to what purpose. It was such a passive-aggressive way to begin married life. A couple needed all possible respect and gentleness from the git-go, and even that guaranteed nothing.

"Hey," Stacy said after several minutes. "I forgot to tell you."

"What?" Sam's heart jumped. Had Lee called while she was in the shower?

"So I looked kidney problems up in my Louise Hay," Stacy continued.

Sam looked over at her assistant. After her call from Cynthia, she had told Stacy about Libby's illness and how her sister needed an organ transplant.

"You two must have some past-life karma," Stacy had said.

Well, forget past life. They had plenty of karma in this one. Next to astrology, Stacy trusted most the New Age healer-guru for all manner of life information. Last April, when Sam had twisted her ankle, Stacy had informed her that, according to Louise, ankles represented mobility and direction and Sam's swollen joint meant she was changing direction in her life. When Carl was suffering from low back pain,

Stacy had told Sam that it represented his fear of money and lack of financial support. "So do you want to hear what she says?" Stacy asked.

"About?"

"About kidneys."

Not particularly, Sam thought to herself, but she knew there would be no stopping Stacy.

Stacy unfolded a slip of paper. "Problems with the kidneys represent disappointment, failure, and shame," she read.

"Shame?"

"Yes."

"Well, if that were true, Catholics and Jews all over the world would be standing in line for dialysis," Sam said.

"There's more," Stacy said. "If you want, I could bring the book in tomorrow."

"Actually," Sam said, "I find people like Louise Hay offensive. What, you get kidney failure because you're disappointed? It's that whole blame-the-victim thing. It's not someone's fault if they get cancer or break a leg."

"She's talking about energetic levels. About patterns behind disease."

"A rose is just a rose," Sam said, "and a disease is just a disease."

"I'm only trying to help," Stacy said.

Before Sam could reply, the phone rang.

"Want me to get that?" Stacy asked after the third ring.

"I've got it," Sam said. Libby or Lee? she wondered. She had to remind herself to breathe.

"Golliwog's," she said into the phone.

There was a pause.

"Golliwog's Cakewalk," she repeated. "Hello."

"Samantha?" A male voice—not Lee.

"Yes."

"It's Richard."

Sam sank back in her chair. "Hello," she said. She picked up her mug, took a slug of coffee.

"I just got in and heard your message."

"I'm glad you recognized my voice," Sam said. "I realized after I hung up I hadn't left my name." Across the room, Stacy pretended not to listen.

"We have caller ID," he said. "And you left your name."

"Oh," Sam said. "Good." The 5 × 7 card was still upstairs. She set down the mug, jotted quick notes. *Keep cool.* "How are you?"

"I'm doing okay, given the circumstances."

"And the twins?"

"They're off at school."

"How's Libby?"

"She's holding her own, but everything is progressing a little faster than we'd hoped."

"Is she there? Can I talk to her?"

Richard hesitated. "She's not home right now," he said.

"Oh," Sam said. It occurred to her that he might be lying, that Libby might not want to talk to her.

"Have you spoken to her at all?" Richard said.

"I haven't. She left a message a couple of weeks ago."

"And you're just now returning her call?"

Don't be defensive, Sam reminded herself. "Cynthia called yesterday. She told me about the dialysis."

Stacy had given up all pretense of not listening.

"I see," Richard said.

"When will she be back? I can call later."

The line hummed. "I'm not sure."

"You're not sure when she's coming home?" She fired the questions, as if she had a right to ask, despite the six years of silence.

"She's—she's at dialysis right now."

"Richard," she said. "Is something wrong?"

"What do you mean?"

"You sound funny, that's all." There was something he wasn't telling her. What did he mean, things were progressing faster than expected? Wasn't Libby on dialysis? Although she knew nothing about this, Sam assumed that once a person was on dialysis, the progress of the disease was slowed or halted.

Another silence. Then: "I'm just worried about Elizabeth," he said.

"Naturally."

"It's been a stressful time," he said.

"I can only imagine," Sam said. "Would it help if . . ."

"What?"

"If I came out there?" The words were out before she could reconsider or retract them. "I could fly out."

"There's no need for that," Richard said.

"If you're sure," Sam said, ashamed to feel relieved.

"If you're sure," Sam says.

They are sitting in Sam's bedroom. The smell of bacon and coffee rises up to the bedroom. The others—Richard and the twins and Jay—are downstairs preparing the holiday breakfast. Food first and then the gifts is the prescribed order, their family tradition.

"Yes," Libby says. "Absolutely."

The box is small and it is wrapped in the lavender paper with silver filigree ribbon that Libby has chosen for her presents this year.

"I shouldn't wait until we're downstairs with the others?" Sam asks.

Libby plops down on the bed next to her. "No. I want you to open it now, while it's just us."

Their heads are nearly touching. Sam can smell the peach-scented shampoo that Libby uses. For the first time Sam notices fine lines fanning out from her sister's eyes. "Okay," she says, then giggles. She and Libby are famous for their inability to keep surprises from each other. It is a family joke that they give birthday gifts months before the actual date. She tears the paper off. Inside she finds a small velvet box. Jewelry, no doubt. She bites her lip. She and Jay are on a firm budget. They have argued about how much she should spend on gifts and he won. Her gift for Libby is a collection of poetry by Mary Oliver that she found in a secondhand bookstore.

"Go on," Libby says.

Sam flips open the box, sees inside a narrow gold band. She catches her breath, recognizing it even before she has slipped it out of the box, even before she has checked the entwined initials of her mother and father. "But this is yours," she says.

"And now it's yours," Libby says with a soft smile.

For a moment, Sam can't speak. She remembers the call that came in after their parents' funeral. The jewelry store manager asked if someone was going to pick up their mother's ring, left there for alterations. Their mother's knuckles had swollen over the years, he told them, and the day before their mother took the trip to Colorado, she had left the ring there to be enlarged.

"I can't take this," she finally manages.

"Yes, you can," Libby says.

"I always knew you were the one she'd want to have it. I got it by default, because I was the oldest daughter." She removes the ring from the box and slides it on Sam's right hand. It fits perfectly.

"I don't feel right about this," Sam says.

Libby curls her hand over Sam's. "Do you remember what Mother used to say about it?"

From the bottom of the stairs, Jay yells that breakfast is waiting, people are starving down there.

Sam closes her eyes. "She said she'd never need a four-leaf clover or rabbit's foot as long as she had this." A wave of loss overtakes her. When their mother— in an aisle seat of row 23—had really needed her charm it had been sitting in a jeweler's workroom.

"This ring was about the only thing I ever heard her be sentimental about," Libby says. "Her good-luck charm."

"And what?" Sam says, attempting a joke. "So you think I need luck right now?"

Before Libby can answer the twins fly into the room.

"Come on," Matthew says, pulling at Libby.

"We've been waiting for hours," Mercedes says, reaching for Sam.

Libby circles them all with her arms. "You're my good-luck charms," she says. "The three of you are all I'll ever need."

Libby

. . . .

Libby lay tensed until after the maid's cart had wheeled past her room and down the corridor. She'd hung the Do Not Disturb sign on the doorknob, but that didn't guarantee anything. The Libertyville motel, chosen because Richard would never think of looking for her there, was two steps above seedy, the kind of low-cost motor inn parents stayed at when they came to see their sons and daughters graduate from basic training at Great Lakes, and nothing was guaranteed, not even cleanliness. There were ancient stains on the carpet—she didn't even want to *think* of their origins—and a buildup of dust around the baseboards where the chambermaids had missed with the vacuum. Libby could only imagine what she'd find if she took a look at the mattress, let alone under the bed. And the flimsy paper strip encircling the toilet seat didn't ensure anything, certainly not that the fixture had been sterilized.

The room was narrow, with simple furnishings: a double bed—where Libby now lay—a nightstand, one chair upholstered in a faded maroon fabric, and a three-drawer maple dresser on which perched a television. Remnants of last night's dinner—take-out pasta—and a partially consumed bottle of red wine remained on the nightstand. The wine, the first she'd had in months, had resulted in a bitch of a headache.

She picked up the remote and flipped on the television, pretuned to a cable station that specialized in sensational news. She stared at the picture—obviously shot from a helicopter—of a car chase in Texas that, according to the anchorman, had been going on for more than two hours, during which the semi involved had sped through intersections and on and off highway ramps, trailed by a half-dozen police cars with dome lights flashing. "This is unbelievable," the reporter was shouting as the rogue flatbed barreled head-on into a stream of traffic. "He just crossed the median strip and now he's going the wrong way on the interstate. Unbelievable!"

This was not the kind of thing Libby normally would have watched, but anything, even this, was preferable to the scene she had been replaying in her head for the past day and a half: Richard with his arms around Sarah James, his cheek resting against her temple, his eyes closed; then, as Libby fled, the sound of his voice calling out her name.

She could fully picture how things would have unfolded if she had stopped, turned, waited for him. He would have reached for her, mouthing predictable explanations and proclamations of innocence. The sad thing was, part of her would have *wanted* to believe him, would have embraced his words instead of challenging them, would have sought the comfort that could be found in hiding behind militant denial. But another, wiser inner knowing wouldn't have bought one word of his earnest explanations. *Fool me twice, shame on me.*

For Richard had fooled her once. She had believed him then, even when all the evidence pointed to a train wreck waiting just round the bend. She had wanted to believe him and so she had and it was that simple. (Who was it that said the most damaging lies are those you tell yourself?) But even her denial hadn't been strong enough to prevent either the wreck or the chain reaction collision that followed. In the years that followed, they had both worked on patching together their marriage and rebuilding trust.

Libby reached for the remote, turned down the sound. On the

screen, the semi was now off the highway. It tore down a two-way street, careened past a yellow school bus, all in eerie silence. What had set off the chase? Was the driver drunk? On drugs? Certainly he couldn't believe escape was possible. The end was inevitable. He'd either crash or run out of gas. He was going down and the only question was how many people he'd take with him. Libby's stomach tightened and her head throbbed, although she continued to watch, unable to turn away. She clicked the volume up.

"It's a miracle no one has been hit," the anchorman was saying.

A miracle, Libby thought. How easily we throw the word around, often when it was really a matter of luck. But what was the difference between good luck and miracles? Was it a question of degree? Divine intervention? If you believed in that kind of thing. She stared at the flatbed as it cut through a parking lot. If bad luck was the opposite of good, she wondered, did "miracle" have an antonym? People spoke of the miracle of birth, but she had never heard anyone talk about the miracle of death. She was sure not even Jesse and her prayer group talked about that.

Her mother used to say you made your own luck. Had she made her own luck, both the good and the bad? Was it bad luck yesterday that had caused her to drive to the college to find Richard just when he was giving the lesson? Or had it simply been bad timing? Was everything that capricious? Or was there something larger, more complicated at work?

If she was dividing her life into two sections delineating times of good and bad luck, the line would be drawn horizontally, not vertically. The early years had been charmed. The later ones, less so. If luck ran in streaks, she had been on a bad streak for years. Losing her parents in the plane crash. Her disease, which even Carlotta said was bad luck. The incredibly bad luck six years ago.

What were the chances of Sam leaving class early that night and returning home? What were the chances that Libby herself would be so susceptible to Jay's flattery? Only that one time, she'd thought, as if the sin would be lesser for having occurred only once. He had come on to her and she had been drunk and vulnerable because of Richard's betrayal. But these familiar excuses were poor even to her own ears. There was no justification for what she had done.

In spite of her headache, she reached for the bottle on the night-stand and poured two inches of wine into the tumbler. Perhaps, she thought, perhaps there is no such thing as luck. Perhaps it is just a word made up to explain what is no more than life unfolding.

Outside, in the hall, the maid's cart rolled back down the corridor. It did not slow as it passed her door. Libby wondered how long she could remain holed up in this room. Tomorrow she was scheduled for dialysis. What would happen if she skipped her session? How long could she live without the treatment? One day? Two? A week? She had no idea. The subject had never come up with Carlotta. She had heard that kidney failure was easy. Relatively painless. You fell asleep and didn't wake up. Could that be true? Could it be that simple?

And if she died here in this room, who would mourn her? The twins, certainly, but after the first shock of loss and paralyzing grief, they would go on, as she had after her parents' deaths, gradually re-absorbed by life—with, occasionally, pockets of pain, triggered by memory. Memory. In a sophomore anatomy course she'd learned that memory lay in the limbic system, one of the deepest, oldest parts of the brain. And she had heard or read somewhere that memory held only the story one could bear to know, but she knew the lie of that. Her memory was full of things she couldn't bear to know but couldn't forget.

In the end, what saved us? Faith, as people like Jesse believed? Or creativity, as Professor Rauh had said? But faith had never pre-vented even the most devout of believers from dying, nor had any act of creation. As in the drama playing out on the screen in her hotel room, the end was inevitable.

The semi was pulling back onto a four-lane highway, pursued by the patrol cars. Cars swerved off the road and onto embankments as the caravan passed. Libby stared at the picture. She was gripped by cold desperation. She didn't know whether it was for herself or in empathy for the unknown truck driver barreling across Texas in a race he was destined to lose.

Sam

. . . .

Through the night, Sam tracked the full moon as it crossed the sky. At eleven o'clock it shone through the south-facing windows. By two, it hung fat and golden in the west, witness to her sleepless night. This time of year it seemed nearly possible to touch it. Was it the harvest moon? Or was that in September?

When she was a girl and sharing a room with Libby, on nights like this the two of them would get out of bed and cross to the window seat, where they would curl up on the padded bench. Then Libby would make up a story about the moon as it passed through its monthly phases, speaking in a whisper so their mother wouldn't hear and make them go back to bed. One time, Libby told her the moon was made of salt and that a herd of cattle roamed the sky, cows exactly like the ones they saw every day in Mr. Farnham's pasture. Each night, like the Farnham's Holsteins at a salt lick, the cows lapped the moon, until it gradually disappeared. Another time Libby told her that the reason the moon grew smaller each night was because it was really a ball of the finest, silver silk and an old woman who stitched for the fairies flew there and clipped away material she used to make gossamer gowns, and blankets for their babies.

When Sam was in the second grade, her teacher, Miss Granger, showed the class a newspaper picture of astronauts on the moon, one driving an LRV. A Lunar Roving Vehicle, Miss Granger explained in a big voice. To Sam it looked like something she could have made with her set of Legos. She'd tuned out Miss Granger and her talk about moon rocks and manned lunar missions and looked out the window, where it had started to snow. She much preferred to listen to Libby's stories about a moon made of silk or salt or sugar than one formed of rock.

Even after Sam had outgrown fairy tales, Libby continued to draw her to the window seat on full moon nights. Now she told Sam about the moon's powerful force that controlled not only the motion of the sea but the monthly cycles of women. She said that its energy was female and ancient goddesses were named for it. When Sam was fourteen she had woken in the night to find Libby writing in the moonlight. "What are you doing?" she asked. But that night her sister did not invite her to join her at the window. "Go back to sleep," Libby said. The next day, when her sister was off with Russell Fuller (leaving her behind, as she did more and more lately), Sam had found Libby's notebook and read her poem: "Wandering Hecate." The poem made her feel even lonelier than her sister's date with Russell. She couldn't figure out what it meant and couldn't ask Libby, since that would mean confessing that she'd snooped in the book.

The moon slid further through the western sky. A lovers' moon. Sam wondered if six states away in Annapolis, Lee was awake and watching it, too. The day before, he'd left for Maryland to conduct another yacht survey. He had slept over the previous night, but things had seemed different between them. Something unresolved. It wasn't that he was cool, just quieter than usual. More reserved.

"Are you sleeping?" he asked her around midnight.

"Not technically," she said.

He turned to her and held her. "I've been trying to imagine how I'd feel if, say, I found you with my brother."

"And?"

"And I guess what I came up with is that I'd be angry and I'd be hurt."

She snuggled closer. He did understand.

"But," he continued, "I want to believe that eventually I'd forgive him. I'd remember that our whole history was about more than one betrayal and I'd want to hear his side of it."

"I hate it when you do that, Lee," she said.

"What?"

"Try and take away my anger."

"That's not what I'm trying to do, Sam. I'm just saying that families are about people who fail and who make mistakes. But when all is said and done, we have to work together."

"How nice for you that you never had to find out how you'd really react," she said. She turned away from him, stiffening when he tried to embrace her.

In the morning, he'd left without waking her. She tried to read nothing into that, only that he was being considerate and letting her sleep. Later, on the kitchen table, she'd found the stone he had picked up that night on Silvershell Beach, the one she had thought was for Alice. She'd brought it upstairs and now it lay on her nightstand. She reached for it and cupped it in her hand. It was nearly flat and it fit neatly in her palm. She traced the white band in the center with her finger and wondered why he'd left it for her and why Alice believed such markings meant good luck.

Libby used to know all the symbols for good luck. Four-leaf clovers, elephants with upturned trunks, rainbows, horseshoes, shooting stars, the number 7. Their mother's wedding band.

Sam twisted the ring on her hand.

Libby.

Always Libby. Thoughts of her—a ghost who had never left—crowded the room.

Despite the six years of silence between them, despite her determination never to speak to Libby again, Sam could no more exorcise her sister from every part of her life than she could carry water in her hand. Over the years, Josh had updated her with news. She knew when the twins graduated from high school and how Matt had given his parents a little trouble in his senior year and where each was going to college. Mercedes was at Brown, Matt at Cal Tech. Josh knew about Sam and Libby's fight—although neither had told him the specific details—but he refused to take sides. I love you both, was all he ever said. She assumed that over the years he'd told Libby news about her, about her divorce, her move to Sippican—a move her brother had disapproved of. Too small-town to sustain her business, he'd told her. She should consider Boston or Cape Cod, or at least New Bedford. When the *Globe* article had come out, she'd clipped it and sent it to him. She wondered if he had mailed that along to Libby.

She wondered, too, how Libby had explained their estrangement to Richard. Had she told him the truth? If not, how had she accounted for the fact that they no longer spoke? Had she in some way blamed Sam?

She cupped Lee's stone between her hands, felt it draw warmth from her body, tried to draw comfort from it. She wished she could talk to Lee. She wanted the reassurance of hearing him tell her that he loved her.

She regretted not asking Richard more questions during their brief phone call. Exactly how sick was Libby? How long had she been on dialysis? What was wrong with her? Sam had automatically assumed it was diabetes, but now she thought it could be something else. Cancer. She felt heaviness inside her chest, as if a rock, the mate to the one she held in her hands, had lodged there.

At four, the moon now low in the western sky, Sam made a decision, and having made it, could at last fall asleep.

In the morning, Stacy hadn't even poured herself her first cup of coffee when Sam brought up the subject.

"I'm going away for a few days."

Stacy smiled. "You and the Hottie taking a vacation?"

"No. Lee's in Annapolis. I'm thinking of going out to the Midwest." She handed Stacy a steaming mug. "To my sister's."

Stacy raised an eyebrow and continued to spoon sugar into her mug. "When?"

"Tomorrow." She did not tell Stacy she had made the reservation earlier that morning, made it and paid for it before she could reconsider or get cold feet.

"Tomorrow? For how long?"

"I'm not sure. Three or four days? A week?"

Stacy crossed to look at the work calendar. "What'll you do about the Chaney wedding?"

Sam picked up the sketch and passed it to Stacy. "I've already made the sugar-paste roping and the tassels."

Stacy didn't take the drawing. "Yeah?"

"Do you think you could finish it?"

"You're kidding, right?"

Sam shook her head. "You've seen me do it a million times."

"Jeez," Stacy said, looking at the drawing. "You think I can do this? What have you been smoking?"

"Of course you can do this. If you can put on eyeliner, you can decorate this cake."

"I don't know," Stacy said.

"On Friday you use an offset spatula to spread sugar paste over the layers. Then you paint the stripes on with food coloring. Use a string for a guide. Silver-dust lines go between the stripes. They don't have to be perfect. Use royal icing for the pearl designs.

"Saturday morning, you'll get to the reception early and assemble the cake there. You've helped with that before, so you know how to do it." Sam pointed to a detail in the sketch. "Once the layers are assembled, you just have to pipe a border along the bottom edge of each tier, attach the roping to alternate layers, and you're done."

"That's all?" Stacy said. She combed her fingers through her gel-spiked hair. "Why don't I make the bride's gown while I'm at it?"

Sam flicked her hand, a don't-be-silly gesture. "You finish up by gilding the rope and tassels. I know you can do it. Taken in steps, this is an easy cake. And I can hire Tricia Nelson to come in Saturday and help."

"I don't know," Stacy said again. "What if the bride complains because you're not there?"

"You've been at enough weddings to know that the bride is far too crazed to be worrying about whether or not I'm there. As long as the cake is there, she wouldn't care if Charles Manson brought it." It's the bride's mother you've got to watch out for, she thought but knew better than to say. "Besides," she added, "it's my cake, my design they want, not me."

"Don't kid yourself," Stacy said. "They want you there."

"Listen, if you're worried, I can call Liz Chaney and tell her I have a family emergency and have to be out of town, but you'll be there. After the wedding, I'll give her a discount if she isn't happy. But she will be, because it's a gorgeous cake and you'll do a great job putting it together."

Stacy looked unconvinced. "Can't you wait until Sunday to go?"

Common sense said that she could. What was the rush? She'd stayed away for six years. What was one more day? She couldn't explain to Stacy the urgency that had overtaken her at dawn and compelled her to make a plane reservation. She didn't really understand it herself. She just knew she needed to go to Libby immediately.

She was scheduled for a six a.m. flight, the only seat she could get on such short notice, which meant she had to set the alarm for three. After Stacy left and she'd finished for the day, she called Lee, reaching him on his truck cell.

"Hold on a sec, Sam," he said. Before he lowered the volume, she heard Bon Jovi blaring in the background.

When she told him her plans, he was silent for a moment.

"Lee?" she said.

"Listen," he said, "call Alice. She'll drive you to the airport."

"That's silly," she said. "There's no reason for her to do that. I'll drive to Providence and leave my car at Green. No big deal."

"Sam, let her do this," he said. "And let me know when you're coming back. I'll pick you up." He paused. "Unless you want me to join you out there."

"No. I mean, I don't know what I'll run into when I get there or exactly when I'll be back. Probably two or three days at the most."

"What about the wedding on Saturday?"

She laughed. "Stacy's covering for me."

"You're serious?"

"If she doesn't have a coronary first."

"She'll do fine," he said.

She wondered why Lee had so much confidence in people's abilities. Why was he so sure that she could sail and Stacy could manage the wedding cake? Why was he so certain that she could mend the past with Libby?

"What about when you get there?" he asked. "Is someone meeting you at O'Hare?"

"No. I thought I'd rent a car when I landed." She didn't tell him that she hadn't told anyone out there that she coming.

"Are you nervous? About flying?"

"No." Everyone assumed that because her parents died in a crash, she was phobic about air travel. She wasn't nervous. At least not about flying—but the thought of seeing Libby again made her stomach churn. If she was a smoker, she'd definitely be reaching for a pack.

"Listen" she said. "Please don't bother Alice. There's no point in her getting up that early when I can easily drive to Green."

"She'll want to," Lee said. "That's what family's for. So call her, okay?"

"Okay," Sam said.

"Promise?"

"Promise."

"And phone me when you get there."

"I will." She pressed the receiver against her cheek, reluctant to let him go. "I love you, Lee."

"I love you, too. And Sam?"

"Yeah?"

"I'm proud of you. You're doing the right thing."

After they hung up, she went up to her bedroom to pack. Lee's praise warmed her. *You're doing the right thing.* Why was it, she wondered, that the right thing to do was always so hard?

Libby

. . . .

*L*ibby woke in the night with a raging headache, from the wine, she suspected, which probably also explained the metallic taste in her mouth. Without bothering to switch on a light, she stumbled to the bathroom and turned on the cold tap until the water ran icy. She took two sips and then held a facecloth under the flow. She wrung it out and folded it into a compress and returned to the bed. She placed the cloth over her eyes and temples, and eventually, her headache only marginally better, drifted off to sleep. When she woke again, her breath came in short gasps, as if she had been running. She sat up, and this immediately eased her breathing, but made her headache worse. She felt slightly nauseated.

When she swung her feet to the floor, the nausea increased and so she sat for a moment before heading for the bathroom. Using the toothpaste she'd purchased from the motel front desk and her finger (they hadn't had any brushes), she cleaned her teeth. She swished with water and spat in the sink. Beneath the flavor of mint, her mouth still held the metallic taste.

Back in the bedroom, she checked the alarm clock on the nightstand and saw it was after nine, later than she had slept in years. She couldn't go home—she hadn't the energy to confront Richard—but she certainly couldn't stay holed up in a motel for one more day.

She crossed to the window, drew back the curtains. The sky was the Wedgwood blue she always associated with autumn and was spotted with billowy clouds. "Islands on a dark-blue sea." Was that Byron? Wordsworth? One of the Romantics, she knew. Shelley, she suddenly remembered. The Romantics had always set her teeth on edge and Shelley with his sanguine sunrises and burning plumes was the worst of the lot.

In the parking lot her Volvo, identical to Richard's except that it was a year older, was parked in the slot reserved for her room, one of only a handful of vehicles in the lot. Next to her Volvo was a brown van with bumper stickers that read: "Proud Parent of a Winston Elementary Honor Student" and "Choose Life, Your Mother Did."

Actually, Libby thought, her mother had chosen to fly to Colorado instead of driving and so, as it turned out, had unknowingly chosen death, but somehow she didn't think the parent of a Winston Elementary School honor student would care to hear this story.

As Libby watched, a family with three young boys came out of the motel and crossed the lot to the van. While the father unlocked the doors and loaded their luggage, the mother fussed with the younger boy's hair, smoothing down a cowlick that Libby could see even from a distance. After he had taken care of their suitcases, the father buckled the boys into the backseat. Once Libby had *been* that family, had combed Mercy's hair and fastened the seat belt around Matt and doled out juice boxes and snack packs of raisins while Richard had settled into the driver's seat, unfolding the road map to check their route one final time. Those were the best days, Libby thought, she just hadn't been wise enough to realize it at the time. But wasn't that the story of her life, appreciating what she had only after it had been taken from her? The van backed out of its parking place and pulled out of the motel lot. It had Ohio plates.

Her roommate during her freshman year at Oberlin had come from Ohio. Julia had been a voice major, a soprano who knew nearly word-perfect all the Gilbert and Sullivan comic operas and a heap of country-and-western songs with lyrics like "Sometimes you're the windshield/Sometimes you're the bug." She spoke with determined authority about everything, and, although she dated a pre-law student at Ohio State, rumors flew that she was a lesbian. She had come from Twinsburg, Ohio, Libby remembered now. Julia'd told her that her town was famous for the number of twins who lived there.

A twin would be perfect, Carlotta had said.

The oddest memory surfaced suddenly: she and Sam, legs bound by scarves, playing Siamese twins. She swallowed against the pain, then closed the curtains, as if the past and all the hurt and loss it held could be erased as easily as that.

It was nearly ten, two hours past her scheduled time for dialysis.

"You choose," she'd said to Richard when they were first married and they faced any decision.

"Making no decision *is* making a decision," he'd said, in a maddeningly superior way.

"Don't be so fucking condescending," she'd replied. It had been their first fight, or, rather, her first fight since Richard had walked away, refusing to be drawn in. Arguing with him had been like quarreling with a cloud, even when they had something serious to deal with.

She had never told anyone about Richard's affair with the student, certainly not any of her friends in Lake Forest. She recalled how ashamed she had been, as if it were her fault. He had promised her it had only happened that once. He hadn't begged for her forgiveness or wept—she had done the crying for them both—but he had vowed it would never happen again and she had believed him. Again she thought about the teenage girl who had broken into a boy's home and super-glued all the zippers on his pants. That girl would have glued shut more than Richard's fly. How could she have lost that part of herself? When had it happened?

She switched on the TV to a talk show. The host was talking to five obese women. As each woman talked, her weight flashed on the screen. Three hundred and forty-nine pounds. Four hundred and fifty-five. Two hundred and eighty. Libby couldn't imagine how they managed the simplest of tasks, like lacing up shoes.

She listened as they talked about failed diets and binge eating and how they loved their chips and pizza, their bacon and cheese-cakes, and how they hid wrappers of fast food the way an alcoholic hid empty bottles and avoided air travel because they couldn't fit in the seats. One of the women, confessing that her twelve-year-old daughter already weighed two hundred pounds, began to sob. The few times Libby had seen talk shows, she had felt dismissive—nearly disdainful—of the people who blurted their intensely personal stories of rape and incest and addiction in front of national audiences, but now, watching the obese women, she was moved to tears.

Be kind to everyone, her father had told her when she went away to college, because everyone is carrying a personal hurt. She thought of Hannah Rose and Gabe. She thought of Jesse and Eleanor.

She thought of Sam.

When she was eighteen, Libby hadn't believed her father, but now it seemed to her that he had been telling a great truth—everyone did carry a personal pain—and this knowledge was suddenly too grim a burden to be borne.

Sam

. . . .

$\mathcal{T}$he trip, with a connection in Atlanta, took forever. It never made sense to Sam that, on a flight from Rhode Island to Chicago, the plane would have to go to Georgia. No wonder airlines went bankrupt. It was nearly three when she landed, and by the time she had picked up a rental car and headed north out of the city, it was after four.

She hadn't eaten much beyond coffee and an airport bagel earlier that morning in Providence, but she didn't stop for lunch. She doubted she could keep food down. Just call it the Visit Your Sister diet, she thought. She regretted now that she hadn't thought about this trip for a day or so instead of acting on impulse. But then, if she had thought about it, she wouldn't have come.

Fifty minutes after she left the airport—long before she was ready—she saw the exit sign for Lake Forest. She was tempted to keep driving, just head on up to Milwaukee. At the last moment, she turned off the highway. She passed the hospital and middle school and made the turn onto North Green Bay. She had visited Libby only twice in the past, yet she remembered the way to her sister's house without one false turn.

The street was lined with maple trees and expensive homes in a variety of styles. English Tudor cottages and Italian manors, stucco coach houses and pseudo-French estates. She recalled that when Libby moved to Lake Forest, she had told her that it was one of the wealthiest suburbs in the Midwest. Trust Libby to land herself smack in the middle of the honeypot. Sam slowed as she approached Libby's house, an imposing Queen Anne, white with green shutters and two-car garage. There was a gray Volvo in the driveway. Sam went numb right down to her shins. She drove past. She was not ready for this. A half mile down the road, able to breathe again, she made a U-turn and retraced her path past the house, then circled back to the center of town. Although coffee was the last thing in the world she needed—her nerves were twitchy enough—she found a Starbucks down the block from Marshall Field's. She backed into a parking space. Even in late afternoon the coffee shop was busy, filled with housewives in expensive shoes. She'd never seen so many twin sweater sets in her life. She thought they had stopped making them sometime back in the fifties, but evidently not. And the hair on these women! What Stacy called helmet hair. Even two young mothers dressed in sweat suits and pushing strollers looked like they'd just had their hair professionally blow-dried. Feeling rumpled and pudgy, Sam took her double latte back to the car. She scalded her tongue on the first sip. A tall, good-looking man walked out of the bank across from the coffee shop and looked in at her, smiled. She remembered then that she had promised Lee that she would call. She dialed him on her cell.

"Well, I'm here," she said.

"Hey," he said, his voice turning soft. "How're you doing?"

"Okay." Of course, she wasn't. She was scared, sad, and nervous. And that was just for starters.

"Where are you? At O'Hare?"

"No. I landed around three and got a car. I wanted to get out of the city before the commuter traffic got crazy." She blew into the coffee, chanced another sip.

"So where are you now?"

"Lake Forest. Actually, I'm sitting in my car outside a Starbucks, drinking a latte and trying to . . . I don't know. Get my courage up, I guess."

"Trying to find the groove?" he asked.

She smiled. "Yeah."

"I wish I were there with you."

"Me, too."

"Have you called her yet? Does she know you're in town?"

"No."

"Sam?"

"Yeah?"

"Are you sure you don't want me to come out? You don't have to do this alone, you know. I can catch an early evening flight and be there by tonight."

"I know. But really, I'm fine."

"Are you staying at her house?"

"I'll probably get a hotel room somewhere. I'll let you know when I'm settled."

"I love you."

"I love you, too."

"Call me later, will you? After you've seen her."

"I will. And Lee, will you give Stacy a call and see if she needs anything? Give her some moral support."

"My specialty."

"Don't I know it." A wave of longing swept her. She set the coffee on the dash and dug through her bag until she found the stone.

"Guess what I'm holding?" she said.

"Animal or mineral?" he said.

She had to laugh. "No hints." She folded her fist around the rock.

"Let's see," he said. "You're holding a . . ." He paused and hummed as if concentrating. "You're holding a good-luck stone."

How did he do that? "You cheated," she said, laughing.

"No way," he said. "Listen, I've got to run, but call me later, okay? Don't forget. And Sam?"

"Yeah?"

"What you're doing is a beautiful thing."

"Glad you think so because I don't have a clue what it is I am doing."

"Well, I can think of a half-dozen things."

"Just tell me one." Tell me one thing, she thought, that will give me the courage to see this through. She squeezed the stone.

"You're giving your sister a chance to make things right," he said.

"Maybe," she said. She wasn't so sure. What if some wrongs couldn't be made right?

Sam pulled into the drive and parked behind the gray Volvo. She sat for a minute and stared at the house, needing a clue that would tell her how to begin, but all she saw was a well-maintained house where people with no financial worries lived. But a façade never revealed what was going on inside. She knew that for a fact. Each house held its own story, kept its own secrets.

Finally she got out of the car and climbed the steps to the porch. There was a wreath made of bittersweet vines on the front door. Ten to one, Libby had made it. Sam ran the bell, bracing her knees to keep them from shaking.

Richard answered. "Samantha?" he said.

"Hi."

He stared at her, not moving. "I didn't know you were coming," he said.

He looked much the same as she remembered. A good-looking man, aging well—skin still taut—except for a slight thickening through the waist. Sam had never really connected with him. He'd always seemed a cipher to her, remote, withholding. An awkward silence stretched on until she broke it.

"May I come in?"

"Oh, sorry," he said, stepping back and motioning her in. "Is Libby expecting you?"

"No," she said.

"Oh."

She could read nothing in this response. "I should have called," she said. I shouldn't have come, she thought.

"No. No, this is fine. I'm just surprised to see you." He recovered smoothly. Her recollection of Richard was of a man always at the top of his game. Self-assured and self-contained, the way those born to wealth often are. Once, early in their marriage, Libby had confided that all he needed to make him content was his music. Now he looked . . . what? Nervous? He had just shaved. She could smell his aftershave.

"Have you eaten?" he asked. "Can I get you something?"

"No. I'm fine."

"How about coffee?"

"All right." How about a shot of Johnny Walker? She followed him into the kitchen. Dirty dishes lay on the counter and in the sink. Two days' newspapers were stacked on the table.

"Is Libby here?" Sam asked.

"No." He spooned grounds into a coffeemaker.

"How is she? I mean, I know she's sick, but I don't know anything about what's wrong with her."

"She has a disease called focal sclerosing glomerulonephritis," he said. "FSGS, for short."

"That sounds serious."

"It's not hereditary," he said, as if that was her concern, as if that was why she was asking.

"When Cynthia said something about her kidneys, I thought maybe she had diabetes."

"No."

The conversation was beginning to feel somewhat surreal. "How long has she been sick?"

"It was diagnosed a year ago. She started dialysis this fall. She goes three times a week"

"How's that going?"

"To be honest, she's having a hard time with it." He got mugs out of the cupboard, then opened the refrigerator and held up a pint of cream, raised his eyebrow in question.

She shook her head. "Black's fine." She listened for the sound of a car pulling into the drive. "Cynthia told me she needs a transplant."

"Her doctor recommends it." He poured coffee into the mugs. "I'd give her one of mine," he said, as if she had asked, "but our blood types aren't compatible."

She felt faint suddenly. Thinking about blood always did that to her. "The bathroom," she said. "Down that hall?"

"First door on the right."

Inside the powder room, she snapped to. There were lace-edged hand towels in a delicate moss green on a shelf by the marble vanity, a bouquet of dried roses in a cut-crystal vase, and a small china dish of egg-shaped soaps. Were these soaps meant to be used? What did you do after you used one? Throw it away? Certainly not put it back in with the others. Martha Stewart had a lot to answer for. But then, Sam remembered, Libby arranged things like this long before Martha Stewart *was* Martha Stewart. She ran cold water and splashed her face.

"Where is Libby now?" she asked when she returned to the kitchen. "Dialysis?"

He paused, and for a moment she could have sworn he was going to tell her a lie. Then his shoulders slumped. "I don't know," he said.

"What do you mean?"

He shrugged. "I don't know where she is."

What did that mean? That she was shopping? Had they had a fight? "You don't know where she is?" she echoed.

"No." He avoided her eyes.

She sat opposite him. "Richard, what the hell is going on?"

"I don't know," he said. "She left."

"When?"

"Two days ago."

"What did she take with her?"

"I don't know. Nothing seems to be gone."

"And you don't have any idea where she is?"

He shook his head.

"Have you called her friends?"

He nodded. "I checked with a couple of them. The thing is, she hasn't been seeing them lately. When she got ill, she didn't want anyone to know." He stood up and began pacing.

"Why would she just take off like that?" Something about his story wasn't adding up.

Again he avoided looking at her. He crossed to the table, picked up his mug, fiddled with the handle. His fingers had always struck Sam as elegant, a word she had never used in regard to any other man's hands. She thought of Lee's, calloused and thickened by work, and went weak with missing him.

"Richard?"

"You have to understand," he said. "She's been upset all fall."

"Naturally."

"Well, she stopped by the college and saw something, well, something that she completely misunderstood. Before I could stop her she took off."

Sam understood perfectly. Had it been another professor, she wondered, or a student that Libby had seen him with? She would have thought this news would bring her grim satisfaction, but instead she felt pierced by sorrow.

When the phone rang, they both started. Richard picked it up on the second ring. "Yes, hello," he said, his voice tinged with hope. "Not interested," he said curtly and hung up. "Telemarketer," he told Sam.

"What about the twins?" she said. "Would she have gone to one of them?"

"That's another problem," Richard said.

"What do you mean?"

"Well, I thought of the twins, of course, and called them. Matt hadn't heard a word from her."

"And Mercedes?"

"I finally reached her roommate."

"And?" she prompted.

"And it appears that Mercedes is also among the missing."

Libby

. . . .

*I*t was after five and the bedside lamp cast a milky glow in the room. Earlier, unable to endure one more talk show or afternoon soap—they only magnified her headache—Libby had switched to an FM station on the television and within minutes had drifted off to the sound of Haydn's *London* Symphony. Now she woke to Hector Berlioz's *Symphonie Fantastique*. A memory stung, banishing the last trace of sleep. The first time she had gone to bed with Richard, Berlioz had been playing on the stereo. Tears flooded her eyes and she brushed them away impatiently. She couldn't afford to sit on the pity pot. That was a one-way path to self-destruction.

She switched the selector abruptly, actually found a country station, which was more in sync with her mood and exactly the kind of thing that Richard couldn't abide. The blues he understood, even appreciated. He owned a couple of Muddy Waters CDs as well as the complete recorded works of Sonny Terry, and he had once lectured her on the form's basic structure—twelve-bar chorus consisting of three-line stanzas with the second line repeating the first with subdominate harmony. But to his ear, country was nothing but crude and sentimental tripe. Good enough reason to listen, Libby thought; in fact, precisely what was called for. Patsy Cline, tales of cheating men and the sad-hearted lovers who threw them out. She turned up the volume and listened to a woman singing a tale of betrayal and revenge.

Lord knows, Libby wanted revenge. She wanted to make Richard pay, big-time. She wanted to call the college and report him, and then phone the twins and tell them what a son of a bitch their father was. She wanted to pour sugar in his gas tank. The way she felt, he'd better hope every store in a hundred-mile radius was out of superglue, because she was in no mood to stop at zippers. That would be a country song she'd like to sing. *Take your home-wrecking pecker out of my back door 'cause when I'm done with you it won't work no more.* But underneath her outrage, a bud of worry grew. She had to face Richard sooner or later—and then what? What *was* she going to do? Leave him? Throw him out? Forgive him? Again.

A small bug tapped at the inside of the lamp shade, circling the light, drawn to the heat that would kill it. Moth or butterfly? she wondered as she watched it flit about the bulb. Once Richard had told her how to differentiate between them: one rested with wings closed, the other with wings open; but she couldn't recall which was which.

A woman's voice broke into her thoughts. It was outside her door, the tone urgent.

"Hold on."

Libby cocked her head, listened for more. She was sure she knew that voice. She got up, rising so fast that momentarily she felt lightheaded, and crossed to the door. She unhooked the safety latch and checked the corridor, but found it empty. The words echoed clearly in her mind. Hold on, the woman had cried. Who had she been talking to? Why had she sounded so urgent and where had she gone? Or could the voice have come from a television in another room? But why had it sounded so familiar?

Hold on. Hold on to what?

Well, I've held enough in my life already, she thought as she relocked the door and crossed back to the bed. She'd held her temper and she'd held her breath, too many times to count. In her life, she had held on, and held in, and held out.

She conjugated the verb. I hold, I held, I have held.

As if a gate had been opened, memories long ago sealed off spilled out. She remembered being ten and holding her breath beneath the surface of Walker Pond, absolutely certain that it was possible for humans to breathe water, that it was only fear that held one back. She remembered holding on to the towrope on the baby slope at Mount Mansfield for too long and causing a pileup when she finally let go. She remembered holding up her hand in fifth-grade geography and being ignored by Mrs. Mumsford, who always called on the boys. She remembered crossing to Sam's bed and holding her sister when Sam was five and afraid of the night. She remembered holding her tongue when she wanted to scream at her mother.

She remembered holding Matt and Mercy, one in each arm, immediately after their birth. She remembered holding the joint she had found in Matt's backpack, waiting for him to explain. She remembered holding on to Richard's hand as they walked down the center aisle after Reverend White had declared them man and wife, and holding out an olive branch—her body—after an argument with him, and holding on to his hand at the memorial service for her parents, and again on the way into the center the first day of dialysis.

Hands held power of destruction and creation, her father had once told her. She held her hands, palms up, in front of her, saw the bulge of the shunt in her forearm. Not every wound showed, she thought.

A sigh, thin as old hope, slipped from her lips.

Hold on, the voice had said. But to what?

Hope? Faith?

She'd long ago felt the falling away of both. Illness and betrayal had come into her life uninvited and filled her with struggle, with questions for which she had no answer. So we hold out, she thought, and we hold on, and in the end what is left?

It came to her then with a shock of recognition. The voice in the hall had belonged to Hannah. Libby was certain of it.

How was that possible? Eleanor Brooks had said Hannah was in a coma. Had she recovered? But even if she had, what could she possibly be doing in this motel?

—

Libby got the number from information. She told herself she was calling Gabe to find out about Hannah, not to bother him with her problems.

"Gabe?" she said when he answered.

"Elizabeth?"

She was astounded that he knew her voice. She'd believed she was strong, that she needed no one, but at the sound of his voice, hers broke.

"Are you all right?" he asked.

She started to sob, unable to reply.

"Elizabeth," he said. "What's wrong? Where are you?"

Hold on, a voice echoed. *Hold on.*

Sam

. . . .

"Hold on a minute," Sam said. "What are you saying? Mercedes has disappeared, too?"

"Well," Richard hedged, "I probably shouldn't have said she disappeared. According to her roommate, she's just off campus." He refilled his cup, offered her more. Sam shook her head.

She waited for Richard to continue but he just drank his coffee, apparently finished with the subject. After a moment she asked, "And the roommate didn't tell you where? Does she know?"

"If she knew, she wasn't telling me."

"Is there any chance she could be coming here?"

"Mercedes?"

No, Santa Claus, she thought, but bit back the retort. "Yes."

Richard shrugged. "It's possible. Both of the twins have been upset about their mother's illness. Mercy more than Matt, I think."

"Have you checked with anyone else at the college? A resident adviser or anyone?"

Richard shook his head. "I think, at this point, that's a little premature."

Premature? Back when they were still speaking, Libby had told her what a wonderful father Richard was to the twins. Engaged in their lives, she had said. If he was so damn wonderful, so *engaged*, why wasn't he on his way to Mercy's college right now? "How long did the roommate say she'd been gone?"

"Two days."

"Two days? And you're not worried?"

"Look," he said, his manner that of a professor explaining a problem to a particularly obtuse student. "I suspect the roommate is covering for Mercedes. I wouldn't be surprised to learn there's some boy involved. If I went storming out there, it would only embarrass her. Libby and I have always tried to honor her independence."

Sam tried to remember how old Mercy was. Eighteen? Honoring independence was one thing, but what if Mercedes needed him? What if she was hurt?

A memory, long forgotten, surfaced.

It is after three in the morning. Sam is curled up in the corner of the upstairs landing, eavesdropping, although her parents believe she is asleep. At first their voices are soft and Sam has to strain to hear, but the talk quickly turns heated and now she can clearly hear both of their voices, raised in anger.

Her father wants to call the police. He is certain Libby has been involved in an accident and is at this moment lying in a hospital. Or worse, he says. (Sam won't allow herself to even consider what worse *could mean. The thought of Libby hurt or in the hospital makes her shiver; she hugs herself tighter.)*

"For all we know," her father continues, "she could be kidnapped."

"For heaven's sake, Peter," her mother says. "Don't be so dramatic. Why would anyone kidnap Elizabeth?"

Sam wants to go down to the living room and bury herself in her father's arms. She wants him to tell her that Libby is all right, but she stays on the landing. She knows if she goes downstairs, they will only tell her to go back to bed.

Her father wants to call the police, but her mother insists they wait until morning. In a tight voice Sam hardly recognizes, her mother says that Elizabeth is probably shacked up at some motel with one of the boys who's been sniffing around ever since Libby turned fifteen.

Shacked up. Sniffing around. Sam can't believe this is her mother speaking.

"If you call the police," her mother continues, "the entire town will know your daughter is a tramp. Is that what you want?"

Sam presses back against the wall of the stairwell, her mother's cruel words stuck in her chest, as if she has swallowed a twig. She waits for her father to insist on calling the police, but he caves to their mother's will.

In the morning, Libby comes home. She is grounded for a month but whispers to Sam that it was worth every minute.

"Look," Richard said. "Mercedes is an adult and she has her own life. We need to respect that."

Sam wondered if Libby would agree. She looked around the kitchen as if searching for clues, something that would tell her about her sister's inner life.

"Right now," Richard went on, "I am more concerned about Libby. Her last dialysis session was on Wednesday."

"So she's missed a session."

He nodded.

"How dangerous is that?"

"It depends," he said.

"On what?"

"On what she's been eating. I spoke to a nurse at the dialysis center and she said if Libby has been following her diet and limiting her liquids, one missed appointment isn't critical. I'm waiting for the nephrologist to return my call now." He checked his watch again. "Listen, why don't I go and get your luggage?"

"I thought I'd get a room in a motel. I don't want to put you to any trouble."

"Of course you'll stay here."

She handed him her car keys and he went out to bring in her luggage.

"Anything you need?" he asked when he returned with her bag. "Are you hungry?"

"Not right now."

"Will you be all right if I go out for a bit?"

She nodded. "Of course. You go and I'll stay here by the phone." She imagined he was going to drive around, canvass the town, look for Libby's car.

He scribbled down a number. "If you hear anything, you can reach me on my cell phone."

She took the paper.

He checked his watch again. "I'll be back in two hours at the most. We're usually finished no later than nine."

She raised an eyebrow in question.

"A rehearsal," he explained. "We have a concert next Sunday."

"Your wife and daughter are missing and you're going to a rehearsal?"

"What would you like me to do? Shall I put my life and job on hold because Elizabeth has decided to take off?"

"Under the circumstances, maybe you should."

Richard gave her a hard look. "Isn't it a little late and out of character for you to be flying in here and putting on the concerned sister act?"

"I am concerned. A hell of a lot more concerned than you seem to be."

"You're no one to be judging anyone, Samantha. You weren't here when Elizabeth needed you. You certainly had no compunction about cutting her out of your life because you didn't get your way."

"My way?"

"She told me how you cut her out of your life because she chose not to pay for your training. She wanted more for you, you know. She wanted you to live up to your potential and she thought you could be more than a cook."

"That's what she told you?"

"Yes."

"Just to set the record straight, not that I care what you think, but first of all I'm not a cook, I'm a pastry chef—"

He waved his hand wearily. "Whatever."

"And second, that wasn't what our fight was about."

"Let's forget it," Richard said. "It's beside the point now." He picked up his car keys and headed for the door. "I'll be back by nine. Call me if you hear anything."

Sam watched from the front window as he backed out of the drive. She wondered if he really had a rehearsal or was going to the woman Libby had seen him with. It was not her business, she said to herself. Nothing that happened here was. But it wasn't that simple. Libby was in trouble. And who knew what the story was with Mercedes.

She returned to the kitchen and poured another cup of coffee. The wall clock said it was nearly seven, which would make it eight on the East Coast.

Lee didn't pick up on his cell and no one answered at either his house or the boatyard. Finally she called Stacy's number. Carl answered and she held on while he turned down a ball game that blared in the background.

"It's Sam," she said. "Can I talk to Stacy?"

"She's not here. She's over at your place tonight. She's working on some wedding cake."

Sam had completely forgotten about the Chaney wedding. She dialed her own number. Stacy picked up on the second ring.

"Hey," Stacy said. "How'd you track me down? Let me guess? You called Carl, right?"

"Right. Is he angry 'cause you're working at night?"

"Are you kidding? He's thrilled to have me out of the house while he's watching the damn game. He gets mad because I root for the team with the cutest uniforms and the best butts."

Sam smiled. "How are you doing? Everything okay?"

"Not to worry. We've got it all under control."

"We?" Now Sam could hear other voices, music.

"My crew," Stacy said. "Wait a minute. Someone wants to talk to you."

"Hello, dear."

"Alice?" Why in the world had Stacy called Lee's mother? "Is everything okay?"

"Everything's fine here," Alice said. "You should see the cake. You'd be proud of Stacy."

"It's done already?" The last-minute assembly should have waited until tomorrow.

Alice laughed. "She made a practice cake, the smart girl." She added something, but the words were muffled.

"What?"

"There's someone else here who wants to speak to you. Hold on."

"Hey," Lee said.

"You're there, too? What's going on?" Sam asked. "Are you having a party or what?"

"Just giving Stacy a hand," Lee said. "Not that she needs it. She's doing a terrific job. In fact, I think you're going to have to consider giving her a raise."

Stacy said something in the background that Sam couldn't catch, and she heard Alice laugh.

"God," Sam said. "I'm sorry she bothered Alice."

"Here," Lee said. "I'm going to hand the phone back to her and let you try and tell her that."

"Tell me what?" Alice said.

"I'm sorry," Sam said. "I had no idea Stacy would call you. I told her to call Tricia Nelson."

"Are you kidding?" Alice said. "I'm having the time of my life. We've sent out for Chinese and I'm in charge of cleanup."

Lee got back on the phone. "See," he said. "She would be insulted if she wasn't here to help."

There were more muffled words in the background.

"Alice said to tell you that's what a mother's for," he said.

Sam let the words spill over her. *What a mother's for.* A wave of loss for her own mother washed over Sam, taking her by surprise.

"How are things out there?" Lee asked, bringing her back.

"Where do you want me to start?" She took a deep breath.

"Problems?"

"Libby has disappeared."

"Disappeared?" Lee echoed.

"That's just the start of it. It appears that my brother-in-law is having an affair, and my niece is missing from her dorm. In fact, she's been gone for two days, not that Richard seems overly concerned."

"Where is he now?"

"He's gone to a rehearsal."

"Let me get this straight. Your sister and your niece are missing and your brother-in-law is at a rehearsal?"

"You got it."

She heard Lee exhale. "I'm coming out," he said.

"No, really. There's no need. There's nothing you could do here. I'll keep you informed."

"I love you."

"Love you, too."

After she hung up, she roamed the house, finding memories everywhere: her mother's china cabinet in the dining room and her silver tea set on the sideboard, a collection of blown-glass paperweights that had been in the family, a pair of chairs that Sam remembered Libby had caned herself.

Shortly after nine, Richard returned. "Anyone call?" he asked.

"No. So how was rehearsal?" She didn't try to ease the sharpness in her voice.

He took her question seriously. "Not as good as it should be at this point. The concert is a week from Sunday. It's a Brahms piece. Difficult."

Sam remembered Libby once telling her that all Richard really cared about was his music. She had thought her sister was exaggerating, but now she believed her.

"I'm going to have a glass of brandy," Richard said. "Can I get you one?"

She knew brandy would mean she wouldn't sleep well, but she nodded.

He was pouring when the phone rang. The liquor slopped over the top of the snifter, dripped on his hand—the first sign he'd given that he was not as calm as he appeared.

"Hello?" he said.

Sam listened openly.

"She is? Should I come now?" There was a long pause while he listened to the caller. "In the morning then," he said. "If you're sure." There was another pause. Then he said, "Oh, will you give her a message? Tell her that her sister is here. Yes. Samantha. Here. At the house."

After he hung up, he poured the other glass of brandy. Sam waited.

"That was a friend of ours," he said as he handed her a glass. "Libby's safe. I'll get her in the morning." He headed into the living room.

Sam followed. "Not tonight?" she said.

If he heard her, he gave no indication. He knelt before the sound system, pushed buttons, adjusted a knob. Music flowed into the room.

Sam turned and walked away. She carried the brandy up to the room where Richard had left her bag. The sound of a string quartet floated up the stairs and she closed the door to shut it out. She thought about Lee and Alice and Stacy sitting in her kitchen, eating Chinese takeout and working on a wedding cake. She would have given anything to be back with them. It was a mistake to have come to Illinois.

Libby

. . . .

*B*y the time Libby arrived at Gabe's, a light drizzle was falling. If the temperature dropped another ten degrees, there would be snow. A pickup truck occupied the narrow drive, so she parked on the street. The bungalow had a wide front porch with window boxes filled with frost-killed geraniums. A screen was still in the combination door; soon the weather would call for a storm insert. A bench fashioned of twigs and tree limbs occupied one side of the porch, and she knew without being told that Gabe had made it.

Almost as soon as she rang the bell, the porch light flicked on and the door opened. On the way over, she had practiced what she was going to say, but now nothing seemed right.

Gabe opened the door. A greyhound, so old her muzzle was nearly white, bounced over and pressed her head against Libby's leg.

"Don't mind Lulu," Gabe said. "She has to check out everyone."

Libby found her voice. "I'm sorry. I know you've got your own troubles, but I didn't know where else to go."

"That's all right," he said. He didn't ask for an explanation. She had the sense that if she'd showed up with an entire Girl Scout troop, he wouldn't have been caught off balance. "Come on in."

The living room was large. It had once been two rooms; Libby could see where the wall had been knocked down and a supporting beam set in. The east-facing window was filled with spider plants and flowering hibiscus. Oversize oil paintings covered the walls. The largest of them depicted a forest with trees composed of human torsos. It might have been grotesque but was lyrical, lovely, powerful.

The room was sparsely furnished. Futon couch, platform rocker, morris chair. Unpainted planks for a bookcase. Early-marriage decorating, Libby thought, a stage of skimping, of castoffs from parents and cheap casseroles, that she and Richard had never gone through. She wondered now if it would have made a difference if they'd had to struggle. Would it have made them closer, more prepared to weather hard times?

She sank into the morris chair. Lulu plunked down at her feet, licked her hand.

"She misses Hannah," Gabe said. "She tolerates me, but she's really Hannah's. She's a rescued greyhound. Hannah says as soon as she gets well, we're getting another one."

"How is Hannah?"

Gabe looked off, focusing for a moment on a place he alone could see. "They tell me things don't look hopeful," he said. "So much is going wrong at once."

"I'm so sorry," she said. Sorry. A feeble, empty word in the face of such pain.

"Her parents are with her now. We've been taking turns. They'll call if there's any change." He drew a deep breath. "The nurses tell us she's unresponsive, but this afternoon, when I was holding her hand and talking to her, I swear I felt her fingers tighten on mine. No one understands what a fighter she is. Hannah won't give up."

There was so much hope on his face, Libby had to look away. She thought about hearing Hannah's voice in the motel corridor and wondered if she should tell Gabe, then decided against it. "I shouldn't have come."

"No, I'm glad you did. Really. Hannah would be glad, too."

She sniffed the air. "I'm not sure but I think something's burning," she said.

"Jesus," he said, bounding from the room. "I was frying up some bacon and eggs when you came."

Alone in the room, Libby remained pinned in the chair by the weight of the greyhound, who now lay across her feet. From the kitchen she heard sounds of a window being opened, water running in a sink. She looked around the room, settled her gaze on a stack of books piled on the side table, saw they were poetry. Donald Hall. Sharon Olds. Richard Wilbur. Marianne Moore. Auden. Neruda. She remembered how Gabe had recited poetry the other day on the prairie.

She picked up the Neruda. *Twenty Love Poems and a Song of Despair.* When she opened it she saw Gabe's name written in firm script on the inside cover. She turned to the final poem; her eyes fell on a phrase: "Sadness stunned you."

The great poets always got it right. That was exactly what sadness did. It stupefied and stunned one.

"You like Neruda?" Gabe said. He was holding a cup.

"You'd have to be in a coma not to," Libby said and could have slit her tongue.

"He's Hannah's favorite." He handed her the dish. "Applesauce," he said. "That should be okay for you."

She swallowed, her throat suddenly tight, and took the cup.

"How many have you missed?" he asked.

"Pardon?"

"How many treatments have you missed?"

She wondered how he knew. "One," she said. "This morning."

She hadn't thought she was hungry but the applesauce was cool in her throat and she ate it all.

Saying nothing, he watched her until she finished.

"Does Richard know you're here?"

She shook her head.

"You should let him know. I'm sure he's worried."

"Do you want me to go?"

He shook his head.

She relaxed. The old greyhound pressed closer against her legs. She could feel the warmth through her pant leg.

"You need to call Richard."

"Will you?" she said.

She gave him the number and listened as he told Richard where she was, that she was all right.

"He's going to come and get you in the morning," Gabe said after he hung up.

"Did he say anything else?"

"He was relieved to know that you're safe," he said.

Libby nodded. What had she expected of Richard? That he'd insist on coming over? That he'd fly to her rescue?

"Oh," Gabe continued. "He also wanted me to tell you that your sister's here."

"Samantha?"

"Yes. He said to tell you she's here. At your house."

Libby was shocked into silence.

Sam

. . . .

*T*he guest room was at the far end of the upstairs hall and was considerably larger than Sam's bedroom at home. It was decorated in lilac and white with accents of green—Libby's favorite colors, Sam remembered suddenly—and held a king-size bed. Action beds, Lee called them. A wash of longing came over her and she would have called him right then, just for the comfort of hearing his voice, but she held back. If she phoned again she knew he would insist on flying out. It was ridiculous, this foreboding she had about Lee meeting Libby. This was Lee, for God's sake, her Lee, but she couldn't rationalize the fear away.

She wandered into the guest bathroom, investigated the miniature mauve bottles amassed in a basket on the vanity. Shampoo, bath gel, conditioner, body lotion. There was a gray stone dish on a shelf by the sink holding an oval of soap tied in twine, a sprig of dried lavender caught in the knot. She could picture Libby picking the herb, tying the twine. There was a stack of towels, soft as velvet. So unlike the rough, line-dried towels of their childhood.

—

Can't you put them in the dryer? Libby begs. I should say not, their mother says. Do you know how much electricity a dryer uses? Well, I'll always dry mine in a dryer when I grow up, Libby says.

In the medicine cabinet Sam found toothpaste and dental floss, a toothbrush still in cellophane, a small bottle of mouthwash, an aerosol container of shaving cream, and a new razor. Behind the door, there was an oversize terry robe hanging on a brass hook. Trust Libby to think of everything. There were tony hotels that weren't this well appointed.

Sam hadn't planned for a long visit and it took her little time to unpack her one bag. Ordinarily on trips she lived out of her suitcase, but under the influence of Libby's immaculate home, she put her things away in the closet and dresser, neatly, as if later there would be an inspection.

She found the booklets in the second drawer of the dresser. "Your Kidney Transplant—Every Step of the Way" was the title of the first. The second, smaller one was "Kidney Transplantation: Information for Potential Living Donors." Sam's first reaction was anger. How like Libby, she thought, to put them where I was bound to find them. Cynthia's words echoed: *I hope she hasn't guilt-tripped you into being tested.* But then she realized she was being paranoid. Libby'd had no idea she was coming.

Just the titles made Sam queasy. She shoved the booklets back in the drawer, out of sight, then stripped down for a shower. The shower-head was as big as a skillet and she turned her face up to the stream of water, letting the warmth of it relax her. The scent of the bath soap was familiar. Definitely herbal. Not lavender. Rosemary. That was it. Expensive, she was certain. Nothing but the best for Libby.

Like the bed linens, she thought minutes later as she slipped between the sheets. Probably eight hundred count. Was there such a thing? She lay in the dark, enfolded by the luxury of her sister's life. An old ember of anger glowed. Libby had everything, why hadn't that been enough? Why had she needed to take the only thing Sam had?

She took a deep breath—it was supposed to help but never did— and waited in the stillness for sleep. But it wasn't really still, for

208 • Anne LeClaire

silence never was, and sounds rose up, infiltrating the quiet. The creaking of a floorboard, the faint melody of Richard's music floating up from the living room, and, in counterpoint to it, a distant train whistle and the rhythmic rolling of wheels on tracks. She remembered seeing the depot in the center of town, a picturesque station that looked like part of a children's game. She listened to the wheels circling on and on in the distance, endlessly. She recalled Libby once saying that the train from Wisconsin to Chicago was one of the longest in the nation. She wondered if that was true.

Once Sam had believed Libby's every word was gospel, but that was another time, back when she trusted her sister, when she thought Libby would lie to anyone but never to her. She thought about the story Libby had made up to explain their estrangement to Richard, and a flush of anger heated her chest. Wouldn't she like to just storm down the stairs and hand him the flat-out truth. Sleep now impossible, she sat up and flicked on the bedside lamp.

It had been a huge mistake to come. She would leave in the morning. Or the afternoon, she decided. After she had seen Libby. She supposed she owed her at least that.

Downstairs, the music shifted, grew louder, tempestuous, near violent. Sam listened for a moment, then, as if in some way propelled by the music and deprived of all will, she got up and crossed to the dresser, opened the second drawer. *What are you doing?* a voice in her head demanded. The booklets were glossy, in full color. "Now I know that dreams do come true," declared a cover quote on "Your Kidney Transplant—Every Step of the Way." She picked up the other booklet, the one intended for donors, and returned to the bed. She scanned the table of contents—"Effects of Kidney Donation," "Initial Evaluation," "Making the Decision," "Hospitalization for Donation Surgery," "Recovery"—then flipped to the introduction. She read the first paragraph:

> This book is intended to provide some answers for you as you consider donating one of your kidneys to a loved one who has lost their kidney function and is facing dialysis treatment. Presently, a kidney transplant is the best chance for rehabilitation and long-term survival.

The print swam before her and she had to close her eyes. *Long-term survival.* Until that moment, reading those words, Sam had not allowed herself to believe Libby was seriously ill. It had not seemed real.

She swallowed past the burning in her throat. The bedside extension rang and the booklet fell from her fingers. Libby? Mercedes? On the second ring, she reached over and lifted the receiver. She held her breath and listened. Richard's voice. And a woman's. The doctor getting back to him about Libby? She should hang up. She pressed the receiver to her ear.

"Sorry I'm calling so late," the woman said, "but I was concerned about Elizabeth. We were all so worried when she wasn't at the center today. Is she all right?"

"She's fine," Richard said.

Fine? What planet was he from?

"Well, no need to bother her if she's sleeping," the woman continued. "Just tell her Eleanor called. And tell her Jesse wanted her to know the prayer group put her in the circle tonight and that they're praying for her."

Sam set the receiver back on the cradle. If the caller had said the tooth fairy was thinking of Libby, Sam couldn't have been more astonished. Had illness made her sister turn to religion? Sam supposed that wasn't unusual. But Libby? Libby the Irreverent? The religious renegade?

A memory surfaced, sweeping her back.

She is eleven, Libby thirteen.

She waits while Libby tells their mother they are going to visit one of Libby's friends—a brazen lie, told with a guileless face. Sam doesn't know how her sister does this. Their mother always knows when Sam is fibbing.

"Come on," Libby calls over her shoulder once they are out of sight of the house. "We're going to be late."

At St. Martin's Cemetery they chain their bikes to the rail fence. While Sam waits, Libby slips off her backpack and takes out a pair of two-inch heels, so new the black soles are perfectly smooth. She removes her sneakers and puts on the new shoes, then hides the backpack behind a grave marker. On the next grave, a statue of Mary looms, sorrow on her face, as if she knows exactly what they are up to. Sam's narrow shoulders slump with the weight of guilt and fear.

In the short time it takes to reach the wide granite steps of the church, she begs Libby to change her mind. "What if we see someone we know?" she pleads, near tears. Her protests are useless, as they always are when Libby has her mind set. This is all the fault of that stupid, stupid Janice McKenney.

The stone church is larger than the Congregational church they attend on occasional Sundays and on Christmas and Easter holidays, the front door so massive it takes both of them to open it. They step into a hollow of cold air and stand for a moment, as if waiting for instructions. Sam expects a hand to grip her shoulder. She would not be surprised to hear a disembodied voice demand that they leave. And she wants to go, truly she does, but Libby grabs her arm and marches them straight inside.

"It smells funny," Sam whispers, but Libby shushes her, tells her it's only incense. Sam thinks her sister has said "incensed," a word her mother uses when she is really angry, and her stomach gives a little jump. If Libby didn't still have hold of her arm, she would bolt for sure.

Midway down the aisle, Libby chooses a pew and slides in. An old woman, who smells like wet wool and bacon, moves over, making room for them. Libby nods her thanks, but the woman is now kneeling on a narrow wooden bench and Libby quickly kneels, too. But within minutes they are back sitting on the pew, and just as Sam is settling in, everyone stands. It is so confusing, it gives Sam a headache—standing, kneeling, sitting, making the sign of the cross. She thinks people are looking at them, but Libby pays no attention.

At last comes the part of the service Libby has been waiting for. Pew by pew, people stand, slide out to the center aisle, and file to the front. Libby pushes Sam into the line and they take their place, inching forward toward the priest.

Sam hates Janice McKenney. Stupid, know-it-all Janice McKenney who acts like she's Boss of the World and is totally responsible for their being here.

"The Communion wafer is the actual body of Christ," Janice told Libby one day on the way home from school. "If you chew it, it's as if you are biting into the flesh of Jesus."

"It's just chunks of Wonder bread," Libby had replied, but Sam could tell by the way Libby held her mouth that Janice's superior attitude was getting to her sister.

"That's all you know," Janice said. "Anyway, you can't take Communion in our church because you aren't Catholic."

"I can so," Libby said.

"It's a sin," Janice repeated firmly. "Everyone knows that."

Why didn't Libby just laugh in her face? For a fact, Libby didn't even like to go to church. She could have cared less about stupid things like Communion. But of course she wouldn't walk away. She never did. Their mother said Libby was born with her fists raised.

"I could if I wanted to," Libby told Janice, "and you couldn't stop me."

"That's all you know," Janice said. "It would be a sin."

"So what if I did?"

"The nuns told us," Janice said, her voice filled with importance. "Flames would shoot out of your shoes."

That was all Libby needed to hear.

So here they stand, within a few feet of a stern-faced priest who is passing out wafers that are "the actual body of Christ," a priest who will surely see immediately they are not Catholic. Sam hasn't wet her pants in years, but she is afraid she will now. She wonders if the priest will call their parents. Or the police.

Libby goes first. Sam can hardly bear to watch. Her sister raises her head. She pokes out her tongue, way out like when the doctor says to say aah. Her face is clear of guilt, just as it is when she tells her mother a lie. The priest places a wafer on Libby's tongue.

Sam drops her eyes to her sister's feet. Flames would shoot out of your shoes. Libby is tapping her toe. Just by the tick-tick-ticking of the shoe tip against the floor, Sam can tell her sister is smiling.

Now the priest is in front of Sam. She presses her lips tight. She'd rather swallow dog doo than take the body of Christ into her mouth. Libby tugs at her sleeve, sharply. The priest looks at her, waiting, just the edge of impatience showing around his mouth.

The wafer is thin as skin and dry, not like the little squares of soft bread the deacons pass out at the Congregational church. It sticks to the roof of Sam's mouth. She tries to dislodge it with her tongue, afraid she will chew it by mistake. Biting into the flesh of Christ. When they are back in their pew and she thinks no one will notice, she tries to dislodge it with her finger.

"Flames will shoot out of your shoes," Libby says later as they unhitch their bikes from the fence, her voice all spooky and deep, like a cartoon witch, and then she starts to laugh. Sam looks around to see if anyone has heard.

"Just remember," Libby says in her regular voice as she straddles the banana seat on her bike. "Everything anyone tells you about this stuff is a bunch of crap."

The sorrowful gaze of Mary follows them as they peddle off down the street.

Sam hadn't thought about that day in years. She could still taste the sawdust dryness of the wafer in her mouth, could still recall her terror as she waited for fire to spark out from the toes of Libby's black shoes.

When she was in high school, she had told her mother about what Janice had told them would happen if they took Communion and how she and Libby had done exactly that.

"Oh, well, Catholics," her mother had said, rolling her eyes.

Now Libby was in a prayer group. Go figure.

Once Sam had thought she knew everything about her sister. She knew Libby liked garlic, but not onions, and that she would do absolutely anything on a dare. She was the first person who knew about Libby's secret book and the poetry she wrote on its pages. And—two months before the twins were born—Sam was the one Libby had confided in and told she wasn't sure she really wanted children.

Now Sam didn't know the first thing about her sister. Except this. The girl she had been wasn't the woman she had become.

She replaced the booklet in the dresser drawer, turned out the light, and tried to sleep.

In the morning, Sam woke earlier than usual, but Richard was already up, the coffee made.

"Eggs or cereal?" he asked as he handed her a mug.

She shook her head. "Just coffee."

"You sure? No juice? Or toast? There's English muffins, too. You should have something."

"Toast," she said.

"Rye or wheat or white?"

What was this, a short-order restaurant? "Wheat. I can get it."

But he was already putting a slice in the toaster. He cupped his hand along the counter, brushing up stray crumbs, dropping them in the sink. There was something so . . . so *contained* about him that it set her teeth on edge, provoked her.

"So who did she see you with?" she asked.

"Who?"

"Libby. Last night you said she saw something she *misunder-*

stood." Sam emphasized the word. "Something that made her run off."

For a moment she thought he wasn't going to reply. He got out a plate for her toast, took butter from the refrigerator. She waited.

"I was giving a student a private lesson in the chapel," he said finally. "Libby misinterpreted what she saw."

"Misinterpreted," Sam said.

He flushed.

"What was it she *misinterpreted*?" she pushed.

The toast popped up and he buttered it, placed it before her. "I was helping a student with her bowing," he said. "I had my arms around her. Libby saw this and jumped to a conclusion. She wouldn't wait for me to explain."

Sam tried to picture the scene. "Why would Libby jump to that conclusion?"

He didn't answer.

She understood then. "Because it happened before," she said in a flat voice.

"Once." He looked straight at her. "Only once. A long time ago."

"When?"

He stared at the ceiling, as if history were written there. "Six years ago."

"Six years ago?"

"It was a mistake. I apologized." He leaned forward. "No matter what you think, I don't make a practice of getting involved with my students."

"You wouldn't be the first who did," she said. "It's not exactly an original situation, is it?"

"Well, I don't."

He folded the newspapers that were scattered on the table, set them on the floor by the back door.

"What did Libby do?" Sam asked.

He sighed. "Just what she's doing now. She took off. Left me and went to visit you. That was the time the two of you had the fight. The one about you becoming a cook."

A chef, Sam thought, a pastry chef, but did not bother correcting him. What was the point?

"Surely you remember," Richard went on. "That was the time you stopped speaking to her and cut her out of your life."

The tangled web of deception, Sam thought, then wondered why Libby had never said anything to her about it. So Richard had cheated on her. It still didn't justify what she had done.

Richard dumped the rest of his coffee down the sink. "It's getting late. We'd better get going."

We? "You want me to come with you, then?"

She had expected him to go alone to pick up Libby. She had thought she would have more time, time to get prepared.

"I thought you'd want to," he said. He waited at the door while she got her coat.

Libby

. . . .

*L*ibby dreamed someone was scratching at her door. Someone *was* at the door. It took a moment for her to orient herself, to recall that she was at Gabe's. She rolled over and pulled the covers over her head, like a child who doesn't want to go to school, which was exactly what she felt like. She didn't want to face any of the day that waited for her. Not Richard. Not Samantha. Let them go away. Let the two of them run off together—there was a certain ironic justice in the thought. Yes, let them disappear together and take Richard's cello-playing girl toy with them. She would stay here, move in with Gabe and Hannah.

The scratching continued—obliterating her daydream—and she surrendered and got up to open the door. Lulu bounded in, swishing her tail and barking. Libby could have sworn the greyhound was smiling—just the kind of thing pet owners were always saying. Dogs did not smile.

The greyhound pressed into her, licking her hand and sniffing at her gown. Smelling Hannah, Libby realized. Last night, Gabe had given her one of Hannah's nightgowns to sleep in, and although it had been freshly laundered, the fabric carried a sweet odor that was Hannah's scent. Libby's own body smelled odd this morning, metallic. Her mouth tasted like old pennies. The ever-present headache tightened its band around her forehead.

She padded down the hall. The greyhound followed her, trailed her right into the bathroom, then circled several times in some doggy ritual before collapsing on the bath mat. Libby stripped, stepped over the dog and into the shower. She dressed again in her badly wrinkled clothes—the third day she had worn them. She applied lipstick, the only makeup she carried in her purse, and pushed at her damp hair with her fingers, trying to fashion it in some sort of style. She looked a wreck. Her face was bloated. The last time Sam had seen her she was fit, thin, her hair highlighted. Well, her sister would find some satisfaction in seeing her now at her worst.

She descended to the kitchen, Lulu at her heels. There was a note from Gabe on the table telling her he had gone to the hospital. To Hannah. He said Richard had called earlier and would be along to pick her up and had emphasized that she was not to drive herself. Underlined. Beneath the note was the slim volume of Neruda's poems. *Twenty Love Poems and a Song of Despair.* A yellow Post-it was affixed to the cover. "For you," he had written. "Remember, love always outweighs despair. Gabe."

Did it? Libby wasn't so sure.

She stood at a front window, watching for Richard, although she was perfectly capable of driving herself. She slid her fingers over the access shunt and checked for the rushing sensation that let her know the blood was still flowing. This precise sensation was known as a *thrill*, Carlotta had told her. "The thrill is gone," Libby sang. At her feet, the dog thumped her tail against the floor. But the thrill—at least the one Carlotta meant—wasn't gone. Her blood hummed along beneath her fingertips, proof that the access wasn't clogged, proof she was alive.

She missed the moment Richard parked at the curb. By the time she saw him, he was already coming around the front of the Volvo, opening the passenger door. Sam stepped out. A queer mixture of excitement and anxiety rose in Libby's chest. She swallowed, felt the weight of the greyhound against her ankle, and was surprised to find comfort in it and more surprised when she stooped and gave the dog a quick hug. Then she opened the door and stepped out.

Dried moths littered the porch floor like confetti and their brittle bodies crunched beneath her shoes as she crossed to Sam.

"You came," she said in a dry voice.

"Yes."

There might have been more, but Richard was there, telling her they were late. Carlotta had arranged for a special dialysis session, not wanting to wait until the scheduled one on Monday. The staff was waiting for them at the center. He dictated arrangements. Libby would ride with him. Samantha would follow, driving Libby's car.

"No need," Libby said. "I can drive my own car. I'm perfectly fine." Except for the headache. Except for the fact that her kidneys had shut down. Except that her heart was aching.

Richard insisted, and it was easier to give in than to fight. She had no fight left in her. He pulled out onto the street. Through the back window, Libby watched Sam follow.

"When did she arrive?" she asked.

"Yesterday."

"Did you know she was coming?"

"No. She just showed up."

"Just like that?"

"Yes."

He flicked on a turn signal, slowed after the turn, checked to make sure Sam was behind them.

"She looks good," Libby said.

He concentrated on driving, said nothing.

"Doesn't she?" she pressed. "Doesn't she look good?"

"I guess," he said.

"She looks"—she searched for the word—"happy. She looks happy." She waited for him to comment, but he remained silent. He needed a haircut, she noticed. In the back, at his neck, hair curled over his collar. There were slight pouches beneath his eyes. Good. She hoped that was the beginning, that jowls would follow, and nose hairs, and droplets of egg yolk on his cuffs.

"Elizabeth," he said, turning to her. "Libby. I want—"

"No," she cut him off. "I don't want to talk about it. Not now."

Later, of course, they would have to. There were decisions to be made.

When they arrived at the center, she spoke before he could even switch off the ignition. "Go home," she said. "There's no sense in both of you staying here. Sam can stay."

"Are you sure?"

She thought he looked relieved. "Yes. Positive."

"Well, then." He paused. "Call if you need me."

She waited by the door while Sam parked and then they walked in together. The Saturday staff was unfamiliar to Libby. She had never seen the charge nurse before; he was a short black man named Everett. She left her handbag with Sam and followed him into the exam room. She got on the scale, watched while he slid the pound marker along the bar. She'd gained weight. He opened her folder and made a note. She sat on the edge of the table while he read over her chart.

"You missed yesterday's appointment?" he asked.

"Yes."

He picked up the blood pressure cuff and strapped it on, pumped the bulb, then released it.

"Your pressure's high," he told her.

"Bad?"

"Higher than your chart shows you've been running. Any blurred vision? Nausea? Vomiting?"

She shook her head.

"Itching?"

"No." Well, there had been a little, but Libby was sure it was nothing more than dry skin.

"What about headaches? Any trouble there?"

"A little." Like constant.

He made a note in the chart, then set the folder down. His fingers were softer than she had expected and he took more time with the exam than Kelly did. He was gentle as he palpated her neck, her stomach, her thighs and ankles. "There's fluid buildup," he said.

There was a sharp rap on the door. Clare Anderson came in. Libby hadn't seen the social worker since their appointment after her first session, although she had been in touch twice by phone. "We need to talk," Clare said.

"It'll have to wait," Everett told her. "I want to get Mrs. Barnett started."

She sat in a different bay, surrounded by unfamiliar faces. She missed Eleanor and Jesse. She missed Hannah.

"You're still using the catheter?" Everett asked.

"For one more week."

He lifted her forearm and checked the site of the shunt.

After he inserted the tubes in the catheter, he asked if she was feeling all right.

"I'm a little cold," she said.

Everett ambled off. When he returned he carried a blanket. He tucked it around her. His kindness reminded her of Gabe.

Clare appeared, pulled a chair close. "What you did was dangerous. I'm not going to lecture you. Some people don't adjust well to dialysis. I understand. But it's your best hope now. You have to stay compliant."

"I know."

"You took a chance. Your blood pressure is up, fluids are up, that's hard on the body, on your heart."

"Okay." So much for forgoing the lecture.

"I know Dr. Hayes has you on a donor list. One of the things that is of concern when you are considered for transplantation is whether you've been compliant with dialysis." Compliant. A good little soldier. "They figure that if you aren't, there's a good chance that you won't follow procedure after transplant. That you're not a good risk. Capeesh?"

Libby nodded.

"I know this isn't easy. But we need you on the team, committed."

"Okay."

"You look tired," Clare said. She patted Libby's knee. "I'll let you get some rest. Is there anything you need?"

"My sister came with me today. She's out in the waiting room."

"You want me to get her?"

"Her name's Samantha. It's her first time here."

"I'm on my way," Clare said.

Libby saw Sam before her sister saw her. She looked afraid and ready to bolt. Libby could sympathize.

Sam came to Libby's station. She kept her arms stiff and close to her sides. "God," she said, the word coming out in an exhalation.

"You don't have to stay," Libby said.

"No. It's okay. Can I sit?"

"Of course."

Around them, machines beeped.

"So here we are," Libby said after a minute.

"Yes."

"You look good."

"You, too."

"Yes. Well."

Six years. A bridge too large to span? Anna Rauh once had told the class that some poems couldn't be fixed, that it was best just to toss them. Was that true of relationships? Were there some that could not be fixed?

"It's been a long time," Libby said. "Josh tells me you're successful."

Sam shrugged. "I do all right."

"He told me you got divorced."

"I'm sure there was no surprise there."

"Still. I'm sorry, Sam."

"Yes. Well. Probably for the best."

"Is there anyone now?"

Sam nodded.

"Someone good?"

"Yes." Her soft smile told Libby this was true.

"I'm glad."

Over at the nurses' station, a glass shattered and the explosion might have been a gunshot, the way they jumped. They watched while one of the technicians brought over a broom and dustpan.

"Afterwards," Sam said, "I broke glass."

"What?"

"After you left. After I threw Jay out. I broke glass." Libby still did not understand. "I was so angry." Sam's voice was soft; she watched the girl sweep up the glass. "I'd never been so furious. I didn't think I was capable of that kind of rage."

"I'm sorry," Libby said. "I wish we could have talked."

"I could understand how someone, some ordinary person, could be capable of murder. You know?" Sam continued without waiting for Libby to reply. "I drove out to a construction site in Fairhaven. It wasn't spur of the moment. I planned ahead. Wore gloves, brought a bag of rocks with me."

"Rocks?"

"To throw at the windows. To break glass."

Libby stared at her.

"I broke every window in the place. I didn't know what else to do."

"God, Sam."

"It was a big house. One of those new trophy places every millionaire with a small dick is building. Double-hungs. French sliders. Skylights. There had to be at least seventy of them. Maybe more. I wasn't counting."

Libby was speechless.

"I can't tell you how gratifying, how *satisfying* the sound of it was. All that glass shattering. When I was finished, I drove home as if I'd done nothing more than run to the corner store for a quart of milk. I remember . . ." Her voice turned dreamy. "I remember looking in the mirror and not even recognizing myself. I looked like an animal. A tiger or something. Powerful. Of course, later I felt horrible. I was actually sick about it. I wanted to send the contractor a check for damages. God knows what they were. But I was afraid if I sent a bank check or money order there would be a way it could be traced to me. I was terrified I'd be caught. That someone had seen my car there or something. I was afraid I'd be arrested and it would be in all the papers: 'Sippican Pastry Chef Jailed for Vandalism.' "

Libby couldn't help it, she started to laugh.

"What?" Sam said.

"You," Libby said, laughing harder. "Miss Goody Two-shoes. Miss Never-Skip-School. Breaking all those windows."

Sam started laughing, too. Other patients stared at them now, but they were beyond stopping, hysterical.

There was a warning, the quick flash of something not right, then the first cramp took hold. It seized her calf muscle, just as it had when she was pregnant and she'd have to jump out of bed in the middle of the night and put weight on her leg, trying to release it. Then the pain was everywhere, gripping every muscle, every cell. Her fingers curled in spasm. The alarm on her machine sounded. Everett was there at once, adjusting her saline solution, soothing her, stroking her shoulder, rubbing her shin, telling her to hold on. Through the curtain of pain, she heard someone telling Sam to go out to the waiting room. She opened her eyes and caught a glimpse of her sister's face contorted with terror.

It's okay. Libby tried to push the words out, to console Sam, but the pain robbed her of speech.

Sam and Libby

. . . .

*S*am pushed her way through the waiting room, out to the parking lot. The image of Libby—mouth a twist of agony, body one single spasm—burned beneath her eyelids. The alarm echoed in her ears. "Oh, God," she said, the words a sob. She doubled over, sucked air.

"Miss? Are you okay?"

A hand cupped her shoulder. "Take a couple of deep, gentle breaths. Easy now."

She forced herself to obey. Her breathing slowed, but not her heart, which thumped wildly beneath her ribs, a small animal bent on escape.

"Better now?" It was the black nurse who had cared for Libby.

She straightened up, turned to him. "My sister—" Words clotted in her throat. Again she heard the urgent ringing of the alarm, saw Libby in spasm. "Is she—?"

"She's fine," he said. "She's resting."

She searched his face for a lie. "Honest?"

"Cross my heart." He smiled warmly, then leaned over and picked up Libby's tote, which had slid off Sam's shoulder when she doubled over. He handed it to her.

"What happened in there?"

"Her saline levels went out of balance and she cramped up."

"Jesus. Does that happen often?"

"Occasionally. We've adjusted it. She's all right now."

"Really?"

"Why don't you go see for yourself?"

"Maybe in a minute." She felt the heat of shame, knowing she couldn't face it again. The buzzers and bells and people in green leather chaises hooked up to machines, blood running through tubes. She hadn't realized it was going to be anything like this. How could he bear to work here? How did people take these jobs? Like the technicians who euthanized stray animals. What kind of heart did you have to have? Incredibly hard? Or soft?

"I've got to get back," he said, and, taking her arm, he led her inside. She sank down on a chair in the waiting room, dimly aware of the curious stares from others.

"Can I get you anything?" he asked. "Water? Or we have some soda in the staff refrigerator. Ginger ale. Coke."

"No. No, but thanks."

The others in the room had come prepared for the long wait. A woman was knitting, several were reading. One—a young woman—sat nodding in time to music pouring into her ears from a headset. Sam didn't want water or Coke or something to pass the time. She wanted Lee. She clutched her hands in her lap to stop their trembling. She regretted leaving her cell back at the house. She needed to talk to him. She leaned over to a man seated on her left. "Excuse me," she said. "Do you know if there is a public phone around here?"

He shook his head. "If it's an emergency, they'll probably let you use the one at the desk."

"That's all right," Sam said. "No emergency."

She lifted the heft of Libby's tote, wondered if her sister carried a cell. Probably. Judging from the weight of the bag, it probably held just about everything but a vacuum cleaner, but knowing her sister, maybe that, too, one of those Dustbusters. She opened the flap.

A slender softcover book of poems lay on top. Poetry was Libby's thing; Sam had never gotten its appeal. Except for the simplest, most direct—Emily Dickinson, say—it was a language she couldn't decipher. Whenever she tried to read it, she just ended up feeling stupid. Libby had once tried to explain it to her, but even the words she used were maddening. Iambs. Trochees. Quatrains. Couplets.

Sam stared at the cover: A dark-haired man in profile, thin slash of an eyebrow, Roman nose, chin resting on cupped hand, was sitting by the bed of a sleeping woman whose hair was the same shade as Libby's. She read the title: *Twenty Love Poems and a Song of Despair.* There was a Post-it stuck to the inside of the cover and she read it before she realized it was personal. "Remember, love always outweighs despair. Gabe."

She slipped the book back into Libby's bag. It was none of her business if Libby had a lover, but still, the softening in her heart she'd felt toward Libby since the first second she'd seen her earlier that morning toughened.

She continued rooting through the bag in search of a phone and found a second book, also poetry. Was this from the mysterious Gabe as well? Inside, in purple ink, was stamped "Northampton Public Library, Northampton, Massachusetts." She turned back to the cover and read the title. *The Will to Change,* by Adrienne Rich. A door to memory opened and she recalled the monumental fuss this book—or rather its absence—had caused. At first there had been numerous calls from Mrs. Stinson, the librarian, informing their mother the book was weeks overdue and requesting its return. Libby had denied having it. Maybe you lost it, their mother had said, but no, Libby said, she'd never taken out the book at all. Mrs. Stinson's calls had been followed by a registered letter requesting payment for the book. It was the only registered letter Sam remembered ever being delivered to their home. Their father had written a check that night.

Sam considered the book. Why hadn't Libby just said she lost it? Why had she lied? Couldn't she have gone to a bookstore and bought a copy? Sam leafed through the pages. Then, on the inside of the back cover, she saw writing that she instantly recognized as Libby's.

Northern lights
Learn Latin

It was typical of Libby's poetry. The Northern lights learn Latin. It made no sense at all, but Sam continued to read.

Swim with the dolphins
Italy
Portugal
Attend a concert at St. Martin-in-the-Fields

Now Sam realized it was not poetry but some sort of list, evidently penned recently, since the ink had not faded. Things Libby had done, she supposed. Fuck my sister's husband, she thought. Her lips tightened. That should be there.

Hold my first grandchild

So, not things Libby had done. But what? Things she wanted to do?

Write a book of poetry

When had Libby written this list? After she got sick? Were these things, then, that she had wanted to do? Things she would never do? Did Libby think she was going to die? Sam returned her attention to the list.

Forgive Richard
Reconcile with Sam

She read the words twice, felt the weight of them settle on her shoulders. Her fingers felt stiff as she closed the book and returned it to Libby's bag. She picked up a magazine from the stack by her chair, opened it, and stared blindly at an article on how to pack healthy lunches for your school-age child.

—

"Sorry you had to see that," Libby said. They were in the car, Sam driving. "It's not always like that."

"I thought you were—I don't know. Dying, I guess." There, she'd said it.

"The first time it happened, I thought so, too."

"It's happened more than once then?" Again the picture of Libby, twisted in agony, flashed before her eyes and she had to blink to clear her vision, to see the traffic around her.

"Twice. So far." Libby dropped her head back against the headrest, closed her eyes.

"How often do you have to go?"

"To dialysis? Three times a week. Four hours each session."

Sam listened while Libby told her about the "part-time job" of staying alive. Libby, voice drained, told her how she had discovered her illness: the exhaustion, foamy pee, swelling ankles.

While Libby talked, Sam glanced over at her. The flesh beneath Libby's eyes was puffy, her face drawn, ashen. Old. As if she'd aged twenty years in one morning. "Sleep if you want to," she said. "I know the way back to your house."

A smile flitted across her sister's face. "Even after all this time?"

"Yes."

Sam drove in silence. Occasionally she glanced over at Libby, but her sister slept.

Reconcile with Sam.

"I never liked him, you know."

Startled, Sam jumped, and the wheel swerved beneath her hands. "Sorry," she said, regaining control. "I thought you were asleep."

"I never liked him," Libby said again.

"Who?" Richard? Sam didn't want to be drawn into their battle.

"Jay," Libby said. "From the first time you brought him around, I thought he was an asshole."

Sam clutched the wheel. "I don't want to talk about it."

"I did try and warn you about him, to tell you not to get married."

In another situation, Sam's double take might have been comical.

"You never did," she said, abandoning her resolve not to discuss this subject.

"You're forgetting."

"When?"

"Well, the last time was when you came here before you eloped. And we were in my bedroom. Remember? You were trying on dresses. I tried to warn you and you got mad."

Sam recalled the morning, remembered the blue dress and the way it hadn't fit quite right. But she did not remember Libby openly warning her about Jay. "Why didn't you like him?"

"Well, for starters, the second time we met, he tried to feel me up, which gave me a pretty good clue he was a prick."

"You're lying."

"Remember the July Fourth picnic at the lake? After we went swimming, you went to the bathhouse to change out of your suit and Richard took the twins for ice cream. Well, your boyfriend Took Liberties." She gave a tired laugh. "God, don't I sound like Mother. Remember how she used to say not to let boys take liberties with us? They say as you age you become your mother. Every girl's nightmare. I still hear her voice in my head. Do you?"

Sam wouldn't be pulled off the subject. "And you never told me about that day at the lake?"

"You were so in love. And we'd all been drinking."

"So if you knew he was such a goddamn prick, why did you fuck him?"

Libby exhaled, a long sigh. "It's a long story. It was a mistake."

"That's it? A mistake?" Sam thought of the list she'd written in preparation for a phone conversation with Libby. *Don't blame. Don't get angry. Don't be defensive. Don't go over old history.* "Is that your way of saying you're sorry?"

"You know I am. God, Sam, if you know anything, you must know how much I regret hurting you. I would do anything to be able to change what happened. Anything."

Reconcile with Sam.

She was not so easily won. Words were cheap enough. She maintained a stubborn silence and heard Libby sigh.

"Who's Gabe?" she asked. She heard in her head the echo of Lee's voice telling her she had the heart of a terrorist.

Libby gave her a quick look. "A friend."

Back in Sippican, on the town square, there was a sculpture formed from woven tree branches, part of the Art in the Park series. A week after its installation, someone had knocked it to the ground. The artist, a local man, had meticulously resurrected it, but the next day it had again been leveled. The cycle went on for a month before they caught the vandals. Two fourteen-year-old boys who couldn't explain their actions. They didn't know the artist, they just wanted to ruin it, they said. It hurt them to look at it. Sam understood.

"This Gabe," she said. "Is he someone's husband, too?"

Libby closed her eyes and turned away. "Yes," she said. "He is."

Had Libby expected it to be easy? Had she thought that after the first awkward moments Sam would say all was forgiven and they would fall into each other's arms like lost girls in a fairy tale? She supposed that she had. How had Sam grown so hard?

She thought of the story Sam had told her about smashing the windows. Once she wouldn't have believed Sam capable of such violence. She reviewed the family myth of them: Josh the action man, adventurer, peace corps volunteer, marathon man, the hero. Libby the rebel, the poet, the bad girl. Sam the baby. The one who needed protecting, their mother's pet. The one who caused no trouble. Over the years, the roles had all been switched.

The car slowed. Libby heard Sam gasp and she opened her eyes just as they pulled into her drive. A truck was parked in front of their house. Sam stamped on the breaks so hard, Libby was jolted against her seat belt. As Sam switched off the engine, the cab door on the pickup opened and a man got out. He was tall and good-looking, with a killer grin, the kind that would stop traffic quicker than a red light.

"Lee," Sam said in a soft-bellied whisper.

"Someone you know?" Libby said, but her sister was already out of the car, running hell-bent into the stranger's arms. He picked her up, lifted her right off her feet, as in some television commercial. He had to be strong to lift her like that, Libby thought. Sam wasn't exactly tiny. The air around them shimmered with such happiness Stevie Wonder could see how in love they were. She swallowed against the hurt that closed her throat.

Finally the stranger put Sam down and turned toward her car. He led the way, Libby noticed. Sam held back. Her sister had said very little about the new man in her life, not even his name. Keeping her life secret. Libby understood, but this knowledge stung.

The man opened the door, held out a hand to her. "You must be Elizabeth," he said. His voice was warm. A good voice. She could see this was a good man.

"Yes," she said.

He pulled Sam to his side, held her hand with his. With his other hand, he helped Libby from the car. "I'm pleased to meet you," he said. "Sam's told me so much about you."

Libby looked at Sam, surprised and absurdly pleased.

Sam held on to Lee, challenging Libby with her eyes, not realizing it was no contest.

This man, thought Libby, looking at Lee's face, this man would never betray her sister. Nor would she, God help her. Not ever again.

Libby and Sam

. . . .

*L*ibby woke to voices in the hall and, sleep-muddled, she thought it was the twins. She surrendered to the quietude she always felt when they returned home from school, the sense that she could breathe fully again because her children were back under her roof, safe. This sensation—peace of heart, she supposed, or the nearest thing to it—always surprised her, for she had never been one of those overly cautious mothers always fretting and stewing.

She nearly called out to them, and then, coming fully awake, she remembered. Not Mercy and Matt. Sam. And Lee. She lay quietly and listened as they passed by her door, followed the echo of their steps on the stairs.

Last night had gone well. Considering. She supposed someone viewing the scene through a camera lens would have seen four people enjoying themselves, with no hint of the truth, the subtext, as she knew it was called in the theater. What actors we are, she thought. Except for Lee.

Earlier in the evening, Sam and Lee had insisted on preparing dinner while she napped. Richard had suggested going out—his treat, he said—but they wouldn't hear of it. Armed with the pages of Libby's dietary restrictions and guidelines, the two of them had fashioned the menu: roast chicken, green beans with mushrooms, green salad with a cranberry vinaigrette. Fresh pineapple for dessert.

The dining room was lit by candles, and by the extra source of light that was Sam in love. Libby could tell from the way her sister's shoulder slanted toward Lee that, hidden from view by the drape of the tablecloth, their hands were interlocked. Richard played the host, serving wine, carving the chicken, steering conversation toward Lee, who, at Richard's prompting, told them about himself and his boatyard.

Richard offered to arrange for them to go sailing on Michigan, and Lee said he'd like that, if not this visit then the next. (*The next.* How she had held on to the promise of those words, taking from them knowledge that Sam would come again.) In answer to Richard's question about why he didn't work on fiberglass crafts, Lee answered that he liked working with wood. Without a scintilla of self-consciousness he'd said, "It takes love to work on wooden boats." He talked about how wood sat in the water in a natural way and how it honored the tree to give it another life.

Then he grinned sheepishly. "I'm talking too much about myself," he said.

Libby liked him enormously then. He reminded her of Richard when they were much younger and he would talk to her for hours about music. Like a lovesick acolyte, she would sit and listen, just as Sam did now, as if every word was a key to the secrets of his heart, while he tried to find the words to share his passion.

"It's like catching a perfect wave, you know," Richard had told her once, and because she had wanted to be flawless for him, to not disappoint him in even an insignificant way, she had nodded, never telling him that she did not surf.

"The power of the music takes you," he'd said. That particular time they had been in his room, both prone on the floor listening to a concerto. He had rolled onto his side to face her. "You almost don't have to do anything," he'd said. "You can't push. The music carries you. You almost cease to exist. It's an organic experience but it requires complete focus. Like being in a trance."

She had stayed silent, letting him talk, but she *had* understood what he meant. It was like that for her when they were making love, or when she was writing a poem.

Now she wondered why she hadn't told him that. Why she hadn't let him know she felt that way about poetry. Had she not wanted to seem to be competing? (Her mother's voice again. *A man likes it when he is the center of your life. Listen, don't talk. That's what they want: a willing ear.* At least Libby had never handed that advice on to Mercy.) When was the last time she'd been lost in a poem? She couldn't remember. Certainly before the twins were born. How was it that Richard had kept his passion alive while she had turned from hers? How did something like that get lost? And once lost, or abandoned, could it ever be reclaimed?

Libby's thoughts returned to last night's dinner. At one point, Lee jumped up, saying he'd almost forgotten he had something for Sam. He left the room, then came back with a photo. Sam laughed out loud when she saw it. Lee passed it to Libby. A Polaroid of a wedding cake. Really stunning. Libby had never seen anything like it.

Sam explained how, because she'd come here, her assistant Stacy had been left to decorate this cake. With help from Alice, she added, and then explained that Alice was Lee's mother, and that led to the story of how they met.

Sam has a whole family of her own out there, Libby thought, and it brought her pain to realize this. Just as it stung to see how completely and obviously Lee loved Sam, hurt because it was something she did not have.

Admit it, Libby said to herself. She stared across her bedroom, watched the sun come through the east-facing windows and play on the furniture. Admit you're jealous. Seeing them together had made her feel old. Used up. She faced an empty future. How had Sam gotten to be the lucky one? Was there some kind of universal balance being struck? Early in their lives she had been the talented one, the pretty one, the one people looked at first. Was it Sam's turn now?

There was a knock on the door, one soft tap, then Richard entered.

"For heaven's sake," she said. "It's your room, too. You don't have to knock." At her insistence, he'd slept in Matthew's bed.

"Did you sleep well?" he asked. He was barefoot, still dressed in pajamas. Pajamas that she had washed and ironed—*ironed*—when she was still a dutiful and trusting wife who cared about such things.

"Yes," she said. "You?"

He came toward the bed. "Elizabeth," he said. "We have to talk. I need to explain. It's not what you think."

She held up a hand, warding him off. "Not now. Really. I can't right now."

He went into their bathroom and moments later she heard him brush his teeth, then the irritating slurp as he drank water from cupped hands. This odd habit—so unlike him—exasperated her no end, though she could not break him of it. There was a glass right there by the sink, for heaven's sake. If he could only hear himself, slurping like a dog at a water bowl.

That reminded her of Hannah's greyhound. If things had been normal between them, she would have told Richard about Lulu, how when she was excited she jumped off the ground with all four feet and how she looked like she was grinning when she was praised or petted. Thoughts of Lulu reminded Libby that she hadn't called Gabe to thank him for taking her in the way he had, and, of course, to ask about Hannah. She hadn't heard a word and she supposed that was a good thing, for if there was news—good or bad—surely Eleanor Brooks would have called. She remembered the look of hope on Gabe's face. Militant hope that would not be denied.

Libby picked up the phone, amazed that she recalled a number she had dialed only once. On the other end, the phone rang on and on. She pictured the empty house and the greyhound sitting by the door, waiting for her mistress to return. Mercedes had always wanted a dog, and now Libby felt a moment's regret that she had never allowed it, just as her own mother had not permitted her to have a pet. For the second time in two days, she thought about how in many ways she had grown up to become her mother. It was not a welcome thought.

She checked the clock. Allowing for the time difference, it was after nine on the East Coast, not too early. She was in the middle of dialing Mercy's number when Richard came out of the bathroom.

"Isn't it rather early to be calling someone?" he said.

She kept her voice cool, distancing. "I'm calling Mercy."

"She's not in," he said, too quickly.

She replaced the receiver. "How do you know?"

"I talked to her last night," he said. "She said she was going out today."

"Oh. When was this?"

"After dinner. When you and Samantha were cleaning up."

"You didn't tell me."

"We haven't had much time to talk."

He looked tired. His shoulders slumped. There was an expression on his face, in his eyes, she could not read but thought was sadness.

She turned away.

Last night, after they had done up the dishes, Sam had pleaded exhaustion on Lee's part. He had driven eighteen hours straight, she said. He needed sleep. Upstairs, in the perfectly outfitted guest room, in the king-size bed, she lay cradled in his arms and, whispering so she would not be overheard, she told him about the dialysis center, the people in wheelchairs, the blood flowing through tubes, the sounds and smells. She told him about the spasm that had seized Libby. He had held her until she was talked out and her tears had stopped.

She told him more details about Richard's involvement with a student that had precipitated Libby's disappearance, and Libby's own apparent affair. And how Mercy was not at Brown, a fact Richard was keeping from Libby. She told him about her own confusing swings of emotion, a flash of love and concern and then a swing back to anger. He listened to everything. "What should I do?" she finally asked him.

"About what?"

"All of it."

"Nothing."

"Nothing?"

"With all that's going on maybe a little nonaction is called for. Just let things be, see how they unfold according to their own timetable."

"What? You mean like Zen?"

He smiled. "Can't hurt." Then he rolled her over onto her stomach. He straddled her and began rubbing her back.

"Aren't you tired?" she said, even as she gave herself over to his touch.

"Shhhh," he said. He used his palms, his thumbs, the edge of his hand as he worked, stroking the length of her back, concentrating on the long muscles that flanked her spine. Then he kneaded her shoulders and neck and she felt her muscles release tension. His hands slowed, massage turned to caress. She became aware of his weight, the heat of his body, and an answering heat was kindled in her belly. A sound—half sigh, half moan—slipped from her lips. He lifted his weight onto his knees, giving her enough room to turn toward him.

And then the action bed got some action.

He woke her early in the morning.

"What time is it?" she said, her voice thick with sleep.

"Nearly nine."

She groped for her watch on the bedside table and squinted at the dial. "It's eight," she said, her voice all outrage.

He laughed. "I guess I forgot to reset my watch."

She groaned. She wanted to sleep another hour. Easy. Maybe two.

"Come on," he said. "We've got places to go."

"Where?"

"You'll see. It's a surprise."

She bargained for more time, but he would not give in. He waited while she showered, then edged her out into the hall, down the stairs, and to the kitchen. There was no sign of Richard or Libby. Sam refused to go any farther until she'd had coffee. He waited impatiently while she drank a mug. She had never seen him this impatient.

They took her rental instead of his truck. "How'd you happen to pick this car?" he asked as he slid behind the wheel, smiling at some joke she didn't get.

"It's what they had for me at the airport. Why?"

"The name," he said.

She still didn't get it. "Dodge?"

"Intrepid," he said. And then: "Everything speaks to us."

They drove through the center of town. Church bells marked their progress. She wondered for a moment if that could possibly be what he had in mind, but he continued past the church.

"Where are we going?" she asked again.

"You'll see."

"Give me a hint. One hint."

"Just one," he said. "It's somewhere Richard told me about last night, a place he said we should see."

"I don't remember him telling you about any place."

"It was after dinner. You and your sister were doing the dishes."

"The lake?" she guessed.

He shook his head and refused to tell her more. At last he turned into a parking lot. Sam looked around but there was nothing in view. "Where are we?"

"The prairie," he said. "Richard said this is one of the last virgin preserves in the state."

"You dragged me out of bed to go for a walk?"

He grinned. "Come on." He made his voice mysterious. "There is more that lies ahead." Then in his normal voice: "I think you'll be glad you came." He took her hand and led her through a meadow to the edge of the prairie. The grasses were dried to shades of bronze and bone. She looked up at him as they walked along the path. She couldn't imagine him truly at home anywhere but near the sea and would have thought he'd have looked alien here in this midwestern flatland, but he strode through the grasses with a quiet grace. And then, in a flash of comprehension, she understood what it was that gave him that quiet confidence. Lee was at ease in his own body. She stepped closer to him, as if she could absorb his confidence. He reached for her hand, smiled at her.

She thought about what he'd said earlier, about letting things unfold on their own timetable. She remembered the list she had found in Libby's book.

Reconcile with Sam.

The hard little marble of resentment rolled in her chest. She reached out and brushed a dried stalk that was nearly as tall as she. "How did you come to forgive your father?" she said.

"Oh, I guess I simply didn't want to carry that monkey on my back."

"What do you mean?"

There was a small, rough-hewn bench, much like a pew, to the side of the path, and he drew her there. She sat with her feet tucked beneath her, leaning against his chest.

"There is a rabbinic story told in the Book of Knowledge," he said.

"Funny, you don't look Jewish," she said, her tone light, joking. They seldom talked about religion, but she knew for a fact that he never went to church. She'd asked him once and he said nature was his parish. He had little use for organized religion.

He smiled, then said, "I'm not telling it in the proper language. The author was more exacting, but basically it's this: If a man comes to you three times and three times asks forgiveness, you're bound to give it to him. If you don't, the thing you won't forgive becomes transferred to you. It becomes the monkey you have to carry."

She did not find comfort in this story. "Where did you hear that?"

"I read it. Mishnah Torah."

Another surprise. She'd only seen him read Clive Cussler novels and old issues of *WoodenBoat*. "You read religious texts?"

"Sometimes."

She took in this information. "So, do you believe in God?"

He didn't answer right away.

"Do you, Lee?"

"Here's what I believe. Or maybe I should say what I know, the kind of knowing that comes from experiencing something, not thinking about it. There have been times when I'm out in deep water, out of sight of land, and it's gotten a little stressful."

"You mean dangerous?"

"Let's say a little intense," he said. "It puts things in perspective. You're called to look at the value of life and what's important." He paused to watch a hawk circle overhead. "And you feel something greater than yourself. You give yourself over to it and you put yourself in the hands of that something, whatever you want to call it."

"I read an article once about the astronauts," she said. "I don't remember the quote word for word, but something like no matter what they believe when they leave earth, there are no atheists among returning astronauts. Something like that."

"That sounds close enough." He reached over and snipped off a tall blade of yellowed grass. She watched as he tore it lengthwise and began plaiting the strands, creating an intricate weave.

"Something you learned in summer camp?" she said.

"Boy Scouts," he said, concentrating on his creation. Somewhere behind them a bird was singing.

"I had pictured this happening differently," Lee said, after a minute. "I had big plans."

"What plans? What're you talking about?"

"But last night, watching you at dinner, seeing you with your sister and knowing what it meant that you had come out here, well, I didn't want to wait. So I had to throw out my script and find another."

"Another what?"

"Another perfect place. Richard suggested the prairie."

He took a breath and rose from the bench. Before she could stand, he knelt in front of her. "Samantha," he said. Then: "Oh, shit. I had this whole thing plotted, but now—don't laugh—I'm too nervous."

She gave a half smile. It unnerved her to see him so anxious. "What is it?"

He held out his hand, palm up, revealing a gold circle. Somehow, out of that stalk of prairie grass, he had fashioned a ring. "Sam, will you marry me?"

She was in lag time, and it took a moment for his words to register. Then she smiled—a smile so wide it was hard to say even the simple word yes.

She would remember this always. The bench that looked like a pew, the morning light that transformed the prairie into a sea of champagne, the ring Lee had created from grass, the bird that could not stop singing.

He took her hand and slid the band on her finger. I'll never lose this, she thought. I'll show it to our children when I tell them this story.

Our children.

A whole future, a future she once believed forever gone, waved before her, as golden as the autumn prairie.

"I take that as a yes," Lee said. He drew her close and bent to kiss her. In the background that crazy bird was just singing its heart out.

After a while he said, "What'd you say we go back and break the news to your sister."

She hesitated, a slight, involuntary holding back. The sun seemed to dim. Lee was different from her. He had a great heart. She wondered what would happen when she disappointed him, when she couldn't match his heart.

"Lee?"

"Yeah?"

"What if you've tried, but you can't?"

"Can't what?"

"Forgive. What if you just can't forgive?"

"Forgiveness is in all of us, Sam," he said.

"You give me too much credit. It scares me."

"You don't give yourself enough," he said. He expected too much of her. "You are as capable of forgiveness as you are of love."

"How do you know this, Lee?"

"You know it, too, Sam. It's in all of us, if we can get quiet enough to listen."

She curled her fingers, felt the scratch of the grass ring against her palm. She thought, what if when you get quiet you don't like what you hear?

Sam and Libby

. . . .

*W*hen they returned to the car, the parking lot was nearly full. The families and the couples with dogs reminded Sam of weekends in Sippican when the beaches were full of people. Lee turned on the ignition and shifted into reverse.

"Wait," Sam said. "Stop."

"What," he said, "you've changed your mind already?"

"Fat chance." She dug in her tote. "Here." She held out her cell. "What's this for?"

"Alice," she said. "She should be the first to know. Before we tell anyone else."

He smiled, then put the car in park and switched off the key. "I better warn you, she'll cry."

"You think?" Sam couldn't picture Alice, all Yankee practicality, crying.

"I can guarantee it. A complete waterworks. She was beginning to give up all hope." He punched in his mother's number. "Fasten your seat belt and get ready."

"For the tears?"

242 • Anne LeClaire

"For Alice in overdrive. Five minutes after we hang up, she'll have the church, preacher, and organist booked. We'll be lucky if she doesn't start putting nursery furniture on layaway."

Sam looked at the grass band on her finger. "Do you want that?" she said in a soft voice.

"Do I want what?"

"A wedding," she said. "For starters."

"I want you." He grinned. "You get to settle the rest of it."

"And kids?" She felt suddenly nervous. There was so much they'd never talked about. "Do you want to have kids?"

"It's not a deal breaker. I mean, if you don't want them, I guess I can live with it, but yeah, I've always thought it'd be great to have a family."

The future that she'd seen on the prairie shimmered before her, so real she swore if she held out a hand she could stroke it.

"Hi," Lee was saying into the phone. "No. Everything's fine. Yeah, she's right here with me. That's why I'm calling. We wanted to tell you something." He listened a moment and then laughed. He turned to Sam. "She says I'd better be phoning to say I asked you to marry me."

"I did," he said to Alice, "and she said yes." He laughed again and said to Sam, "She wants to know what took me so long." He passed the phone to her.

"Hi," Sam said to her about-to-be mother-in-law.

"I knew from the first day I laid eyes on you that you were the one for Hurley," Alice said. "Have you set the date?"

"I warned you," Lee said to Sam after they hung up. "I know I just said the wedding plans were up to you, but I hope this time you aren't set on eloping."

"Why?"

"Because now that we've told my mother, it's not even a remote possibility. I bet she's already calling her friends."

"Stacy," Sam said. "We've got to tell Stacy." She punched in the number for her assistant. "Hi, Stace," she said. "It's me, Sam."

"I was waiting for your call," Stacy said. For a crazy instant, Sam thought Alice had already spread the word. "Well, you don't have to worry," Stacy went on. "They didn't ask for their money back."

"Who?" Sam couldn't stop looking at Lee. She wondered how many kids he saw in their future. Two would be perfect. Maybe three.

"Helloooo," Stacy said. "The Chaney wedding. The cake. Isn't that why you're calling?"

"Wrong wedding," Sam said.

"What do you mean?"

Sam told her the news.

"What did she say?" Lee asked after she hung up.

"You know Stacy. After she finished whooping and hollering, she said, 'Sagittarius and Aries. Fire attracts fire. Your future will burn bright. Lots of passion.' " She didn't tell him Stacy had said half the women in Sippican would be wearing black armbands.

"I like that last part," he said, leaning over to kiss her. "The part about lots of passion."

Her toes tingled with wanting him. Maybe four. Four children and a dog.

He turned on the ignition. "Now let's go tell your sister."

It was nearly noon when they returned to the house. Libby was out and Richard was in his study. The sound of his cello reverberated through the house.

Sam opened the refrigerator. "How about breakfast?" She checked the time. "Or lunch?"

"Maybe later." He wrapped his arms around her. "Right now I think I want to go upstairs and sample some more of that passion Stacy was talking about."

Libby turned back toward Richard. She'd heard the back door close and then the sound of a car starting up.

"Are they going somewhere?" she asked.

He nodded and smiled, and in that moment she caught a flash of the young Richard and knew both the heat of desire and the anguish of loss.

"Last night Lee asked me what I thought was the most romantic spot around here," he said. "I suggested the prairie."

"Most romantic spot?"

"I think he's going to propose to your sister."

"Oh." She again felt that sense of emptiness, of being left behind.

"Are you getting up?" he asked, pausing at the door.

"In a bit."

After he left, she held her fingers over the shunt, felt the rushing of blood. She slid her hand up her forearm, felt the hardness of bone beneath her palm. She thought about Gabe's story of the tribesmen who had survived lightning and so possessed the power to knit bones. She wondered if there were tribal healers who could mend the heart. What you would have to survive to earn that power. From another part of the house, she heard the sound of Richard tuning his cello.

She showered, dressed, and went downstairs, restless in a house that felt too empty. She checked her e-mail, but there were no messages from either Mercy or Matt. Around ten, she tried Gabe again, but there was still no answer. Briefly, she considered driving over to the hospital, but if Hannah remained in a coma, there was little point. Plus, she knew bacteria were rampant in hospitals, carrying the risk of infection, and she certainly didn't need that complication.

She poached and ate an egg, cleaned up the dishes, leafed through the Sunday *Tribune*, did both crossword puzzles. Richard was still holed up in his study; Sam and Lee did not return. Finally she scrawled a note for the others and headed out. She drove down Westminster and stopped at Foodstuffs, where she purchased a spinach-and-chicken casserole with wine sauce. As he'd promised, Gabe's door was unlocked.

As soon as Libby opened the door, Lulu was on her, barking frantically and nearly knocking the bag out of her arms. She had to laugh, the way the greyhound bounced up and down, baring its teeth at her. There was no doubt about it, Libby noted, it was definitely a smile.

She set the casserole in the refrigerator, then looked until she found a retractable leash hanging on a hook by the back door. "Don't get too excited," she told the dog, as she clipped on the leash. "It's just a short one."

They strolled twice around the block, passing two couples who nodded to her and called Lulu by name. Ecstatic to be outdoors, the greyhound darted around, stopping every few minutes to sniff rocks and shrubs. Occasionally, in a fit of ecstasy, she'd snap and bite at the air, which made Libby laugh out loud. She wouldn't have dreamed it could be so pleasurable to walk a dog.

When they returned to the house, she refilled the greyhound's water bowl, then sat at the table and waited while Lulu drank her fill. As she sat there, occupied with nothing except a momentary contentment, a word surfaced in her brain, floating up like a fragment of music. She found a scrap of paper and set it down:

Bonesetter.

She let it roll around in her mind, pleased with the perfect sound of the vowels, the abruptness of the *t*'s, the soft liquid of the *s*. She pictured a scene. At first the details were hazy, but gradually they came into focus. Open mesa. A woman, tall—like her mother—stood alone.

The greyhound came in from the kitchen, did her ritual circling, then settled in at Libby's feet, curling into a ball. Libby bent to stroke her coat, as sleek as a seal's. More words surfaced. She picked up the pen and wrote:

They say when lambent light
Illuminates the heavens.

Too much alliteration, scoffed a familiar voice, the same one that saw all her shortcomings, the one that silenced her. She willed it away. A stronger voice told her it was crucial to keep going, reworking would come later.

They say when sky fire strikes,
Current burns, cracks,
blinds.

Tonight, when brown flesh splits,
Swirls, spins and falls silent, then rises,
They say a bonesetter is born.

She wrote on, re-creating myth, unmindful of the greyhound at her feet or the traffic on the street outside or the ticking of the mantel clock. When she surfaced, she was amazed to see the better part of an hour had passed.

She left a note asking Gabe to call her when he got in, and telling him she'd left food in the refrigerator. Lulu leaned against her leg. The dog cocked her head, raised her ears, and looked up with sad eyes.

"All right, all right." Libby scribbled a postscript to the note. "Just don't get used to it," she said to the dog.

When she pulled into her driveway, she saw that in her absence Sam and Lee had returned. Hours earlier, just the thought of confronting Sam's unyielding anger and Richard's betrayal had overwhelmed her, but something had shifted while she was at Gabe's, something she couldn't put a name to or understand. She felt a strength she hadn't in a long time. In the quiet of Gabe's home, writing those lines of poetry, she had reclaimed a part of herself. She went inside, to the kitchen, where the three of them were having tea.

"I was just about to send out the posse," Richard said. And then: "What's that?"

"Who, not what." Libby was absurdly pleased with herself. She unclipped the leash. "This is Lulu."

"Where did you find her?" The greyhound insinuated herself between them.

"She's Hannah's," Libby said.

"Who's Hannah?" Sam asked.

Richard stroked the greyhound's head. "I always wanted a dog," he said.

"You did?" Twenty years she'd lived with him and he'd never once mentioned it. She wondered what else she didn't know about him, what else she hadn't seen. Was it because he had withheld or because she hadn't looked? Lulu darted from one of them to another, poking her muzzle in their thighs and licking their hands. Then she stood by Richard and put her head in his lap.

"Who's Hannah?" Sam asked again.

"A friend," Libby said. She crossed to the sink and filled a bowl with water, set it out for the dog. "She's in the hospital and Lulu was so lonely without her, I couldn't bear to leave her alone."

"How's Gabe doing?" Richard asked.

"He's with her. Hannah's parents are there, too."

"A couple we know," Richard explained. "Gabe works for the Open Lands Association. Hannah was on the same dialysis schedule as Elizabeth, but she's in a coma now."

"Oh," Sam said in a quiet voice. A flash of comprehension crossed her face. She wouldn't meet Libby's eyes.

Is he someone's husband? she had said.

Libby rested a hand lightly on her sister's shoulder, stroked her hair back from her forehead. It's all right, she wanted to say. Sam still would not look at her, but she did not pull away. Libby remembered a lecture Anna Rauh had given the class on Keats's theory of negative capability. You have to be empty, the professor had said, and only then can you fill with understanding and sympathy for the subject. She'd been talking about poetry, but Libby thought maybe it was as true of life. Did you have to experience a great emptiness—a loss of certainty—in your own heart, for it to be receptive to others? Were pain and loss the lightning one had to survive in order, like a bonesetter, to heal the heart?

"On a happier note," Richard said, "we were waiting for you to return to begin a proper celebration."

"Celebration," Libby said.

Sam extended her hand. "My engagement ring," she said.

Libby looked at the grass band on Sam's finger.

"Until the real thing comes along," Lee said, looking sheepish.

Sam looked at him, her face luminous. "This is the real thing," she said.

"Congratulations." Libby was amazed to find she meant it, completely. She leaned over and gave Sam a hug and then crossed to hug Lee. "Welcome to the family," she told him. "Such as we are."

They had a celebratory meal of leftover chicken and salad, and Richard found a bottle of champagne for the toast. Libby allowed herself one sip. While they ate, she told Lee stories about Sam, about the summer Sam made money by selling the neighbors floral bouquets, the catch being she'd cut the flowers from their gardens.

"I never did," Sam protested.

"And another time," Libby said, "she got up in the night and cut my hair with our mother's sewing scissors."

"I did not," Sam said, truly shocked.

Libby looked at her. "You don't remember?" she said. "I had long braids and you cut one right off. We found it on your pillow in the morning. Mother was furious."

"I really did that?" Sam said.

Libby nodded. "I can't believe you've forgotten."

"What about the time you made me go to St. Martin's Catholic Church?" Sam told Lee and Richard the story of taking Communion and of her fear that Libby's shoes would go up in flames, consuming them both as well.

"Snotty, know-it-all Janice McKenney," Libby said. "I haven't thought about her in years." She looked at Sam. "I wouldn't have done it if you hadn't been there."

"Because I was your audience?"

"Because you gave me courage. I always felt stronger when it was the two of us."

"I gave you courage?" Sam said, eyes wide in astonishment. "I was always afraid of everything."

"You loved me," Libby said.

Lee left shortly after lunch. The others tried to talk him into waiting until the next morning, but he had appointments he couldn't reschedule. And then there's Alice, he said, winking at Sam. He told them he had to get back and get his mother under control before she made all the wedding arrangements.

When he went upstairs to pack, Sam followed him. Part of their conversation drifted down to Libby. She heard him ask Sam how long she was going to be staying, and her answer: I don't know. Then a door closed and she could hear no more.

"Don't forget I owe you a sail on the lake," Richard said. They were standing on the porch, saying good-bye.

"I'm glad I finally got to meet you," Lee said to Libby, and she could tell he meant it. "Take care of yourself. Get well."

Then he and Sam walked down the steps to the truck. Libby saw them kiss. Watching them, strengthened by the reflection of their love, Libby permitted herself to believe pain and loss were really in the past. She allowed herself to hope.

And then the phone rang.

"I'll get it," Richard said.

She waited.

"Hello, yes?" he said, his customary opening. He listened for a moment, and his face altered, as if for an instant the fiber holding flesh to bone had given way. Libby felt a rusty band circle her heart.

"I see," Richard said. And then: "I'm sorry. Yes, I'll tell her. Yes, of course. As long as you want. No." He hung up and turned to her. She felt the band tighten.

"Who was it?"

"Gabe," he said. "Hannah's passed."

Libby and Sam

. . . .

Shortly after Gabe's phone call, Libby went up to her room, taking the greyhound with her. "For a nap," she said, but an hour later, when Sam walked down the hall past her sister's room, she heard Libby crying. She hesitated, debating whether or not to go in, then tiptoed past.

Alone in the guest room, Sam curled up on the bed, but she could not rest. She missed Lee, although he had been gone only an hour. She crossed to the dresser and picked up the ring he'd given her. It already felt more brittle than it had been that morning and was fragile in her fingers. There must be some kind of fixative, she thought, that would preserve it. She would ask Lee. She set it carefully back on the dresser, then looked at her watch. Right about now, if he hadn't run into any holdups, Lee should be halfway through Indiana. She'd made him promise he would stop somewhere overnight and not drive straight through.

She found her cell, called him.

"Hey," she said when she reached him. "Guess who."

"Could I possibly be speaking to the future Mrs. Hardwin?"

Mrs. Hardwin. Samantha Hardwin. If she'd had a pencil she would have doodled the words like a teenager.

"I bet you say that to all the girls," she said in a voice belly-soft.

"Only one," he said. "Only you."

"Where are you?"

"Indiana," he said. "Home of James Dean and David Letterman."

"I mean specifically. What town?"

"Just west of South Bend," he said. "I'm making good time."

"When are you going to stop?"

"I'm not sure. I'll see how it goes. Probably around Cleveland. Or maybe as far as Youngstown."

"But you're not going to drive straight through, right? You promise?"

"Hey," he said. "Are you going to be a nagging wife?"

"Count on it," she'd said.

"I am," he said.

At six, she went back downstairs and found Richard in the kitchen preparing dinner. Libby was still in her room.

"Is she sleeping?" Sam asked.

"I don't think so. I heard her a while ago talking to the dog."

"Have you told her about Mercy?" Sam kept her voice low.

"No," he said. "That's the last thing she needs to be thinking about now. She's taking Hannah's death really hard."

"Were they good friends?"

"Hannah's younger. In her twenties, I would guess. I think they became close while they were at the center having treatments."

Sam crossed to the stove and put the kettle on to heat. "Want some tea?" she asked.

"Yes, thanks. Listen, has Elizabeth mentioned anything about the bonfire to you?"

"No," she said. She found mugs and tea bags, a jar of thyme honey, and set them out.

He told her about the annual event. "It's tonight," he said. "I think it would do Elizabeth good to get out of the house. See if you can talk her into it."

"Talk me into what?" Libby stood at the door. Lulu was at her side.

"The bonfire," Richard said. "I was just telling Samantha about it. I thought it would be a good idea if you went."

She surprised them both by saying yes.

There was no moon; the meadow was cloaked in shadows. Sam was aware of a crowd but had no idea of its size. Flashlights bobbed and weaved in the dark as people approached. It had turned chilly in the past hour. She shoved her fists into her pockets and hunched her shoulders against the cold. "Are you okay?" she asked Libby.

"I'm fine," Libby said.

There was an uneasy truce between them; things had softened but were not resolved.

Two men with spouted gallon cans circled the pyre, sending arcs of kerosene over the stacked wood. Sam could smell it from where she stood. Parents pulled their children back. The crowd stilled. Flashlights were flicked off. It grew quiet, as if everyone had drawn one long breath of anticipation. Then a match was struck, torches were lit. The fire starters held the torches to the pyre. There was a hollow whoosh—the roar of combustion—and the flame leapt upward. Sam jumped back involuntarily. Several mice ran from the pile, and a squirrel. Three or four songbirds flew from the top.

From somewhere behind her came the sound of a single bagpipe. Then, in the distance, an answering call. Sam's breath caught in her throat. Libby hadn't told her about this. She wished Lee could have stayed, could have been here with her. She wanted to share everything with him.

She looked over at Libby. For a moment, she nearly didn't recognize her. In the leap and flicker of the flames, her sister's face had been transformed into a mask of sorrow, bones etched with grief. Sam looked back at the fire, as if the flames were capable of burning away the image of Libby. A spasm of pain, nearly electric in nature, shot through her chest, and for a moment she wondered if she was having a heart attack. Wouldn't that be the perfect irony, she thought.

She dared another look at Libby, saw a tear trace down her sister's cheek.

Three times, Lee had said. Three times to grant forgiveness.

The flames leapt as if their hunger would never be assuaged. Sparks flittered up into the night like fireflies. The echo of pipes faded into the moonless sky.

She turned to Libby, uncertain. What could she say? How could she find the words that would explain away six years of silence?

In the end, there was no need. She slipped her hand into Libby's, felt the shock of recognition, the cellular memory of Libby's skin that even when she was a girl had been as soft as talcum powder. For an instant, there was no response, and then Sam felt her sister's fingers curl around her own.

Lee was right, Sam thought. Forgiveness carried its own freedom. She felt light, released from the weight she had borne too long.

The spasm in her chest released. A piece of her heart had come home.

Sam and Libby

. . . .

When they returned home from the prairie, they found cans of dog food stacked on the counter.

"What's this?" Libby said.

"I ran down to Jewel's while you were at the bonfire," Richard said.

Libby looked over at Lulu, ensconced on a heap of blankets in the corner of the kitchen. "And you put down my good blankets?"

"It was that or the couch," Richard said. "Greyhounds don't have much flesh on their bones. They need a lot of cushioning." The dog, as if understanding she was the center of this conversation, got up and stretched, then crossed to Libby and pressed her muzzle into her groin, until Libby stroked her. Satisfied, Lulu returned to the makeshift bed and curled into a ball.

"She's had a long day," Richard said.

"Haven't we all," Libby said.

"How was the bonfire?" he asked.

"Beautiful," Sam said.

"Was there a crowd?"

"Same as usual," Libby said, stifling a yawn. Her face was drawn with exhaustion. There were deep circles under her eyes.

"If you want to go to bed, go ahead," Sam said. "You don't have to stay up for me."

Libby shook her head. "I want to. Stay up, that is. If you're not too tired, I'd like the company."

Without asking, Richard poured some brandy into a tumbler for Sam. "Tea or juice?" he asked Libby.

"Tea," she said, then added, "thanks." She rubbed her hands to remove the chill of the prairie.

He measured a half cup of water, poured it into a mug, added a tea bag, then set the mug in front of Libby. "I guess the two of you can get along all right without me," he said.

"We'll try," Sam and Libby said in perfect unison, then laughed. The greyhound cocked her head and watched him leave, then heaved a doggy sigh and dropped her head on her front paws.

The two sisters lapsed into silence.

Libby spoke first. "Sam," she said, "I want to explain—"

"Don't," Sam said. "You don't have to say anything. What's past is past. It doesn't matter."

Libby searched her face. "It does matter. I need you to know how sorry I am, how much I've hated myself, how guilty I've felt."

"Listen," Sam said. "Jay was a shit. I was just beginning to find that out when you came to visit. The end was inevitable."

"Maybe, but not that way."

"No. Not that way."

"Can you forgive me?"

Sam slid her hand in her pants pocket, felt the smooth hardness of the stone Lee had given her. "I already have," she said, and knew that was the wondrous truth.

Tears welled in Libby's eyes and she lifted a hand to brush them away. "Sorry," she said. She bent her head over her tea.

"No need." Sam got up and tore a paper towel off the roll. She handed it to Libby.

"God," Libby said. "I think I've cried more today than I have in months."

"I'm sorry about your friend Hannah," Sam said. At the sound of

Hannah's name, the greyhound raised her head. "And I'm sorry about yesterday, when I said—"

This time Libby interrupted. "It's all right. I can't blame you for what you thought. You didn't know."

Sam took a sip of her brandy. "Richard said she was on dialysis and that you got to know her at the center."

Libby nodded. "The first time I went, I didn't think I was going to get through it. Then I looked up and saw Hannah and, in a way I can't explain, she helped me. I wish you could have met her. In some ways she reminds me of you."

"Of me? How?"

"There was this essential goodness about her. You have the same thing."

The compliment confused and embarrassed Sam. "I seriously doubt it," she said.

"You do."

Sam switched subjects. "Richard tells me your doctor wants you to get a transplant."

"Let's take a break on that topic, okay?" Libby said. She brushed a thumb over the shunt.

"But I want to hear about it. I want to know."

"Tomorrow," Libby said. "Tomorrow, I'll tell you every gruesome detail. More than you want to hear, believe me."

"Are you sure?"

"Positive. I'm so tired of it, Sam. Just for tonight, let's pretend I'm healthy as a Green Bay running back."

Sam rose and went to stand behind Libby. She massaged her shoulders. "Is this too much pressure?"

"No. It feels glorious. I almost made an appointment for a massage about a couple of weeks ago, but I felt like such a freak with the catheter sticking out of my chest. I didn't want anyone to see me like that. It's bad enough I have to look at it."

"I'm sorry," Sam said.

"Hey, It's not your fault."

Sam kneaded Libby's neck, rubbed her temples. She ran her fingers through Libby's hair. It was a shade darker than when they were children, but still pretty. "That story you told Lee this afternoon, was it true I cut off your hair?"

"Lord, yes," Libby said. "I can't believe you've forgotten. Mother was absolutely furious. She took me to the beauty shop and I cried the entire way. I had to get one of those ugly bowl cuts."

"Why did I do it?"

"I think you thought you could glue it on your head."

"But why?"

"You said you wanted to look like me."

"God, I can't believe I've blocked this whole thing. Were you mad at me?"

"For about a week," Libby said. "But you were so sad and I finally figured, hey, hair grows out."

"Really? You didn't hate me?"

"I could never hate you, Sam."

Now Sam was the one who fought tears. Libby passed her the makeshift tissue. "We're the pair," she said.

"Do you know what I could use right now?" Sam asked.

"What?"

"Cookies. Brownies. Hot fudge sauce. Anything with sugar."

"Cupboard next to the oven. Second shelf. In the back."

Sam crossed to the cupboard. "These?" she said. "Fig Newtons? These aren't cookies. These are health food."

"I'm afraid that's the closest you're going to get." Libby watched as Sam set the package on the table. "I could never do that."

"What?"

"Eat whatever I wanted."

"You mean get fat?"

"No. First of all, you're not fat. Secondly, that's not what I meant. I meant eat whatever I wanted. Even before I got sick, I never allowed myself to. I honestly can't remember the last time I wasn't on a diet. Better to have enjoyed it all."

Sam shoved the package toward her. Libby took one. Sam lifted her eyebrows, waited. Libby took two more.

"Do you remember those tap-dancing classes Mother made us take?" Sam said.

"God, yes. Old Miss Nickel-and-Dime. I think she was probably still terrorizing children when they folded her in her coffin." She sipped her tea and ran a finger absently over her shunt. "Tell me about your business," she said. "I want to know everything. And then I want to hear about Lee. All the juicy details."

"Well," Sam, said, knowing now she could tell Libby anything, that she had nothing to fear. "The first time I met him, he was standing in his mother's kitchen, and when he smiled at me I felt the kind of wanting that you feel in your knees."

"That good?"

"Better. Twenty on the scale of one to ten."

Sometime after midnight, Sam went upstairs. She stared at the bed that was much too large for one person. She wondered how far Lee had driven, where he was sleeping. She knew it was late to call, but she gave in to the impulse.

"Hello?" he said. A television was on in the background.

"Hi," Sam said.

"Hi."

"So tell me again why you want to marry me."

"Hold on," he said. "Give me a couple of minutes. The voice is familiar."

"Funny guy," she said. "So where are you?"

"Ohio."

"Home of?"

"Let's see. John Glenn. Neil Armstrong. George Custer."

"Ah. Frontiersmen."

"And very appropriate, I might add," he said.

"How's that?"

"Because right this very minute, I'm thinking of a frontier I'd like to explore."

"Hold that thought."

"How long?"

"Just a couple more days."

"I'm holding my breath. How was the bonfire?"

"Spectacular. There were bagpipes." She thought of telling him about the moment she had reached for Libby's hand, but kept silent, keeping it to share when they were together. "I wish you could have been there."

"Next time," Lee said.

"Yeah." She took the beach stone out of her pocket and set it on the dresser, right next to her ring. "Lee?"

"I'm right here."

"Tell me something I don't know."

"Like what?"

"Anything."

He thought a minute. "Okay," he said. "Robins only sing when they're mating. Otherwise, they're mute."

"Is that true?"

"Absolutely."

"I love you, Lee."

"I love you, too, Sam."

When she hung up, the king-size bed seemed a shade less lonely. She undressed and slipped into the bed. She listened to the creak of the hall floorboards as Libby came upstairs and heard the scratchy sound of greyhound toenails trailing behind.

Somewhere in the distance, a train whistle sounded. Down the hall, a toilet flushed. She lay and let the day replay in her mind. She remembered going to the prairie with Lee, the sun warming her while they sat on the bench, the bird singing, Lee weaving her a ring. She remembered the sound of Alice's voice on the phone, all happiness at their news, and Stacy's delight, too, and the zodiac's promise of passion for them. She thought about the celebration over lunch and the four of them laughing and sharing stories, and how she had observed Richard looking at Libby, had seen the concern on his face, seen him anticipate her needs, and had realized that whatever was going on between them, it was more complicated than she had thought. She thought about the grief that came with the news of Hannah's death. And she recalled the bonfire on the prairie and the moment she'd slid her hand into Libby's, and then returning to the house and sitting in the kitchen and talking.

She had been absolutely astonished when Libby told her she was like Hannah because they both had essential goodness. It wasn't true, and she wondered how Libby of all people could think that. And if Libby really did believe that, how could she have betrayed her? But maybe it was easier to betray someone if you believed they were intrinsically good, maybe you thought they would more readily forgive you. Anger thickened in her chest, heated her face. She willed it away. She did not want to lift that burden again.

The day seemed a single confusion of joy and sorrow. She got out of bed. She hadn't done this since she was a child, but, feeling only slightly foolish, she knelt by the bed and clasped her hands in the steeple position, palms together, fingers pointed straight up. The child's prayer came automatically to mind. "Now I lay me down to sleep. I pray the Lord my soul to keep. If I should die before I wake, I pray the Lord my soul to take." How that phrase had terrified her. *If I should die before I wake.* She remembered being afraid to fall asleep after she had recited the prayer at her mother's insistence, crying until Libby came to her and held her and promised that she would not die. Libby wouldn't let her. Only then could she sleep.

Really, what a dreadful bedtime prayer for a child.

She had not said a formal petition in a long time and did not know how to begin. And then she thought of Stacy.

"I'm grateful for . . . ," she began. The kaleidoscope of events swirled in her head. "I'm grateful for this day."

Then, without forethought, she stood and crossed to the dresser. She opened the drawer and took out the brochure for organ donors that she'd found the day before. She bunched her pillow up against the headboard and settled in to read.

"Presently, a kidney transplant is the best chance for rehabilitation and long-term survival," she read. *Long-term survival.*

"For some, a new kidney means a chance to spend more time with their family, for others it may mean a chance to return to work, a chance to travel, or perhaps a chance to start a new way of life."

A chance to travel. Sam thought about the list she'd found in Libby's book. Italy. Portugal. St. Martin-in-the-Fields. She continued reading.

"An overwhelming 90% of donors report that the experience was positive and worthwhile. Furthermore, many report that having gone through it, they would do it again."

She turned to the next page. "Any healthy family member who has a compatible blood type and compatible HLA tissue typing may be considered as a possible kidney donor." She sat up and leaned forward, pressed her palms against her back where she imagined her kidneys were. According to the booklet, a kidney was approximately the size of one's fist. She leaned back against the pillow and held her hand in front of her face, clenched it.

She reread the sentence. "Any healthy family member who has a compatible blood type and compatible HLA tissue typing may be considered as a possible kidney donor." She absorbed information about the required steps in the initial evaluation, about testing for blood type, and the test for white cell cross-match. She read about the minimal effects of donation on the donor. (Of course they would say minimal.) "The donor's remaining kidney," she read, "is able to do approximately 80% of the work that the two kidneys had done previously." Again she formed a fist, cupped it in the other hand, imagined it being taken from her body. Her eyes returned to the page.

"There is a perioperative mortality of .03% or 5 in 16,000, less than the risk of a woman in pregnancy." At the last word—"pregnancy"— her throat closed.

Children. It wasn't a deal breaker, Lee'd said, but he'd always thought it would be great. Sam thought of Alice and how Lee had said that she'd probably already be putting bassinets on layaway.

A question for Solomon. Do you save your sister or a child not yet conceived? How could she make that choice? How could she not help Libby? But how could she sacrifice the chance to have a child? Tears blurred the page and she blinked them away. Then she read the next sentence.

"Women who donate a kidney do not have any increased risks in pregnancy or childbirth."

She read the sentence three times. "Women who donate a kidney do not have any increased risks in pregnancy or childbirth." She did not have to make a choice. Take it easy, she thought. There's no rush here. Think about it. Talk it over with Lee. Get more information. Don't be impulsive.

She rose, put on the terry robe, and went out to the hall. The light shone in the crack beneath Libby's door. Sam knocked softly.

"Yes?" Libby said.

"It's me. Are you up?"

"Sure. Come on in."

Libby lay in bed. The greyhound was curled beside her.

"I want to do it," Sam said.

"Do what?"

"Be your donor. I want to be your donor."

Libby looked down at her hands. She ran her fingers over the shunt.

"Did you hear me?" Sam said. "I want to give you my kidney."

"Oh, Sam-I-Am," Libby said. "Let's talk in the morning."

Sam crossed to the bed and sat next to her sister. "I want to, Lib. I won't change my mind."

"I don't know what to say," Libby said.

And then the phone rang. They both started and, moving as one, they turned and looked at the clock.

It was *one a.m.*

Lee, Sam thought, and then breath came again as she remembered that she had just spoken with him, that he was safe in a hotel in Ohio.

Mercy, Libby thought. *Matt*.

Libby and Sam

. . . .

"*M*om?"

"Matt?" Libby's heart thumped, blood pulsed in her ears. "Are you all right? What's wrong?"

"Nothing's wrong, Mom."

"It's nearly one in the morning and you're calling to say nothing's wrong?"

Richard appeared in the doorway. "It's Matt," Libby mouthed at him.

"Sorry to be calling so late, but I thought you might be worried about Mercy. I wanted you to know she's okay."

"What do you mean, Mercy's okay?"

"She's here. With me."

She turned to Richard. "Matt says Mercy's with him," she said, her voice betraying her confusion. He looked down at the carpet.

"Mercy's out there?" she said to Matt. "In Pasadena?"

"Yes. I didn't want you to worry," he said. "I thought you might have tried to reach her at school. She said she left without telling anyone there where she was going."

"But why is she there with you? Put her on the phone. Let me speak to her."

"She's sleeping, Mom. She's pretty tired. She drove about three days without much sleep."

"She *drove* out there? To Pasadena?" She sat up fast, startling Lulu, who gave a high yip.

"What was that?" Matt said. "Was that a dog?"

"Yes," Libby said.

"You've got a dog?" His voice was incredulous.

"No. I mean she's not ours. I'm watching her for a friend."

"I don't believe it. You've really got a dog there? What kind?"

"A greyhound."

"Is she lying on your bed?"

"As a matter of fact, she is."

He gave a short laugh. "Did she have to wipe her feet first?"

"Matt, why did Mercy drive out there?"

"She's trying to sort some things out, Mom. She needs some time."

"But why didn't she come home?"

"She didn't want to bother you. She knows you've got a lot on your plate right now."

"For God's sake, Matt. What's going on?" Libby heard the sharp tone enter her voice.

"I really don't want to get into it, Mom. You need to talk to her about this."

Twin loyalty in action. They wouldn't rat on each other with a saber to their throats. "Have her call me first thing."

"She will. And Mom?"

"Yes?"

"She's had a rough time of it. Go easy on her."

A rough time. That could mean anything. Was Mercy flunking a course? Boyfriend trouble? If it was Mr. Tongue Stud, good riddance to him. A breakup with him was nothing to be crossing the continent for.

"How are you doing?" Matt asked.

"I'm fine."

"How is dialysis? Any infections? Are your numbers good?"

She had to smile. Matt, her scientist. Of course he would have researched the disease. She remembered how, the day after she told him about going on dialysis, he'd called and said he'd done some checking and that a donor only had to be eighteen and he was old enough. She'd told him they weren't at that stage.

"I'm going to be fine, Matt. Really."

"You don't have to do that, Mom."

"Do what?"

"Protect me. Or Mercy. We're not little kids."

Of course she had to protect them. That's what parents did. "I know you're not, dear. I just don't want you worrying about me."

"Do you think if you don't tell us what's going on, we won't worry? The thing is, we probably worry more. Don't you get it? We need to know what's happening with you."

"Is that why Mercy's out there? So you two can talk about my disease?"

"She'll call you tomorrow, Mom."

She gave up. "Do you want to talk to your dad?"

"I'm pretty beat, Mom. I'll talk to him tomorrow. Okay?"

"Sure."

"Everything else okay there?"

"Yes." She looked across the room at Sam. "Oh, your aunt is here."

"Aunt Sammy?"

"As far as I know she's the only one you've got."

"Aunt Sammy's there? I thought you two weren't speaking."

"Well, now we are."

The wire hummed. "And she's there with you now?"

"Right here, even as we speak."

"Mom?" he said in a ten-year-old's voice.

"What?"

"You aren't dying, are you?"

"No, Matt," she said. "I'm not dying."

"I just wondered. You know. You having a dog there and Aunt Sammy and everything. It weirded me out."

"Everything's fine. I promise." You promise, she thought. Because they need you to. They need your certainty.

When Matt was eleven, he'd come home from school and marched straight up to Libby. "You and Dad will never get divorced, will you?" he'd asked. Billy Madison's parents had just split. "But you and Dad," he'd persisted. "You'll never get divorced, will you?" And she had said no, absolutely. Because he didn't want to hear that nothing in life was certain, no guarantees issued with birth certificates, or marriage licenses for that matter, and that even strong love can die. People, too. No matter what the question, that is not the answer they want.

"Mercy's out in Pasadena," she said when she hung up. "She drove across the country. Drove right through Illinois without even calling us. Matt says she'll phone in the morning. What do you think it is? Oh, God, you don't think she's in trouble at school, do you?" Or something else? The image of Mercy with the punk boyfriend sprang again to mind, and with it a terrible thought. Could Mercy be pregnant? She pushed the idea aside. She couldn't bear to consider it.

"Let's wait and see," Richard said, interrupting her musing. "At least she's all right. We know where she is."

Libby studied him with narrowed eyes. He couldn't meet her gaze.

"You knew," she said. "You *knew*."

"I didn't know she was with Matt. Only that she wasn't at Brown."

"How long exactly have you known this?"

"What does it matter?"

"How long, Richard?"

"Three days."

"And yesterday morning, when I was going to call her and you told me you'd talked to her? You were lying then?"

"I was just trying to protect you."

"Protect me? I'm your wife. When one of our kids goes off somewhere, you tell me, you don't protect me."

Sam made a small sound. "I'm going to let you two sort this out." She bent and gave Libby a kiss, patted the dog. "I'll see you in the morning."

"This can wait until morning, too, Liz," Richard said after she left.

"No," Libby said. "It can't. Do you know how it makes me feel when you say you lied to protect me? It feels like I'm a child." She stopped, caught her breath. Was this what Matt meant when he said he didn't want Libby withholding things? Was this how he felt?

Richard crossed to the bed. "How come you get to decide who gets handed what information and who gets shut out?"

"Who have I shut out?" Her voice rose. The greyhound whined, inched closer, laid her long muzzle on Libby's leg. She softened her voice. "Who?"

"Our friends, for starters. Me."

"I haven't shut you out."

"Yes, Liz, you have."

"Well, if I have it's because you like it that way. It fits your agenda."

He pinched the bridge of his nose. "I think we should really wait until tomorrow to have this conversation. We're both tired."

"So you felt left out," she said. "Is that why you . . ." She couldn't finish.

"Why I what?"

"That girl. Because you felt 'left out'?"

"What girl?"

She waited.

"Sarah?"

She stared at him.

"There's nothing there, Liz."

"I saw you, Richard. I *saw* you."

"She's a student, for God's sake. She's Mercy's age. Do you seriously think I'd get involved with a girl our daughter's age?"

"I saw you. You had your arms around her."

"You saw me giving her a lesson."

"With your arms around her? With your eyes closed?"

"I was showing her a passage, helping her with the bowing."

She stared at him.

"I'm not going to do this, Libby. I'll say it once. There was nothing there. I'll swear on a Bible or my life or whatever you choose. And you can decide whether to believe me or not. I made one mistake years ago. There's no excuse and I'm not offering one. But that was in the past and I've never done it again, no matter what you think. And I can't go on paying for a mistake I made six years ago."

"We both made mistakes," she said, her voice a whisper. "You weren't the only one." She dropped her head, covered her face with her hands, too exhausted to go on.

"Liz? Are you all right?" he asked.

"Just tired. It's nearly two. I've got dialysis in the morning."

"I don't have classes," he said. "I'll drive you."

She started to say, no, that was all right, Sam could drive her, or she would do it herself, but she stopped. *You decide who gets shut out.* "Thanks," she said. "I'd like that."

"We should leave by seven."

"Yes." Then, "Richard?"

"Yes."

"Before Matt called, when Sam was in here, she told me she wants to be tested. She wants to be a donor."

"God." He exhaled a long breath. "That's great, Liz."

"But can I ask that of her? Can I really let her do that?"

"Yes," he said, and reached for her hand. "Yes, you can."

Sam and Libby

. . . .

he flight into Providence was thirty minutes early, but when Sam arrived Lee was there, waiting. He stood at the bottom of the airport escalator holding a half-dozen Mylar balloons, a bouquet of roses, and a sign like the one limo drivers held to signal arriving passengers. It said: "Girl of My Dreams." People smiled at him and several stopped to see who he was waiting for. When he greeted Sam with a kiss, they applauded.

"You make me feel like a star," Sam whispered, only slightly embarrassed.

"Not too OTT?"

"I love it."

"The champagne's chilling at home," he said. He kissed her, then handed her the flowers and took her bag. "Anything in baggage claim?"

"This is it," Sam said.

"Then let's get out of here."

Once in the truck, he drew her to him. "The balloons were just a warm-up," he said. He gave her a long kiss.

"Mmmm," she sighed. "I don't suppose I could talk you into turning in at the first motel we see."

"You could, but you'd have to explain it to a couple of people who have dinner waiting for you."

"Alice?"

"And Stacy. They've been cooking all day."

"Your mother and Stace?"

"In action. The last I heard they were deciding whether to have four or five courses."

"Sounds like they've become friends."

"You don't know the half of it. They're inseparable. Peanut butter and jelly. Gin and tonic. Rock 'n' roll."

"Alice and Stacy," she repeated. "I can't imagine."

He ran a finger down her cheek, kissed her again. "They'd kill me for telling you, but they're planning an engagement shower."

"They are?" Sam grinned. "A real shower? Sheet cake? Racy girl talk? Lots of lacy lingerie?"

"A guy can only hope."

She laughed, delighted.

"And speaking of engagements," Lee said. He reached over, unlatched the glove compartment, and handed her a small velvet box.

"Oh," she said in a small voice. She felt like she was sixteen. Lee made everything new.

"Are you going to open it or just hold it?"

She lifted the top. "Oh, Lee. It's—it's stunning."

He took the ring, a single pear-cut diamond, slipped it on her finger.

"It's beautiful." She turned her hand so the stone caught the light. "And it fits perfectly. How did you know my size?"

"I have my spies," he said.

"Libby," she guessed.

"You got it." He lifted her hand to his mouth, kissed the hollow of her palm.

"Lee?"

"Yes?"

"Can we talk about it now? I want to tell you more about what the doctor said, everything."

He hugged her close. "I want to hear."

The day before, at Carlotta's office, Sam and Libby had waited for the results of the preliminary tests. The nurse had suggested that Libby wait in the outer office, but Sam insisted that her sister be there for the report. "We're in this together," she said.

The doctor looked up from the folder as they came in. "Step one accomplished," she said.

The two sisters smiled at each other; both were nervous.

"Your blood type is A," Carlotta said to Sam, "your HLA tissues are compatible, and the white cell cross-match was negative."

Sam had forgotten what the last test was for.

"Your blood cells and Elizabeth's are mixed to see if they're compatible, that is, that Elizabeth does not make an antibody response to your antigens," Carlotta explained.

"And the test was negative?"

"It was perfect. You and your sister are a six-of-six match."

Sam reached over and held Libby's hand.

Carlotta flipped a page in the folder. She smiled at Sam. "You're in good health. Your blood pressure's normal and your diabetes test was negative. So far, you're a textbook donor for Elizabeth."

Sam squeezed Libby's hand. "Where do we go from here?" she asked.

"That completes the initial screening test. Now we set you up with your own team."

"My own team?" Sam said. "Won't you be my doctor?"

"No. I'm heading Libby's team. Each donor has to have a separate team consisting of a clinical transplant coordinator—that's usually an RN trained specifically for transplantation—a transplant nephrologist, a urologist, and a transplant social worker."

Sam chewed her lip. Libby had said Carlotta Hayes was wonderful. She trusted her. "But you can be on my team, can't you?"

"No."

"Why?"

"The hospital's bioethics committee insists that the donor's team be independent of the recipient's."

"Why do I need a social worker?" Sam asked.

"Again for ethical reasons." Carlotta leaned forward toward Sam. "Organ donation is emotionally complicated. A social worker conducts screening to evaluate the donor's motives and psychological state. They want to eliminate any possibility that you might feel pressured into donating. Now, Elizabeth tells me you're from Massachusetts."

"Yes."

"What part?"

"Southeastern."

"Have you given any thought to what hospital you want to use? Boston's Beth Israel Deaconess is one of the best in that area."

Libby spoke for the first time. "We want to be in the same hospital. If Sam chooses Beth Israel, can you go there?"

"That won't be a problem."

"No," Sam said. "I'll come here." She spoke impulsively, regretting it almost immediately. She should have checked with Lee. She would need him there.

Carlotta gave her a steady gaze. "You don't have to make that decision today. You will probably want to talk it over with your nephrologist, and with your family."

Sam nodded. "Would you recommend a doctor?"

"I can give you some referrals."

"Thanks. And what's the next step?"

"You make an appointment."

"Okay." Sam swallowed.

Carlotta made a note. "In the meantime, why don't you return to Massachusetts and clear your calendar. Depending on whether you have an open or a laparoscopic nephrectomy, recovery time ranges from two to four weeks. That is something you and your doctor will determine."

"What's the difference?"

"One is more invasive than the other. Both have pros and cons. As I said, you'll want to make this decision with your own doctor. I imagine that, even if you choose to have the operation here in

Chicago, some of the tests—the EKG, the twenty-four-hour urine collection to assess kidney function, chest X rays, sonogram—can be done at a hospital in your area before you return. Again, that's something to discuss with your doctor."

"Is there anything I need to do?"

Carlotta smiled. "Take good care of yourself. Get a dental checkup. Start exercising if you don't already. We've found pre-op exercise shortens recovery time."

"Exercise?" Sam turned to Libby. "You'll owe me big-time for this."

"Yes," Libby said. "I will."

Later, as they drove home, Sam had turned to Libby. "Are you okay? You're awfully quiet."

"In there," Libby said, "listening to Carlotta, it hit me what I'm asking you to do. Are you sure, Sam? Are you absolutely sure you want to do this?"

"More than anything, Lib," Sam said. "More than anything in the world."

"Lee?" Sam said. They were still in the airport parking lot. Lee had held her while she told him about all Carlotta said. "I know when I asked, you said it was my decision and you'd support me no matter what I decided, but I need to know that it's really all right with you about me being a donor."

He drew a finger along her palm, tracing the lines that represented love and life and destiny.

"Because it affects us both," she said.

He looked at her. "There were women before you, Sam. That's no state secret. But no one like you. I fell for you the moment I met you and I've been falling ever since. I love the way your nose crinkles when you laugh, and the way your hair spreads out on your pillow when we're in bed. I love the little birthmark on the small of your back, and the way you bite your lower lip when you're concentrating."

"Oh," she said softly.

"Don't interrupt," he said. "I'm just getting warmed up. I love that you're an artist."

"I'm not. I just make cakes."

He pressed a finger against her lips. "I love that you're an artist," he said again. "That reporter was right. Your cakes are art. I love the way you're so sweet to every bride. I love your innate kindness. I love the way you don't get mad at the chipmunks for eating the birdseed, you just put out extra for them. I love you for giving Stacy a job after a lot of people including her own mother had given up on her. I love the way you hum in the morning when you first wake up. I love the way your body feels next to mine, the way we fit. I love you more than I thought it was possible to love anyone. But this past week, watching you with Libby, I gave you a part of me I didn't even know I was holding back. I knew I could trust you with my heart."

She was crying and he wiped her tears. "Now I think we'd better head home before my mother has an APB out for us."

"I want three," Sam said, her face radiant.

"Three what?"

"Kids. Three kids. And a dog."

They were on the highway when she took out her cell. "I promised Libby I'd let her know I got home okay.

"Hi," she said when Libby answered. "It's me. Just wanted to let you know our kidney landed safely in Providence."

"Lee met you?" Libby said.

"Indeed. With balloons, flowers, and a ring."

"Tell him I send my love. And I'll see you in a couple of days." Libby paused. "Sam? If you change your mind about this, I understand. If you change your mind at any time, I'll understand."

"I won't change my mind." Sam reached over and laid her hand on Lee's thigh. He covered it with his.

"Just so you know," Libby said.

"I know."

"And you'll call me with your arrival time and the flight number?"

"I'll call you."

"Richard will meet you at O'Hare."

"Okay." Sam heard the rattle of dog tags. "How's Lulu?"

"She misses Hannah. Every time someone walks in the door, she looks up, then she kind of sighs and drops her head."

"The service is this afternoon?"

"At four."

"I'll be thinking of you."

"Thanks. Me you, too."

After she clicked off, Sam turned to Lee. "Hannah's memorial service is this afternoon. It's going to be hard on Libby."

The notice had requested that in lieu of flowers, contributions be made to Greyhound Rescue or to the scholarship fund set up in Hannah's name, but even so, the front of the funeral parlor was filled with floral arrangements. The room was oversweet with their scent and windows had been opened to let in fresh air. People had been filing in steadily for the past forty minutes. The staff had had to set up additional folding chairs.

There was a guest book in the entry and Richard signed for them both, then guided Libby into the room, past a table with framed photos. Hannah as a child. Hannah at Halloween, dressed as a fairy with gossamer wings as big as she was, waving a flyswatter wand. Hannah with Lulu. Hannah with Gabe. After one glance, Libby turned away. She could not bear to look at them. She kept seeing Hannah as she had been in the dialysis center, smiling with a calm knowingness. Richard found two seats. Libby recognized people from town and the staff from the center. Jesse and Eleanor sat two rows in front of her. They had seen her come in and now shifted in their seats to smile at her. Gabe sat in front, Lulu resting at his feet. Hannah's parents, shrunken with grief, sat next to him.

Libby held Richard's hand so tight, her knuckles were white. The service began. The minister rose and said the usual thing about everyone gathering not to mourn but to celebrate Hannah's life. There was a click as the sound system went on, and then the first notes, the low call of the tuba, then trumpet and trombone. A low-down, bluesy rendition of "Just a Closer Walk with Thee." There was poetry, read by Hannah's closest friends. Auden and Dickinson and Neruda. Someone from the local greyhound rescue chapter spoke. Libby's mind drifted. Her gaze kept returning to Gabe and to Hannah's parents. She wondered how they could bear the loss of a daughter. She didn't know how they managed to breathe. The thought of anything happening to Mercedes made her feel faint. Tomorrow, she thought. Mercy will be home tomorrow. She needed her daughter, wanted to hold her. She floated away from the unbearable poignancy of the funeral, replayed Mercy's phone call in her mind.

"Mom?" Mercy had said.

"Hello, dear." Libby had resolved to stay calm, no matter what Mercy had to tell her.

"Matt told me he called you last night," her daughter said.

"Yes."

"Are you mad at me?"

"No."

"Is Dad?"

"Neither of us is angry with you. We're just wondering, if you have a problem, why you couldn't come to us." A note of reproof had crept into her tone.

Through the connection, Libby heard Mercy draw in a breath. "I knew you'd be upset."

"I'm not upset, Mercy. I'm concerned." Libby marshaled her thoughts.

"I know you're really going to be mad," Mercy said.

"Mercy. Listen to me. I won't be angry. I promise. Whatever you have to tell me, I won't get mad." Libby looked across the kitchen. Lulu looked up from her bed and flapped her tail several times against the floor. Whatever Mercy tells me, Libby thought, whatever it is, I'll stay calm.

"Mom," Mercy said.

"I'm here."

"I'm quitting school."

Libby sat down. Jesus, she thought. I can't take this. I can't take one more thing.

"Mom?"

"It's okay," she said. But it was not okay. At that moment, she wanted to kill Mercy.

"Mom?" Mercy said again.

She steadied her mind, tried to find the right thing to say. The greyhound got up and came to her, put her narrow muzzle on Libby's lap, rolled her eyes up. Libby stroked the soft coat.

"Just come home," she said. "Come home and we'll talk about it. Okay?"

"Will you tell Dad? Oh, God, I'm so scared of what he'll say."

"He'll be fine, Mercy. He loves you. We both do. Just come home. Do you want to fly? I can get a reservation."

"I'll drive. Matt said he'd come with me."

"Be careful."

"I will. Oh, God, I feel terrible—I haven't even asked how you are. How are the treatments?"

Libby started to say that she was fine and then remembered Matt telling her they did not need protecting, that they needed to know the truth. She took a deep breath and said, "Well, dialysis has its good days and bad." Like life, she thought. "My doctor thinks the sooner I get a transplant, the better it will be."

"That's what I've been reading, too," Mercy said. Her voice was steady. "Matt got all this stuff about it off the Net."

"Your Aunt Sam wants to be the donor," Libby said.

"She does?"

"Yes. She's already had the preliminary tests."

"When would it happen?"

"Soon."

"I'm glad I'll be there."

"Me, too."

I can't handle this, Libby thought after she hung up. But of course she would. She knew that somehow one always handled what life doled out. Even the things that leveled you. A lump in the breast. A midnight phone call. Betrayal of love. Positive test results. A daughter dropping out of school. Death.

Now Hannah's father was walking to the podium, a tall man shriveled by grief, his steps slowed by the weight of sorrow. He gripped the edges of the podium and looked straight out. He did not read from notes.

"Hannah's mother and I and Gabriel thank you for coming." He stopped, looked down, gathered himself. Libby could not imagine the courage it took for him to speak.

"I guess I could stand up here all day and talk about Hannah," he went on. "But it wouldn't be enough." He paused. His eyes clouded, looked off somewhere none of them could see, and the air seemed to go out of him. Then his gaze cleared. Even from where she sat, Libby could see the visible effort this cost him, this coming back.

"Bear with me while I tell you a story," he said.

A man to her left sighed. Libby gave him a dirty look.

"When I was five," the father began, "my grandmother died."

Libby liked the way he said "died" straight out, dispensing with euphemisms. Around her, people sat up a little straighter, leaned forward, listening.

"She was Welsh. After some discussion, it was decided that my mother and I would fly to Wales for the funeral. It was December," he said, and then he smiled. "A child's Christmas in Wales.

"My grandmother lived in a village near Cardiff. We arrived the day before the service. I couldn't understand anyone and so was mostly frightened, but what really unnerved me was my grand-mother's coffin that had been set on a table in her living room. The first night, the house was filled with people. At one point, there was a knock on the door. Everyone fell silent, then the oldest woman I'd ever seen came in. She was so tiny, I could have looked her in the eye, had I dared, which I didn't. She looked exactly like the witch in my illustrated book of fairy tales."

Around Libby, people were leaning forward, intent on his story. At some point, Richard had put his arm around her.

"No one said anything to her, not a word, they just parted and made way for her to reach the coffin. A saucer had been placed on top of the casket, and the old lady reached up and grasped it. She brought it to her lips and ate what it held. And then, as quickly and as word-lessly as she had arrived, she disappeared."

He stopped and looked down at the row where his wife sat. She nodded at him, a slight bend of her head. He took a breath and con-tinued.

"Years later my mother told me it was a Welsh custom. The old lady was a professional sin-eater. The saucer held salt, and the belief was that all the sins of the dead were contained in that dish of salt. When the sin-eater ate the salt, it absolved the dead woman of her sins."

He turned toward the coffin. For the first time, his voice failed. He looked down, took a breath, then continued. "We wouldn't need a bowl of salt or a sin-eater for Hannah, because she never sinned."

Libby brushed away tears. Richard slipped his handkerchief into her hand.

"I know what you must be thinking," Hannah's father continued. "You must be thinking, oh, that's a father talking. But if you think for a moment about Hannah, you'll know it's true. She never sinned. Not the big ones like lying or stealing or hate. Or the small, mean ones like gossiping or envy. Or withholding love. She was filled with such goodness and sweetness." He looked over at Hannah's casket. Every eye in the room followed. "If there were a saucer on her coffin," he said, "it would surely hold sugar, not salt.

"In her last weeks with us, she told her beloved Gabriel that they didn't have time to feel sorry for themselves. They only had time for the good thoughts. She said that every day must be one of the good ones."

He walked to his daughter's coffin and laid a hand on it, bowed his head. His wife rose. She held a hand out to Gabe. Together, with the greyhound, they joined her husband to stand beside Hannah's coffin.

Hannah's father turned to face the people who had come to mourn her death and to celebrate her life. "That's what she would want you to remember," he said. "Every day must be one of the good ones."

And then the service was over.

Libby and Sam

. . . .

"How do you feel about it?" Sam asked Libby. They were in the outer office, waiting for the nurse to call Sam's name. She had returned to Illinois, having decided to have the tests performed there after all, rather than in Boston. During the past week, she had completed the final round and met with the members of her transplant team. Today, after Dr. Forest gave her the final okay, they would set the date for the surgery.

"How do you think I feel?" Libby said. "I mean Mercy's only eighteen." She breathed a long sigh. "What will she do? Work at Starbucks? God, this would have killed Mother."

"If she weren't already dead," Sam said. They both started to laugh. An older patient, overhearing, glared at them and muttered the words "no respect" just loud enough for them to hear. Libby snorted, which made Sam laugh harder. As children, she and Libby would occasionally start laughing over some silly thing—uncontrollable laughter, the kind that one of them could set off in the other by just giggling, the kind that always ended with their mother sending them to their room. Until they could behave, she said. Until they could control themselves.

Sam felt that hysteria coming on. "Be right back," she gasped, and fled to the hall to regain her composure. She found a water dispenser and drank two cups. As she swallowed, she thought as she often did these days of the everyday miracle of functioning kidneys.

"So will Mercy come back home and stay with you?" she asked Libby when she returned.

"I guess so. I'm hoping she will."

"Really?" Sam arched an eyebrow.

Libby gave her a rueful smile. "Mostly. Ninety percent of me."

Sam nodded.

"Mercy says she'll have to think about it," Libby continued. "She's struggling between wanting to be independent and needing us. I'm trying to give her room to make the decision—what is it psychologists say? Give her space. But I don't see that she really has any choice. She can't touch the trust fund her grandparents set up until she's twenty-five. She'll have to find a job." She sighed again at her daughter's impulsive decision.

"How's Richard doing?"

"Probably better than I am, which surprises me. I thought he'd get all professorial and heavy-handed, but he's been really good."

"He's changed," Sam said.

"I know. He's more present than he's ever been. More like I remember him from when we were young."

"They say age doesn't change people, that they stay themselves, only more so. I think that's true of grief, too."

Libby stared at her. "Do you think so?"

"Absolutely. Like elements fired in a crucible. Grief refines us to our essential self."

"Samantha?" The nurse approached.

Sam stood. She turned to Libby. "Are you coming?" she asked.

"Do you want me to?"

"Of course I do. We're in this together."

Before Libby could rise, the nurse intervened. "Dr. Forest prefers to see you alone," she said to Sam in an officious tone.

Sam started to protest.

"That's okay," Libby said. "I'll wait here." She winked at Sam and shrugged, as if to say, Rules, go figure.

"Don't run off with any sailors while I'm gone," Sam said.

When she entered his office, Dr. Forest rose. He was stocky, with silver-streaked black hair and hands with capable, blunt-tipped fingers. From their first meeting he had reminded Sam of her father.

"Please," he said. "Sit down." He indicated the leather chair by his desk.

Carlotta Hayes had recommended three doctors. Sam had picked Dr. Forest simply because of his name. She thought of the trees Lee converted into boats, the way he spoke of uniting elements when a boat slid into water. It seemed an auspicious name. It had turned out to be a good choice.

"My sister Elizabeth is in the waiting room," Sam said. "Can she be here, too?" He had not yet met Libby. "She's the one who'll be getting my kidney." *Our kidney*, they now called it.

Dr. Forest's gaze flickered, dropped, and then he lifted his eyes and looked straight at her, but that momentary hesitation was all that was needed.

"What is it?" Sam said. "What's wrong?"

He didn't sidestep the question or equivocate. "I'm sorry, Samantha. I wish there was an easier way to tell you this. You can't be your sister's donor."

Sam stared at him, stunned by words that didn't compute. She and Libby were a six-point match. They had told her she was the *text-book* donor for her sister. A *perfect* match, they'd said. She had done everything *right*. She had exercised. She'd stopped drinking alcohol, had even lost five pounds. There had to be a mistake. She remembered suddenly that Libby had told her that when she'd first learned about her disease, that had been her initial thought: There had to be a mistake.

"Why?" she asked. "Oh, God. Do I have the same disease?"

Dr. Forest shook his head. "No. In fact, you're in extremely good health."

"I don't understand, then. What's the problem?"

He opened her folder, pulled out the sonogram, and pushed it across the desk to her with the hands she had once thought she could trust.

"You can't be a donor for your sister because you only have one kidney."

She did not touch the printout. She blanked for a split second. "What?"

"You only have one kidney," he said.

"How can that be?" she said.

He leaned forward slightly. "It's more common than you might think. Some people live their entire lives without discovering it. It turns up in the autopsy."

She twisted the ring on her finger, pressed the stone in against her palm. The doctor's words echoed in her brain. She tried to make sense of them. "What does this mean?" she asked.

"Nothing about your life has to change," he said. "Your kidney has served you well for thirty-eight years. There's no reason to think it won't continue. You're in good health." His voice turned reassuring. "You can still get pregnant, have children."

Sam remembered that during their first meeting, she'd asked him if there would be any problem getting pregnant after she gave Libby her kidney. He was thinking of that now.

"I still don't understand. How could I never know this?" She thought of the physicals she had had each year since childhood.

"You've never had surgery or given birth," he said, "so there was never any reason for a sonogram. As I said, basically nothing has changed."

He was so wrong.

Everything had changed.

Sam could no longer donate a kidney, could no longer save her sister.

"Can I get you something?" he asked. He was a kind man. "Water?"

She shook her head and, after a moment, rose. Now she had to go out and tell Libby.

"I'm fine," Libby said. "Really. I just need to be alone for a little bit." She and Sam had returned to the house and were standing in the kitchen. Libby saw the hurt in her sister's eyes, knew she felt rejected, knew this was hard for her, too. Sam's face had been so ashen when she'd told her about the sonogram results that Libby had been afraid she might faint. "I'm so sorry," Sam kept saying, as if it were her fault, but Libby couldn't take care of her sister now. She could barely take care of herself.

She picked up Lulu's leash. After the funeral, Gabe had asked them if they would keep the greyhound for a while. He'd tried taking Lulu home, but she had whined and cried, refused to eat. At least at Libby's she ate, although she was listless. She didn't beg to go for a walk or give anyone her doggy smile. For a while, in the days after Mercy returned home and until she left for Brown to formally withdraw from school, the greyhound had shadowed Mercy, following her everywhere, even sleeping on her bed. Although the comforter on her daughter's bed had cost close to three hundred dollars, Libby didn't say anything. What did it matter?

Now, leash in hand, she headed for the door. "I'll take Lulu with me," she told Sam, and she headed out.

She drove down Deerpath, toward the lake, but as she neared the turnoff that led to the lake's parking lot, she kept going. She drove past the gated mansions that lined the road, immense, palatial homes that reminded her of the mansions at Newport. She seldom came this far down Lake Road, but when she did, she always was struck by these homes and wondered who lived there. Captains of Industry, Richard had once told her, his voice capitalizing the words. The road ended at the cemetery and she drove through the stone arches, turned right on the drive toward the lake and around the loop, toward Hannah's grave. She parked and let Lulu out of the car. She supposed there was a rule prohibiting dogs, but she didn't care. What did it matter?

She stared at the stone, erected since the funeral. "Hannah Rose, beloved wife of Gabriel." A lifetime in a handful of letters. Lulu sniffed at the ground and then began tugging at the leash, as if to say, Come on, let's walk. Well, what had Libby expected? That the dog would whine and cry, paw at the ground, knowing Hannah lay there?

Libby wandered about, looking at the monuments, the majority of which were large and ornate. Mounted on top of one stone there was a half-size bronze statue of a deer that looked not unlike the greyhound that trotted at her side. Another granite marker had been carved into a graceful bench. All so we do not forget, she thought, for beyond death was the other death where one was lost to memory, consigned to oblivion. She thought of all the stories that lay in the ground beneath those stones. People who had fallen in love because of the line of a jaw or the tenor of a voice, who had been disappointed because of the color of a dress or a lost dream. People who had loved and grieved over things both minute and immense, none of which could be captured on a stone, no matter how imposing or expensive. The thought made her too sad to continue. She should not have come here. She turned back toward the car. Still, she was not ready to go home. She could not face Sam's need for consolation. And so, once again, she returned to the prairie.

When Libby opened the car door, Lulu did not run on ahead. She looked up, head cocked, her eyes sad. Libby clipped on the leash. With the greyhound at her side, she walked through the meadow, past the charred remains of the bonfire, onto the prairie. She turned up her collar against the chill. Soon winter would really set in. The ground would be covered with snow, deeper than the dustings of the last week, and the grasses would be sheathed in ice, morphing the prairie into a crystal palace. Eventually spring would follow, *that* at least one could count on. As there was every April, there would be a controlled fire, the grasses burned. And then, within days, new growth would thrust up through the ashes.

"What looks like devastation is but a single stage," Richard had told her once. "Only one period in a cycle that leads again to life."

Sometimes.

Sometimes devastation was just devastation, Libby thought. Sometimes it led to nothing. It circled in on itself. A hard, black, bitter knot of nothing.

She walked until she came to a bench. Lulu sat at her feet and leaned against her legs. A meadow vole scurried out from a clump of grass, but the dog did not stir.

I can't be your donor, Sam had cried, her face wet with tears.

Libby had heard people say that news like that clobbered one in the solar plexus, but really it struck like a blow to the entire body. Like lightning. It took time to recover. She thought ahead to the things that needed to be done, phone calls to be made. She would have to tell Richard. Carlotta. The twins. She noted these things in one part of her brain, but mostly she felt dull, insensate. Shock, she supposed. More by habit than conscious intent, she slid her hand beneath her coat sleeve and laid her fingers on her forearm, felt the buzz. Some portion of her mind registered the fact there was no clot in the shunt. Her body felt heavy.

It was a joke. A terrible cosmic joke. To be reconciled with Sam, to have a chance at life, her body functioning, and then in a snap, in a capricious turn of fate, to lose it. Lose the hope. She couldn't bear it. Could. Not. Bear. It.

Once, when she was ten and Sam was eight, they had been promised a trip to the Eastern States Exposition. Libby had saved her allowance for weeks, planning how she would apportion it between the amusement rides, the souvenirs, the chili dogs and spun candy. And then Sam caught the chicken pox and the trip was off. "It's not fair," Libby had screamed. "Why do we all have to stay home just because she's sick? Why can't she stay here with a babysitter? Why can't Daddy and me go? I want to go." Her tantrum accomplished nothing and she'd been banished to her room. "Think of your sister," her mother said. "She's disappointed, too, Elizabeth. It's not her fault. Don't be selfish." The sour taste of disappointment had risen in Libby's throat. What's wrong with being selfish? she had wanted to scream at her mother. The next day, she went to the pantry and took down her mother's favorite teapot, the one with pink rosebuds on the side that had belonged to their grandmother. Deliberately, she broke off the handle, then set the pot back on the shelf. When the china had snapped, she had known the momentary flash of satisfaction, but it changed nothing. She did not get to go to the exposition.

Across the prairie, a man in orange work overalls—not Gabe—was pruning back a hawthorn. She thought of the day, on this same bench, when Gabe had shared an apple with her and told her about the bonesetters and they had seen the deer. It had been, what . . . six weeks ago. So much had happened since then. It felt like that afternoon had happened in a dream. She tried to recall the fleeting moment when she'd thought she understood it all, the connection of life. That moment was far remote.

Libby swallowed against the bitterness. How had Hannah held on to hope when she knew she was dying? When all her hopes and dreams were already dead? How did one stand fast and hold on to that kind of faith?

The oppression of lost hope weighed in Libby's chest.

Promises were only a setup for disappointment. It was better not to wish for anything, not to hope.

Sam walked into Libby's den. She was filled with worry about her sister and could not stop wondering where Libby had gone and when she would return. It had occurred to her that Libby could be holed up in a motel, running off as she had earlier that fall. The thought left her limp, helpless. She wondered when Richard would be home. Or maybe Libby had gone to him. That wasn't out of the question. They had seemed closer in recent days, warmer toward each other.

Sam reached around and pressed a palm against her back, poked her fingers into the flesh on either side of her spine. It felt the same as it always had. It occurred to her then that she didn't even know which side of her body held her one kidney. She hadn't asked the doctor, nor had she looked at the sonogram he had pushed across the desk. Outside in the street, a car slowed, and she felt the catch of hope in her throat, but by the time she got to the window and looked out, the car had passed by.

She crossed to the leather chair that had once belonged to their father. She missed him terribly, more as the years went on, which seemed strange to her. She would have expected to feel the loss lessening by now. "We're orphans," Libby had said to her during a call after the plane crash, and at the time it had sounded melodramatic, but the truth of it grew with each passing year, as if all that counted in her past was being gradually erased, leaving her at sea.

At last she dialed Lee. When she heard his voice, her brittle self-control shattered. Between sobs, she told him the news Dr. Forest had given her. He listened, and his voice reached across the miles to console her.

"It'll be all right," he said. "Listen to me, Sam. It'll be all right."

"How?" Sam cried. "How will it be all right? Do you know the odds of Libby getting a kidney? Do you know how long the list is? There are thousands and thousands of people waiting for a transplant. Nearly sixty thousand people are waiting for a kidney every year. Every year, Lee. Do you know how many donors there are? About eighteen thousand. And that's counting cadavers."

"I know."

"I was her only hope."

"Not her only hope," he said.

"God, Lee. I feel so terrible."

"I know."

"And I'm scared. What will happen to her now?"

"Have faith." His voice was confident.

"I'm trying," she said. She ran her fingers over the brass nail-heads on the chair arm.

"There's no try," he said in his best Yoda imitation. "There is only do."

How do you *do* faith, she wanted to ask.

After they hung up, as she waited for Libby to return, she kept picturing how her sister had looked when she learned Sam couldn't be a donor. Her face had crumpled and then hardened, set due north. It had made Sam's blood run backward. In that moment she knew Libby had given up.

Sam pressed her face against the leather wingback, smelled the scent of her father's cigar. After all these years, she was amazed it was still there. Have faith, Lee had said, so like something her father would have said. She wondered what her father would do. He certainly wouldn't give up. He would never give up. Just that knowledge gave her strength.

After several minutes, Sam picked up the phone again and dialed her brother's number.

"Josh," she said when he answered. She couldn't believe she was actually getting through to him. Cynthia must be out. "It's Samantha."

"Hey, Sam," he said. "It's good to hear from you. How're you doing?" His voice sounded all Colorado health. "I just got back from a run."

"I'm at Libby's," she said.

"In Illinois?"

"Yes." They hadn't informed Josh of her decision to be Libby's donor. On the advice of both Carlotta Hayes and Dr. Forest, she and Libby had agreed to wait until all the tests had been completed and the date for surgery set before saying anything to other family members and friends.

Now she told her brother everything, proud that her voice held steady and she did not cry.

He asked Josh-like questions about what the doctor had said. "God, what bad luck for Libby," he said.

"That's why I'm calling, Josh," she said.

"Why?" His voice was suddenly wary.

"Will you be tested, Josh? Just to see if it's even possible for you to be a donor for Libby?"

"Sam—"

"It doesn't mean that you're making any kind of commitment," she said, cutting him off. "Just be tested." If he would just agree to this, it would be the first tiny step in getting him to change his mind.

"Why?"

"To see if you are even a match."

"Why?" he repeated. "There's no point if I'm not going to be a donor."

She swallowed. "If you could just see her, Josh. It would break your heart."

The wire hummed. "Listen, Sam," he finally said. "I'll come out there, if that will help. I'll hold her hand. Hell, I'll hold both of your hands. I can send some money if that's a problem. But I'm firm on this. I can't be a donor."

"Because Cynthia won't let you." Her voice was flat, accusing.

"Don't blame this on Cynthia. It's my decision."

Sam thought about what the social worker had told her. Choosing to be a donor was a deeply personal, complicated, and emotional decision. Some people couldn't do it, not even for a person they loved. It wasn't a question of being selfish, the social worker had said, although it had seemed so to Sam. Still seemed so.

"She's your sister, Josh. Don't you love her?"

"That's below the belt, Sam."

No, it isn't, Sam thought. No matter what the social worker had said, if you loved someone, it wasn't about how could you think of giving a kidney, it was how could you not.

"I'm not going to defend myself on this, Sam," Josh said.

"Okay," she said. She heard the resolve in his voice and admitted defeat. What did Libby call him? Switzerland. The neutral nation.

"Any other news?" he asked, as if this were now an ordinary conversation.

"Not that you care," she said. "But I'm getting married."

"I care, Sam. Don't punish me because I can't do this thing you want."

"I'm sorry," she said. But she wasn't.

"Married, huh?" he continued. "Who's the lucky guy?"

"His name's Lee." She couldn't go on. "I'll write you all the details."

"And you'll let us know the big date?" he said. "You'll send us an invitation to the wedding?"

"Of course."

"Okay, then. Well, give Libby my love."

But not your kidney. "I will," she said.

Don't sit around waiting for an invitation, she thought after she hung up. I'd invite the ghost of Richard Nixon before I'd ask you to my wedding. But of course, she would. For better or worse, she was not a neutral nation.

Sam and Libby

. . . .

Richard woke suddenly in the night and threw back the blankets.

"What is it?" Libby mumbled, surprised to find that she had fallen asleep after all. The strain of the previous evening—the three of them pretending everything would be all right—had brought on a bout of insomnia.

"Noises," Richard said. He cocked his head, listening, then looked toward the ceiling. "I think it's coming from the attic."

"Are you sure?" Libby held her breath, listened.

"There?" he said. "Did you hear that?" He got up and pulled on a robe.

From the space above her head came a faint scrabbling sound, barely discernible. How on earth could such a muted noise have woken Richard from sleep? She stayed in bed while he went to investigate, listened to his footsteps on the attic stairs, then the creaking of beams as he crossed directly overhead. What was up there? Mice? She shuddered at the idea.

"We've got a squirrel problem," Richard announced when he returned minutes later.

"Terrific," she said. "All we need now is vermin chewing up the attic." It seemed the last straw. She suddenly remembered how Carlotta had told her that one crisis in a family would sometimes precipitate another one, often setting off a domino effect, with one calamity following another, until it felt like the trials of Job had befallen them—although she supposed a squirrel in the attic didn't qualify as a catastrophe. At the time of that conversation, she had been telling Carlotta about Mercedes leaving school. She had said she felt like she'd been dropped into the middle of a soap opera. In fact, if all this had been written into a script in one of the daytime soaps, Libby would have flicked the television off, impatient with the impossible drama of it all. And then Carlotta had said it wasn't completely unpredictable that Mercy should behave this way. "It is not at all unusual for a child to act out when a parent is seriously ill," she'd said. "Wreck a car or get into drugs. Or for a spouse to have an affair." On that scale, Libby supposed, Mercy's dropping out seemed relatively minor.

"Actually," Richard was saying, "it looks like we've got a family of them."

"A family?" Libby had lost track of the conversation.

"Of squirrels."

"How long do you think they've been there?" Libby asked. She thought about the boxes stored up there. Christmas decorations, summer clothes. Odd furnishings. "How do you suppose they got in?" An accusatory tone crept into her voice, as if he were to blame. "Have they done any damage?"

"I don't know, Elizabeth," Richard said. "It's the middle of the night. I didn't take an inventory."

His tone was sharp, but she preferred it to the solicitous way he'd spoken to her lately, as if she would break if a breeze swept though the room.

"I'll take care of it in the morning," he said, now contrite. "I'll get a Haveahart trap."

"I don't care if you get a I-Don't-Give-a-Shit Trap. Just get them out of there."

She slid out of the bed.

"Where are you going?"

"Downstairs."

"Now?"

"I won't be able to get back to sleep."

"Want me to come with you? I could heat some milk."

"There's no sense in both of us being up."

"Are you sure?"

"I won't die if I go to the kitchen unescorted," she said.

"Lib—," he began, but she didn't wait for him to finish.

There was a ribbon of light beneath Sam's door, and for a minute Libby paused. Then she continued down to the kitchen. In the corner, Lulu lifted her head and gave a few halfhearted thwacks with her tail, but did not get up. Chin on crossed paws, the greyhound watched as Libby flicked on the lamp on the side table.

She couldn't believe how much had happened in the last twenty-four hours. Had it been just yesterday morning when they'd sat at the table eating breakfast, too excited to do more than nibble on toast? Was it just yesterday that the future had seemed so promising? When they had talked about "our kidney" and joked about joint custody?

"Hey." Sam entered the kitchen.

"Hi," Libby said. "Did Richard wake you?"

"Richard?"

"I thought maybe he woke you when he went up to the attic."

"No. I was awake. I couldn't sleep."

"He heard noises up there. Squirrels. Would you like some tea? There's decaf and herbal."

"I can get it." Sam crossed to the range. "You don't have to wait on me."

Libby sat at the table and watched as Sam moved about the kitchen, turned the gas on beneath the kettle.

"Lib?"

"Yeah?"

"What are you going to do now?" Sam crossed to stand behind Libby's chair and began to massage her sister's neck.

Libby shrugged. "I don't know."

"I think you should send Josh that book for organ donors," Sam said after a minute. "Get him some information."

"Forget about Josh, Sam. I'm not going to beg."

"Well, someone should. He's your brother."

"And he has a right to not want to do this."

"I can't believe you can accept that so easily. You'd be there for him. You know you would."

Libby reached a hand up and stroked Sam's fingers. "Not everyone has the same idea of family obligations," she said. She wasn't sure she did herself. What, if anything, did a person owe other family members?

"Christ, every time some famous athlete or actor needs a kidney, people line up to donate one, but Josh won't even *consider* giving one to his own sister." Sam spread her fingers over Libby's scalp, massaged her temples. "Maybe you should try and find someone willing to sell you one."

"Great idea. Unfortunately, it's illegal."

"Well, they should make it legal. They should let you be able to pay someone for an organ."

Libby stayed silent. This thought had occurred to her.

"I mean, they let women rent their bodies for surrogate births, don't they? They let you sell your blood, for heaven's sake. Why not a kidney?"

The kettle was spewing steam and Sam went to get the tea. Libby started to laugh.

"What?" Sam said.

"I was just thinking of back when we were young. Remember how we were in search of the perfect orgasm?"

Sam turned, smiled. "Yeah. When two people making love come at exactly the same instant, right?"

"Yes."

"God, we pursued that like it was the holy grail of sex." Sam tilted her head in question. "What made you think of that now?"

"I was thinking that it was a waste of time."

"Because it doesn't matter that much?"

"Because we could have spent the time forgetting the perfect orgasm and searching for the perfect organ."

It wasn't that funny. Probably no one else would have laughed, but it set them off, made them helpless with laughter, until suddenly Libby was weeping and Sam could only hold her.

While Sam packed, Libby looked on. Sam knew her sister was resisting the impulse to take over the job herself. No one could pack a suitcase like Libby.

"Are you sure you don't want me to stay on for a few more days?" Sam said. "I could manage it. I don't have to go back. Honestly."

Before Libby could answer, the phone rang. They both jumped. Libby grabbed it before the second ring; Sam stopped folding a pair of jeans. She held her breath.

"Hello?" Libby said, unable to keep an edge of eagerness from her voice.

Sam watched her sister's face, and although she knew it was improbable if not impossible, she prayed that it was Carlotta calling with the news that a match had been found. Then Sam wondered if that was the way it was going to be every time a call came into the house. The insurmountable, heartbreaking pull of hope.

"She's right here," Libby was saying. She handed the receiver to Sam.

It was Lee.

"I'll give you some privacy," Libby said and turned toward the door.

"That's okay," Sam said, reaching out a hand to stop her, but Libby had already left.

Sam shoved the suitcase aside and sank down on the bed. "Hi," she whispered, overcome with longing.

"Hey," he said. "How's it going?"

"It's so sad, Lee," she said. "It about breaks my heart."

"I know."

"And I'm so scared. What if she doesn't find a donor?" She waited for him to tell her to keep the faith.

"The very reason for my call," he said.

"What?"

"Listen, don't say anything to Libby until we have more info, but we're getting tested."

"Who's we?"

"My mother and me. To see if we're a match."

"A match?" It took her another moment to take in what he was saying. And then the immensity of it stunned her. "Alice," she said. "And you."

"And Stacy."

"Stacy?"

"Yes. We'll all getting tested."

For one minute she let the beauty of what they were offering surround her. And then she let it go for the impossible dream that it was.

"Just hear me out, Sam," Lee was saying. "This isn't a snap decision. We'd all talked about it earlier."

"You did?"

"Well, at first it was just kind of a what-if scenario, like what if a sibling needed an organ, would you do it. And then it got more specific. Like what if Sam can't be a donor for Libby. Trust me, Sam, we've really thought about this."

They didn't understand what they were offering. The hugeness of it. "You can't," she said.

"Why can't we, Sam? Weren't you going to?"

"That's different. I'm her sister. I mean, your mother and Stacy don't even know Libby."

Lee laughed. "Mom said that's exactly what you'd say. She said to tell you we're family. And that's what families do. They're there for each other."

Sometimes they are, Sam thought, thinking of Josh.

"And Stacy?" she asked. "What about her?"

"She says she's family, too. She says to tell you she's a water sign. She only needs one kidney. Sam? Are you there?"

"I'm here," she said. "Tell her . . . tell her I'm grateful. She'll understand. Tell her I'm full of gratitude."

And she was. She wept at the beauty of their offer, the magnificent generosity and wild love of it. For a minute, she let herself be cradled in the power of their love, even if the odds were surely against any one of them being a match for Libby.

Sam and Libby

. . . .

"Are you afraid?" Richard said.

"A little." A lot, really, but what good did it do to share that?

They were alone in the room now. He was sitting on the edge of her bed, holding her hand. Mercy and Matt had just gone off to get coffee, finding strength in each other as they always had. Gabe had been in earlier with an orchid, which now sat on the windowsill. Carlotta had dropped by, along with the anesthesiologist, who had told Libby exactly what she could expect in the next hours and had given her a form to sign. Eleanor Brooks had stopped by, too. She'd left an affirmation card for Libby. "Hold on to your dreams," it said. "They are your transport to the stars." Libby had Richard tape it to the wall over her bed, right next to the good-luck card Jesse's prayer circle had sent.

"Richard?"

"Yes."

"I just want you to know, if anything goes—" She stopped. She had taken care of things. Earlier in the week she had signed her will, as well as the paper making Richard her medical-care proxy and stating that, if something should go terribly wrong, under no circumstances was she to be put on life support. There *were* things worse than death. She had filled out an organ donor card. Once that would have chilled her, if she had considered it at all, but now it had brought her a measure of quiet satisfaction.

She had cleaned out her underwear drawer. (She couldn't imagine anything more depressing than having to sort through someone else's worn underpants.) And she had unearthed the diary she'd kept during the bad time six years ago and burned it, while contemplating the human compulsion to write down those things that could not be spoken.

The twins were no longer children, and that gave her great consolation. These last few days, reflecting on the past, she had realized with some surprise that she'd lived a good life. A good life, not just a good-enough life. A full life. Rich with both joy and sorrow.

She didn't actually believe she was going to die. Carlotta had been thoroughly reassuring on that point. Still, she had written a letter to each of the twins. She was not being melodramatic or morbid, just covering the bases. No matter what reassurances Carlotta gave, surgery involved risks.

"Nothing will go wrong," Richard said, as if reading her mind. He was fiddling with her Walkman. He'd prepared a tape of music for her to listen to during the operation. Some Schumann, some Mozart.

"But I'll be under anesthesia," she'd protested when he gave it to her.

"Play it anyway," he'd said. He'd been researching on the Web. There was evidence that surgery was easier and recovery swifter when patients listened to music, even while unconscious.

The floor nurse poked her head in and told Richard he'd have to leave.

He bent and kissed Libby. "See you in the recovery room," he said.

"I never got to write you a letter," Libby said, reaching for his arm. "Or Sam. I never got to write to Sam."

"There's no need," Richard said. "We know."

"Where is Sam, anyway?" Libby said.

"I saw her in the corridor," Richard said. "She just got here. She's gone across the hall. She'll be here in a minute."

Sam opened the door quietly.

"Hi," she said.

"Hi," Lee said.

She wondered if his smile would ever lose the power to heat her belly, turn her knees liquid. "I've only got a minute," she said as she kissed him. "They're going to be kicking us out pretty soon."

She crossed to the bed. "How are you doing?" she said to Alice.

Alice smiled. "To tell you the truth, I've been wondering exactly how much a kidney weighs. This could be the easiest diet I've ever been on."

Sam laughed. She stroked Alice's hand. "Do you need anything?"

"Not a damn thing," Alice said. "I want you all to know that just because Libby's getting my kidney no one has to feel pressured into naming the baby after me."

"What baby?" Sam asked.

"Yours and Lee's."

Lee laughed. "What did I tell you," he said to Sam. He turned to Alice. "Have you ordered a bassinet yet?"

"Why on earth would I do that?" she said. "There's a perfectly fine one at home in the attic. It held you and your brother and it will hold my grandchild, too."

Sam dug in her purse, found what she was looking for. "Here," she said.

Alice took the stone. She ran a finger over the white line in the middle. "Why, this is your lucky rock," she said.

"It's yours," Sam said. "It was meant for you all along."

"Thank you," Alice said. Then she added with Yankee firmness that no one could dispute: "I'll take it, but I won't need it. I'm going to be just fine."

The nurse came in and shooed them out.

"Will you wait for me downstairs?" Sam said to Lee.

"I'll be getting coffee," he said. "Take your time."

Sam slipped into Libby's room and found her sister was alone. "Hey," she said.

"Hey."

"I thought Richard would be here," Sam said.

"He just left."

Sam crossed to the window and looked up. "A full moon," she said. She loved it when the moon was visible in the daytime sky.

"You know what that's made of, don't you, Sam-I-Am?"

"Let's see. Spun silk or cotton candy, or the salt lick for cows." Sam opened her tote. "I have something for you." She handed her sister a gift bag.

Libby looked inside. "A book," she said.

"It's made by hand," Sam said.

"It's beautiful." Libby opened it, saw the blank pages.

"Do you know what it's for?"

"A diary?"

"It's for your poetry, Lib. For your book of poems."

Libby ran her hand over the pages. "Thank you," she said, meaning for much more than the book.

"There's one more thing," Sam said. She handed Libby an envelope.

"What's this?" Libby said. "A letter? I was going to write one for you, too. I feel bad I didn't."

"Open it," Sam said.

At first Libby didn't understand. "Tickets?" she said.

Sam grinned, so pleased with herself. "Air tickets to London," she said. "And the winter schedule for concerts at St. Martin-in-the Fields."

"How did you know?"

"Everything is waiting for you, Lib," Sam said. "All your dreams are still ahead."

What was ahead? Libby hadn't allowed herself to think too far into the future, to consider the possibility her body would reject the transplant. One day at a time.

She was staring at the tickets when she heard the voice. It was so clear she turned to see if Sam had, too, but her sister was leaning over to kiss her.

"See you when it's over," Sam said. "We'll all be waiting." She blew a kiss from the door and was gone.

But Libby *had* heard it. Hannah's voice. *Hold on,* it had said, just as it had in the hotel corridor weeks before. *Hold on.*

A nurse entered the room. "Time to get you ready." Libby let her take the envelope and book and place them on the bedside table. "You're going to feel a little pinch," the nurse said, and she injected the sedative into Libby's arm. "This is to relax you. In a few minutes, you'll feel drowsy."

The nurse explained the procedure as she accomplished each step: inserting the IV tube to keep Libby from getting dehydrated and to increase her flow of urine; shaving and disinfecting the area of the surgical site. Her hands were sure, her motions efficient. She hummed while she worked.

Libby lay, perfectly calm, waiting for what was to come. Hold on, Hannah had said. To what?

To dreams? On the wall over the bed she saw the card Eleanor Brooks had brought. *Hold on to your dreams. They are your transport to the stars.* She wondered how Hannah had held on to her dreams in the face of her death, had talked about opening a nursery when she knew she would not have children. This seemed to Libby a courageous thing.

Hold on.

To hope?

To every good deed and promise?

To love?

To life?

A single life seemed so fragile, at once insignificant and magnificent. She wondered how one had the fortitude to bear any of it, let alone all of it. "Life is messy," a minister had once said back when she and Richard still attended church. "It's messy and complicated and difficult at times, but it is not without a pattern. If you stand apart and look back at it from a distance, there is always a pattern. Have faith in that," he'd told the congregation. "Hold true to that faith, even when the warp and weft are invisible to your sight. Especially then."

The sedative began to take effect. She closed her eyes. Against the darkness of her lids, she saw . . .

A spider's web.

It spread out in an intricate pattern, just like the one she had seen on the prairie in September. She could remember it so clearly, that garden spider's web with the zigzag in the center. It was nearly two feet across. Its myriad threads had been woven with great and tender care into an unmistakable design and, as fragile as they appeared to her eyes, they held the tensile strength to withstand the fiercest of winds, the worst of prairie storms.

A miracle.

Really.

When you thought about it.

Acknowledgments

. . . .

My gratitude to The Ragdale Foundation for providing me with a nest at the edge of a tall grass prairie in which to give birth to this book, and to The Virginia Center for the Performing Arts for granting me the gift of time and space in which to write major portions.

I am indebted to the transplant patients and donors who were willing to share their experiences with me. I am especially grateful to Jim and Marcia Smith, John and Judy Delehanty, and Brian Baltz for their enormous generosity in this regard.

A number of people were invaluable in educating me about the intricacies of kidney disease, pastry making, boat building, sailing, and prairies. The knowledge and kindnesses are theirs. Any mistakes should be laid solely at my door. My thanks to Dr. Tyler Miller, my steadfast guide through the complicated territory of kidney disease; Kim Smith, director of the Lynchburg Dialysis Center in Amherst, Virginia; Brad and Mike Pease at the Pease Boat Yard, Chatham, Massachusetts; pastry chefs Tracy Maes and Diane Bliss; Jeremy Batson at the Open Lands Association in Lake Forest, Illinois; and Daniel Adams.

Additionally, I am particularly grateful to Susan Tillett, Zack Linmark, Constance Alexander, Rev. Christopher Leighton, Ronna Wineberg, and Marilyn Kallett, all of whom shared long conversations with me about forgiveness and families, and to Alice George and Peter Saunders for poetry consultations. Thanks to the staff at Lovells of Lake Forest, who were gracious and accommodating.

Thanks to Kay Ruane for the beautiful art that graces the cover and to Margaret Braun, whose magnificent book, *Cakewalk*, was the inspiration for Sam's cakes.

As always, I thank Deborah Schneider, agent extraordinaire and wise friend, and the dream team at Ballantine: Maureen O'Neal, Gina Centrello, and Kim Hovey.

I thank, too, the usual cast of characters who enrich my writing and my life: Ginny Reiser, Margaret Moore, Jebba and Larry Handley, Ann Stevens, and Jackie Mitchard, and my assistant, Jean Needel, who keeps things running smoothly.

Lastly, and always, I thank my family. Their love and support sustains me.

About the Author

ANNE LECLAIRE is a novelist and short story writer who teaches and lectures on writing and the creative process. She also has worked as a radio broadcaster, a journalist, an op-ed columnist for the *Cape Cod Times*, and a correspondent for the *Boston Globe*. Her work has appeared in the *New York Times, Redbook*, and *Yankee* magazine, among others. She is the mother of two adult children and she lives on Cape Cod.